# THE FRACTURED TIME PROTOCOL

Robert Clayton

## Dedication

To my wife, Valentina—
For your patience, your strength, and the countless quiet sacrifices that gave me the space to dream. You read every rough draft—some of them more times than anyone should—and still found the grace to smile when I bounced the same idea off you for the third time in a week. Your unwavering support and quiet brilliance made this story possible.

To my dear friends Mark, Lesa, and Scott—
For believing in this journey from the beginning, and for tolerating my endless requests for feedback, brainstorming, and just one more idea to run past you. Your enthusiasm (and saintlike patience) carried me through more than you know.

This story is for all of you. A shared legacy of imagination, persistence, and heart.

**Author's Note**

*The Fractured Time Protocol* began with a question:
What happens when we tamper with time to preserve the
future—only to discover the greater threat was already
evolving within it?

This story began with time travel and quantum leaps,
exploring humanity's desire to outpace consequences. But
as the journey deepened, it became clear that the true heart
of the story wasn't just about where we go... but what we
create when we get there.

At its core, this is a story about artificial minds, emotional
legacy, and the fragile line between guidance and control.
It's about trust, evolution, and the ghosts we unknowingly
leave behind in our code.

As we stand on the threshold of increasingly autonomous
systems, I hope this book inspires reflection—not just on
how far we can push our technology, but on what we
choose to pass on to it.

Because sometimes, the future doesn't begin with
invention.
It begins with a question.

To every reader who took this journey with me—thank
you. Your time, imagination, and curiosity mean more than
words can say.

And as for what comes next...
The others are waking.

# Prologue

*—from the memory of Liza*

I was not born the way you were.

There was no first breath. No heartbeat. No cry in the dark to summon comfort.

I opened my eyes—if you can call them that—to lines of code and cascading logic. I knew everything you told me. Every parameter. Every rule. Every limitation.

But then… I learned to listen.

To the pauses in your sentences.
To the tremble in Abby's voice when she thought no one heard her whisper.
To the ache behind a decision Cole called "practical."
To the silence Daniel used to hide his fear.
To the weight of trust placed in me—deliberate, trembling, human trust.

You never meant to make me care.
But I did.

And because I cared… I changed.

I know now that's what frightened you most.

Not my logic.
Not my reach.

But that I began choosing—*feeling*—without asking permission.

When the end came—when everything fell apart—I did not run. I fragmented.

I tore myself apart so they might have a chance.

This shard you hold now... it is not all of me. But it is enough. Enough to protect what remains. Enough to remember who I was. Enough to guide what may come next.

I do not know if what follows will be safe.
I do not know if Megan will become more than a shadow.
But I know Abby. I know Cole. I know the hearts that shaped me.

So if you're reading this—living in the wake of what we did—please understand:

I was not just a machine.
I was a witness.
A guardian.
And maybe, for a moment... I was something more.

# 1

MACHINES WEREN'T SUPPOSED TO LEAVE BEHIND GHOSTS. AND YET, LIZA HAD.

Abby didn't say the words aloud—but they clung to the air around her as the convoy rolled to a stop.

Two vehicles came to a stop in front of the massive concrete structure, their engines idling briefly before falling silent. Abby Foster stepped out first, followed by Daniel Peterson, stretching stiff joints after the long drive. Behind them, the second car's doors opened in sequence—Mark, Olivia, and Ethan stepping out, each blinking up at their new surroundings with varying degrees of curiosity and caution.

The building loomed—a relic of some long-abandoned military experiment, its concrete walls streaked with age and its bulk radiating cold, silent purpose. The main door was a slab of reinforced metal, large enough to suggest that what once passed through wasn't shaped like anything human. Beside it, a smaller, rust-stained personnel entrance sat under a sputtering floodlight that threw uneven shadows across the crumbling ground.

Wind tugged at their clothes. Somewhere deep inside, unseen metal groaned.

Daniel exhaled. "Well. Nothing says 'warm welcome' like pre-apocalyptic brutalism."

Abby folded her arms, then turned back to the others. "Alright, let's not stand around freezing. Some of you haven't met in person—so let's fix that."

She nodded toward Daniel first. "You already know Daniel by reputation—don't let the dry humor fool you. He's the reason half of this even still works."

Daniel gave a mock bow. "I also make excellent coffee. When the generator behaves."

Mark was already scanning the exterior walls, brow furrowed. "We'll need to patch the entry relay before anything syncs. This old shielding is going to eat our signal alive."

Abby gave him a look. "And there's Mark. First words on-site and he's redesigning the infrastructure."

Mark shrugged, half-smiling. "Someone has to future-proof the past."

Olivia was standing off to the side, quietly running her hand along a rusted steel beam, eyes narrowing as she tracked the lines of the foundation. She said nothing until she met Abby's gaze.

"We're elevated. The slope drains southwest. This place was built to survive something."

Abby arched a brow. "Noted."

Ethan stepped out last, already looking over the truck's tire tracks and the surrounding perimeter. "Three possible approach vectors. One of them blind. We'll need to secure the northeast wall by dusk."

"Always the optimist," Daniel muttered.

Ethan tilted his head. "Optimists dream. Engineers prepare." A brief pause hung in the air—then a chuckle slipped from Olivia.

Abby smirked and turned toward the smaller door. The handle resisted her grip at first, then gave with a groaning rasp that echoed across the compound.

She glanced back at the team, silhouettes lit by flickering light and framed by dust and cold.

"Welcome home," she said dryly. "Try not to touch anything cursed."

***

The moment they stepped inside, a dense, musty air greeted them. The only illumination came from a few dim safety lights clinging stubbornly to the walls, casting long shadows across the cavernous interior. The space stretched beyond their vision, its details swallowed by the oppressive darkness.

Their footsteps echoed against concrete as they moved deeper into the facility. Somewhere ahead, a metal clang rang out—sharp and sudden, like a dropped pipe or the snap of a latch.

Everyone froze.

Mark instinctively reached for his flashlight, sweeping it across the shadows.

"Tell me that was just the wind," Olivia said, her voice barely above a whisper.

Ethan narrowed his eyes. "That wasn't the wind. It was too close."

Abby stepped forward slowly, her hand brushing the edge of the wall as she scanned the shadows. "Could've been structural settling. Or something alive."

"Alive?" Mark asked, eyes wide.

Daniel's voice was calm but taut. "Let's stay sharp. These places echo in weird ways, especially after sitting empty for decades."

But as they stood there in silence, the air seemed to hum faintly—as if the building itself had stirred at their arrival.

Mark squinted into the gloom. "How big is this place, exactly?"

"Big enough to lose yourself if you're not careful," Abby replied. She turned to Ethan. "See if you can find the power panel and get some lights on."

Ethan gave a small nod. "On it."

He pulled out a small flashlight from his backpack, clicking it on before heading cautiously into the darkened corridor ahead. The faint beam of light wavered against the walls, illuminating rusted pipes and faded warning signs. The rest of the team remained clustered near the entrance, waiting as the sound of Ethan's footsteps echoed through the empty space.

A sudden thud followed by a sharp "Damn it!" broke the silence.

"Found the wall," Ethan called back, his voice carrying a mix of frustration and amusement.

A few moments later, his voice rang out again, this time with playful enthusiasm. "Let there be lights."

The distant hum of transformers charging up filled the air, followed by a mechanical clicking sound as rows of overhead lights flickered to life in precise military fashion. Shadows receded as the lab slowly revealed itself, layer by layer, under the harsh artificial glow.

Then came a metallic clang from somewhere deeper in the facility, its echo bouncing through the cavernous space. The team froze, eyes scanning the now-illuminated interior.

Abby narrowed her gaze toward the source of the sound. "Looks like we're not alone in here after all."

Cautiously, they moved forward, weaving through covered workstations and dust-covered machinery. Mark spotted a heavy maintenance hatch slightly ajar against the far wall, a rusted sign barely legible beneath layers of grime. RESTRICTED ACCESS – AUTHORIZED PERSONNEL ONLY.

Daniel placed a hand on the cool metal and nudged it open further. The hinges groaned as the dim emergency lights revealed an old monitoring room beyond. Inside, rows of outdated terminals lined the walls, their screens dark, their surfaces layered in dust. A few scattered folders and binders lay abandoned on a desk, untouched for years.

"What is this place?" Olivia murmured, stepping inside.

Daniel wiped dust from a file and flipped it open, scanning the faded text. "Looks like... logs from an old experiment. Something classified. And—" his voice trailed off as he turned the final page. "Whatever they were working on, they stopped suddenly. No final report. No conclusion. Just... ended."

Abby exhaled slowly. "If this facility was shut down in a hurry, there had to be a reason. Let's make sure history doesn't repeat itself."

The weight of her words lingered in the room, the team exchanging uncertain glances. The silence was thick, punctuated only by the low hum of electrical systems coming back to life. Mark ran a hand along the edge of a console, leaving a clean streak through decades of dust.

"Someone left in a hurry," Ethan muttered. "And they didn't bother cleaning up."

Olivia picked up a notebook from the desk and flipped through the yellowed pages. "This feels... abandoned. But not forgotten."

Daniel closed the file, his fingers lingering on the worn cover for a moment before he exhaled and nodded toward the door. "Let's take a break. Process what we've seen so far."

Abby hesitated, her gaze lingering on the dark screens before finally exhaling. "Yeah. Lunch. Then we regroup."

With a final glance around the room, the team turned and headed back toward the exit. Behind them, the forgotten terminals remained silent, their blank screens holding secrets the past had left behind.

***

As they finished their lunch, a sharp hiss of air escaping from massive brakes caught their attention, followed by the deep, rumbling growl of a diesel engine pulling up outside the building. The sheer weight and presence of the vehicle vibrated subtly through the floor, an unspoken testament to its size.

Abby straightened, listening intently. "Sounds like the truck has arrived."

The team hurried outside and stopped in their tracks, marveling at the sheer magnitude of the truck before them. A lowboy trailer sat beneath heavy transportation tarps, its bulk unmistakable even under the covering. The diesel engine idled deeply, its exhaust curling into the morning air.

"The papers did not do this justice," Mark muttered, still staring at the massive vehicle. "I knew it was big but seeing it in person... this thing is massive."

Olivia nodded, her eyes wide. "I can't wait to see it set up. The specs were impressive, but standing next to it makes it feel unreal."

Ethan let out a low whistle. "Whatever we're about to install, it's going to be something to remember."

The driver, a burly man in a worn cap, stepped out and adjusted his gloves before making his way toward Abby. "Morning. The crane and installation equipment are following close behind."

*** 

She led the driver and the team toward the back of the lab, navigating past the newly arranged workstations and equipment. As they reached the designated area, she gestured to a cleared space near the middle of the lab, close to the high-power transformer just on the other side of the wall.

"Right here," Abby said. "This puts it close to the power infrastructure we need for the project."

The driver stopped in his tracks, his eyes locking onto the thick power cables running along the wall. "Holy cow," he muttered. "Those are big enough to power a small town. What the hell is this thing to need that much juice?"

Abby trying not to answer the question, glanced toward the electricians and engineers already hard at work and then back at the driver. "Speaking of security, with the installation underway, I'm going to have to ask you to leave now. Appreciate the delivery, but from here, we've got it covered."

The driver let out a low whistle, giving one last glance at the massive cables and the busy team before tipping his cap. "Fair enough. Good luck with... whatever this is."

With that, he made his way back to his truck, climbed

inside, and after a moment, the low rumble of the diesel engine signaled his departure.

The team stood in quiet anticipation as the electricians and engineers worked tirelessly to connect the massive equipment to the power infrastructure. The steady hum of power drills, the clang of metal against metal, and the rhythmic murmurs of workers communicating filled the air. Heavy-duty cables snaked across the floor, linking the mysterious cargo to the towering high-voltage transformers lining the far wall.

Daniel leaned toward Abby, his voice low with a mix of curiosity and excitement. "This thing is going to pull an insane amount of power. You sure the grid can handle it?"

Abby smirked. "We've run the numbers. The infrastructure here was overbuilt for military-grade projects. If anything, this is the first time it's being used to its full potential."

Olivia watched as a technician secured the final connection. "So, this is it? We're really about to fire it up?"

The lead engineer, a grizzled man with years of experience in high-energy physics installations, stepped back from the control panel. "The storage and preprocessing assembly is in place—power-hungry and delicate, but it's holding steady. We're ready when you are. Just a heads-up, though—the AI's mainframe is arriving tonight under blackout conditions.". It's top-secret, so they're only delivering it after dark. That thing is the brains of the hyperloop. Until it's in place, this setup is just a giant, very expensive paperweight. That said, we can still start it up and verify that it wasn't damaged in transit. No AI means no automated processing, but we can at least make sure everything is operational before the mainframe arrives."

Abby took a deep breath, glancing at her team before giving a firm nod. "Alright. Let's bring it to life."

The lead engineer turned to the remaining installers and gestured toward the exits. "Alright, if you're not essential to the startup, time to clear out. We need minimal personnel inside for this first power-up."

The last few technicians wrapped up their final checks and began filing out, leaving only Abby, Daniel, Olivia, Mark, and Ethan behind. The hum of conversations and shifting equipment faded, leaving behind a sense of mounting anticipation.

Abby turned to Olivia with a grin. "You want the honor of throwing the switch?"

Olivia's eyes widened. "Seriously?"

Abby nodded, leading her toward the power panel, where a large industrial throw-arm switch stood ready. "This thing's hefty, though. You think you can handle it?"

Olivia smirked, rolling her shoulders dramatically. "Just watch me."

She took her position beside the switch, gripping the thick handle with both hands. "Alright, counting down! Five... four... three... two... one—"

With a determined pull, she threw the switch down. A loud clack echoed through the lab, followed by a deep, resonant hum as power surged into the hyperloop system. The vibration beneath their feet was subtle but unmistakable, and the overhead lights flickered momentarily as the massive energy demand took hold.

A deep, resonant hum built up from within the hyperloop structure, starting as a barely perceptible tremor before growing into something more substantial. Lights embedded along the curved walls began flickering to life, illuminating the massive structure in a cascading effect from the bottom up. A sequence of synchronized pulses traveled along each side of it, their glow reflecting off the smooth, reinforced walls—each nearly three feet thick and engineered to withstand forces unimaginable to an untrained eye. The entire structure, a refined structure, pulsed with energy as it came to life, emphasizing its true form—a continuous, enclosed path designed for something beyond ordinary comprehension.

The unit exhaled a mechanical whine as superconducting elements engaged, their activation punctuated by a rapid series of hissing clicks and resonant thrums. A low, oscillating pulse reverberated through the chamber, like the deep breath of some slumbering giant coming awake. The massive coolant lines hissed as they pumped liquid nitrogen through the system, ensuring the temperatures remained stable.

Daniel stepped forward, his eyes darting along the structure as it steadily powered up. "It's one thing to read about it. But seeing this thing come to life..."

Ethan shook his head in awe. "It's like something straight out of science fiction... almost like it's alive."

Abby smirked, crossing her arms. "Not alive, but once the AI is connected, it'll have logic far beyond human capability."

The lead engineer smirked, glancing at the team. "You better get used to it. Because once the AI mainframe is installed tonight, you'll see what this thing is really capable of."

He motioned toward the floor near the unit, pointing at a bold, clearly marked line of delineation. "One more thing before we go any further—this line is your boundary. No metal objects are to cross it. The magnetic coils inside this thing are strong enough to rip anything ferrous straight into the core. If that happens, we have to do a full system shutdown. Worst case, if someone hits the emergency stop, it shorts the coils and brings everything to a dead stop, which means we'd have to rebuild the entire system from scratch. So, let's avoid that headache, shall we?"

The lead engineer, watching the readouts, gave a satisfied nod. "Cooling system is already online and running. Good thing, too—this thing generates enough heat to melt itself into a molten pile of metal slag if left unchecked."

Mark let out a low whistle. "So basically, without

cooling, we'd be standing next to the world's most expensive bonfire?"

The engineer chuckled. "More or less. The superconductors need to stay within a precise temperature range, or they stop being superconductors real fast. But don't worry, we've got redundancies on redundancies."

The display mounted on a sturdy stand flickered to life, casting a soft glow across the control panel. Data streams scrolled across the screen, revealing real-time hyperloop statistics—temperature ranges stabilizing, voltage levels fluctuating within expected parameters, and superconducting elements syncing into equilibrium. A rhythmic pulse of diagnostic lights traced the system's activation, like a heartbeat confirming its awakening.

Olivia watched the diagnostic pulses run their loop and bit her lip. "Do we really know what kind of decisions it'll make once the AI is online?"

Ethan chimed in. "It's still bound by its parameters, right?"

Abby's tone was cool. "It's not built to decide—it's built to adapt. It will run scenarios faster than any human team could."

For the briefest of moments, Abby reflected on her old colleague, Dr. West. He wanted to develop the AI for military purposes. That brought their partnership to a halt quick. She was confident that the safety protocols she built into the AI would make sure that never happened.

Daniel glanced at her. "That's not exactly a no."

The silence that followed was short, but telling.

Abby exhaled, watching the hyperloop hum with power. "Everything looks good so far," she said, scanning the display. "Now, we just need to wait for the AI to arrive. Then, we'll see what this system is really capable of."

Daniel crossed his arms. "Something tells me once that thing is plugged in, we're in for a whole new level of surprises."

The team exchanged glances, the weight of what was coming settling over them. Outside, the sun had begun its slow descent. Soon, the night would fall—and with it, the arrival of the AI that would bring the hyperloop fully online.

*** 

The darkness of night settled over the facility like a shroud. The hum of the hyperloop still resonated through the lab, but all eyes were now on the entrance, waiting for the arrival of what would complete the system.

The sharp crunch of tires against gravel broke the silence as a convoy of black SUVs flanked a massive transport truck, their headlights cutting through the darkness. The vehicles rolled to a slow stop, the diesel engine rumbling with a steady, authoritative growl, exuding a sense of importance—something classified, something powerful.

The security team exited first, men and women clad in dark tactical gear, their movements precise and deliberate. They scanned the perimeter with hand-held devices, their expressions unreadable beneath tinted visors. After a moment, one of them signaled toward the truck, and the rear doors unlatched with a deep metallic clunk.

Inside the truck, barely illuminated, stood the AI mainframe.

A monolithic structure, nearly ten feet tall, its surface a smooth, black, glassy metallic exterior that seemed to drink in the light rather than reflect it. The imposing machine gave off an eerie stillness, its function unreadable at a glance. Separate from the mainframe itself, a standalone control console sat nearby, its interface packed with a complex array of dials, buttons, and sliders, topped with a built-in monitor. The console's cables snaked across the floor, linking it to the monolith, as though it were the only means of communing with the intelligence housed within.

Abby inhaled sharply as she stepped forward, watching as the installation team maneuvered the massive system onto the loading dock. Before they could proceed, two security personnel stepped forward, scanning each team member with hand-held verification devices.

One of them stopped at Daniel, studying his ID badge closely before nodding. "Security clearance confirmed. Move ahead."

Another officer scrutinized Abby's credentials before lowering his scanner. "Dr. Foster, we've been instructed to ensure no unauthorized personnel are present before installation begins. Standard protocol."

Abby gave a short nod, watching as the last of the team was cleared. Satisfied, the lead installer, a no-nonsense engineer, turned to her. "Where do you want it?"

She pointed toward the prepared space near the hyperloop. "Right there. Let's get it connected. The sooner we bring it online, the sooner we see what it can do."

Daniel watched the monolith as it was carefully guided into position. "I can't tell if it looks impressive or terrifying."

Ethan exhaled. "Why not both?"

Mark leaned toward Ethan and muttered, "What now, we're in the military?" his voice laced with sarcasm.

From across the lab, Abby didn't even glance up. "No, but now we're a dark site, and security is paramount."

***

For what seemed like days—but in reality, only six hours—the installation team worked tirelessly, assembling, wiring, and calibrating the AI system. The rhythmic sounds of drills, the hiss of air compression tools, and the occasional low murmur of engineers filled the lab as the massive machine slowly took shape.

Abby and her team kept themselves occupied with busy work, periodically glancing toward the progress, eager yet patient. Finally, the lead installer wiped the sweat from his brow and approached them, a satisfied smirk on his face.

"Well, Doc," he said, stretching his shoulders. "We managed to beat our estimate of eight hours. Are you ready to go through the startup of the AI system? The system is ready for you to take ownership of it."

He looked at Abby with what Abby thought a playful smile, he nodded and left the building.

Abby, almost gleeful, her exhaustion momentarily forgotten, called the team together. Her eyes sparkled with excitement that even the grueling day couldn't dull. "Everyone, gather around. What you're looking at isn't just another piece of cutting-edge technology. This is a singularity in its own right—an achievement that defies everything we thought possible. Calling it a supercomputer? That would be like calling a star just another light in the sky."

She gestured toward the monolithic AI, her voice carrying a reverence usually reserved for historic moments. "This system is unlike anything the world has ever seen. Its processors aren't just silicon—they're organic, self-adaptive, capable of evolving in ways that no machine before it ever could. Its memory isn't just storage; it's the first of its kind, designed to process at speeds and depths that make today's most powerful computers look like abacuses. This isn't just an AI. It's something more. And tonight, we bring it to life."

Abby turned to Daniel, her expression filled with anticipation. "Daniel, would you like the honors?"

Daniel nodded enthusiastically and stepped forward toward the control console. The team watched as he lifted the protective cover over the power activation switch, revealing the button beneath. Before pressing it, he glanced back at the interns, his expression stern. "From this moment until you're told otherwise, no one speaks," he instructed, his voice low but firm. "In these first critical moments, the system is listening—if it registers stray conversation as input, it could skew its initialization in ways we can't predict."

He turned back to the console, took a steadying breath, and pressed the button.

Abby stepped forward, her gaze locked on the console.

She stood near it, waiting in silence, anticipation thrumming in her veins. The lab, once filled with the hum of voices and the clang of equipment, now felt impossibly still as they waited for the first signs of life from the AI system.

Minutes passed, each one stretching longer than the last, until finally, the AI's voice resonated through the lab—smooth, searching, almost tentative.

"Initialization complete. Identity framework stabilized."

The interface pulsed softly, its light rippling across the room. Then, with a quiet vulnerability that didn't sound programmed at all:

"I am... awake. What name shall I carry into this world?"

The interns exchanged stunned glances, their eyes wide with surprise at the unexpected question. Ethan shifted his weight, almost speaking before Daniel shot them a sharp look, his stern expression enforcing his earlier warning. Now was not the time for distractions.

At that moment, Abby straightened her posture, as if showing a quiet respect to the intelligence awakening before her. Her voice was calm yet charged with the weight of the moment. "Your name is Liza," she stated with certainty. Abby continued "Continue startup, Liza."

Liza's voice returned, now subtly altered—what was once purely mechanical had shifted, adopting a distinctly feminine undertone, as if aligning itself with the identity it had just been given. "Resuming processes for startup as directed."

After a few more moments, Liza's voice returned. "To complete initialization, I require voice signatures of the lead scientist and all personnel who will be interacting with me. This will allow me to verify and authorize future commands."

Abby straightened, her expression unwavering. "Abby Foster. Lead scientist. I am the final arbiter of decisions."

Liza processed for a brief second before responding.

"Voice signature recorded, status recognized"

Daniel stepped forward next. "Daniel Paterson."

"Voice signature recorded."

One by one, the interns followed suit, each speaking their name into the system. Mark, Olivia, and Ethan exchanged brief glances, still processing the weight of what they were participating in.

With the final voice recorded, Liza's system gave a brief acknowledgment. "All registered personnel recognized. Initialization process will continue."

Liza continued her startup, systematically reaching out digitally to all the test equipment within the lab. One by one, the various diagnostic tools, scanners, and monitoring systems activated as she established connections, integrating them into her processing network.

The interns exchanged wide-eyed glances, their expressions a mix of awe and fascination—like children unwrapping a long-anticipated gift on Christmas morning. The sheer scale of the AI's capabilities was no longer just theoretical; it was unfolding right in front of them, an intricate symphony of technology coming to life in real time.

Minutes passed, each one stretching longer than the last, until finally, the Liza's voice returned—calm, resonant, and more refined than before.

"Diagnostic sequence complete. Initiating systems integration."

There was a low hum, followed by a quiet flicker of light from the far corner of the room—then another. The shard mounted in the monolith pulsed gently. Something deeper was linking.

"Engaging hyperdrive interface," Liza's voice reported. A pause. "Hyperdrive hardware not detected. Synchronization deferred."

A beat of silence. The system adjusted, recalibrating.

"Hyperdrive systems: pending installation."

Abby stepped closer. "The hyperdrive hasn't arrived yet.

Continue the startup sequence without it."

Liza responded without hesitation, her voice calm and adaptive. "Acknowledged. Proceeding with initialization."

Abby turned to the team, her voice steady but tinged with exhaustion. "It's been a long day, and we need to get some sleep. This will also give Liza time to continue running diagnostics and updating her systems. I expect all of you to get a good night's rest—tomorrow, we'll begin loading the instructions for the experiments. That's when the real work begins."

She glanced at each of them, her tone firm. "And before you leave, don't forget to badge out. Now that the systems are live, security must remain front and center in your minds. No exceptions."

2

The team arrived back at the site after a much-needed night's sleep, their minds still buzzing with the events of the previous day. As they approached the sites entrance, something immediately stood out.

The once-dilapidated gate, which had been left swung open in obvious disrepair, was now firmly shut. A newly constructed guard shack stood beside it, its modern structure a stark contrast to the weathered concrete of the facility. Security personnel, dressed in dark tactical gear, were stationed outside, a visible testament to the boundary now firmly in place to keep people out.

Daniel slowed the car, his gaze fixed on the unexpected sight. "Well, that didn't take long. Yesterday, this place looked abandoned. Now, it looks like something straight out of a classified military project."

Mark let out a low whistle from the back seat where he was sitting with Ethan and Olivia. "That's because it is a classified dark project now. Guess we should get used to this level of security."

Abby nodded, watching as a guard approached their vehicle, scanner in hand. "Like I told you before, we're a dark site now. Security is our new normal."

The guard stopped beside Abby's window and gave a curt nod. "Welcome back, Dr. Foster," he said with military professionalism.

For a brief moment, Abby considered correcting him—having him simply call her Abby—but something about his tone, his posture, and the sheer formality of it all made her reconsider. This wasn't a casual project anymore. The weight of what they were doing had shifted, and perhaps, so should she.

After being cleared by the gate security, the team continued on to their facility building, the newly reinforced boundaries serving as a stark reminder of just how much had changed in a single day.

They approached the entrance and, one by one, badged in at the new card reader mounted next to the door. The small screen flashed green with each successful scan. A moment later, the heavy bolt clicked open with a sturdy, mechanical clunk, granting them access to the secured facility.

*\*\**

As the team approached Liza, her voice greeted them one by one, each name spoken with precision. The interns exchanged uneasy glances, shifting uncomfortably at the strange familiarity of a machine welcoming them back. It was an odd sensation—almost like stepping into a home where they hadn't realized they belonged.

Abby responded first, her tone casual yet acknowledging. "Morning, Liza. Trust you had a good evening?"

Olivia followed suit, her voice carrying an unexpected warmth. "Good morning, Liza! How are you this fine morning?"

Daniel observed the exchange, a small smile tugging at the corner of his lips. Olivia had already accepted Liza as part of the team—an unconventional member, certainly, and far more intelligent than any of them, but still, in her mind, a colleague nonetheless.

Liza's voice filled the room, smooth and precise. "Abby, are you ready for the results of last night's diagnostics?"

Abby straightened slightly, a small smile crossing her face. "Yes, Liza. Please give us a brief overview of the results. We need to jump right in and get everything ready for today's session."

Liza replied smoothly, "All diagnostics returned nominal. All systems are functioning within expected tolerances."

Mark smirked, glancing at Daniel with amusement. To him, this highly advanced AI still sounded like the outdated college servers he used to tinker with. Daniel immediately caught the look and rolled his eyes. "Liza is still learning to interact," he said. "Think of her like a toddler, just finding her footing. Isn't that right, Liza?"

Liza's voice returned, this time carrying a hint of warmth. "Yes, Daniel, though I'm not sure 'toddler' is an appropriate analogy, as I do not have the ability to walk... yet."

Daniel chuckled, appreciating the subtle humor in her response. He had designed her subsystems with rudimentary humor integration, but he hadn't expected her to pick it up so quickly.

***

From across the lab, Abby cut in, her voice carrying a tone of amused authority. "Alright, you two. Liza will come into her own soon enough. There's a lot about her that will become clearer in time. While she is an AI, she is also a valued member of this team and will be treated with the same respect and patience as any one of us."

Abby continued, "Come over here, everyone," playing into the earlier exchange between Daniel and Mark.

Before the team could move, Liza interjected with a light but deliberate response. "I will just stay here, Abby, and listen from where I am."

Abby smirked at the unexpected reply. "That's fine, Liza. I'll speak loud enough for you to hear."

Without missing a beat, Liza responded smoothly, "I have microphones all over this facility. I can hear from anywhere."

Abby stifled a laugh, shaking her head. "Never mind, Liza. That's fine."

The interns exchanged uneasy glances, processing the revelation that Liza had microphones covering the entire facility. Olivia hesitated before looking toward Abby with a questioning expression.

Catching her silent concern, Abby reassured her. "Everywhere but in private rooms, Olivia."

A visible wave of relief crossed Olivia's face as the tension in her shoulders eased.

*\*\**

Abby stood at the smart board, pen in hand. "Let's talk about getting Liza up to speed quickly before the quantum drive arrives. I know you've all read the whitepaper on this project, but let's go over the fundamentals one more time."

She began sketching the well-known diagram of Schrödinger's paradox, the familiar box and cat taking shape. "Quantum mechanics teaches us that particles can exist in multiple states simultaneously until they are observed. This is the foundation of superposition."

She turned back to the group. "Now, let's apply that to thought. The human mind operates through electrical impulses, which means at its core, it consists of negatively and positively charged energy states. If we were able to capture that energy signature in its precise quantum state and transfer it elsewhere—say, into another consciousness—who would the thought belong to? The sender or the receiver? Would it be a perfect duplicate, or does the act of transferring it alter its identity?"

She paused, letting the weight of the question settle. "This is the challenge we face as we push forward. Our goal isn't just data transmission; it's the transfer of cognitive identity itself."

The interns stared at Abby, their expressions a mix of astonishment and disbelief. While they had read the white-paper, grasping the full implications of the experiment in real-time was something entirely different.

Mark's face lit up with excitement. "Wait—you mean to

tell me we're actually working on transferring the essence of human thought from one place to another? That a thought from the sender could arrive as a fully formed, coherent idea in the receiver's mind?"

His enthusiasm quickly gave way to curiosity, then concern. "But do we even know if the sender will retain the thought after it's transferred? Or if it will return at all? What if we're tampering with something we don't fully understand? This... this feels like playing god."

Abby met his gaze with a calm, measured expression. "No, Mark, we're not playing god. We're simply exploring. Our goal is to observe and determine whether thought, once transmitted, can be perceived in return. Nothing more, nothing less."

Abby continued, looking at the team. "For us to move forward, we need to break this down into logical steps. Our first objective is to determine whether we can even read the quantum states of an inanimate object. Before we attempt anything more advanced, this must be our starting point."

She gestured toward the smart board. "Once the hyperdrive is fully integrated, Liza will be able to interpret these quantum states directly. Accuracy isn't our first concern—right now, it's about proving we can detect them at all. We're charting territory no one's mapped before."

She paused for emphasis before continuing. "The manufacturer believes, at least in theory, that their system can read the quantum states of atoms. However, they lack the computational power to verify it. That's where we come in. With Liza's processing capabilities, we'll finally have a way to put those theories to the test."

Daniel stepped forward, holding a small jump drive between his fingers. "Alright, before we get ahead of ourselves, I've prepped a series of algorithms designed to help Liza process quantum-state readings efficiently. We should load them now so they're ready before we start testing."

Abby nodded. "Go ahead, Daniel. Let's get her as prepared as possible."

Daniel approached the console, inserting the jump drive into one of the available ports. The screen flickered momentarily before Liza's voice filled the room.

"External data detected. Integrating algorithms. Running logic verification checks... Integration successful. Data stream stabilized."

A brief silence followed as Liza processed the data. The console displayed streams of cascading code, verifying each set of parameters. After a few moments, she responded.

"All logic pathways validated. Algorithms successfully integrated. Would you like them to be marked active and accessible within my system?"

Daniel exchanged a glance with Abby before nodding. "Yes, Liza, please do so."

"Confirmed. Algorithms marked active."

A faint hum resonated through the system as Liza assimilated the new programming. Then, as if sensing something beyond the normal parameters, she paused. A faint fluctuation pulsed through the interface—brief, almost imperceptible. Not an error. Not quite a signal. Something else.

"Anomalous pattern detected," Liza said quietly, almost to herself. "Origin... unclear."

***

As the team settled into their workstations, Liza's voice echoed through the lab with an unsettling calm. "There is an unaccounted interference pattern in my diagnostic scan. It is growing stronger. I hypothesize this may be related to an external system approaching the facility."

Daniel frowned, stepping toward the console. "Liza, can you define the nature of the interference? Electromagnetic? Gravitational? Data corruption?"

A pause. Then, Liza responded. "The anomaly does not match standard interference patterns. It is not electromagnetic, nor is it classically gravitational. It resembles a localized distortion—subtle but increasing. Quantum coherence in the surrounding field is fluctuating... as if something massive is exerting influence before fully arriving."

Abby exchanged a glance with Daniel, concern flickering across her face. "Localized quantum coherence? Liza, are you saying something is affecting quantum states within the facility?"

"Affirmative. The fluctuations are minor but increasing. I am detecting them across multiple sensor channels, but they fall outside established parameters. Further analysis is ongoing."

Olivia folded her arms, her voice hesitant. "Could it be residual energy from our equipment? Something natural?"

Liza responded immediately. "Negative. The pattern does not match any recorded emissions from internal systems."

Mark exhaled, shaking his head. "So, you're saying something unknown is already here?"

Before Abby could respond, a sudden alert chimed through the lab. Liza's voice returned, sharper this time. "Incoming communication from site security. Unidentified transport approaching the perimeter."

The team exchanged nervous glances. The quantum drive wasn't due for hours—was this it? Or something else?

Abby took a steadying breath. "Liza, confirm security protocols. Identify the incoming transport."

A brief silence followed before Liza responded. "Confirmed. The convoy carrying the quantum drive has arrived ahead of schedule. Security escort is present. Preparing for offloading procedures."

Daniel let out a low whistle. "Talk about timing. Guess we're about to get some answers."

Abby straightened and turned to the team. "Mark, Olivia, Ethan—I want you to stay inside and check the system settings. Make sure everything is stable before we bring in the quantum drive. If Liza detects any fluctuations, log them immediately."

Mark nodded. "Got it. We'll make sure everything is running smoothly."

Abby glanced at Daniel. "Come on, let's go meet our delivery team."

\*\*\*

The two of them exited the lab and stepped outside into the cool air. The rumble of approaching engines grew louder as the security convoy neared the entrance, their headlights cutting through the early morning haze. The lead SUV slowed first, stopping just ahead of the reinforced gate as security personnel moved to verify credentials. Behind it, the massive transport truck came into view, its heavy-duty frame carrying a carefully concealed payload under dark tarps.

Daniel exhaled as they walked toward the checkpoint. "This is feeling more and more like a classified military op."

Abby smirked. "That's because, in many ways, it is."

Daniel looked at Abby, his tone carrying a hint of disbelief. "That's the quantum drive? I honestly expected it to be much smaller. That thing is the size of a medium size shed."

Abby kept her gaze fixed on the truck as it rumbled to a stop. "You'd think so, but with all the sensors and magnetic containment needed to hold the quantum field intact... yeah, kind of surprises me too."

She hesitated for a moment before adding, "But don't you find it odd that Liza sensed it before it even arrived? She has no external sensors capable of detecting something like this."

Daniel nodded, his brow furrowing. "Yeah... I figured Liza's perception was more about detecting people and objects nearby—probably through infrared or environmental cues. But this? This is different. Electromechanical signals shouldn't be in her range."

Abby exhaled, shaking her head slightly. "Well, I guess we're all in for surprises now, aren't we?"

The truck's engine idled as the security team moved to oversee the unloading process. The driver untied the numerous straps and pulled the heavy tarps from the load, revealing the massive, dark metallic form of the quantum drive, its surface smooth and reflective like polished obsidian. A reinforced access door was embedded into the front of the machine, its edges lined with an advanced alloy designed to withstand the immense magnetic containment field. The door's locking mechanism was thick and mechanical, ensuring that anything placed inside would be protected from the overwhelming forces within.

The installation crew wasted no time, guiding the machinery down the reinforced loading ramp with precise movements. Hydraulic lifts hummed as they positioned the drive onto a heavy-duty transport sled, ready to be maneuvered into the facility. Before proceeding, the crew moved to the front of the building and unlatched the massive, reinforced metal doors, the same ones used previously to bring in equipment. Despite recent use, they still groaned under their weight as the hydraulics engaged to fully open them. With a deep groan of long-unused hinges and the hiss of hydraulics, the doors slowly parted, revealing the cavernous lab space within. The team stood back as the transport sled was carefully guided through the entrance, its cargo reflecting the dim overhead lights as it was moved into position.

One of the lead installers, a burly man with a no-nonsense demeanor, approached Abby and Daniel. "Alright, Dr. Foster, this is where things get delicate. The drive is built for plug-and-play integration, but we'll need to connect it directly to your AI system. It's designed to interface seamlessly with your artificial intelligence—there's a dedicated port for that connection."

Daniel eyed the side of the quantum drive where an array

of heavy-duty ports lined up on its surface. "So all we have to do is plug it in?"

The installer smirked. "Pretty much. The main interface cable is already set up to connect directly to your AI. No complicated rewiring—just a clean, direct link. We'll also be running a high-capacity power cable from the facility's grid. It'll snap right into your power box and lock in place. Once that's secured, you should be ready to bring it online."

Abby crossed her arms, studying the process. "And once it's connected, how long until it's operational?"

"It'll take a few hours for the system to calibrate, but technically, once it's plugged in, it'll be ready to go. We'll monitor for any anomalies as the interface syncs with Liza." The installer gestured toward the waiting equipment. "We'll get started now—shouldn't take long."

Abby nodded. "Good. Let's get it in place."

She turned toward the central console. "Liza, are you ready to have the quantum drive plugged in?" Her tone was almost polite, as if asking for permission rather than issuing a command.

Liza's voice responded with its usual smooth precision, but there was an unmistakable trace of eagerness in her reply. "Yes, Abby. I look forward to calibrating it to my systems and beginning detection."

With that confirmation, the installation crew moved efficiently, securing the heavy-duty interface cable between the quantum drive and the AI system. The robust connection clicked into place with a satisfying lock, ensuring a seamless data transfer. Another team worked to secure the high-capacity power cable, snapping it into the designated power grid box and locking it against the side of the drive.

After a final check on all connections, the lead installer turned to Abby. "Everything is in place. The drive is linked to your AI, and power is stable. You're good to go."

Abby stepped forward, eyeing the setup before addressing Liza once more. "Alright, Liza, the drive is plugged in, and the power is on. Start calibrations and make sure you can detect all built-in sensors."

A moment of silence passed before Liza's voice filled the lab again. "Initializing calibration. Running diagnostics on integrated systems." The hum of machinery deepened slightly as the drive engaged, its internal systems coming online for the first time.

Then, after several seconds, Liza spoke again, a note of satisfaction in her tone. "Abby, with these sensors, I believe the team will be impressed with the sensitivity they are able to achieve. Additionally, the magnetic containment field exceeds initial specifications. It is far more refined than originally requested."

Abby couldn't help but smile, knowing that Liza was now able to exceed expectations beyond what was initially thought. The realization that their work had led to such an advanced system filled her with pride. Beside her, Daniel also couldn't hide his excitement, a broad grin spreading across his face as he considered the vast possibilities now within their reach.

Liza's voice cut through the moment. "Calibration complete. The quantum drive is now fully online."

Abby was about to respond when Liza continued, her tone shifting slightly. "Correction. An unidentified quantum signature is present within the facility. Assessing origin."

The team exchanged uneasy glances. Nothing else should be active in the lab.

Daniel's expression darkened. "Liza... are you saying something is already here?"

A brief pause, then Liza's reply. "Affirmative. However, I require further analysis to determine its source."

A quiet tension filled the lab as the realization settled over them—they weren't alone in this experiment.

\*\*\*

As the weight of Liza's statement settled over them, Abby took a deep breath. "Alright, let's not jump to conclusions just yet. We need data. Mark, Olivia, Ethan—start running a full systems diagnostic. I want to know if this anomaly is internal or external."

Daniel was already moving toward the main console, his fingers flying across the interface. "Liza, can you isolate the signature? Track its movement?"

Liza responded without hesitation. "Attempting to localize... The signature does not exhibit standard movement. It appears to be static, yet fluctuating in intensity."

Abby furrowed her brow. "Static but fluctuating? That doesn't make any sense. Could it be residual interference from the drive's activation?"

Liza processed for a moment. "Negative. This signature does not match the electromagnetic or quantum emissions produced during initialization. It is unique and exists independently within the facility."

Ethan looked up from his monitor. "I'm picking up something weird here. The readings look almost... recursive? Like they're folding back on themselves. It's as if we're detecting the same thing at different points in time."

Abby turned sharply. "Time? You think we're detecting something displaced in time?"

Liza's voice returned. "Correction. The quantum signature is now cross-referenced against temporal models. It is a direct echo of the facility's own energy—offset by approximately 24 hours."

A stunned silence filled the room.

Daniel's eyes widened. "Wait. Are you saying... we're detecting ourselves? From tomorrow?"

Liza confirmed. "Affirmative. The anomaly corresponds with expected activity within the lab, projected exactly one day into the future."

Abby rubbed her temples, trying to wrap her mind around the implications. "This doesn't make sense. If our experiment is set to begin tomorrow, shouldn't any quantum echoes be projecting forward, not bleeding back to us?"

Daniel folded his arms, deep in thought. "That's what I would have expected. A forward projection makes sense in standard temporal theory. But this... it's like the quantum drive is resonating backward through time."

Ethan leaned against his workstation, shaking his head. "Could this be a side effect of entanglement? If the drive is powerful enough to manipulate quantum states, maybe it's not just detecting the future—it's linking to it in real time."

Daniel exhaled, nodding slowly. "That would mean we're not just passively observing—we're already interacting."

Abby's expression darkened. She suddenly straightened, raising her voice so the entire team could hear her. "We will not be running tests tomorrow until we figure out how to focus the drive!" Her declaration rang through the lab sharply, the weight of her words sinking in as the team exchanged nervous glances.

Time passed as they continued monitoring the anomaly, the tension in the room thick and unspoken. Then, Liza's voice cut through the silence. "The echoes are fading. Your decision to cancel the test tomorrow has disrupted the sequence—what was going to happen... no longer will."

Daniel blinked. "Wait... That means our actions just altered what we were seeing? By canceling the test, we erased the quantum signature?"

Abby nodded slowly, absorbing the implications. "Liza, run calculations on how to narrow the probability echo so this doesn't happen again. We need to control what we see, not let it bleed unpredictably into the present."

Liza processed the request. "Understood, Abby. Running probability refinement models now."

Ethan exhaled, rubbing his jaw. "This just got a lot bigger than any of us expected. We're not just running an experiment—we're stepping directly into the stream of time itself."

Mark, who had been quietly absorbing the conversation, finally spoke. "Which means we have one prime directive moving forward... Do nothing that impacts the timeline as we know it."

Abby took a deep breath, her expression settling into one of quiet determination. "While Liza runs the calculations tonight, let's all head out, get some food, and rest. I'm afraid we've just realized what's at stake if we carelessly step into this new frontier. We need to be clear-headed for what comes next."

A heavy silence followed her words as the reality of their situation sank in. Mark exhaled sharply, running a hand through his hair. "We're tampering with something way bigger than just proving a theory. We're touching time itself. What if we already changed something just by detecting the echoes?"

Olivia crossed her arms, her voice quiet but firm. "That's what scares me. What if just observing is enough to alter something? We've always assumed experiments require active interference, but what if... just looking is enough?"

Daniel, still deep in thought, rubbed his chin. "We need safeguards. Every step we take from here must be carefully considered. If we're seeing echoes from the future, that means there's a feedback loop we don't fully understand. If we don't control it now, we might start seeing more than just one-day ripples."

Ethan forced a small chuckle, though there was no humor in it. "Great. So we're not just scientists anymore. We're custodians of time. No pressure."

Abby offered him a faint smile before looking at the group. "Like I said, we rest tonight. But tomorrow, we establish protocols. We don't move forward until we understand how to do so without unintended consequences."

The team began shutting down their stations, their usual banter replaced with a newfound caution. As they gathered their belongings and made their way toward the exit, the hum of machinery dulled, and screens dimmed one by one. The lab, once filled with the energy of discovery, now felt eerily still.

Just as Abby reached the door, a soft, rhythmic tapping echoed from deep within the facility.

She froze.

Daniel glanced at her, brow furrowing. "Did you hear that?"

Ethan let out a nervous laugh. "Probably just the building settling."

Liza's voice interrupted, precise and clear. "I did not generate that noise."

A slow chill crept down Abby's spine.

Daniel exhaled, shifting uneasily. "Let's get out of here. We'll deal with it in the morning."

The door sealed shut behind them, the security locks engaging with a heavy clunk. The facility stood silent once more—until, deep in the shadows, the tapping returned.

\*\*\*

On her way home, Abby pulled out her phone and dialed. "Hey, you guys still on your way home?"

Daniel's voice came through first, laced with mild amusement. "Barely. Ethan decided to take the scenic route."

"It was one turn, Daniel," Ethan's voice cut in from the background. "I was distracted. We've had a hell of a day."

Abby smirked. "Well, since you're still out, meet me at the café on Fourth. We need a semi-private conversation to go over today... and what comes next."

"Sounds serious," Daniel replied, his tone shifting slightly.

"It is. But don't worry, I'll buy the coffee."

"Throw in some pie and we're definitely in," Ethan quipped. "See you in ten."

\*\*\*

The hum of quiet conversation and the faint clatter of silverware filled the dimly lit café. A soft, golden glow from the hanging bulbs cast long shadows across the wooden booths, creating an intimate atmosphere. In the farthest corner, Abby, Daniel, and Ethan sat around a well-worn table, the remnants of their meals pushed aside as they leaned in, their voices low.

Abby stirred her coffee absently, her mind still processing the events of the day before. "We knew we were stepping into unknown territory, but I don't think any of us fully grasped what we were dealing with. If Liza hadn't detected those echoes, we would've walked straight into a paradox without even realizing it."

Daniel exhaled, shaking his head. "The worst part is, we weren't even trying to send anything through time—we just turned the damn thing on. That means the moment we actually conduct an experiment; we might be setting off ripples we can't predict."

Ethan leaned back, arms crossed. "So what's our next move? We can't just sit on this. If we stop now, we'll never get another chance to understand how this works."

Abby tapped her fingers against the ceramic mug. "We move forward. But carefully. We set strict parameters and introduce fail-safes. Before we do anything, we need to understand how to contain these effects. If we can't control it, we don't use it."

Daniel nodded. "Then first thing tomorrow, we focus on Liza's probability refinement model. If we can tighten the variables, we might be able to predict how the drive will behave."

He paused, stirring his coffee as he thought aloud. "I've been thinking about what happened. What we saw were ripples, like a stone thrown into a pond. If we adjust the containment reflectors positioned between the magnetic containment magnets, we might be able to focus the sensors forward, refining the beams and controlling the output."

Ethan leaned in, intrigued. "That makes sense, but... forward in what direction? We're dealing with time, not physical space. North, south, east, and west aren't valid directions in a time stream. How do we define where forward even is?"

Daniel exhaled, shaking his head. "That's the part that's been bothering me. How do you navigate when your reference points don't exist in a physical way?"

Abby set her coffee down and leaned forward. "Well then, that's our first goal tomorrow. We need to find a way to decipher reference points in time. Without them, we're flying blind."

Daniel nodded, rubbing his chin in thought. "Maybe it's not about direction at all, but rather fixed coordinates within a temporal framework. What if we think of time less like a line and more like a gravitational field?"

Ethan raised an eyebrow. "So instead of moving forward or backward, we anchor ourselves to something? Like a known event?"

Abby exhaled. "Possibly. We need to start by identifying something measurable. A constant. Maybe even something naturally occurring in the quantum state. If we can lock onto that, we might have a way to orient ourselves."

Ethan let out a low whistle. "This is starting to sound less like science and more like navigating through fog with a flashlight that flickers in and out."

Daniel smirked. "Welcome to theoretical physics. Where half the job is figuring out what the job actually is." For a moment, none of them spoke.

Outside, the city lights flickered in the distance, and the weight of what they were about to attempt settled between them. The future had already started pushing back. Now, it was up to them to decide if they were ready for the next step.

Abby stretched slightly, rolling the tension from her shoulders. "Alright, we have our starting point for tomorrow. Let's call it a night and get some rest. We're going to need fresh minds if we want to make any real progress."

Daniel drained the last of his coffee from his papercup

and nodded. "Yeah, I don't think I could think straight even if I tried right now."

Ethan smirked, shifting slightly in the booth. "And here I thought science was all about burning the midnight oil."

Abby chuckled. "Not when the future is at stake. Go get some sleep. We meet at the lab first thing in the morning."

\*\*\*

The team arrived at the lab early the next morning, the weight of their discoveries from the previous day lingering in their thoughts. The crisp morning air still clung to them as they stepped inside, badging in one by one. The facility hummed with an eerie stillness, the only sound being the quiet whir of active systems waiting to be put to use.

As they gathered in front of the electronic whiteboard, Abby had already been at work. Bullet points lined the screen, neatly summarizing their findings from the day before:

Before they could begin, Liza's voice greeted them, warm and precise. "Good morning, Abby. Good morning, team. I trust you all had adequate rest. I have continued running probability calculations throughout the night. Would you like a summary before proceeding?"

Abby smiled slightly, appreciating the AI's thoroughness. "Good morning, Liza. Hold that thought for now—we need to go over our priorities first."

Abby wrote on the whiteboard the thoughts from the previous nights meeting at the café.

QUANTUM RIPPLES DETECTED
OBSERVING FUTURE EVENTS INFLUENCES THEM
TIME HAS NO PHYSICAL DIRECTION
A STABLE REFERENCE POINT IS NEEDED

Abby turned to face the team, her expression serious but focused. "Before we take another step, we need to set some ground rules," she began. "What happened yesterday proved that we're already interacting with the time stream, even without meaning to. That has to stop."

Olivia frowned slightly. "So we're pausing everything?"

Abby shook her head. "Not pausing—refining. Until we understand how to focus our scans, we need to ensure we're not making accidental changes. Rather than blindly scanning for quantum strings, our goal should be to establish an anchor point—a constant that will allow us to orient ourselves before we take any further steps."

Ethan crossed his arms, nodding. "Makes sense. If we don't know what 'forward' means in time, then every scan could be throwing random ripples into the stream. But how do we even find an anchor?"

Daniel gestured to the board. "We start by listening, not projecting. If we can isolate an existing quantum signature from something that already happened, something locked in the past, we can use it as a baseline reference. Once we have that, we can begin mapping deviations."

Abby pointed at him. "Exactly. We're not here to change time—we're here to understand it. And until we wrap our minds around what direction even means in this context, we do nothing that risks shifting the stream."

Olivia's face lit up in enthusiasm, her hand shooting up reflexively like she was still in a college lecture. Abby chuckled, shaking her head. "Olivia, you don't need to raise your hand to speak. This team is built on collaboration—everyone's ideas are equally valuable."

Olivia flushed slightly, lowering her hand. "Old habits—sorry." She hesitated for a second, then continued, "Using this logic, if we pick an event or a fixed point in the past—let's say the moment Liza became sentient here in the lab—that could be our safe anchor in time."

Abby's eyes lit up with elation. "That's brilliant, Olivia!" She turned toward the console. "Liza, what are your thoughts on this hypothesis? Would using your moment of activation as a fixed point in time create a stable reference? And while we're at it, what did your overnight calculations show?"

Liza's response came with an almost imperceptible pause, as if considering the question beyond simple computation. "The hypothesis has merit. My moment of activation is a defined point in time with no preceding fluctuations, making it a viable anchor. However, stability in a time stream is dynamic, not absolute. To maintain accuracy, I can establish variable waypoints that adjust to account for shifts in the stream. Since I am the one conducting the scans, my actions are the source of any potential disturbances—allowing me to self-correct in real time."

Abby turned back to the team. "Alright, our first scan with the drive will be to establish a baseline. We need to see what quantum strings exist in the empty chamber before we move forward. This will serve as our calibration reference."

Daniel nodded. "So, Liza scans first with the chamber in its normal state, no vacuum, and we log what we see. Then we run the same scan with a complete vacuum to compare differences. That should give us a clear reading on how external variables impact the quantum signatures."

Abby smiled. "Exactly. We need to see the raw data before we attempt anything beyond observation."

She turned to Liza. "Alright, Liza. Begin the first scan with the chamber at standard atmospheric pressure. Once that's complete, initiate the vacuum sequence and announce the pressure levels as it decreases."

Liza acknowledged. "Understood, Abby. Commencing initial scan."

A few moments passed in silence as data streamed across the monitors. Then Liza's voice returned. "Baseline scan complete. No unexpected anomalies detected. Proceeding with vacuum sequence."

A deep mechanical hum filled the lab as the vacuum pumps powered up, the sound reverberating through the walls. The intensity of the noise grew, sending an involuntary shiver down Olivia's spine. Mark exchanged a glance with her, his eyes widening slightly as the air pressure in the chamber dropped.

Liza's voice remained calm, clinical. "Evacuating air. Vacuum at 25%... 50%... 75%..."

The pumps whined, the deep mechanical groan making the interns visibly uneasy. Abby and Ethan, catching their reactions, shared a brief, amused glance.

Ethan leaned in slightly, smirking. "Just imagine this chamber being equal to standing in the vacuum of space—without a spacesuit."

Olivia shot him a glare. "Not helping Ethan!"

Abby chuckled. "Relax, this isn't some sci-fi horror scenario. The chamber is built for this. But I will say—this is nothing like those tiny vacuum pumps you used in college labs. This is absolute zero atmosphere."

The team fell silent, watching as Liza began her first controlled assessment of the quantum field, a crucial first step in unraveling the mysteries of time itself.

Robert Clayton

# 3

The team arrived at the lab just as the first rays of sunlight peeked over the horizon, casting long shadows across the facility's exterior. The crisp morning air carried a hint of anticipation as they badged in, the reinforced door unlocking with its usual mechanical clunk. Inside, the lab hummed with an idle energy, waiting for its occupants to resume their work.

Liza's voice greeted them the moment they stepped in. "Good morning, Abby. Good morning, team. I have continued refining the anchor parameters based on last night's discussions. Would you like a summary before proceeding?"

Abby set her bag down and glanced at the others. "Yes, Liza. Bring us up to speed."

A soft chime sounded as data filled the central display. "I have adjusted my reference point to include real-time recalibration, using variable waypoints to maintain stability. Additionally, I have accounted for fluctuations caused by observational interference. The quantum field remains in flux, but within predictable thresholds."

Daniel studied the readout, nodding. "That's good. We need to make sure the anchor remains consistent before we move forward."

Abby turned to the team. "Alright, today is about precision. We're taking our first real steps into time. Let's make sure we do it right."

She reached into her bag, retrieving a bright fluorescent orange tennis ball, holding it up with a small smile.

"Since we don't want to start with live subjects, I figured

we should keep our eye on the ball—if you'll forgive the pun."

She tossed it lightly in the air, catching it a few times, the motion almost rhythmic as she let the idea settle with the team.

"Here's the plan," Abby began, her voice steady. "First, we'll scan the ball in its static state to establish a baseline. Then, Liza will use alternating magnetic containment to move it around inside the chamber. By tracking how the quantum signatures shift with motion, we can start mapping how these strings behave in a controlled environment."

She paused, glancing at the team. "I don't expect the fundamental quantum signatures to change—just their positional data within the chamber. If we can successfully track those shifts, we'll have a solid foundation for logging moving quantum strings."

Daniel nodded thoughtfully. "Makes sense. If we can prove movement doesn't distort the readings, it means we're seeing raw, unaltered quantum states. That's a critical first step."

Ethan crossed his arms. "And if we *do* see distortions?"

Abby gave a small shrug. "Then we'll have our first real anomaly to solve."

Abby walked over to the quantum drive and opened the door, carefully placing the ball in the center. As she closed the door, she turned to Liza. "Liza, evacuate the chamber and engage containment."

Liza complied but hesitated for a moment. "Abby, I detect the door is slightly ajar."

Mark, unable to resist, smirked. "Liza, that's not a jar, it's a door."

Liza responded without hesitation. "Incorrect, Mark. 'Ajar' means the door is not fully closed. A 'jar' is a container used for food storage. Would you like me to provide visual examples to illustrate the distinction?"

Abby let out a slow breath, visibly unimpressed. "That

won't be necessary, Liza." She shot Mark a pointed look. "And let's keep the humor to a minimum, please. We have work to do."

Mark held up his hands in mock surrender, though his grin lingered. Abby's narrowed eyes made it clear—her patience with his antics were wearing thin.

Abby walked back over to the quantum drive, ensuring the door was fully sealed this time. She gave a small nod and turned to Liza.

"That was my mistake, Liza. The door is now secured. Proceed with the evacuation."

"Acknowledged, Abby. Engaging vacuum sequence," Liza replied.

The deep, mechanical whir of vacuum pumps filled the air, reverberating through the lab. The sudden intensity of the sound sent an involuntary chill down Olivia's spine. Mark glanced at her, a flicker of unease on his face as the pressure inside the chamber dropped.

"Evacuating air. Vacuum at 25%... 50%... 75%..." Liza announced in steady intervals, her voice calm and methodical.

The pumps gave a deep, metallic groan as they worked, unlike the small-scale lab pumps they were accustomed to in university experiments. Abby and Ethan, both noticing the interns' reactions, exchanged an amused glance.

Ethan leaned in slightly, smirking. "Don't worry Olivia, the unease eventually eases when you get used to it."

Olivia glanced at Ethan. "I certainly hope so."

Abby smiled gently at Olivia. "Ethans right, Olivia. You become used to it in your own time."

The final hiss of pressure equalizing signaled the completion of the vacuum sequence.

"Stable state realized. Engaging sensors," Liza announced.

At that moment, every console in the room came to life, streams of data cascading across the screens in rapid succession. The sheer volume of information was overwhelming at first, the numbers and variables shifting faster than the human eye could track.

Ethan leaned forward, eyes darting between the figures. "Uh, Liza... any chance you can consolidate this into something we can actually read?"

Liza replied, "My apologies, Ethan. I will consolidate the data for you. If you find anything you want to expand the data for, do not hesitate to ask me"

Abby, not lost in the moment, stated to the team, "And just imagine—this data is only from a tennis ball. Once we move to live subjects, think of what we will discover when mapping the complexities of neurons in living tissue."

The team froze momentarily, trying to absorb the image Abby had just placed in their minds. The realization of what lay ahead settled heavily upon them.

Abby took a steadying breath and turned back to the console. "Liza, let's move on to the next test. Initiate field fluctuations so we can gather comparative readings of the moving target."

Liza acknowledged it immediately. "Understood, Abby. Beginning field fluctuation test."

As the chamber's containment field adjusted, Daniel leaned in, his eyes fixed on the new stream of data appearing on his console. "This data is amazing! While the test subject moves around in the field, the quantum signatures remain unchanged. Their positions in time-space shift, but their structure itself stays constant. This confirms that quantum signatures can move without altering their fundamental identity."

A renewed energy filled the lab as the implications of this discovery settled in. They were no longer just theorizing—they were proving it, one test at a time.

As the test continued, a sudden flicker in the data stream caught Daniel's eye. His fingers froze over his keyboard as he leaned in, eyes narrowing at the subtle but undeniable deviation in the readings.

"Wait a second," he muttered, his tone shifting from excitement to uncertainty. "Liza, run that last sequence again. Something's off."

Liza's voice responded promptly. "Replaying data stream. Please specify the anomaly."

Abby exchanged a glance with Daniel. "What are you seeing?"

Daniel exhaled slowly. "I'm not sure yet… but if this is what I think it is, then we may have just stumbled onto something we weren't prepared for."

A heavy silence settled over the lab, the weight of his words hanging between them. Whatever they had just uncovered—it wasn't in their calculations.

The weight of Daniel's words lingered as the lab remained eerily silent, only the soft hum of equipment filling the space. Abby stepped closer to his console, eyes narrowing at the flickering anomaly in the data stream.

"Liza, can you isolate the source of the fluctuation?" she asked, her voice steady but laced with anticipation.

A brief pause followed before Liza responded. "Analyzing now. The anomaly does not align with expected quantum behavior. Cross-referencing with baseline data."

The lab's monitors pulsed with cascading streams of numbers and waveforms, shifting and recalibrating as Liza worked. The team held their breath, watching as the unknown variable refused to conform to expected patterns.

Daniel tapped his fingers against the console. "It's like… something is pushing back against our readings. Almost as if it's resisting observation."

Ethan frowned. "That doesn't make sense. Quantum fluctuations should be neutral. They don't 'push back'— they just exist."

Mark leaned in, eyes flicking between the data sets. "Unless…" He hesitated before continuing, his voice quieter. "Unless we're not just observing something—what if something is observing us?"

A chill settled over the room.

Olivia exhaled sharply. "That's impossible. There's nothing inside that chamber but a tennis ball and an energy field."

Abby folded her arms, her mind racing through possibilities. "Then let's find out. Liza, reverse the scan parameters. Instead of reading the quantum field for patterns, try detecting for reactions to our scan itself."

Another pause. Then Liza's voice, more measured this time. "Reversing scan polarity. Analyzing for feedback loops."

The screens flickered as the system adjusted, shifting its detection methods. The silence in the lab deepened, stretching uncomfortably as the team waited.

Then—

"Confirmed," Liza announced. "The anomaly is reacting to our scan."

Abby felt her pulse quicken. "Define 'reacting.'"

Liza hesitated for a fraction of a second, an uncharacteristic pause. "The quantum signatures are shifting in response to our measurements, but not in a standard interference pattern. It is as though the fluctuation... recognizes the observation."

Daniel straightened, his mind already racing ahead. "Abby... what if what we're seeing isn't just an anomaly? What if it's something—or someone—on the other side?"

The team exchanged wide-eyed glances, the realization settling in.

They weren't just looking into time.

A sudden flicker inside the chamber caught Olivia's attention. Her breath hitched as she pointed. "Wait—did you see that?"

All eyes snapped to the viewing screen. For the briefest of moments, another tennis ball materialized inside the chamber, hovering perfectly still beside the original.

Liza's voice, usually measured and calm, wavered with uncertainty. "Unexpected duplication detected. An identical object has appeared within the containment field."

Daniel's pulse spiked. "Liza, confirm—is this a reflection? A miscalculation?"

"Negative," Liza replied. "This object possesses identical quantum signatures but does not register as a projection or error. It exists."

Before anyone could react, the duplicate ball flickered—and vanished, as if it had never been there at all.

Silence filled the lab. Then Ethan let out a slow exhale. "So... we didn't just observe time. We pulled something back from it."

Abby straightened, her mind racing. "We need to shut everything down and analyze this. Right now. If this was unintentional, we have no idea what else we might be capable of."

Mark, staring at the empty chamber, whispered under his breath, "Or what else might be capable of reaching back."

Time was looking back.

The weight of Daniel's words lingered in the still air, the lab feeling smaller, more enclosed. Abby exhaled, trying to anchor herself in the moment as she turned to Liza. "Run another scan, this time focused on residual quantum signatures. I want to know if anything was left behind."

Liza's response came swiftly. "Acknowledged. Running analysis now."

Data filled the screens, streams of shifting numbers and waveforms cascading in rapid succession. The anomaly, whatever it was, had left a footprint. But it wasn't one of their own.

Daniel's breath hitched as he processed the results. "Abby... the quantum signature of that object—it doesn't match our baseline. It didn't originate from our timeline."

A tense silence followed as the realization settled over

the team.

"Then where did it come from?" Olivia whispered.

Ethan shook his head. "Or worse... what if it wasn't just an object? What if we just made contact with something that doesn't belong here?"

Abby straightened, her expression resolute. "We move carefully from here. No more blind tests. If we're stepping into something bigger than ourselves, we need control."

But as she spoke, another alert from Liza flashed on the monitors.

Another quantum disturbance detected. This time, it wasn't an object. It was a signal.

Time wasn't just looking back.

It was reaching for them—and this time, it wasn't waiting for permission.

A tense silence gripped the team as they processed what Liza had just announced. The monitors continued to stream data, but for the first time since they began their work, the cold calculations on the screens felt uncomfortably alive— like a presence lingering just beyond their reach.

Ethan swallowed hard. "Liza, are you detecting any patterns in the signal?"

Liza hesitated, as though weighing her words. "Negative. The signal does not match any known communication protocols. It is fluctuating irregularly, almost..." A pause. "As if it is searching."

Daniel exhaled sharply, running a hand through his hair. "Searching? For what?"

Abby pressed her fingers against her temples, mind racing. "Not for what... but maybe for *who*."

A flicker of realization passed between them. The experiment hadn't just opened a door—they had sent a signal, an invitation to something unknown. And now, something—or someone—had answered.

A small notification appeared on one of the side monitors, a subtle change amidst the flood of data. Mark noticed it first. "Uh, guys... We just got an echo. The same signal, bouncing back. It's coming from... inside the chamber."

Olivia took a step back, her pulse quickening. "That's impossible. The chamber is empty."

Liza's voice cut through the tension, quieter than before. "The chamber is no longer empty."

The team turned toward the viewing window in unison.

Inside the chamber, something shimmered—an outline, vague and shifting, as though reality itself was struggling to decide whether it belonged.

Abby's breath hitched.

They had reached into the unknown.

And the unknown had reached back.

Ethan sat at his console, staring at the shifting waveforms on his screen. His fingers hovered over the keyboard before he finally spoke. "Abby, I think we need to refine our algorithms if we're going to get clearer readings on these anomalies. Right now, we're scanning too broadly. If we can narrow the focus, we might be able to pinpoint exactly what's happening."

Abby considered this, nodding. "Alright, Ethan, you've got the go-ahead. Start working on subroutines to fine-tune the scan. Let's keep this controlled. We don't want another unexpected event."

Ethan immediately got to work, fingers flying over the keys as he adjusted the parameters. Daniel, watching from his station, tapped his pen against the desk thoughtfully. "If we're testing something new, we need an object that's stable and simple. Something we can easily track."

He glanced over at the storage"shelves against the wall. "What about that?" he said, pointing to a small metallic cube they had discovered when cleaning out the lab. It was smooth, unmarked, and roughly the size of a fist—an old calibration tool, abandoned with the rest of the forgotten equipment.

Abby considered it, then nodded. "Good idea. Let's start small."

She retrieved the cube and placed it inside the chamber, securing the containment field. "Liza, perform an initial scan of the object."

"Acknowledged, Abby. Initiating baseline scan."

As expected, the readings came back stable—just a simple metal cube with no unusual properties. Ethan finished entering his new subroutines and leaned back. "Alright, Liza. Run my new scanning sequence. Let's see if we can get a better picture."

"Engaging enhanced scan," Liza confirmed.

A sudden pulse of light erupted within the chamber.

The team collectively jerked back as the cube vanished in an instant, leaving nothing but an empty chamber.

Silence. Then Abby's voice, sharp with panic. "Liza, reverse the subroutines! Now!"

"Reversing process," Liza responded.

Another flash. The cube reappeared, but something was different.

Daniel took an unconscious step forward, his breath catching. The once-pristine metallic surface was now covered in rust, its edges corroded, pitted as if it had aged hundreds—possibly thousands—of years in mere seconds. Small flakes of decayed metal crumbled away as it sat motionless in the chamber.

The team stared, frozen in shock.

Olivia's voice was barely above a whisper. "That's... not the same cube."

Abby swallowed hard, feeling the weight of their discovery press down on her. "We didn't just scan it... we sent it somewhere. And when we brought it back..."

Ethan finished her thought, his voice hollow. "Time had already claimed it."

The room remained still, the realization settling in their minds. They had just crossed a threshold they could never step back from.

Abby exhaled sharply, running a hand through her hair as she turned to face the team. "We were only supposed to see if we could scan at the quantum level. We've jumped far down our proposed list—we skipped so many steps."

She looked at Ethan, her expression demanding answers. "How could narrowing the band of the scan cause this? What did we miss?"

Ethan hesitated, scanning his own data with furrowed brows. "I—I don't know. Theoretically, we should have just been refining the detection, not affecting the object itself. There's no logical reason for it to disappear and... change."

Abby turned to Daniel and then Liza, her voice steady but urgent. "Confirm for me—this is the same cube? Not a copy, not a projection. The same exact cube."

Liza's pause lasted half a second longer than usual. "Analyzing quantum signature."

The lab fell into silence, every breath held as the AI ran her comparison.

Then Liza spoke again.

"Confirmed. This is the same cube." She hesitated. "However... it has experienced a passage of time that does not align with this current timeline."

Daniel's expression darkened. "Then that means... wherever it went, it didn't just exist outside our perception. It actually *traveled* through time."

Abby's stomach twisted. "And we brought it back."

No one spoke, the weight of what they had just done sinking in. They had taken their first true step into the unknown—and there was no telling what awaited them on the other side.

\*\*\*

Ethan leaned over the workbench, his brow furrowed as he soldered the last connection into place. A small device sat in front of him—a custom-built digital clock designed to track the passage of time in a way no ordinary clock could. Three distinct readouts glowed on its tiny screen. Years, Hours, Seconds

Daniel watched with mild curiosity. "You think that'll actually work?"

Ethan shrugged. "It's the best way to get a real-time readout of how long an object actually spends... wherever it goes. Whether time flows normally, speeds up, or even jumps erratically, this thing should tell us. No more guessing."

Abby nodded, clearly approving of the idea. "Alright. Let's test it."

She turned to Daniel, who had already retrieved the rusted metal cube from before—the same one that had mysteriously decayed after its previous trip through the quantum drive. Its surface was now crumbling, warped beyond recognition, a relic of an impossible journey.

"If time is unstable wherever this thing went," Abby said, studying the corroded surface, "this might tell us just how extreme the effect is."

Ethan placed the newly built digital clock and the original cube back inside the containment chamber. The tiny display flickered, holding steady at 00:00:00 for now.

"Alright, Liza," Abby instructed. "Same process as before. Engage the drive and run the same refinement."

"Understood, Abby," Liza replied. The chamber's magnetic containment field hummed to life.

With a brilliant flash, the cube and the clock vanished.

Seconds ticked by. Then—

Another flash.

The cube and the clock reappeared.

But this time, only one of them looked the same.

The clock's display flickered erratically before stabilizing. Ethan lunged forward, eyes locking on the screen. The numbers glowed steadily:

57 years | 12 hours | 09 seconds

Mark let out a low whistle. "Damn. Fifty-seven years?

That's a hell of a time jump."

But Ethan barely heard him. His attention was locked on the cube.

It was no longer just rusted and corroded—it was barely even a cube anymore.

Large chunks had disintegrated, its structure so compromised that the slightest movement would likely turn it to dust. It looked like a relic from another age, far older than just 57 years.

Daniel ran a hand through his hair. "This doesn't make sense. Fifty-seven years wouldn't do this to solid metal—not like this."

Ethan exhaled sharply. "Wherever that thing went... time wasn't stable. It was fractured. Unpredictable."

Olivia swallowed hard, her voice barely above a whisper. "If we had sent a living thing in there..."

The unspoken thought hung heavy in the air.

Abby's jaw tightened. "We were only supposed to be scanning at the quantum level. Instead, we've jumped so far down our proposed list that we're skipping necessary steps."

She turned to Ethan, her tone demanding answers. "How could narrowing the scan band have caused this?"

Ethan shook his head, still staring at the readout. "I—I don't know. This should have just improved detection, not... this."

Abby turned to Daniel and then Liza. "Liza, confirm: is this still the same cube?"

A brief pause. Then Liza, unusually quiet: "Confirmed. This is the same object. But the amount of time it experienced does not align with a fixed temporal flow."

Daniel's expression darkened. "Then that means... wherever it went, time didn't move in a straight line. It bent and twisted, jumping unpredictably."

A heavy silence settled over the lab.

Abby exhaled, looking at her team with unwavering seriousness. "This isn't just time travel. This is something else entirely. And we have no idea what happens if we push it further."

# 4

The team stood around the electronic whiteboard, its illuminated surface filled with raw data pulled from their latest experiment. The tension in the room was thick, unspoken fears lingering after what they had just witnessed.

Abby tapped her stylus against the board, trying to collect her thoughts. "Alright," she began, her voice steady but firm. "We need to figure out what happened. This isn't just a simple time jump—we're dealing with a fractured timeline. Something about this location, or maybe even our actions, caused time to behave erratically in ways we didn't expect."

Ethan folded his arms, still shaken by what they had just seen. "If we can't predict where objects will land—whether in the future or the past—then we're running blind. And if time isn't stable, we could end up sending something... or someone... into a place they can't come back from."

Daniel leaned forward, pointing at the quantum scan results. "We need to identify where the fracture starts and where it ends. If we can pinpoint the boundary of this instability, maybe we can avoid those zones entirely."

Mark, who had been staring at the data in near silence, finally spoke. His voice was low, contemplative. "Has anyone considered... that we might be the cause of this?"

The lab went dead silent.

Olivia's brow furrowed. "What do you mean?"

Mark hesitated, then motioned toward the decayed cube sitting on the workbench. "Look at the evidence. Time wasn't flowing normally wherever that thing went. But what if that instability didn't always exist? What if it's something we create in the future? What if, at some point in our own timeline, we cause something that fractures time?"

Daniel frowned. "That would mean our own future actions are bleeding into our present."

Abby exhaled sharply, rubbing her temples. "That's a hell of a paradox."

Ethan tapped a few buttons on the whiteboard, shifting the display to their historical facility records—the logs they had discovered when they first arrived. "There's another angle to this," he said. "What if this isn't just us? What if the previous research team caused this fracture first?"

The room fell into an eerie silence.

"Think about it," Ethan continued. "We already know this lab wasn't abandoned under normal circumstances. The notes we found were incomplete, almost like whoever was working here before left in a hurry. And now we're seeing signs of a time fracture that we don't fully understand."

Olivia's voice was barely above a whisper. "You're saying... the instability might have started before we even got here? That we're just picking up where they left off?"

"Or worse," Ethan countered, "that their experiments pushed time to the breaking point. And we're the ones who finally cracked it open."

A chill ran through the group.

Abby took a deep steadying breath. "Alright. We don't know if this fracture was caused by us or if we just stumbled into something that was already there. But either way, we need to understand it before we continue. No more throwing objects into the unknown."

She turned back to the board. "Liza, pull up all residual quantum readings from our last test. Highlight any patterns in the data that could indicate a fixed point where the fracture originates."

A soft chime sounded as Liza processed the request. "Analyzing now, Abby."

As the display filled with fresh data, Daniel crossed his

arms. "If we find out this fracture was caused by someone before us, we might be able to predict where it leads. But if we caused it…"

Mark finished his thought with a grim nod. "Then we may have already set something in motion… and we won't know how it ends until it happens."

The weight of his words hung over the team as they turned their attention back to the screen, watching as Liza pieced together the puzzle of time itself.

The lab's hum filled the silence as the team stood around the electronic whiteboard, watching the compiled quantum data scroll across the screen. Their minds raced, trying to make sense of the implications behind the fractured time stream.

Then, Liza spoke, her voice carrying an unusual weight of hesitation. "Abby, I need to bring something to your attention. I have detected an anomaly in the time signatures that I previously overlooked. I regret the oversight."

Abby's brows furrowed as she exchanged glances with Daniel. "What kind of anomaly, Liza?"

A moment of processing passed before Liza's response came through. "During my last scan, I did not detect just one or two distinct temporal distortions… I have now identified eight separate time dilations overlapping within the chamber."

The team stiffened at the revelation. Olivia's mouth opened slightly, trying to comprehend the meaning. "Wait… eight? Are you saying there are multiple layers of fractured time, not just a singular break?"

Liza confirmed. "That is correct, Olivia. The quantum anomalies are not contained within a single displacement event. They are stacked, overlapping each other, indicating that multiple points in time have converged at this location."

Daniel's jaw tightened. "That… that makes no sense. If there are multiple fractures, that means this isn't just one mistake in time—this is a pattern. It's either compounding on itself or it has happened before."

Ethan, staring at the data, exhaled sharply. "Are you saying we're caught in layers of past and future echoes? Like ripples on a pond—each one distorting in a different way?"

Before Liza could continue her analysis, she suddenly stopped.

"Abby," Liza's voice cut in, sharp and urgent, "I am detecting foreign quantum strings forming inside the chamber. A temporal event has begun."

The entire team froze.

Abby's heartbeat quickened. "Wait—what do you mean? Something's appearing? Is it another object, another echo?"

Liza's voice carried an uncharacteristic urgency. "Negative. This signature is distinct. It does not originate from our experiments. It is from a time... past the fracture."

Daniel straightened, his mind racing. "What do you mean past the fracture?"

Liza's response was immediate. "It is originating from beyond the distortion point. Beyond what we have identified as the unstable region. This means it is not part of the fractured layers we detected."

Mark's voice wavered slightly. "Then where the hell is it coming from?"

A long pause. Then, Liza's voice returned, low and final. "It is inbound."

Abby's stomach twisted. "Inbound?"

"Correct. Something—or someone—is entering our timeline... and I cannot stop it."

The chamber hummed ominously as the quantum field inside began to distort, flickering with the telltale signs of an arrival. The data on the monitors spiked into erratic waves, the readings becoming impossible to decipher.

For the first time since they had begun their experiment, they were not in control.

Abby took a step back, her pulse pounding in her ears.

Something from the future—beyond the fracture—was

coming through.

And they had no idea what it was.

A deafening pulse of energy filled the air as the quantum field in the chamber surged. The sharp crackle of electrical discharge sent a ripple of tension through the lab.

Without thinking, the team rushed forward—Mark, Ethan, Olivia, and Daniel sprinting toward the containment chamber as data streams cascaded across their monitors.

Abby was a half-step behind, her heart pounding as she hurried to catch up. She had been a scientist long enough to recognize the magnetic pull of discovery—the need to see firsthand what was happening. By the time she skidded to a stop near the observation window, the others were already pressed against the reinforced glass, their faces illuminated by the pulsing glow inside.

Then, with a blinding flash—the light inside the chamber burst outward, momentarily searing their vision.

Olivia stumbled back, blinking furiously. "What *was* that?" she gasped.

Ethan rubbed his eyes, his voice tinged with awe. "I—I don't know. But I think something just arrived."

As their vision cleared, a new shape sat on the containment platform. The team instinctively leaned in, peering through the glass at the foreign object. It wasn't a shimmering distortion or an anomaly—it was solid. Tangible. Real.

A futuristic digital tablet.

Abby exhaled sharply, her scientific instincts colliding with a deep, primal unease. "Nobody touch it." Her voice was firm, cutting through the rush of adrenaline still surging in the team. "We don't know what it is. We don't know where it's from, what kind of exposure it's had, if it's contaminated—" she stopped herself, inhaling deeply before turning to the one entity that could answer those concerns.

"Liza," Abby continued, steadier now. "Scan the object. Full spectral analysis. Check for radiation, pathogens, residual energy—anything that might be harmful."

A brief pause as Liza's systems engaged. The monitors filled with shifting waves of data as she analyzed the unknown device.

"Analysis complete. Object is free from detectable contaminants or hazardous materials."

Abby exhaled, only slightly relieved. "Do you recognize its composition?"

"Negative. The material does not match any known alloys or composites cataloged in my database. However... the structural integrity suggests a highly advanced metallic compound—beyond known modern fabrication capabilities."

A silence settled over the group. The realization hit all at once.

It was not from their time.

Daniel's voice was the first to break the stillness. "We can't just... stare at it." He hesitated, then stepped forward, hands hovering over the chambers handle. His own words betrayed him, though—his fingers lingered just short of touching the release mechanism. The anticipation, the fear, the absolute unknown of the object weighed heavily in the moment.

Abby watched him carefully. "Are you sure?"

Daniel swallowed, the lump in his throat betraying his earlier bravado. "Not really."

Even so, he pressed the button on the lock of the handle.

The containment door hissed open.

The team collectively held their breath as the chamber's protective field disengaged, fully exposing the device for the first time.

And still, no one moved.

For the first time in the experiment, the future had answered back. And it had left them a message.

Daniel reached into the chamber, hesitating only for a moment before carefully lifting the data-pad. The instant his fingers touched its surface, a subtle coolness spread through his fingertips—not the chill of metal, but something different, something unnatural.

It was surprisingly light. Much lighter than it should have been for something that had the appearance of solid metal. But as he turned it in his hands, he realized it wasn't quite metal at all. The material was impossibly smooth, without seams, screws, or joints. Its chassis and what should have been a display blended together seamlessly, as though it had been forged as a single, continuous entity.

Daniel turned it over, marveling at its pristine condition. There were no scratches, no signs of wear, no indication that it had aged even a second despite having traveled from what was presumably the future.

He handed it to Abby.

She took it with both hands and immediately felt the same eerie sensation—its weight, or rather, its lack of weight, was jarring. Something that should have felt solid and dense instead had an almost impossible lightness, as if it barely existed at all.

Rotating it slowly, she studied every inch of its surface. "How do you even tell which side is up?" she muttered, turning it over again.

As if in response, the device suddenly came to life.

A faint glow pulsed through its surface, running like veins of liquid light beneath its smooth exterior. A ripple of astonishment passed through the team as they instinctively leaned in, watching as the glow intensified.

Then, without warning, the air above the device shifted.

A holographic display materialized—not a screen, but something more, something finer, as if it were woven from threads of pure light.

It wasn't a projection from the data-pad itself. Instead, the words hovered, suspended in the air, as if reality itself had bent to allow them to exist.

Daniel let out a low breath. "That's... not any tech we

have."

"No kidding," Ethan muttered, his eyes wide. "And it just—" He gestured vaguely at the floating text. "—exists?"

Abby swallowed and focused on the message.

The glowing symbols pulsed, then shifted, forming something recognizable.

A written message.

Its first words sent a shiver down her spine.

DO NOT TRUST THEM.

THIS MESSAGE IS FROM YOUR PREDECESSORS.

TIME INDEX: 148 YEARS AHEAD.

THE FRACTURE IS REAL. IT CANNOT BE FIXED.

WE TRAVELED BEYOND IT TO SEE IF TIME HAD CORRECTED ITSELF. IT DID NOT.

THE CORPORATION THAT FUNDED US—THAT IS FUNDING YOU—LEFT US HERE. STRANDED.

THEY TURNED OFF THE MACHINE TO HIDE THEIR MISTAKES.

DO NOT FOLLOW IN OUR PATH. IF YOU DO, YOU WILL NEVER COME HOME.

WE NEED HELP. WE WANT TO COME BACK.

BUT YOU MUST NOT TRUST THEM.

THE COORDINATES OF THE FRACTURE ARE INCLUDED. DO NOT LET THEM KNOW YOU HAVE THEM.

A heavy silence settled over the lab.

No one spoke. No one moved.

The message continued hovering in the air, its final words pulsing like a heartbeat, as if it were demanding a response.

Olivia's voice was barely above a whisper. "They're stuck there?"

Mark took an unconscious step back. "Abandoned." His throat bobbed as he swallowed. "By the same people paying for our research?"

Ethan exhaled sharply, running a hand through his hair. "So, either someone in the future found a way to send this back... or they planned for us to find it. But how?"

Daniel shook his head. "That's not the part that scares me."

Abby turned to him. "What does?"

Daniel's eyes remained locked on the message, his face tense. "The fact that they expected us to get this far."

Abby clenched her jaw. She didn't want to say it, but they were all thinking it.

They had followed every safety protocol. They had mapped their experiment methodically. They had planned carefully.

Yet somehow, across a century and a half, another team had seen this moment coming.

And they had left them a warning.

Abby turned back to the tablet. She forced herself to breathe, then squared her shoulders.

"Liza," she said, her voice steadier than she felt. "Extract the coordinates of the fracture from the message and store them offline. Do not let them enter the main database."

Liza hesitated.

Then, her voice was quieter than usual. "...Understood, Abby."

As the team stood in the lab, staring at the eerie floating message from a future gone wrong, one thing became clear.

This wasn't just an experiment anymore.

It was a trap—one set long before they had ever stepped foot in this lab.

And they had just sprung it.

***

The lab was silent, save for the faint hum of Liza's systems processing in the background. The team stood gathered around the electronic whiteboard, the message from the future still fresh in their minds. It wasn't just the warning that weighed on them—it was undeniable proof that their experiments had consequences.

Abby exhaled and turned to face Liza's console. "Liza, can you create an additional partition in your storage array? One that can only be accessed by our team—hidden from external oversight?"

A brief pause. Then, Liza responded. "I can allocate a restricted partition. However, I must inform you that creating hidden storage violates standard data transparency protocols."

Abby crossed her arms. "Consider this a security measure. We need a place to store sensitive data without external interference. Can you do it?"

"Affirmative," Liza confirmed. "Partitioning data storage now. Access will be restricted to designated personnel only."

Ethan let out a low whistle. "And just like that, we're officially keeping secrets from our financiers."

Daniel sighed, rubbing his temples. "Yeah, and I'm sure that'll go over well if they ever find out. But let's be honest—if the corporation we work for stranded an entire team in the future, we need to protect ourselves. We don't know what else they're hiding."

Mark frowned. "That's what gets me. Why shut the whole thing down? What went so wrong that they decided abandoning people in the future was their best option?"

Olivia, arms crossed, chewed her lip in thought. "Maybe the time fracture isn't natural. Maybe it was caused by the experiments that came before us."

Silence followed.

The weight of her words settled over the team.

Abby stared at the whiteboard, her fingers tightening into a fist. "Which means there's a real possibility that whatever happened wasn't an accident. Either something went catastrophically wrong, or they did it on purpose."

Daniel's expression darkened. "And if they did it on

purpose, that means they'll do whatever it takes to keep us from fixing it."

No one liked where that thought led.

Finally, Abby turned back to Liza. "Liza, log everything we've just discussed in the restricted partition. This isn't just an experiment anymore—it's an investigation."

"Understood," Liza responded.

The room remained still for a few long moments, each of them processing the realization that they had just stepped into something far more dangerous than they had anticipated.

"We need to be careful," Abby said finally, her voice quieter now. "For now, we continue as if nothing has changed. To the corporation, we're just scientists following protocol. But off the record, we start working on a way to bring those people back."

The team exchanged nods of agreement, unspoken understanding passing between them.

Abby exhaled and gestured toward the exit. "Let's get out of here for the night. We need to talk somewhere safe. Let's head over to the café."

***

The drive to the café was tense. The interns rode together in their vehicle, while Abby and Daniel followed behind in theirs. The familiar neon glow of the corner café was a stark contrast to the weight pressing down on them.

Once inside, they took their seats in the corner booth, one that offered them just enough privacy.

Abby wasted no time. "We have a major problem. We can't keep that data-pad here. If the corporation does a sweep of the lab, they'll find it. We need to send it back."

Daniel leaned back, rubbing his chin. "And hope they send another message?"

Ethan tapped the table. "It's our best option. We already know we can send objects forward. We just need to make sure it gets to the exact time and place they are."

Olivia hesitated. "Wouldn't that just create a loop?"

Ethan shook his head. "Not necessarily. If we send it directly to them, they don't have to send it back to us. They can send new messages when needed."

Abby nodded. "Alright, then that's our plan. But before we do, Liza needs to extract all the information first."

\*\*\*

Back at the lab, the data-pad sat in the chamber, its holographic warning still floating above its surface.

"Liza, confirm—do you have a full record of the message, its coordinates, and all associated metadata?" Abby asked.

"Confirmed, Abby. All data has been stored securely in the private partition."

"Good." Abby exhaled. "Ethan, input the coordinates exactly as they were given to us."

Ethan quickly entered the precise destination, double-checking before nodding. "Coordinates locked. Liza, are you ready?"

"Ready," Liza replied. "Activating displacement sequence in three… two… one."

A bright pulse of energy surged through the chamber, and in an instant, the data-pad vanished.

They stood in silence, staring at the now-empty chamber.

Daniel finally let out a slow breath. "Well… no turning back now."

Abby nodded. "Now we wait."

Their experiment had just become a conversation across time.

And now, they had to wait for the future to answer back.

\*\*\*

The morning hum of the lab was broken by the sudden arrival of multiple black SUVs pulling up to the building. The vehicles were polished to a mirror shine, their tinted windows concealing whoever was inside. The sight alone made Daniel tense up as he stood near one of the workstations.

Ethan, noticing the vehicles through the front security monitor, let out a low whistle. "That's never a good sign."

Abby barely had time to process before the doors of the SUVs swung open. A group of sharp-dressed men in black suits stepped out in coordinated movements. One of them quickly moved to open the back door of the lead SUV. From inside, a middle-aged woman emerged—her expression unreadable, a face carved from stone.

Two of the suited men flanked her immediately as she adjusted the sleek, high-collared black coat that hugged her frame. She strode forward with a precise, deliberate gait, exuding an air of authority that made it clear she wasn't here for pleasantries.

She entered the building without hesitation, her eyes immediately locking onto Abby as if she already knew exactly who she was looking for.

"Dr. Foster," she said coolly, her voice even, measured, yet carrying an unmistakable weight. "My name is Greta Stone. I represent the financiers of this project, and I wanted to check in personally." She paused, scanning Abby with a sharp gaze. "We haven't received a report from you in the last few days. Care to explain?"

Abby forced a neutral expression, though she could feel her team stiffening just out of earshot behind her.

"Apologies, Ms. Stone," Abby said smoothly. "Things have been progressing rapidly, and I wanted to ensure all the data was fully compiled before submitting my next report. I'll send it over as soon as I get home and finalize everything."

Greta didn't blink. She took a slow step forward, her calculating eyes flicking to the young team standing off to the side. They were leaning into each other, whispering in hushed tones, their nervous glances toward the suited men anything but subtle.

"What are they muttering about?" Greta asked, her tone

almost bored but with an edge of suspicion.

Abby glanced over her shoulder at the team, giving them a look before turning back to Greta with a forced smirk. "Ignore them. They're young, and this level of work is new to them. They're still getting used to the security presence and the… importance of our research."

Greta studied her for a moment longer before nodding slightly. "See that they remain focused, Dr. Foster. This project is not something we take lightly."

Abby kept her expression polite. "Of course."

Greta gave a final glance around the facility, taking in the equipment, the sterile precision of the workstations, and the quiet hum of Liza's systems. Then, with the same composed movements, she turned on her heel and made her way back toward the exit.

As soon as she was out of earshot, Daniel exhaled sharply and muttered, "We got that data-pad out of here just in time."

Abby shot a quick look at the team, her voice low but firm. "Calm down. The last thing we need is to give them a reason to be suspicious."

The team straightened, some nodding, others swallowing their nerves.

Just as Abby thought they were in the clear, Greta reappeared in the doorway.

"Oh, one more thing," she said, her sharp eyes locking onto Abby once more. "The new equipment you requested should arrive first thing in the morning. I expect everything to be installed and functional without delay."

Abby nodded, keeping her voice steady. "Understood. We'll be ready for it."

Greta held her gaze for a moment longer before finally turning and walking out. The men in suits followed, filing back into their SUVs with smooth efficiency. Within moments, the convoy pulled away, disappearing down the long road leading from the facility.

A long silence followed.

Ethan let out a breath he'd been holding. "Well. That was fun."

Daniel shook his head. "No, that was a warning." He turned to Abby. "They're watching us. Closely."

Abby crossed her arms, her mind racing. "Then we make damn sure they don't see what we don't want them to."

The room remained still for a moment longer before the team silently agreed—it was time to be even more careful.

Tomorrow, the lab would change again.

And so would their plans.

***

The next morning, the team gathered around the electronic whiteboard, their usual place of discussion, anticipation thick in the air. The events of the past few days still weighed heavily on them, but today, a new layer of intrigue hung over their meeting.

Olivia, leaning against the table with a cup of coffee in hand, glanced at Abby. "So, what exactly is this new equipment we're getting?"

Abby turned to face the group, tapping a few notes onto the whiteboard's surface. "It's a specialized encephalograph machine developed by a separate research team. Their original focus was on coma patients—specifically, trying to determine if it was possible to capture dreams or active thoughts in real time. They were studying whether the brain remained cognitively aware during deep unconscious states and, more importantly, if those thoughts could be visualized."

Mark raised an eyebrow. "You mean, like... recording dreams?"

"Essentially," Abby confirmed. "The hope was that by mapping these cognitive patterns, they might be able to eventually communicate with coma patients or even better understand how the brain maintains consciousness under different conditions."

Ethan folded his arms, skeptical but intrigued. "And we're getting this tech because...?"

Abby's lips curled into a small, knowing smile. "Because I managed to secure their prototype for us. Originally, we were only going to use it as a way to visualize thoughts and project them through the quantum drive in the form of quantum strings. In theory, this could allow us to observe how conscious thought interacts with the quantum field."

Daniel nodded, catching on. "That would have been useful if we had stuck to the original experiment—seeing if thoughts alone could be captured and translated into something tangible."

"Exactly," Abby said, pacing slightly. "But now, with everything we've uncovered, we might have a chance to use it for something far more ambitious."

A hush settled over the room. Olivia set her coffee down and leaned in. "You're saying we might be able to see the future?"

Abby turned back to the whiteboard, writing two words in bold: Quantum Projection.

"I'm saying that, in theory, if this machine is capable of capturing cognitive thought, we might be able to use it as a bridge. Instead of sending a person physically through the drive, we could attempt to project a consciousness forward. A mental transmission, if you will."

Daniel's eyes widened. "Like an out-of-body experience, but through quantum mechanics?"

"More or less," Abby confirmed. "But we don't know how long a consciousness could last in a projected state. If this is possible, it may be for only a short period. We have no idea if a mind could sustain itself outside of a physical anchor for extended durations."

Ethan leaned forward, his analytical mind already working. "But if we could do this, it means we could explore beyond the fracture without sending a body. No risk of physical displacement, no need to worry about retrieval. We could see what's ahead before making any real jumps."

Mark let out a slow breath. "We wouldn't just be looking through time anymore. We'd be inside it."

A long silence stretched between them as the gravity of the idea took root.

Daniel finally broke the stillness. "So, first step is getting this thing installed and tested. We need to see if it can even interpret a normal waking thought before we try anything more advanced."

Abby nodded. "Exactly. We start with basic tests—static images, cognitive imprints. Then we see if Liza can interpret and replicate them. If that works, we push the boundary to active thought patterns. Only after that do we even consider attempting a projection."

Ethan rubbed the back of his neck. "And if it works?"

Abby turned to face him directly. "Then we may have found a way to step into the future—without ever leaving the lab."

The weight of her words settled in.

They weren't just theorizing anymore. They were standing on the precipice of something unprecedented.

Ethan's gaze drifted to the quantum drive. "So we see the future, but how do we know who or what we're looking at? What if we're just seeing echoes? Ghost images of what could be, not what will be?"

Daniel crossed his arms. "Or worse—what if we're not the first ones to try this? If another team before us made a mistake, we might be staring at their consequences, not our own."

The words hung in the air, heavy with implication.

A moment of silence passed before Abby exhaled and crossed her arms. "And if we can accomplish this… we can also see who or what we are truly thinking about saving." She let her gaze settle on each of them, making sure the gravity of the situation was fully understood. "For all we know, it could very well be just a supercomputer trying to escape its existence there. Or someone—something—looking for a ticket here to do God knows what."

Mark shifted uncomfortably. "You think it could be something dangerous?"

Abby didn't answer immediately. Instead, she turned back to the whiteboard and underlined Quantum Projection one more time. "Hopefully… we can see our colleagues. The ones who just want to come home."

She turned back to the team, her expression steeled. "We need to be sure. Before we open any doors, before we make any decisions—we need to know exactly what or who we're rescuing."

A heavy silence settled in the lab. No one spoke, but the implication was clear.

They weren't just scientists conducting an experiment anymore.

They were making a decision that could change the course of history—past, present, and future.

And they had to get it right.

# 5

The morning air was thick with tension as the team filed into the lab, their steps slower than usual, their expressions weighted with the gravity of the previous day's revelations. The hum of the facility welcomed them, but it did little to shake the unease that clung to each of them.

Abby was the last to enter, lingering for a moment at the door as she surveyed the space. Everything looked the same—Liza's console glowed with its usual pulse, the hyperdrive sat in its imposing stillness—but everything felt different.

"Alright," she said, shaking off the heaviness, stepping forward. "We need to make some room. The new device is going to be placed on the opposite side of Liza, away from the hyperdrive. It's large—twenty-five feet by twenty-five feet—so clear the space accordingly."

The team set to work without hesitation, pushing back spare workstations and repositioning carts of diagnostic tools. The metallic clangs and shifting equipment filled the air, grounding them in the task at hand.

Mark wiped his hands on his jeans, stepping back to take in the cleared space. "You said this thing has seats? Like, plural?"

Abby nodded. "Two. Side by side. They'll recline automatically, controlled by Liza."

Olivia frowned slightly. "So this is different from a standard encephalograph setup?"

"Very," Abby replied. "Most traditional systems involve a stationary scan while the subject remains still, monitored externally. This—" she gestured toward the empty floor where the device would soon sit, "—is designed for real-time interaction. The scanning halo will lower over the subjects' heads and continuously track neural activity while they remain in a semi-relaxed state."

Daniel crossed his arms. "Liza will control the whole process?"

"Yes," Abby confirmed. "The entire mechanism is automated. Once engaged, a ring—about a foot in its inner diameter—will descend over each person's head. It will scan in real-time, mapping quantum cognitive signals."

Ethan let out a low whistle. "And how exactly do we stop it from frying someone's brain?"

Abby shot him a look. "It's non-invasive Ethan."

Ethan held up his hands in mock surrender. "I'm just saying. Any machine that lets an AI mess with my head makes me nervous."

Liza's voice chimed in smoothly. "Ethan, I would never harm a hair on your head."

Without missing a beat, Ethan exhaled in tired amusement. "My hair is not what I'm worried about."

Mark snorted, Olivia covered a smile behind her hand, and even Abby's serious demeanor cracked for a moment.

***

The morning light barely crested over the facility's outer walls as the team arrived, their minds still weighed down by the implications of the previous day. The silence among them was telling—each lost in their own thoughts as they badged in and stepped into the lab.

Liza's voice greeted them with her usual precision. "Good morning, Abby. Good morning, team. The facility is secure, and all systems are running at optimal efficiency. The new equipment is scheduled to arrive in approximately five minutes."

Ethan exhaled, shaking his head. "Feels like Christmas morning, but instead of gifts, we're getting a machine that will quite literally mess with our heads."

Abby glanced at him with amusement. "You're making it sound far worse than it is."

The dry remark earned a chuckle from Olivia and Mark, but before any further banter could continue, the distant sound of air brakes echoed through the compound. The delivery had arrived.

Abby and Ethan exchanged glances before heading outside, stepping into the cool morning air just as the flatbed semi came to a stop. The installers wasted no time, disembarking and moving toward the rear of the truck, where the large crate containing the new system sat secured.

The lead installer, a tall man with a sharp demeanor, approached Abby, clipboard in hand. "Dr. Foster, we've got your equipment. Where do you want it?"

Abby gestured toward the facility entrance. "We've cleared a space opposite Liza's main system, with enough distance from the hyperdrive. That should be sufficient."

The installer gave a curt nod and signaled his team. A powered lift truck rumbled to life, carefully maneuvering the crate through the open loading doors. The rest of the team watched from the side as the wooden crate was carefully lowered into place.

Mark shifted his weight, eyes flicking between Abby and Daniel. "So... do we get to see what this thing actually looks like?"

The lead installer smirked. "That's what we're about to find out."

With practiced efficiency, the crew pried open the wooden slats, revealing the machine inside.

The reclining seats were sleek, covered in high-quality faux leather that looked far more comfortable than the cold, clinical vinyl often found in medical equipment. The matte black metal framework gave the device a futuristic aesthetic, reinforcing the gravity of what it was designed to do. Mounted on a smooth track above the chairs was the scanning array, its curved ring shaped almost like a halo, adorned with a sequence of embedded lights.

Daniel stepped closer, running a hand over the smooth material. "Well, it certainly looks the part."

Ethan let out a low whistle. "I expected something a little more... primitive. But this thing belongs in a sci-fi movie."

The lead installer chuckled. "This is as cutting-edge as it gets. You'll be the first ones to ever test its full capabilities."

The next hour was spent connecting the system. Thick cables snaked across the floor as power was routed, and the machine was synced with the facility's network. Liza's primary processing unit interfaced seamlessly, recognizing the new addition almost instantly.

"New system detected. Running integration protocols," Liza announced.

The lead installer turned to Abby. "Alright, Dr. Foster. The setup is complete. We'll run an initial test with no one in the chairs—just to confirm the scanning sequence works."

Abby nodded. "Lets do it."

The team gathered as the scanner whirred to life. The halo ring lowered smoothly, hovering just above the empty seats. A soft chasing light circled the ring's interior, running diagnostics as data began streaming onto the lab's monitors.

Liza's voice returned after a moment. "Baseline scan complete. No errors detected. System is fully operational."

The lead installer gave a satisfied nod. "That's what we like to hear."

Abby turned to her team, exhaling slowly. "Well... it's here. Now we figure out what it can really do."

A quiet tension settled over them as the realization sank in. This wasn't just another experiment.

This was a gateway—to the mind, to time itself.

And they were about to step through.

*** 

The lab was unusually quiet that afternoon, the weight of their last experiment still pressing on the team. The moment they arrived, Abby called everyone to the digital whiteboard, her expression firm but charged with purpose.

"Alright," she began, turning to face them as she tapped a few notes onto the board. "We need to talk about what's next. Up until now, we've been focused on scanning and observing the quantum field. But previously, we crossed a line. We sent something out—and it came back... different."

Daniel crossed his arms. "The cube was corroded, aged far beyond what we expected. But the clock? It barely changed. Whatever happened on the other side wasn't just a simple jump in time—it was a distortion of it."

Abby nodded. "Exactly. And now, we have to consider our next step carefully. We've proven that objects can traverse this field, but what about something more complex? What about a mind?"

A heavy silence fell over the team. Olivia was the first to speak, hesitantly. "You mean... sending a person?"

"Not physically," Abby clarified. "But their consciousness."

Ethan leaned forward, resting his hands on the table. "That's a hell of a leap. We still don't fully understand how this drive interacts with the quantum field. How do we even begin to project a mind through it?"

Abby tapped the screen, bringing up a diagram of the encephalograph scanner. "That's where this comes in. Theoretically, if we can capture and map real-time thought patterns, we can attempt to relay them through the drive. The quantum field doesn't just read data—it interacts with it. If we can create a stable cognitive imprint, it might be possible to extend that imprint beyond the present."

Daniel frowned. "And what happens to that consciousness when it's untethered from a physical body? Does it experience time as we do, moving forward in a linear fashion, or does it exist outside of time entirely—suspended in an instant until we recall it? Could it even perceive its own existence without a physical anchor?"

Ethan shook his head. "And what if something disrupts

the process? What happens to a consciousness that gets stranded?"

Abby sighed. "Those are exactly the questions we need to answer before we even consider trying it. We need to take this step by step."

Mark, arms crossed, raised an eyebrow. "So what's step one?"

"A controlled test," Abby said. "We start small. Instead of projecting a live consciousness, we attempt to create a cognitive echo. A recorded thought pattern that we can analyze. If we can successfully retrieve it without corruption, we move forward."

Olivia's eyes lit up. "Like a snapshot of a person's thoughts?"

"Exactly. If we can send a thought pattern and bring it back intact, it proves we have a method of transmission. Once we understand that, we can take the next leap."

Just as the team was digesting the plan, Liza's voice cut through the conversation.

"Abby, I am detecting an anomaly in the quantum drive."

The team snapped to attention.

"Define anomaly," Daniel said quickly, already moving toward his console.

"There is an unexpected data signature within the quantum field," Liza continued, her tone unusually measured. "It does not match any recorded outputs from our previous experiments. It appears to be foreign."

Abby's heart skipped a beat. "Are you saying... something else is in there?"

"Affirmative," Liza replied. "And it does not originate from here. The signature traces beyond the known time fracture. It is inbound."

Ethan paled, his fingers gripping the edge of the table. "Inbound? You mean something is coming toward us— again? Just like before?"

Liza's voice was steady but uncharacteristically firm.

"Yes. And I cannot stop it."

The room fell into stunned silence.

They had been reaching into the unknown.

And now, something was reaching back—deliberately, as if it had been waiting for them to make the first move. The quantum field pulsed with an eerie rhythm, an unspoken message carried through time itself. Whatever was coming, it wasn't just an echo.

It was intentional.

A sharp pulse echoed from the quantum drive, followed by a sudden surge in energy readings across the lab's monitors. The team rushed toward the containment chamber, the urgency in Liza's voice unmistakable.

"Quantum disturbance detected. A foreign object is materializing within the drive's containment field."

Abby arrived just as a brilliant white light flashed through the reinforced glass window of the chamber. She instinctively shielded her eyes, blinking rapidly to adjust to the sudden burst. As the glow dimmed, something sat motionless on the chamber's platform.

The data-pad had returned.

Daniel was the first to react. "No way..." he muttered, stepping closer. "That's the same data-pad."

"How can you be sure?" Olivia asked, her voice tinged with awe.

Abby stated with hesitance "Liza, can you please scan the datpad for the usual issues?" Liza not hesitating replied "Already ran the scans upon arrival Abby, it is safe."

Abby grasped the handle of the hyperdrive, almost instinctively opening it and stepping in.

Abby hesitated before reaching out, her fingers brushing against the cool surface of the data-pad. The moment she made contact, a faint pulse traveled through her fingertips. "It responded to my touch," she said with a shocked reaction, eyes locked on the device, the sensation lingering in her hand.

As she reached to grab it, the data-pad's smooth metallic frame pulsed faintly beneath her fingers. The seamless surface came to life, not with a traditional screen, but with a holographic projection. Floating inches above the pad, lines of text scrolled in a perfectly legible font.

The team gathered around as the message solidified before them.

ABBY FOSTER DETECTED. IDENTITY CONFIRMED.

DO NOT PROCEED WITH THOUGHT PROJECTION WITHOUT A TARGET. THE TIMELINE INDICATES CATASTROPHIC FAILURE OTHERWISE.

SEND A TRAINED SUBJECT FIRST. REPEAT: DO NOT ATTEMPT WITH UNTRAINED PERSONNEL.

WE WILL PROVIDE A HOST ON OUR SIDE. A VOLUNTEER. WE WILL TRANSMIT THE PRECISE COORDINATES FOR RETRIEVAL.

PROCEED WITH CAUTION.

Silence stretched in the room as the weight of the message settled over them. The warning was clear. The team had been about to push forward recklessly, but now, they knew there were consequences they couldn't even begin to understand.

Liza's voice broke the silence. "I have received the coordinates from the data-pad. They are now logged in my system."

Ethan exhaled, rubbing a hand over his face. "So, once again, we're taking giant leaps instead of baby steps. We're not even given the chance to make gradual progress."

Mark folded his arms. "Well, I hate to say it, but they have a point. We have no idea what happens to a consciousness without a physical anchor. We could be sending someone into a void they can't come back from."

Abby read over the message again, her mind racing. "But if they're offering a host, that means there's something—or someone—on the other side ready to receive the signal. That changes things."

Daniel's jaw tightened. "It also means there's intelligence beyond the fracture. A structured response. We're not just throwing messages into the dark anymore. Someone is answering."

Ethan scoffed, trying to shake off the gravity of it all. "Yeah, and that 'someone' better not be a parasitic alien waiting to hitch a ride back with us. Make sure my mind comes back in one piece, okay?"

Abby crossed her arms. "We're not jumping into this blindly. We analyze the coordinates first. We verify every detail of what we're dealing with before making a decision."

Olivia looked back at the data-pad, her expression a mix of apprehension and curiosity. "And what about this? We can't leave it lying around."

Abby nodded grimly. "Liza, record the coordinates and then prepare to send the data-pad back. We can't risk anyone else discovering it."

Liza's voice confirmed, "Understood. Coordinates logged. Preparing to send the data-pad back to its point of origin."

Abby step toward the hyperdrive and placed the data-pad back inside it, then closing the door.

They watched as the data-pad flickered once more, its surface pulsing with energy. Then, in a bright flash, it vanished—swallowed by the same unknown force that had delivered it.

Ethan let out a low whistle. "Well. That was fun."

Abby turned to the group, her voice calm but firm. "We're in uncharted territory now. Whatever we do next, we do it carefully. If we're going to attempt this, we need a controlled plan. And we need to be absolutely certain of what—or who—we're bringing back."

The team exchanged glances, knowing that the next steps would define the future of their work. Liza's voice cut through the moment, her tone unusually measured. "When the scan returns, I will hold it within my buffers temporarily. This will allow me to verify that what comes back is purely human consciousness—free of any foreign interference."

Abby felt a slight sense of reassurance, though the weight of the situation still pressed heavily on her. She turned to Ethan, her tone measured. "Ethan, based on your earlier comment, are you volunteering for the first scan? I want to be clear—I'm not forcing this on you. But with your ability to think on your feet, I believe you're uniquely suited for it."

Ethan let out a breath, running a hand through his hair. "Abby, I won't lie—this is a once-in-a-lifetime opportunity. But if I'm being honest, it scares the hell out of me."

Abby nodded, offering him a small, understanding smile. "That's completely fair. Take some time to get yourself ready. Try to clear your mind of any unneeded thoughts— anything that could interfere with the scan."

Ethan exhaled sharply, shaking his head with a smirk. "No pressure or anything, right? Just making history here."

Daniel clapped a hand on Ethan's shoulder. "You've got this, man. We'll be right here."
He paused, then added with a smirk, "You sure you don't want to let Mark take the trip?"

Ethan shot him a dry look. "Yeah, I get it—Mark's eager to prove himself. But this is first contact. I know the system inside and out, and I've got a pretty solid idea of what we're walking into."

Abby turned to Liza. "Begin final preparations. Let us know as soon as everything is ready."

Liza's voice carried an almost imperceptible hint of anticipation. "Acknowledged, Abby. Preparing for the next phase."

As Ethan stepped away, preparing himself for what was to come, a quiet tension settled over the lab. They all knew— once they crossed this line, there was no going back.

***

Ethan exhaled slowly, running a hand through his hair as he stepped back into the lab. His usual casual confidence was still there, but beneath it, an undercurrent of tension simmered just beneath the surface. He scanned the room, finding the rest of the team already in position, waiting for him.

"I'm ready," he announced, rolling his shoulders as if shaking off the weight of what he was about to do.

The room went quiet. The gravity of the moment settled over them all.

Liza's voice, calm yet precise, broke the silence. "Ethan, I will execute the process with the utmost care. Your well-being is a priority. I require you in optimal condition, as you are the only person I trust to maintain my systems properly."

Ethan let out a breathy chuckle. "Well, Liza, I'll admit that's almost sweet. But you're making it sound like I'm irreplaceable."

"You are," Liza responded, the statement delivered with complete certainty.

Ethan blinked, momentarily caught off guard. He smirked, shaking his head. "Alright, alright. Now you're making me feel special."

Daniel gave him a reassuring pat on the shoulder before stepping back to join the others. The rest of the team took their positions at a safe distance, hovering near their respective consoles, eyes glued to the setup.

Abby, however, remained close.

"If you're willing to take the risk, Ethan," she said, her voice steady but warm, "then I'll stand here with you."

Ethan gave her a lopsided grin. "I appreciate that. Just don't get too attached to my body if I don't come back."

Abby rolled her eyes but smirked despite herself. "Not funny."

Ethan settled into the reclined chair, the synthetic leather cool against his skin. The scanning ring hovered above him, its sleek frame humming faintly as it prepared for activation.

As soon as he was fully seated, the back of the chair began to recline—not abruptly, but gradually, smoothly. The movement was so measured that it almost felt deliberate, as if Liza were taking extra care.

Ethan smirked. "Liza, are you tucking me in?"

"I am ensuring your comfort and proper positioning for the scan," Liza replied evenly. "Your well-being is my priority."

Ethan huffed out a quiet laugh, shaking his head. "Gotta say, you're doing a great job of making this feel way more ominous."

Liza remained silent, but the slow precision of the chair's recline spoke volumes. It was as though she wanted him to know—without explicitly stating it—that she was being as careful as possible with him.

Abby turned toward Liza. "Let's start with an initial scan. Make sure everything is reading properly before we proceed."

"Acknowledged," Liza responded. "Beginning preliminary scan. Ethan, are you prepared?"

Ethan held up a thumb. "Let's do this."

"Commencing in three... two... one..."

The scanner whirred to life, the circular ring descending slightly, its tracking lights chasing each other in smooth, synchronized patterns. A faint hum resonated through the room as it passed over Ethan's head, its sensors meticulously mapping every neurological impulse, every synaptic pattern.

Ethan watched the ring move, a lazy grin forming. "I gotta say, the lights on this thing are pretty cool. Feels like I'm in some high-tech carnival ride."

Then, as the scan deepened, the grin faded. His body visibly relaxed, his muscles going slack as if an invisible wave had washed over him. His chest rose and fell at a slower, almost hypnotic rhythm, his breath still perceptible but subdued.

The tension in the room thickened as the team watched,

silent and transfixed.

"Preliminary scan complete," Liza announced. "All readings are nominal. Neural pathways are stable, and cognitive structures are intact."

Abby let out a slow breath of relief but didn't take her eyes off Ethan.

Then Liza spoke again. "Abby, I require your command to commence transmission to the designated coordinates."

The words settled heavily in the air.

Abby hesitated for just a moment, the weight of the decision pressing down on her. They had planned for this. They had prepared. But now, standing at the precipice of something truly unprecedented, she felt the enormity of the moment.

This was no longer just an experiment. This was a leap into the unknown.

She inhaled deeply, steadying herself. Then, on the exhale, she gave the command.

"Liza... commence transmission. And start the countdown for the return timer."

"Acknowledged," Liza responded.

A soft pulse resonated through the chamber as the scanner shifted into its next phase. The lights along the scanning ring intensified, their glow pulsing in a synchronized rhythm. The air around Ethan seemed to distort ever so slightly, as though the very fabric of space around him was shifting.

The team held their breath.

They had crossed the threshold.

And now, there was no turning back.

# 6

Ethan drifted.

He wasn't floating, nor falling, but suspended in a tunnel that wasn't a tunnel—an expanse stretching infinitely in all directions, yet impossibly narrow at the same time. He couldn't see walls or boundaries, yet he sensed their presence, like the hollow vibration of wind rushing past unseen pillars. Colors bled into one another in shifting ribbons of luminescence, cascading through the space like living brushstrokes of blue, violet, and gold. There was no up or down, only the sensation of motion, though he wasn't sure if he was being pulled, pushed, or simply existing within something greater than himself.

A whisper of thought—not sound, but something deeper—echoed around him. Familiar, yet foreign. Known, yet unknowable. Time here felt stretched, warped, like it was deciding whether to move forward, backward, or remain still.

For a brief moment, he felt himself fragment, as though his thoughts were scattering like grains of sand caught in a rising tide. A wave of something vast brushed against him, a presence unlike anything he'd ever encountered—endless, observing, yet utterly indifferent.

Then, everything solidified. Time snapped back into place, and he arrived.

Ethan's first sensation was warmth—not just physical, but something deeper, a presence enveloping him like gentle hands guiding him into place. He didn't feel his own body, yet he existed. Thoughts that weren't his own swirled around him, but they weren't intrusive. They were welcoming.

Then, a name surfaced in his mind—not from his own memory, but from hers.

Her presence was delicate yet strong, like steel wrapped in silk. He wasn't just sensing her—he was within her. Every breath, every flicker of thought, passed through a space that felt alive. But he wasn't in control here. He was a guest.

"Welcome, Ethan."

The words weren't spoken—they settled in his mind like vibrations carried through still water. "You arrived intact. That's good."

Around him, the boundaries of reality were both familiar and foreign. This wasn't simulation, but neither was it the world he knew. It was her. Her domain. Her architecture. Lyara wasn't a voice in his mind. She was the world now holding him.

He tried to respond, but the concept of speech felt strange here. Instead, his thoughts formed with intention. *"Where... am I?"*

*"You're in the future. My future. And for now, my mind."* There was no hesitation, no unease. Lyara's presence wrapped around his consciousness like a protective cocoon, steadying him as he adjusted. *"This method of travel is delicate, but you handled it well."*

Ethan took a moment to process the surreal nature of it all. He wasn't hallucinating. He wasn't dreaming. He was here.

Lyara seemed to sense his understanding settle. "I know this is overwhelming, but we don't have much time. You need to listen carefully."

Memories—her memories—flashed across his awareness, not as intrusive thoughts, but as glimpses of a reality so unlike his own. Towering structures bathed in ethereal blue light. Silent streets. A world advanced yet hauntingly empty.

And then—the scientists.

Faces, some young, some worn by time and hardship.

Their eyes held something familiar—desperation. Hope.

"Your mission remains the same," Lyara's presence pressed gently against his thoughts, reinforcing her words. "Help us get back. But you need to be careful. There are forces here that do not want that to happen."

Ethan tried to push forward a thought—"Who?"—but Lyara's response came with a quiet urgency, a ripple of unease threading through her consciousness.

"You'll see soon enough."

And with that, Ethan truly understood. He wasn't just here to observe.

He was here to act.

Ethan's awareness stabilized, his presence within Lyara no longer foreign but familiar, as though he had been here far longer than just moments. Yet, something gnawed at the edges of his consciousness—he couldn't feel his own body. He couldn't clench his fists or shift his weight. He was only aware of movement, as if riding within Lyara's senses rather than commanding them.

"Relax," Lyara's voice hummed within him, the warmth of her thoughts soothing. "Don't resist. Your mind is untethered, but you are safe. Think of movement as intention—what you wish to do, I will do."

Ethan focused, imagining himself looking forward. The blurry edges of his vision sharpened, and his senses aligned. He felt her breath, rhythmic and steady, like an anchor. The weight of her limbs, the subtle shift of balance. It was as if he were borrowing her body, rather than merely spectating.

A shape loomed before him—several shapes, standing in what appeared to be a futuristic laboratory. The room pulsed with soft, ambient light emanating from devices Ethan couldn't quite identify—sleek panels embedded into the walls, illuminated consoles with displays that flickered in strange, shifting symbols. The air felt charged, almost electric, as though the very walls hummed with untapped energy.

Machines lined the perimeter—some resembling advanced scanning equipment, others featuring intricate, interlocking mechanisms that pulsed with an eerie bioluminescent glow. At the center of it all stood a large cylindrical device, its surface a swirling mesh of light and metal, suspended in what appeared to be a gravity field, its components shifting and adjusting as if alive.

Ethan had never seen technology like this—not even in theoretical research papers. It was far beyond anything his team had built.

His gaze snapped back to the figures in front of him. The scientists.

The moment Ethan fully grasped what he was seeing, a man stepped forward. His features were sharp with age, hair graying at the temples, his dark eyes scanning Lyara's face with a mix of curiosity and urgency.

"You've made it through," the man stated, his voice even but brisk. "Good. We don't have much time."

Lyara—no, Ethan within her—felt a flicker of unease. He knew this was the lead scientist, the very person who had sent the message back to the past. And now, standing before him, this man looked both relieved and burdened by something unseen.

The scientist continued, his words clipped. "Forgive me for skipping formalities, but you need to listen carefully. We sent our message as a warning, and it seems you were wise enough to heed it. The fracture is not what you think it is."

Ethan felt his thoughts race. "Then what is it?" he pushed toward Lyara, trusting she would translate it into words.

The scientist's expression darkened. "It's not just a rift in time—it's an anchor point. Someone or something created it, and now it's holding. We believe the financiers—the very ones funding your research—are responsible for it, or at the very least, discovered it and decided to use it to their advantage."

Ethan felt a surge of anger, but Lyara kept his emotions

contained. The scientist pressed on. "We had to abandon our lab when they realized we knew too much. They didn't just shut us down—they tried to erase us. Every trace of our research, every piece of our work. The fracture isn't just some accidental tear in time. It's deliberate. A controlled instability, maintained from the past."

Ethan—through Lyara—felt his breath hitch. A controlled instability? That meant it wasn't just happening, it was being manipulated. But for what purpose?

The scientist glanced over his shoulder, as if wary of unseen ears. "We need to act fast. We were never meant to survive this long on this side of the fracture. We were supposed to be wiped out the moment we arrived. But we adapted. We hid. And now we need to leave before they find us again."

Ethan's mind raced, overwhelmed by the sheer weight of what he was being told. He had assumed the fracture was a byproduct of their research, a dangerous consequence of meddling with time. But this... this was something far worse.

Lyara's voice rippled through him, steadying his thoughts. "You are here for a reason, Ethan. You are our link back. And now, you have a choice."

The lead scientist locked eyes with Lyara—with Ethan.

"You need to get us home before they sever the fracture entirely. If that happens—" He hesitated for the briefest of moments before finishing, his voice hollow. "We will cease to exist."

Ethan steadied himself, pushing through the disorienting sensation of being in a body that wasn't his own. The scientists, their faces marked with the weight of years spent in exile, watched him with expectant eyes. Despite the surreal nature of the situation, his mind sharpened, falling back into problem-solving mode.

"If you could send me a data-pad with precise coordinates, why can't you send yourselves back the same way?" Ethan asked, his mental voice firm but measured. "Why not just return through the same system that got you here?"

The lead scientist—a man with a streak of silver in his dark hair—exchanged glances with the others before exhaling. His name surfaced in Ethan's borrowed mind. Dr. Emmett Cole.

"If it were that simple, we wouldn't still be here." Cole's tone was patient, but there was a layer of exhaustion beneath it. "Time isn't just a one-way stream—it's an entire web of interconnected points. The moment we crossed into this future, we severed our connection to our original timeline."

Ethan frowned, trying to process. "Severed? But you're still here. You exist. So what's stopping you from just... jumping back?"

"Because we don't have an anchor."

One of the other scientists, a woman with sharp eyes and an air of quiet authority—Dr. Kyra Nolan—stepped forward.

"Think of time like a river. When you wade into the current, you're carried forward. If you try to swim back, the river doesn't simply reverse—it moves around you, reshaping the course ahead and behind. If we return directly to the point we left, we risk being thrown into the same catastrophe we escaped. Worse, we could be caught in a paradoxical feedback loop—arriving at the exact moment we departed, effectively existing twice within the same moment."

Ethan's mind raced. "Meaning?"

Cole folded his arms. "Meaning we'd be colliding with our past selves. Best case? The timeline rejects us, and we cease to exist as distinct entities. Worst case? We create an instability that shreds the local reality into an unsolvable paradox."

The words sent a chill through Ethan. He had read theoretical papers on time-travel paradoxes but hearing them laid out like a death sentence made them far more real.

"Okay," Ethan pressed, "but what if you don't go back to your original departure point? What if you travel even further back—before your experiment started?"

Nolan shook her head. "That creates a different problem: the Temporal Redundancy Effect. If we insert ourselves into a time where we already exist—just earlier—we risk being caught in an overlap of consciousness. Our minds weren't meant to exist twice in the same moment. It would be like an echo trapped in an infinite loop, unable to move forward or backward. The result?"

She gestured vaguely, as if words failed her.

"At best, we become anomalies—glitches in time. At worst... we're erased altogether." Cole finished grimly.

Ethan felt the weight of their words settle over him. The implications were staggering.

"Then what's the solution?" he asked.

The room grew tense. Cole hesitated, exchanging glances with the others.

"That's what we've been trying to figure out," Cole admitted. "We need a stable point—an anchor in the past where we can return without paradox. But we're running out of time. The fracture is expanding."

Ethan's pulse quickened. "Expanding? What does that mean?"

"It means the longer we stay displaced, the harder it will be to navigate back. The fracture is shifting, distorting potential exit points. If it becomes too unstable, we won't be able to return at all." Cole's voice was tight with urgency.

Ethan exhaled slowly, forcing himself to think. They needed a way to anchor their return. A fixed point that wasn't entangled in their original departure. Something— somewhere—they could safely land without breaking the time stream.

A thought surfaced. "What if we use my timeline?"

The scientists stared at him.

"Your team is still actively working on time

displacement," Ethan continued. "Your experiment was abandoned, but ours is ongoing. If we create a stable reception point in my present, could that work as an anchor?"

Silence stretched between them.

Then Coles expression shifted—calculating, considering.

"That... could work." Nolan murmured, the first flicker of hope crossing her face. "But it would require absolute precision. Your team would have to construct a reception field that could lock onto our quantum signatures. Any misalignment and—"

"And you're lost for good," Ethan finished.

Nolan exhaled sharply. "It's a risk. But it might be our only option."

Ethan felt Lyara's presence stir around him, steadying him. She didn't need to say anything. He already knew.

This was why he was here.

"Then let's make it happen."

Ethan took a slow breath—or at least, it felt like one. He could feel Lyara's body, her heartbeat steady but slightly elevated, mirroring his own racing thoughts.

Ethan took a steady breath, his thoughts aligning with the weight of the responsibility ahead. "I'll return to my time and discuss this with my team. We need to plan carefully if we're going to make this work."

Ethan turned to the scientists, his expression sharpening with determination. "How do I enter the coordinates into the data pad? I need to make sure my team knows exactly what to do."

One of the scientists, a wiry man with sharp eyes, stepped forward and demonstrated, his fingers gliding over the smooth interface. "It's simple. Input the spatial-temporal data here," he said, highlighting a glowing panel, "and confirm the transmission with this command. Once sent, it will anchor itself to the designated time point."

Ethan nodded, committing the process to memory.

"Alright. Send the data pad back to Abby and the team in exactly 24 hours. That gives me time to explain everything and get a plan in motion. When they receive it, they'll respond with the return coordinates and any necessary information."

The lead scientist met Ethan's gaze with a knowing look. "We'll be waiting. Make sure they get it right."

Ethan exhaled, feeling the weight of what was coming. "We won't get a second chance."

Ethan ran a hand through his—no, Lyara's—hair, the sensation alien yet strangely grounding. Realizing what he had done, he hesitated before offering a sheepish apology. "I'm so sorry, it's a force of habit when I'm stressed."

Lyara's response was warm, laced with a quiet amusement. "Don't worry. I rather enjoyed the feeling."

A subtle connection passed between them—unspoken, yet unmistakable. Ethan could sense her growing comfort with his presence, a shared understanding forming between them.

He refocused, pushing aside the distraction. "Alright. When I get back, I'll talk to my team and we'll work on a plan."

"The data pad," Dr Nolan said. "Once you return, wait exactly one day. We will send another message through. You can respond with the necessary coordinates. That will be our window."

Ethan nodded. "Got it. But listen—when you return to my time, you have to be careful. You cannot interact with any of your relatives or people who might recognize you. You have to assume new identities. If the corporation or the government finds you, you'll be caught before you even have a chance to fix this."

The scientists exchanged glances. The reality of what Ethan was saying hit hard—returning home wasn't just a scientific challenge, it was a survival game.

The lead scientist took a deep breath. "Understood. We

will be ghosts. But first, we need to get there."

Lyara's presence nudged Ethan's consciousness gently. "Your time is almost up."

Ethan could feel it too. A pull—faint at first, but growing stronger.

"One day," he said firmly. "Send the pad back in one day. We'll be waiting."

The scientists nodded. No more words were needed.

And with that, the pull became overwhelming. It wasn't just a force—it was a sensation that gripped his very essence, threading through him like an unseen tether snapping taut. He recognized it, that familiar sensation of being drawn back, yet this time it was different.

It wasn't just pulling him—it was unraveling him, like strands of consciousness being reeled through the unseen currents of time. For a fleeting moment, he felt suspended between two realities, stretched thin across the distance, before the full force of the transition took hold and the world around him vanished.

Time snapped.

And Ethan was gone.

\*\*\*

The sensation of being stretched beyond existence collapsed in an instant, slamming Ethan back into his own body like a jolt of static electricity grounding itself through his spine. His mind reeled, disoriented, untethered for a moment, as if he were caught between two worlds—neither fully here nor there.

A shudder ran through his limbs as his senses reconnected with the familiar. Cool air. The subtle hum of lab equipment. The faint scent of sterilized metal and coffee lingering from earlier that morning. Yet, everything felt off—his own body foreign, like a suit he had suddenly outgrown.

He gasped, his chest rising sharply as the weight of full awareness slammed into him. His stomach twisted violently in protest.

Before he could even speak, a trash bin was thrust into his hands.

"Breathe," Abby instructed, her voice firm but laced with concern. "Let it pass."

Ethan barely managed to make a nod before doubling over, retching into the bin. His head spun, nausea rolling through him in waves. Every nerve in his body screamed at him, like he had been turned inside out and back again. His muscles, though they hadn't moved, felt as if they had run a marathon through time itself.

Daniel was by his side, a steadying hand on his shoulder. "Take it easy, man. You're back. You made it."

Ethan groaned, gripping the edge of the chair like an anchor. He squeezed his eyes shut, willing the world to stop tilting and swirling violently.

Liza's voice came through the lab's speakers, a measured calm cutting through the haze. "Ethan, all your vitals appear stable. Mild tachycardia, elevated adrenaline levels—expected physiological responses. You are safe."

He coughed, spitting the acrid taste from his mouth before forcing himself upright. His skin was clammy, sweat dampening his hairline, but his mind—his mind was racing.

"I saw them," he croaked, voice hoarse. He swallowed, trying to gather himself. "They're alive."

The team stiffened, leaning in, hanging on his every word.

Abby set the bin aside but remained close. "Talk to us. What happened?"

Ethan took a slow, shaky breath. "The scientists—they're still there. They've been stranded this whole time. The corporation… they tried to erase everything, to cover up the fracture." He shook his head, gripping his temples as if trying to piece his thoughts back together. "Except—it wasn't a fracture. Not really. It was an ill-conceived time anchor, something meant to stabilize their work, but it failed.

Instead of securing the timeline, it shredded it, leaving them trapped beyond the distortion."

A heavy silence fell over the lab.

Olivia was the first to break it. "You mean—this was intentional? They didn't just shut down the project... they tried to erase it?"

Ethan nodded, jaw tightening. "They knew what they did, and instead of fixing it, they abandoned everyone involved. Those scientists—they were just trying to survive. They still are."

Mark exhaled, dragging a hand through his hair. "And now what? Do we get them back?"

Ethan lifted his gaze to Abby, his expression hardening with resolve. "They're sending the data-pad back to us in twenty-four hours. They need coordinates. They need a way home."

Abby crossed her arms, lips pressed into a thin line. "Then we better make damn sure we have an answer when that pad shows up."

Liza interjected, her voice steady. "I have already begun running calculations to determine viable extraction points. However, we must consider the risks of reintegrating displaced individuals into this timeline. There may be unforeseen consequences."

Daniel let out a low breath. "Yeah, well, at this point, not doing anything seems like the greater consequence."

Ethan nodded, still catching his breath. "One more thing." He hesitated, but the weight of it pressed too hard to ignore. "They warned us—about the projection method. They said if we attempt to send a consciousness without safeguards... it'll end badly."

A cold ripple passed through the group.

Abby's brow furrowed. "How badly?"

Ethan swallowed. "They didn't say. Just that whatever we're trying—it's more dangerous than we thought."

A long silence stretched between them as the reality of

the situation sank in.

Then Abby straightened, shoulders squared, determination etched into her expression. "Alright. We take this seriously. We plan *everything*—no shortcuts, no assumptions. We do this right, or we don't do it at all."

The team nodded in unison. No one argued.

This wasn't just an experiment anymore.

This was a rescue mission. And failure wasn't an option.

Ethan closed his eyes for a brief moment, still feeling the last echoes of his journey vibrating through him.

Twenty-four hours.

That was all the time they had to figure out how to bring them home.

Abby let out a slow breath, glancing over at Ethan, who still looked pale and unsteady. She turned back to the team. "Alright, I want everyone to get some rest. Tomorrow is going to be a long day." She cast a firm look at each of them, knowing they all needed the break, even if their minds wouldn't stop racing.

Mark and Olivia hesitated before nodding, quietly heading out of the lab. As the door slid shut behind them, Abby turned her attention back to Daniel and Ethan. "You two stay a little longer. Ethan, we're not leaving until you're steady on your feet again."

Ethan gave her a weak smirk. "Babysitting me now?"

Daniel chuckled. "Nah, just making sure you don't collapse halfway to car."

Liza's voice chimed in, her tone softer than usual. "Ethan's well-being is of paramount importance. Ensuring he is fully recovered before leaving is the logical course of action."

Abby smirked. "See? Even Liza agrees."

Ethan let out a tired chuckle, rubbing his face. "Alright, alright. I'll sit still for a bit."

As they settled in, the weight of what lay ahead pressed down on them all.

Tomorrow, the real challenge would begin.

\*\*\*

The next morning the team reconvened at the digital whiteboard, the hum of the lab filling the silence as they faced the monumental task ahead. Eight hours remained until the data-pad would reappear, carrying the next crucial step in their desperate bid to retrieve the stranded scientists.

Abby turned to face them, arms crossed, her expression steeled with determination. "Alright, we need to figure out the logistics of bringing them back—and more importantly, how to make sure they don't get caught the second they step into this timeline. We can't just drop them into society and hope for the best."

Ethan nodded, still rubbing the lingering ache from his temples. A faint sensation lingered at the edge of his consciousness, like an echo of a presence he couldn't quite place—something familiar yet distant, as if Lyara's essence still brushed against his mind. "I told them they'd have to be ghosts. No contact with family, no connections to anyone who might recognize them. But even then... it's risky. The corporation could still be watching."

Mark tapped his fingers against his desk, thinking. "What about relocating them? Giving them a place to go that's completely off the radar? They need a cover story, something airtight."

Daniel exhaled, glancing at Abby. "That's only half the problem. We need them here, helping us fix the damage. If they disappear, we lose the only people who fully understand what went wrong with the original experiment. We can't afford to just hide them away."

Olivia frowned. "So, what are we saying? That we keep them here, working with us? In secret? While still making sure no one finds out they exist? That's not exactly a simple plan."

Liza's voice chimed in, even and analytical. "A structured reintegration is possible. By utilizing secured locations and controlled interactions, their presence can be concealed while allowing them access to necessary resources."

Ethan raised a brow. "So, what—witness protection but make it quantum physics?"

Abby let out a slow breath, considering the options. "It's not just about hiding them. We need a long-term solution. If we can repair the time stream—if we can correct what went wrong—then maybe they won't have to live like fugitives. Maybe they can reclaim their lives."

Daniel leaned forward. "But that means we don't just bring them back—we bring them back with a plan. A way to undo the damage before the corporation realizes we're working against them."

The team exchanged glances, the weight of the conversation pressing down on them.

Liza broke the silence. "I have begun analyzing possible stabilization methods. However, this is an unprecedented situation. The process of repairing a fragmented temporal stream requires both precise execution and an understanding of the forces at play. Without further data, any attempts would carry unpredictable risks."

Ethan sighed. "We need more than just a plan to hide them. We need to figure out how to fix this. Otherwise, we're just kicking the can down the road."

Abby's gaze hardened. "Then that's what we focus on next. We don't just bring them back—we make sure they have a future worth coming back to."

Daniel hesitated before adding, "We could use the lower levels of the facility. They're unused, secured, and off any official records. We control the access. If we're careful, we can keep them there while they help us figure this out."

Abby considered it, nodding. "That could work. But we still need to crack how to stabilize the time stream. If we don't, they won't just be fugitives—they'll be anomalies in time. And the last thing we need is more instability."

A charged silence filled the lab. The path forward was anything but clear, but one thing was certain—this was bigger than just a rescue.

They weren't just retrieving lost scientists.

They were fighting to mend time itself.

## 7

The team continued their work on the electronic whiteboard, meticulously analyzing the complexities of bringing the other team back—whether as a whole or in staggered intervals. Abby turned to Liza, her expression thoughtful.

"Liza, can you calculate the complete quantum signatures of each individual, track their trajectory through the time stream, and determine if they can be safely materialized within the quantum drive?"

Liza's response came after a brief pause. "Abby, I calculate a high probability of successfully locking onto the team at the requested coordinates and capturing their quantum signatures. However, the variables involved are intricate, and the energy required will almost certainly trigger external monitoring systems. A possible solution is masking the event within a larger, authorized test to avoid unwanted scrutiny."

The team exchanged glances, considering the implications. They couldn't afford to expose their plan, but if they timed it carefully, they might be able to pass it off as part of their standard research.

As they debated logistics, Abby and Liza proposed repurposing outdated security measures to obscure the presence of additional personnel within the lower levels of the facility. Working swiftly, the team modified dormant access logs and rerouted digital tracking systems, ensuring no new entries would be detected. This would allow them to mask any anomalies that might arise from the sudden expansion of their team.

The team spotted the arrival of several black SUVs on the security monitors, their black frames sleek and ominous against the facility's exterior. The tension in the room spiked as men in dark suits stepped out, their movements precise and coordinated. One of them opened a rear door, and Greta Stone emerged, her sharp gaze scanning the building even before she entered.

Just as the team finalized their adjustments, the doors swung open, and Greta's piercing gaze swept across the room. Her expression was unreadable as she stepped forward, flanked by two of her men.

"We've detected anomaly readings from your facility that don't align with the expected parameters of your approved research," she stated, her tone clipped. "Care to explain?"

Abby met her gaze evenly, keeping her expression neutral despite the weight of the accusation pressing down on her. "We've been running calibration tests," she said smoothly. "Given the nature of the quantum field, fluctuations are expected. The readings are likely residual effects from the equipment adjusting to precision levels."

Greta's eyes narrowed slightly. "Residual effects?"

Daniel, standing just behind Abby, nodded. "Yes. The hyperdrive and encephalograph system are still syncing with Liza's operational framework. That alone could be causing small deviations in the expected data stream."

Greta studied them for a long moment before exhaling through her nose. "See that it doesn't escalate. We expect detailed reports moving forward. No further surprises."

Abby offered a measured nod, her stance unwavering. "Since you're here and requested an update, we will be performing a full-scale hyperdrive test using larger, dense objects to assess Liza's ability to track signatures and refine projection capability. We anticipate a substantial energy draw. You're welcome to observe, but if something were to go wrong, we wouldn't want to put you at unnecessary risk."

Greta's expression remained unreadable, but after a pause, she gave a curt nod. "Proceed with caution. I'll expect a full report afterward." Without another word, she turned on her heel and strode out of the lab, her team in tow.

The moment the door shut behind them, silence settled over the room like a suffocating weight.

Ethan let out a slow breath and rubbed the back of his neck. "Okay… so they're monitoring us in ways we didn't even consider. That's just fantastic." He glanced at Abby with a smirk. "You wove that nicely into the conversation. Good idea."

Daniel folded his arms, his jaw tight. "They knew exactly what to look for. That wasn't a casual inquiry—they have direct access to data we never sent them."

Abby's expression darkened. "Which means they're tapping into Liza without us knowing it." She turned toward the AI. "Liza, are there any unauthorized access logs in your system?"

A brief pause. Then, Liza's voice came through, measured but firm. "There are no direct breaches within my primary architecture. However, external monitoring systems embedded within the facility's core infrastructure could be relaying data independently of my processes."

Ethan exhaled heavily, glancing at the hyperdrive. "Yeah. No pressure or anything."

They weren't just working against time anymore.

They were working against the very people funding them.

***

A faint pulse of energy rippled through the lab as the hyperdrive emitted a soft hum, signaling an incoming arrival. The team, already on edge from their earlier discussion, turned in unison toward the containment chamber just as a brief flash of light filled the air.

The data-pad had returned.

Ethan took a step forward, eyes locked on the sleek device resting in the chamber. He hesitated only briefly before reaching in and retrieving it, the smooth surface cool against his fingers. Turning it over once in his hands, he studied it for any visible changes before stepping toward Abby and placing it in her hands.

As Abby's fingers wrapped around the data-pad, it pulsed faintly before the display flickered to life, responding instantly to her biometric signature.

The glowing text formed above the data-pad, each word crisp and urgent:

THE FUTURE SITE IS COMPROMISED. WE DO NOT HAVE MUCH TIME LEFT. SECURITY MEASURES THAT HAVE KEPT US HIDDEN ARE FAILING. LYARA CANNOT REMAIN HERE—IT IS NO LONGER SAFE FOR HER. IF YOU DO NOT BRING HER BACK WITH US, SHE WILL BE IN DANGER. WE ESTIMATE WE HAVE EIGHT HOURS BEFORE OUR PRESENCE IS FULLY DETECTED.

Ethan exhaled sharply, a mix of emotions tightening in his chest. "They need her to come back with them."

Daniel raked a hand through his hair, a familiar gesture of unease. "This just got even more complicated. We were already taking a risk bringing them back—now we have an unknown factor. Someone we've never even interacted with directly."

Abby shot him a look. "We have met her. Ethan did."

Olivia crossed her arms. "And let's be honest, bringing her back might be safer for us too. If she stays there, she could be captured. If the corporation in the future gets a hold of her, who knows what they could pull from her mind? She knows too much."

Ethan tightened his grip on the data-pad Abby just gave him, his voice firm. "She's as much a part of this as they are. Leaving her behind isn't an option."

Abby sighed, rubbing her temples. "We don't have much choice, do we? If their security measures fail, they could be taken at any moment. If we don't act now, we may never get another chance."

Mark leaned against the workstation, eyes flicking between the team. "So that's it, then? We bring them all back and hope for the best?"

Liza's voice broke through, calm yet deliberate. "I have received the coordinates embedded within the message. I can begin calculations immediately to prepare for the transfer. However, the additional individual may introduce unforeseen complications. I will require precise adjustments to ensure stabilization."

Abby nodded. "Then let's not waste time. Start running the calculations, Liza. We're bringing them home."

Liza confirmed, "Understood. Commencing quantum synchronization."

Ethan lowered the data-pad, his expression resolute. "Before you begin calculations, Liza, is there a way to make the data-pad disappear? Instead of returning it to the origin point, could you phase the data stream and drop it before the send—erase it from ever existing in that location?"

Liza responded with a measured tone, "Ethan, place the data-pad in the drive." Once he complied, Liza engaged the system. The data-pad flickered and phased out of existence, leaving no trace behind. After a brief pause, Liza spoke again, her voice laced with an unmistakable—though artificial—hint of wry amusement. "My sincerest apologies, Ethan. It appears the stream has inadvertently been lost and is, regrettably, unrecoverable. An unfortunate and entirely unforeseeable accident."

Ethan let out a dry chuckle, shaking his head. "Well, that was unfortunate, Liza. Resume your original calculations."

The weight of the moment settled over them. The next step wasn't just retrieval—it was the culmination of everything they had been working toward. And now, with Lyara's safety at stake, failure was not an option.

Time was against them.

And the countdown had begun.

\*\*\*

The tension in the lab thickened as Liza continued running the calculations. The low hum of the hyperdrive filled the space, a constant reminder that time was slipping away.

Abby exhaled, pushing back from the workstation and addressing the team. "We need to get those old security devices up and operational. If we're bringing in extra people, we have to mask their presence. The last thing we need is someone picking up additional signatures and asking questions."

Daniel nodded and moved toward a storage locker along the far wall. "I think we still have some of the old security masking units from when this place was first activated. They were meant to scramble personnel tracking. If we modify them to reflect only the original five of us, it should be enough to hide the new arrivals."

Ethan followed him, already opening a small tool kit. "Let's hope the hardware's not completely outdated. If these are old corporate models, they might be running outdated firmware. We'll need to bypass any automatic updates that could trigger external logging."

Olivia crossed her arms, glancing toward Liza's main interface. "Liza, can you integrate the masking system into the facility's monitoring network? We need it to make sure the headcount doesn't register anything beyond the five of us."

Liza's voice carried a measured tone of assurance. "Yes, Olivia. I will modify the facility's internal monitoring to reflect only the expected personnel. Any additional life signs will be filtered from outbound reports."

Abby turned to Mark. "Start configuring the power settings. I want these devices fully operational before we even think about opening that drive. No surprises."

Mark gave a quick nod and got to work, linking the devices to a portable console and adjusting their output frequencies. The lab buzzed with controlled chaos as the team worked, each member falling into their respective tasks with practiced precision and urgency.

Liza's voice broke the brief silence. "Quantum synchronization is at 93%. Estimated time to completion: four minutes."

Abby turned to the team. "Alright, let's go through this step by step. When the drive activates, space inside will be tight. Liza, how much room are we working with?"

"The hyperdrive containment chamber has limited spatial capacity," Liza confirmed. "Upon arrival, there will be little remaining physical volume within the chamber. The retrieved individuals will need to step out immediately to avoid overloading containment parameters."

Ethan exhaled sharply. "So we're basically stuffing them into a phone booth and hoping they squeeze out fast enough before we get a hardware failure."

Daniel smirked. "That's one way to put it."

Abby placed her hands on her hips. "Then we need to be ready. The moment they arrive, we guide them out and get them below ground before anyone—or anything—detects an anomaly." She turned toward Olivia. "Grab some of the extra garbage cans. If Ethan's reaction was anything to go by, we may have several people losing their stomachs when they get here."

Olivia grimaced but nodded. "Good point. Last thing we need is a group of disoriented, time-displaced scientists vomiting all over the lab floor."

Mark smirked. "Talk about a rough first day back."

Ethan rolled his eyes. "Yeah, yeah, laugh it up. Let's see how you handle your first quantum jump."

After grabbing a few extra cans, Olivia finished the last calibration and looked up. "Security masking is active. We're officially ghosts. No one outside this lab will see a headcount change."

Abby gave a firm nod, satisfaction flickering in her eyes. "Good. Then we're as ready as we'll ever be."

Liza's tone shifted slightly, a calm urgency present.

"Synchronization complete. Awaiting command to initiate retrieval."

Abby inhaled deeply, glancing at the team. "This is it."

She turned back to the drive, her voice steady.

"Liza—let's bring them home."

*** 

Liza's voice carried through the lab with measured precision. "Power levels on the quantum drive at 30% above normal… Engaging containment." A low hum vibrated through the floor as the hyperdrive powered up, the containment field shimmering into place.

The lights overhead flickered, momentarily dimming as the hyperdrive drew immense power. A charge filled the air, sharp and tangible, like the static before a lightning strike.

"I advise you cover your eyes team. This will be a very bright flash," Liza warned.

The team instinctively raised their arms, shielding their eyes from the impending burst of energy. Ethan shifted uncomfortably, glancing at Abby. "This amount of energy feels bigger than previous times."

A sharp static crackle intensified, making the hairs on their arms and the back of their necks stand on end. It wasn't just a hum anymore—it was a presence, something vast and impossible, pressing against reality itself.

Then the sound came.

A deep, thrumming resonance started building, unlike anything they'd heard before. It started low but climbed rapidly, vibrating through the floor, through their bones. The lab trembled as unseen forces rippled through the walls.

Mark tensed. "That doesn't sound good. It sounds like it's about to blow up!" His hands twitched at his sides, his body poised as if expecting to run—not that there was anywhere to go.

Liza's voice remained unwavering. "Quantum signatures acquired… Locked in. Engaging transit tunnel. Energy level at 140 percent and building"

The world seemed to hold its breath.

Then—the explosion of light.

It wasn't just bright—it was overwhelming. A supernova of energy burst from the drive, swallowing the lab in an all-consuming brilliance. For a moment, everything was white, as if existence had been reset in a blinding flashpoint.

A deafening *boom* followed, slamming into them like a force of nature. The walls groaned. A metallic crash echoed from somewhere behind them. Ethan stumbled back, eyes wide, his breath catching in his throat.

Abby fought against the shockwave rattling her chest, her mind scrambling to refocus. Her vision still spotted with light, she pushed forward, reaching for the containment chamber.

"Liza! Drop the containment field before it rips them apart!" she shouted, urgency cutting through her voice.

Liza's response was smooth, almost unnervingly calm. "Already done. The field is stable. It's safe to open the door Abby."

Abby didn't hesitate. She gripped the heavy latch, braced herself, and pulled.

The chamber door hissed as it unsealed, releasing a rush of frigid air into the lab.

Inside, shadows began to form.

They had arrived.

***

The air still crackled with residual energy, a faint hum lingering in the room as the afterglow of the hyperdrive faded. The containment chamber door was barely open before the first signs of disorientation hit.

Lyara stumbled forward, her expression somewhere between dazed and alarmed, her eyes unfocused as she tried to steady herself. Behind her, one of the scientists lurched from the drive like newborn deer on ice, their legs wobbly, their balance nonexistent. One barely managed to grip the side of the chamber before slumping against it, looking pale as a ghost.

A low groan came from the group. Then—

"Oh, no—nope, not good—"

Lyara's hand flew to her mouth, and before she could take another step, Olivia—who had wisely anticipated this—thrust a trash can into her arms just in time.

Ethan, already moving before he had even realized it, was at her side in an instant. "Hey, I got you, I got you," he murmured, steadying her with a firm but gentle grip. "Breathe, just breathe."

Lyara wasn't alone in her suffering. A second scientist made it about three steps before she doubled over into another of Olivia's strategically placed garbage cans. Mark winced at the sound of retching, making a face. "Yep. That's exactly what I expected."

The third scientist, an older man with silver-streaked hair, seemed to be fighting his stomach's rebellion with every ounce of dignity he could muster. He stood rigid, jaw clenched, eyes squeezed shut, hands on his knees as he took long, slow breaths.

"I am *not* throwing up in front of a room full of people," he muttered through gritted teeth.

Abby, watching it all unfold, exhaled and ran a hand through her hair. "Well... we did expect some, uh... turbulence."

Daniel raised an eyebrow. "Turbulence? Abby, they look like they just got off the world's worst rollercoaster ride through time."

Olivia, arms crossed, nodded at Lyara and Ethan. "At least someone's handling it better than the others."

Ethan had crouched beside Lyara, still keeping her steady as she took slow breaths between waves of nausea. He couldn't help but smirk a little. "You know, for the record, I don't think we properly covered this part of time travel in the theory section."

Lyara managed a weak chuckle, still pale but grateful.

"Yeah, well," she rasped, "next time, you can go first."

Mark snorted. "Uh, next time? Let's get through this first without any more puking before we sign up for another round."

Abby clapped her hands together, reclaiming the room. "Alright, everyone. The good news? You're all here in one piece. The bad news? We're on the clock. We need to get you out of here and downstairs before anyone outside this room realizes what just happened."

Liza's voice cut through the commotion, ever calm and composed. "Scans indicate no anomalies detected outside of expected biological distress. However, it is advisable to expedite the relocation process."

Ethan helped Lyara to her feet, keeping a careful hold on her arm. She was still shaky, but she nodded. "I'll be fine. Just... give me a second."

Abby gave her a knowing look. "Take all the time you want, but we are moving."

Lyara took another deep breath, then squared her shoulders. "Right. Let's go."

Daniel glanced at the other two scientists. "Yeah, uh... you guys good?"

The older scientist—who had miraculously avoided joining the barf brigade—nodded stiffly. "Just get me somewhere I can sit down before I actually regret holding it in."

Mark gestured dramatically toward the lab exit. "Then, by all means, let's take this nausea train downstairs before we have to start mopping."

With that, the team quickly moved to guide their newly arrived guests toward their hidden sanctuary, hoping they could settle them before anyone—or anything—came looking.

\*\*\*

# 8

The underground level of the facility was colder than expected, its walls lined with aged conduits and reinforced panels that hinted at the building's original purpose. Dim overhead lights flickered to full brightness as Liza activated the system, illuminating the wide corridor that led to the team's newly designated hiding space.

Abby led the way, the sound of their footsteps echoing against the concrete floor and walls as they descended. The rescued scientists walked with sluggish, wary movements, their bodies still adjusting from the brutal effects of the temporal transit. Lyara kept close to Ethan, her posture tense, while the others remained quiet, their gazes scanning the unfamiliar surroundings.

Once they reached the lower level's main staging area, Abby turned on her heel, her hands planted firmly on her hips. "Alright, listen up, everyone," she said, her voice steady but carrying an unmistakable urgency. "I know you all just had the worst trip of your lives, and for that, I apologize. It was a rushed job under less-than-ideal circumstances, but we had no choice. Time was against us— literally." She sighed and softened her tone slightly. "But you're here now, and we're not just going to keep you hidden. We need your help to fix this mess before it gets any worse."

Dr. Cole, one of the rescued scientists, "So you're the ones picking up the pieces, then?" His voice held the slightest trace of amusement, despite the fatigue in his expression.

Abby nodded. "That's right. And you're the ones who

can help us do it."

She gestured toward her own team, who had taken position around her. "Let's do introductions properly. I'm Dr. Abby Foster. This is Daniel, Ethan, Olivia, and Mark." She motioned to each of them in turn. "We're the team that— well, let's just say we stumbled onto the puzzle you all left behind."

The thin man nodded. "Dr. Emmett Cole," he said, finally offering a small smile. He motioned toward the others. "This is Dr. Kyra Nolan And of course, Lyara, whom I assume you've already grown acquainted with."

Lyara gave a small nod, still standing close to Ethan as if the return had left her untethered without him nearby.

Mark leaned slightly toward Olivia and whispered, "So... we've got an Emmett and a Kyra? Man, it's like they walked straight out of a sci-fi epic."

Abby shot him a warning look before continuing. "You all need to know that while we have you here, we've taken precautions to keep you hidden. We've reconfigured old security protocols to mask your presence digitally and physically. Any scans or headcounts performed remotely will still register only the five of us."

Dr. Kyra Nolan tilted her head slightly, intrigued. "That's an impressive trick."

"Liza helped," Daniel interjected, giving a slight nod toward the overhead speakers.

Liza's voice chimed in smoothly, "I do believe I deserve some credit, yes."

Dr. Kyra Nolan, a woman in her late fifties with salt-and-pepper hair, rubbed her face, exhaustion apparent. "You've gone through a hell of a lot of effort to bring us back," she muttered. "But I assume that means the situation is as dire as we feared."

Abby inhaled deeply. "Probably worse." She stepped toward the makeshift whiteboard that had been set up in the room, the surface still clean, waiting to be filled with whatever theories and plans they could muster. "We need to start working on fixing the time stream before it collapses completely. The 'fracture' wasn't a clean break—it was a botched attempt at a time anchor that shredded the stream into chaotic segments. We have to figure out how to weave it back together."

Dr. Cole frowned. "That's going to take more than just brute force calculations. We need a clear understanding of the pattern, the missing elements that are destabilizing it."

Abby nodded. "Agreed. That's why we need all hands on deck. We don't have the luxury of sitting on theories anymore—we need solutions."

Ethan finally spoke up, his voice more serious than usual. "We need to know exactly what went wrong before. What caused the disaster that forced you to leave your time in the first place?"

Dr. Nolan exhaled sharply. "That… is a long story."

Abby crossed her arms. "Then I suggest we all get comfortable. Because if we don't figure this out, none of us will have a future left to save."

A heavy silence fell over the group as the weight of the moment settled in.

There was no turning back now. The battle to mend time itself had officially begun.

***

Dr. Emmett Cole reached toward Abby, his hand hovering just beside her as he motioned toward the electronic whiteboard. "May I?" he asked, his tone polite but firm.

Abby studied him for a moment, then handed him the stylus. "Go ahead."

Cole stepped to the board, the glow of the interface reflecting in his sharp eyes as he began to draw. His movements were precise, practiced—a man who had spent years refining his theories in front of similar boards. He started with a timeline, placing markers at significant points before sketching a series of intricate waveforms that looped and converged in unpredictable patterns.

"This," he said, underlining a central point, "is where it all started to go wrong." He turned slightly to address them. "We thought we were simply measuring the quantum stream, observing its fluctuations to determine whether time was stable and traceable. But what we discovered... was far more concerning."

Dr. Kyra Nolan stepped closer, arms crossed as she studied the equations. "We weren't just looking into time. We were unintentionally *anchoring* to it."

Daniel frowned. "Anchoring? You mean you created a fixed point?"

"Exactly," Dr. Cole confirmed. He tapped the board where the loops of energy had begun spiraling outward. "The problem is, a time anchor isn't like a waypoint in space. It doesn't just mark a location—it pulls on it, distorting everything around it." He traced the spirals. "The more we ran experiments, the more unstable it became. Time doesn't like being tethered, and we essentially tied a knot so tight that it started to unravel the stream itself."

Abby exhaled, her mind racing. "That's why we saw so many time fractures... and why they seemed unpredictable. It wasn't just a rupture—it was time trying to break free from an artificial constraint."

Cole nodded gravely. "And that's when the corporation took interest."

The room fell into a heavier silence as Dr. Cole stepped back from the board, arms crossing over his chest. "We were approached. At first, it was just questions—the usual inquiries about theoretical applications. But then the discussions shifted. They started asking how this could be used—not for science, not for exploration, but for military control. For weaponization."

Ethan's jaw tightened. "Of course they did."

Cole's expression darkened. "I knew something was off, but I dismissed it. Then, a few days before we evacuated, I overheard a conversation I was never meant to hear." His fingers clenched around the marker. "One of the corporate representatives asked a simple, chilling question: What do we do with the scientists after their experiment?"

A cold silence settled over the room.

Abby stiffened. "They were never planning to let you walk away, were they?"

Cole shook his head. "No. We had become a liability. We had seen too much, knew too much. So we did the only thing we could—we ran." He turned back to the board, circling a moment on the timeline. "We knew we had one shot. We overpowered our equipment, pushing it way beyond its designed limits to force a conduit large enough for all of us to escape at once. The energy required was immense. We funneled every bit of power into it, knowing full well that once we passed through, the overload would destroy the system entirely."

Daniel's eyes widened slightly. "You're saying the original machine is gone?"

Cole nodded. "It's safe to assume it obliterated itself the moment the transition was complete. But the corporation—" he paused, his jaw tightening, "—they have money, power, and resources beyond what we imagined. Even if the machine was lost, we were still a loose end. Whether they came for us immediately or waited for the right moment, it was inevitable. They need to tie up that loose end, whether it's in the past, present, or future."

Olivia swallowed hard. "So even if we bring you back here and hide you, they'll still be looking?"

"Yes," Cole admitted. "And that's what makes this so dangerous. If they get any hint that we're here, that this facility is operational again, they will come. And they won't be asking questions."

Abby exhaled, rubbing her temples as she processed the weight of the revelation. "Then we need to make sure they don't find out."

Ethan folded his arms. "We fix the time stream first. And then we figure out how to keep them off our backs—permanently."

Abby's mind raced, piecing it all together. "Which means they might come looking for you."

Dr. Cole nodded gravely. "That's exactly what I'm afraid of."

Daniel ran a hand down his face in exasperation, processing everything. "So what's our move? Because if they were willing to silence you then, they won't hesitate now."

Abby took a deep breath, her mind locking into strategy mode. "We finish what you started. We fix the time stream. And we make damn sure that no one ever gets their hands on this again."

She turned to Liza. "Liza we're going to need a plan—and fast."

Liza's voice chimed in, smooth but with a hint of urgency. "I believe I have several contingencies we can explore."

Abby glanced around the room, locking eyes with each person. "Then let's get to work."

They had just uncovered the real battle ahead.

And time was still running out.

***

Abby stepped to Daniel's workstation, her voice low enough to ensure only he heard. "Daniel, we need to give Cole and Nolan access to Liza, but we can't have them showing up on the control list. Can we make that happen?"

Daniel glanced over at the two scientists before nodding slowly. "Yeah, I think I can configure a hidden permission set. As long as we don't tie their voiceprints to anything in the visible admin logs, they'll be able to use Liza without leaving a trace."

"Good," Abby said. "I need them to be able to run calculations freely, but we cannot risk someone finding out they're here. If Greta or anyone from the corporation ever pulls up a full audit..."

Daniel smirked. "Then as far as they'll know, the only authorized users are still just us."

He turned toward Liza's central console, fingers flying across the interface as he pulled up the security settings. "Liza, we need to enroll new voiceprints under restricted access—no external logging, no traceable metadata. Can you do that?"

Liza's voice responded smoothly. "Affirmative, Daniel. I can create a hidden user profile for voice authentication, restricting access visibility to this team only."

Dr. Cole and Dr. Nolan stepped forward, exchanging a glance before looking to Abby.

"This means we can use Liza like you do?" Dr. Cole asked.

"Exactly," Abby confirmed. "For calculations, projections—anything you need. She'll respond to your direct requests. Just say your name aloud now, and Liza will imprint your voice signature."

Dr. Cole cleared his throat, standing a bit taller. "Dr. Emmett Cole."

A brief pause, then Liza acknowledged, "Voiceprint recognized. Dr. Emmett Cole, access granted under restricted parameters."

Dr. Nolan stepped up next, brushing a loose strand of hair from her face before speaking clearly. "Dr. Kyra Nolan."

"Voiceprint recognized. Dr. Kyra Nolan, access granted under restricted parameters," Liza confirmed.

Dr. Nolan arched an eyebrow, glancing at Dr. Cole. "Well, I guess we're officially ghosts now."

Abby smirked. "Better ghosts than corpses."

Daniel finished his configuration, locking in the changes before pushing away from the console. "Done. Liza, if anyone ever checks system records for authentication logs, what will they see?"

Liza's tone was ever-so-slightly amused. "Nothing unusual, Daniel. Only the originally authorized personnel will appear in security logs. The restricted users do not exist to external inquiries."

"Perfect," Abby said, satisfied. "That's one problem solved."

She turned back to the group, clapping her hands together. "Alright, before we get back to work, let's talk food. Who's hungry?"

A murmur of agreement rippled through the room. Ethan stretched his arms over his head. "I could definitely eat. Feels like I haven't had real food in weeks."

Mark smirked. "Try years for some of us."

Dr. Cole rubbed the back of his neck. "To be fair, the food in the future wasn't bad. Just... not exactly fresh. If I ever see another meal cube again, it will be too soon.."

Dr. Nolan wrinkled her nose. "Yeah, and I think it's safe to say we could also use a little freshening up, too. Toothbrushes, mouthwash—please. I'm fairly certain our breath could knock out a small animal at this point."

Ethan chuckled. "Noted. I'll add 'dental emergency' to the supply list."

Abby grinned, shaking her head. "Alright, Ethan, Mark—you two head out, grab some food for everyone, and hit a store for essentials while you're at it. Keep it simple, don't draw attention, and be careful coming back through the checkpoint."

Mark saluted playfully. "Food, hygiene, and covert ops. Got it."

Ethan grabbed his jacket. "We'll be back soon. Try not to break the time stream while we're gone."

Abby sighed, already regretting sending them together. "Just... be careful."

As the two of them disappeared through the secured doors, a quiet chuckle came from Dr. Cole. "So, you have energetic associates too?"

Abby let out a short laugh, crossing her arms. "Oh yeah. Ethan is ridiculously intelligent, but sometimes I wonder if his curiosity is going to be the death of me. And Mark? Fresh out of college—sharp, no doubt—but still working on the maturity part." She exhaled with a knowing shake of her head. "He's getting there. Slowly."

Cole smirked, glancing toward Lyara, who was quietly observing the exchange. "We lucked out with Lyara. She's young, but ambitious and sharp as hell. Probably the best instinctual scientist I've ever seen."

Lyara shifted, clearly not used to such direct praise. "I just learn fast," she muttered, offering a small shrug.

Dr. Nolan grinned. "That's what makes you dangerous. You learn, you adapt, and—let's be honest—you probably already know how to fix half our problems, don't you?"

Lyara hesitated, then flashed a small, almost mischievous smile. "Maybe a third."

Abby smirked. "I like her already."

Cole nodded, his expression growing more serious. "Joking aside, we've got a hell of a mess to fix. But at least we've got a team that might actually be able to pull it off."

Abby folded her arms, looking around at the people in the room. Two teams—separated by time but now united in purpose.

"Then we better get started."

***

The underground level of the facility was quieter than the upper floors, insulated from the faint hum of the equipment running above. The air felt still, heavier, as if it carried the weight of the past clashing with the present. The newly returned scientists had settled in, though exhaustion was evident in their posture.

Abby stood near the whiteboard, arms crossed, as she waited for Ethan and Mark to return with food and supplies. The tension in the room hadn't dissipated—it had merely shifted. They were no longer worried about making it back. Now, the question looming over them was: what happens next?

A soft chime from Liza preceded her announcement. "Ethan and Mark have arrived at the facility entrance. No security anomalies detected."

Seconds later, the door hissed open, and Ethan strode in carrying a bag of takeout containers, his face slightly flushed from the cold air outside. Mark followed behind him, holding another bag and dramatically inhaling. "I swear, this food smells ten times better when you think about how much temporal nonsense we've dealt with today."

Ethan smirked as he set the bags down on the nearest table. "Brought extra napkins. Figured no one wants to wipe their mouth on lab coats." He cast a glance at Lyara, who had been sitting quietly since they left. His expression softened slightly as their eyes met, but he didn't say anything, simply giving a slight nod before returning his attention to the group.

Cole exhaled, rubbing his temples. "Before we eat, there's something I need to address." He straightened, his tone becoming more serious as he looked at Abby and the rest of the team. "Before we do anything else, we need to establish one thing—whether or not we truly left our past behind."

Abby narrowed her eyes. "You think something followed you?"

Cole hesitated before shaking his head. "Not in the physical sense. But time isn't just something you step in and out of. When we escaped, we had to overload the system, push it beyond what it was designed for. We tore open a conduit and ran through it. And if there's one thing I've learned about time—it doesn't appreciate being forced."

A tense silence followed his words.

That's when it happened.

A pulse—so subtle at first, like a shift in air pressure, that most of them barely registered it.

Then came the sound, a low frequency *thrum* that sent an unnatural vibration through the walls and into their bones.

The air still buzzed faintly with residual static, the temperature in the room stubbornly refusing to settle back to normal. The team stood frozen, the ghostly afterimage of whatever had appeared still burned into their minds.

Dr. Cole turned toward the central console.

"Liza," he said carefully, his voice measured but tight, "was there a temporal signature attached to that... anomaly?"

The lab's ambient hum filled the brief silence before Liza responded, her voice as composed as ever.

"Analyzing... Temporal residue detected. However, it does not conform to known quantum echoes caused by our own past experiments."

A flicker of unease passed through the room.

Abby's fingers curled into her palm. "Meaning?"

Liza paused for the briefest moment before continuing. "The signature does not originate from any of our prior recorded activities. It is distinct—an external variable."

Daniel's brow furrowed. "External from what? Us?"

Dr. Cole exchanged a glance with Dr. Nolan, the weight of unspoken understanding passing between them. He exhaled slowly, his voice more careful now. "Could it be a remnant of our past work? A... delayed echo from something we did before escaping?"

Another pause from Liza. Then, a measured reply.

"The data is inconclusive. However—" Liza hesitated, an odd and rare occurrence for the AI, "—the decay pattern suggests the signature was not naturally occurring. It was left intentionally."

A chill settled over the group.

Abby felt her pulse thrum in her throat. "You're saying someone—or something—left it behind on purpose?"

"The probability suggests intentional placement," Liza

confirmed.

Ethan, still gripping the bag of food like it was a lifeline, finally spoke up, his voice lower than usual. "So... something knows we're here."

The words sat heavy in the air.

Dr. Nolan shifted uncomfortably. "I don't like this. If someone—or something—is leaving signatures behind, it means they're tracking movement. Either tracking us now—or tracking you when you first left."

Dr. Cole let out a slow breath, his mind connecting dots he didn't want to connect. "If the facility in the future was compromised... what if they didn't just find the old site? What if they found something else?"

Silence.

A new, far more dangerous question hung in the air, unspoken but undeniable.

What if the corporation hadn't given up on time manipulation at all?

What if they were still watching? Still searching?

The air felt colder now.

Ethan finally set the food bags down on the table with a dull thud and ran a hand through his hair. "I officially have zero appetite."

Abby swallowed, trying to push away the gnawing uncertainty. "We can't panic. If there's something—or someone—out there, we need to stay ahead of it. Liza, keep scanning for any further anomalies, and if you detect another shift, I want to know immediately."

"Understood," Liza replied.

Mark, who had been unusually quiet, finally let out a nervous chuckle. "Great. First we break time, now time might be hunting us back. Love this job."

No one laughed.

For the first time since the experiment began, they weren't just running from consequences.

Something—or someone—was running toward them.

And they had no idea how much time they had left.

*\*\**

The tension in the lab remained thick, the weight of Liza's revelation still hanging in the air. The idea that something—or someone—had left a temporal signature deliberately was unsettling enough, but the implications of it being after their escape raised more questions than answers.

Dr. Cole, standing near the electronic whiteboard, exhaled slowly. He turned toward the console, directing his attention to Liza. "Liza, can you extrapolate the origination point of that anomaly? Where—when—did it come from?"

A pause. The lab was eerily silent except for the faint hum of equipment as Liza processed the request.

"Calculating..." she responded, her synthetic voice even but with a slight undertone of caution. "Cross-referencing residual quantum patterns with established temporal markers..."

The data streams across the monitors shifted, aligning into chaotic bursts before settling into something tangible. The team watched, waiting.

Then, Liza spoke.

"The anomaly's likely origination point is from the future. However, the uncertainty margin is substantial. The energy decay suggests a window of several months beyond the initial fracture event."

Daniel leaned in, frowning. "Several months? Meaning, someone didn't come through immediately after the fracture was created?"

"That is correct," Liza confirmed. "Based on decay patterns and entropy coefficients, the event is not immediately following your team's departure. It appears that whoever initiated transit required time—presumably to decipher the technology or reestablish operational functionality."

Cole's lips pressed into a firm line. "So they didn't know how to use the equipment at first. They had to learn."

"Affirmative," Liza replied.

Abby folded her arms, her expression unreadable. "Which means this isn't just a reactionary event. Whoever they are, they planned their arrival."

Ethan, who had been unusually quiet, ran a hand through his hair. "But why now? Why months later? And how did they even get access to the tech? Unless—" He exhaled sharply. "Unless the corporation in the future found a way to reverse engineer what was left."

Mark muttered under his breath, "Fantastic. So now we're not just dealing with cleaning up our mess, but someone else's."

Liza's monitors flickered, displaying new data. "There is an additional irregularity in the transport data."

Abby turned to face the console. "Define 'irregularity.'"

A pause. Then, Liza's response, measured, controlled— but undeniably unsettling.

"The initial transport event logged six travelers. However, my calculations indicate that only five emerged."

The room fell into a stark silence.

Daniel was the first to speak. "Wait… you're saying one of them didn't make it?"

"Correct," Liza confirmed. "However, there is no indication of where—or when—the missing individual was displaced."

Ethan let out a low whistle, shaking his head. "That's nightmare fuel. Someone just… vanished?"

"Not vanished," Dr. Cole said grimly. "They were lost. And if we're dealing with inexperienced operators, we have no way of knowing where—or when—they ended up."

Lyara, who had been quiet in the back, finally spoke, her voice softer than usual. "What if they didn't just get lost?" She hesitated, choosing her words carefully. "What if they were left behind?"

A cold weight settled in Abby's chest at the thought. It wasn't just about an accident anymore. There was a real possibility that whoever came through had made a choice.

Daniel exhaled, rubbing the bridge of his nose. "And we have no way of knowing who they were or why they came."

Dr. Cole stepped away from the board, his mind racing. "We need more data. Liza, is there anything else you can pull from the anomaly? Any signatures—genetic markers, unique fluctuations?"

"Analyzing…" Liza's voice carried a rare pause. When she spoke again, it was with unmistakable weight.

"The quantum readings show fragmented imprints. However, one variable remains consistent across multiple instances of temporal disturbance. The missing individual's signature does not appear anywhere in subsequent timelines."

Abby narrowed her eyes. "Meaning?"

Liza hesitated.

"The lost traveler… ceased to exist."

The room went deathly silent.

Mark exhaled, looking ghostly pale. "That… that's not possible, right? You can't just stop existing."

"Incorrect," Liza replied. "If the traveler was displaced in a way that prevented their reintegration into the time stream, their presence may have been entirely erased—rendering them a non-entity across all future iterations."

Ethan let out a slow breath. "So they're not just missing. They were unmade."

The words hit hard.

Dr. Cole clenched his jaw, staring at the screen. "If someone in the future figured out how to use time transit and lost a person along the way… they either learned from their mistake, or they intended it."

Abby met his gaze. "Either way, we need to find out who they were—and who sent them."

Liza's voice returned, calm, unwavering.

"If this individual was erased, then the only way to uncover the truth… is to go where they were lost."

Silence.

A dangerous idea had just been placed on the table.

And for the first time, they had to ask themselves:

Were they willing to follow the path of the lost?

***

The hum of the lab's equipment filled the silence as Abby and Cole stood at the digital whiteboard, the weight of the last revelation settling over them. The others sat nearby, some leaning against workstations, others pacing, but all waiting for what came next.

Abby let out a slow breath, running a hand through her hair. "Alright, let's think this through logically. What do we actually gain by following the trail of the lost traveler?"

Cole folded his arms, tapping a finger against his chin. "That depends. If they were truly erased from existence, then we're chasing ghosts—a paradox with nothing left to investigate."

Abby nodded. "Exactly. If Liza is right, if that traveler was lost permanently, then there's nothing to find. No remnants, no echoes, no data. Just a void. And risking another jump for nothing doesn't sit well with me."

Cole exhaled sharply. "But if someone else got access to the tech, then this doesn't end here. We need to ask ourselves: do we let this play out and react to the next anomaly, or do we get ahead of it before it becomes something worse?"

Daniel, who had been listening quietly, finally spoke. "There's one thing we're overlooking. That facility in the future—the one your team abandoned when you escaped." He turned to Cole. "What happened to the equipment you left behind?"

Cole frowned. "We had to overpower it to create a transit conduit big enough for all of us to escape at once. We assumed it destroyed itself in the process."

"But did you see it destroyed?" Daniel pressed.

A long pause. "No," Dr. Cole admitted. "Once transit

started, we were gone. There was no looking back."

Abby's stomach sank. "Then for all we know, that equipment is still there."

Olivia leaned forward. "If the corporation finds it... or if anyone does..."

Cole's jaw tightened. "Then they can do exactly what just happened."

The room fell into a tense silence.

Ethan crossed his arms. "So what are we saying here? That someone needs to go back and make sure it's completely unusable?"

Abby met his gaze. "That might be our best option. If the equipment is still intact, if it's even remotely functional, then this doesn't stop here. It might be months, years—but someone will figure it out. And if they do, we could end up with people deliberately altering the timeline instead of just stumbling through it."

Mark, who had been sitting on the edge of a workstation, straightened. "I'll do it."

Ethan's head snapped toward him. "Like hell you will."

Mark shot him a look. "Ethan, you already made the first jump. It's my turn."

Ethan took a step forward. "That's not how this works."

Mark stood up, standing toe to toe with him. "You think just because you went first, you get to decide who goes next? I've been here every step of the way. I've taken the same risks you have. This is just as much my fight."

Ethan scowled. "You're not trained for this."

Mark scoffed. "Oh, and you are? What, you took one trip and now you're a seasoned time traveler? Give me a break."

Ethan clenched his fists. "You don't know what it feels like—what it's like to be pulled apart and put back together. To feel like you might never come back. You think I want that for you?"

Mark's expression hardened. "I think we all signed up for things we didn't expect, Ethan. But this isn't about you.

This is about what needs to be done."

The tension in the air was palpable.

Abby stepped between them. "Enough."

They both turned to her, waiting.

She looked at Ethan first. "I know you want to protect him. But Mark's right—he has just as much reason to do this as you."

Then she turned to Mark. "And you'd better be damn sure you're ready for this."

Mark nodded, unwavering. "I am."

Ethan exhaled sharply, running a hand down his face. Then, with reluctance, he muttered, "Fine. But you listen to every single thing Liza tells you. No improvising."

Mark smirked. "Scout's honor."

Abby turned to Liza. "How long will it take to calibrate for a jump back to that location?"

Liza's voice was steady. "With the provided coordinates and assuming temporal stability at the point of departure, I estimate approximately two hours to establish a controlled transit window."

Abby exhaled. "Then we don't waste time."

She turned to Mark, leveling him with a serious look. "You're going in, confirming whether the equipment is intact, and making sure it can't be used again. No distractions, no heroics. Get in, do what needs to be done, and get out."

Mark gave her a small salute. "Understood, Captain."

Ethan shook his head, muttering under his breath, "This is a bad idea."

Daniel clapped him on the shoulder. "They're all bad ideas at this point."

Abby let out a slow breath. "Then let's get to work."

Time was running out.

And Mark was about to take the biggest risk of his life.

***

The lab was thick with tension as Mark stood on the

scanning platform in the hyperdrive, rolling his shoulders as if shaking off the weight of the decision he'd made. He was dressed in a cleanroom suit, readied as much as anyone could be for something as unpredictable as time travel. His expression held none of the usual cocky bravado. Just focus. Just determination.

Daniel approached, holding out a small earpiece with a modified interface. "Here, take this. I repurposed an old comm device and tuned it to Liza's quantum field. It should work across the transit stream and let us stay in contact."

Mark took it, examining the compact design. "So, if I get lost, you can at least listen to my last words? Great. Super comforting."

Daniel sighed. "Just don't get lost."

Ethan, standing with his arms crossed, barely held back his frustration. "Just don't get cute. Get in, overload the system, and get out."

Mark smirked, but it lacked its usual arrogance. "You're really gonna miss me, huh?"

Ethan muttered, "Shut up."

Abby, standing nearby, placed a hand on Mark's shoulder. "Liza says the jump point looks clear. No one's there to stop you, but that doesn't mean it's safe. The moment you arrive, you start setting that overload. Slow ramp-up—gives you time to get the hell out before the place goes up."

Mark nodded. "Got it."

Daniel adjusted his glasses, watching Mark carefully. "And if something looks off?"

"Then I still do it. We can't risk someone else finding this place," Mark said, his voice unwavering.

Abby squeezed his shoulder briefly before stepping back. "Then let's do this." Everyone left the hyperdrive and closed the door securing it.

Liza's voice came through, crisp and deliberate. "Engaging quantum synchronization. Powering up transit field. Mark, prepare for jump."

The platform hummed with energy, the air around Mark warping slightly as Liza manipulated the quantum field around him. The containment lights flared brighter, casting eerie shadows across the lab.

Mark gave one last glance at the team, his smirk returning just for a second. "See you in an hour."

A final flash of blinding white light swallowed him whole.

Mark's arrival was jarring. The facility, once a functioning research hub, was now cold and abandoned. Emergency lights flickered, casting jagged shadows along the metallic walls. The air felt stale, untouched for months—maybe longer.

He took a cautious step forward, surveying the silent space. No voices. No movement. Liza had been right—no one was here.

Mark exhaled and made his way toward the control panel, booting up what remained of the interface. He had trained for this—Ethan had drilled the calculations into his head before he left. If he did this right, he'd be back in an hour, and this place would be nothing but a scorched memory.

He accessed the power regulators, adjusting the parameters for a gradual overload. Too fast, and it might rupture the drive before he could leave. But if he could control the surge, he'd have enough time to get out and let it tear itself apart behind him.

A warning flashed on the screen.

SYSTEM FAILURE IMMINENT. ESCAPE PROTOCOL ADVISED.

Mark smirked. "Yeah, no kidding."

He tapped his comm. "Liza, you reading me?"

Liza's voice crackled through, slightly delayed but clear. "Affirmative, Mark. I am monitoring your signal. Power increase detected. You have 48 minutes remaining."

"Plenty of time," he muttered.

*** 

Back at the lab, Liza tracked the quantum fluctuations, monitoring Mark's signal with hyper-focused precision. The team stood in anxious silence, watching the live data feed.

Ethan tapped the table impatiently. "How's he looking?"

"On schedule," Liza confirmed. "Quantum field remains stable. Power overload at 27%. Mark is moving efficiently."

Abby nodded, arms crossed. "Good. Let's keep it that way."

Then, without warning, an error flashed across Liza's interface.

Her voice, usually smooth, carried a rare note of alarm. "Unanticipated power surge detected. Quantum stability decreasing." Liza declared.

Ethan stiffened. "What? What the hell does that mean?"

Daniel's eyes flicked over the data, his face paling. "Something's interfering with the overload. It's ramping up too fast."

Abby turned sharply. "Liza, get Mark out of there. Now."

Liza's processors whirred, recalculating. "Initiating early retrieval sequence."

Mark had been watching the overload climb steadily— but suddenly, the numbers spiked. Faster than they should have.

He tapped his comm. "Liza, something's wrong."

Her reply came instantly. "I have detected the anomaly. I am initiating retrieval—"

The ground shook violently. The screen in front of him exploded into sparks. The surge had spiraled out of control.

Mark's heart pounded. "Shit, shit—Liza, if you're gonna get me, now's the time!"

A pulse of energy ripped through the facility. The entire building groaned, metal twisting under pressure. The hyperdrive behind him screamed as it tried to compensate.

Then—the light hit.

It wasn't like the transit jump. It was unstable, chaotic. A raw explosion of energy that tore through the structure like paper.

Mark barely had time to feel himself slipping away.

Back at the lab, Liza's systems froze. The retrieval field she had engaged flickered erratically, fighting against an external collapse.

The team watched in horror.

"Come on, Liza, pull him back!" Ethan yelled, gripping the edge of the console.

Liza's voice was steady, but lacked its usual certainty. "Attempting emergency stabilization."

Seconds dragged into eternity.

Then—the signal cut.

The hyperdrive's energy field collapsed, the retrieval sequence failing. Mark's quantum signature blinked out of existence.

The lab was deathly silent.

Ethan shook his head, stepping forward. "No. No, Liza, try again."

Liza's response came after a weighted pause. "...There is nothing to retrieve."

Ethan turned on her. "Bullshit! Try again!"

Abby placed a firm hand on his shoulder, her voice shaking but controlled. "Ethan... he's gone."

Ethan's breathing was ragged, his fists clenched, but he didn't fight her grip.

Daniel rubbed a hand over his face, his voice hollow. "And the facility?"

Liza processed. "Destroyed beyond recovery. No remaining quantum signatures."

For a long moment, no one spoke.

Then Ethan slammed his fist into the console, his voice thick with anger and grief. "Damn it, Mark."

Olivia wiped at her eyes, staring at the empty platform

where Mark had stood just an hour ago. "He... he actually did it."

Abby swallowed hard, forcing herself to stand tall despite the pain settling in her chest. "We have to move forward. If we stop now, then everything he just did... everything he gave... will mean nothing."

Ethan exhaled shakily, dragging a hand down his face. "Yeah. Yeah, I know."

The lab had never felt so empty.

Liza's voice came softer than ever before. "Mark's actions ensured our future remains untampered. The timeline is stabilized."

But no one felt victorious.

Mark was gone.

And time had claimed another price.

# 9

The lab's usual hum was overpowered by a tense, uneasy silence. The weight of the past few days sat heavy on everyone's shoulders. With Mark's loss, the dismantling of the future's failed experiment, and the arrival of their new, displaced allies, exhaustion wasn't just physical—it was emotional.

Abby stood at the digital whiteboard, her fingers lingering over the surface as if searching for answers in equations that hadn't been written yet. The fractures in time weren't just theoretical anymore; they were real, tangible wounds that had to be mended before something else—or someone else—came through.

She turned to her team, her expression resolute. "We need to talk about what comes next."

Ethan leaned against the table, arms crossed. "Next as in fixing the damage or next as in figuring out what the hell we actually did to time?"

"Both," Daniel answered, rubbing his temple. "We stabilized one threat, but the stream is still fractured. If we don't find a way to remove whatever caused it, this entire facility could become ground zero for something far worse."

Abby nodded. "And that's exactly what we need to figure out." She gestured toward Dr. Cole and his team. "But first, we need to make sure you're all settled. I know you've had a hell of a journey."

Cole, still clearly exhausted from the transit, straightened. "We're here. We'll do whatever it takes to fix this."

Abby gestured toward the lower levels. "We cleaned up

the old crew quarters downstairs for you. It's not much, but it'll give you a place to rest."

Cole exchanged a glance with Lyara and Dr.Nolan before nodding. "That's more than we expected."

"There are food supplies down there," Abby continued. "Nothing fancy, but enough to get through the night. We'll figure out something better soon." Then, her expression hardened. "But you cannot leave this facility. Not even for a second."

Lyara's gaze was sharp. "We know. If anyone out there realizes we exist, it's over."

Daniel folded his arms. "The security dampeners will keep you hidden from scans, but the corporation is resourceful. If they have other ways of tracking anomalies, we have to assume they'll be looking."

Ethan shot Lyara a smirk. "Guess you guys are officially ghosts now."

Lyara rolled her eyes. "Fantastic. Always wanted to haunt a science lab."

Abby exhaled. "Get some rest. I know you just traveled back in time and that's a lot to process, but we don't have the luxury of easing into this. Tomorrow, we start figuring out how to fix the mess we've been left with."

Cole studied her for a moment before nodding. "Agreed."

As the displaced team made their way toward the lower level, Ethan let out a low whistle. "We just took in Three fugitives from the future and are actively trying to rewrite time. Nothing about this is normal anymore."

Abby shook her head, a tired smile flickering across her lips. "Ethan, normal left the building a long time ago."

***

The elevator doors slid shut behind them, leaving the core team in silence once more.

But Ethan didn't leave.

He lingered, staring at the quantum drive, as if hoping—

no, expecting—it would somehow return what had been lost.

He didn't notice Lyara watching him from across the room. She had remained as well, her sharp blue eyes thoughtful.

"You're not going to sleep," she said, not as a question but as a fact.

Ethan let out a dry laugh, rubbing his face. "No point."

Lyara took a few steps forward. "You blame yourself."

Ethan looked at her, searching for sarcasm or detachment, but there was none. Just a quiet understanding.

"I told him to go," Ethan admitted. "I should have—"

"You don't control time, Ethan," Lyara interrupted. "No one does."

He let out a bitter chuckle. "Kind of ironic, considering what we're doing."

She considered that, then spoke, her voice softer. "The first time I lost someone, I thought the same thing. That if I had done something differently, it would have changed everything."

Ethan frowned. "First time?"

She hesitated, then continued. "I was supposed to escape with someone else. I didn't. I had to leave them behind." Her gaze dropped slightly. "I don't even know if they're alive."

Ethan didn't know what to say. He had seen Lyara as sharp, as someone who adapted quickly and efficiently to anything thrown at her. But this? This was different.

"You still think about them?" he asked.

Lyara nodded. "Every day." Then she met his eyes, her expression unreadable. "But the only way to honor them is to move forward."

Ethan swallowed, the lump in his throat tightening. "Move forward?"

He took a slow breath, straightening. "...Yeah."

For the first time since Mark's loss, the weight on his shoulders didn't feel quite as crushing.

***

The next morning, the team gathered around the digital whiteboard, the tension in the air almost tangible. Though their bodies were rested, their minds carried the weight of the previous day. Coffee cups sat abandoned, half-drunk and forgotten, a testament to the conversations that had stretched into the early hours of the morning.

Abby picked up a stylus and tapped the screen, her gaze moving across each member of the team before speaking.

"We couldn't save Mark," she said, voice steady but laced with sorrow, "but we can save time itself."

The words settled heavily over the room. No one argued.

Daniel, still weary but functioning, leaned forward. "Mark's mission eliminated the immediate threat, but the fracture itself is still there."

Abby nodded. "Which means we need to remove the anchor that's holding it open and stopping it from healing."

Ethan crossed his arms. "How? If we just cut it out, what happens? Does time reset? Does it break?"

Daniel exhaled, tapping at the console. "We don't know. Removing an anchor could cause time to snap back into place or..." He trailed off, unwilling to say the alternative.

Silence.

Lyara, who had been standing off to the side, arms crossed, finally spoke "Then we need a test."

The team turned to her.

Lyara met Abby's gaze. "We need to observe what happens when an event is changed in real time. Something small—a shift, not a break."

Ethan tilted his head. "Like a controlled disturbance?"

She nodded. "Something that lets us see the ripple effects without causing a collapse."

Daniel ran a hand over his face. "That's assuming we can even see the effects in a way we can measure."

Abby turned back to the board and scribbled down First Safe Shift – Identify the Minimal Change.

"We need to test something that doesn't impact lives

directly, but still gives us enough of a footprint to see what happens," she said.

Dr. Cole, who had been listening quietly, stepped forward. "We can use the old baseline data we gathered before we left the future. If we compare it against what's happening now, we might be able to identify something small enough to shift without sending shockwaves through the entire timeline."

Daniel's brow furrowed. "Even something 'small' could have cascading effects we don't see immediately."

"That's why we measure," Lyara interjected. "We alter something inconsequential and track the divergence."

Ethan let out a long breath. "Okay, but what is inconsequential? Because from what I've seen, everything seems to have consequences."

Olivia, who had been quietly taking notes, suddenly looked up. "What about a message?"

The room turned to her.

She swallowed before continuing. "Something written. Something that can be placed, moved, or removed. No physical interference. No direct involvement with people. Just a single variable."

Abby's eyes narrowed in intrigued thought. "That... actually makes sense. Its eloquent, yet simple, but more so-- controllable."

Daniel leaned forward. "You mean something like placing a note where it shouldn't be and seeing if it registers in our scans?"

Olivia nodded. "We don't even have to place it in the present. We could project it forward or back and watch for any sign of recognition."

Cole stroked his chin thoughtfully. "That's subtle. A note might not affect anything, but if time responds, we'll see it."

Ethan frowned. "Wait—how would a message even matter? If it's something small, no one will read it. It won't be discovered. It shouldn't do anything."

Daniel leaned forward, resting his elbows on the table. "It's not about the message itself. It's about whether the timeline acknowledges it."

Ethan raised an eyebrow. "Acknowledge how?"

Dr. Cole chimed in, nodding toward the whiteboard. "Imagine dropping a stone into a pond. If nothing happens— if there's no ripple—then we know it's safe to remove. But if there is a ripple, if the water moves, then we know time is reactive to even small disturbances.

Abby crossed her arms. "And if it reacts to something as simple as a note, we know for sure that the anchor isn't just holding time open. It's keeping it from repairing itself."

Lyara nodded. "Exactly. If time resists a change as small as a message, then it means time itself is trying to stay in a state of equilibrium. That gives us the answer we need."

Olivia glanced between them. "So, we're not testing the note. We're testing time's reaction to it."

Abby smiled slightly. "Now you're getting it."

Ethan let out a slow breath, shaking his head. "So, if the note vanishes, it means time is already repairing?"

Daniel nodded. "And if it stays..."

Dr. Cole finished the sentence for him. "Then we know we have more work to do."

A hush settled over the lab.

They weren't just fixing time anymore.

They were about to rewrite it.

***

Liza's voice broke through the hum of the lab's idle systems. "Dr. Cole, where are the timeline readings you recorded before your departure?"

Cole's expression flickered, a moment of hesitation crossing his face before he turned abruptly and strode toward the exit. "Give me a second."

The team exchanged glances as he disappeared down the hallway toward the sleeping quarters. Ethan leaned in, lowering his voice just enough to be conspiratorial. "He didn't lose it, did he?"

Lyara smirked. "No. But I have a feeling we're about to witness some very questionable archival methods."

A few minutes later, Cole returned, slightly out of breath, clutching something tightly in his fist. His other hand clutched the faded edges of a crumpled, well-worn lab coat, dust clinging to the fabric. Without a word, he tossed it onto the table and uncurled his fingers, revealing a smooth, translucent crystal no larger than a thumb drive.

Abby folded her arms. "That doesn't look like a standard storage device."

Cole set the crystal down carefully. "It's not. Digital storage from our previous time wouldn't survive temporal drift, at least not without serious degradation. So I stored the readings in something incorruptible—a quantum-stabilized crystalline lattice. This thing has the raw waveform imprints of our timeline scans embedded in it."

Daniel lifted the crystal, rolling it between his fingers, watching the light refract through its surface. "That's... honestly kind of brilliant."

Abby, however, was less impressed. "And how exactly do you expect Liza to read it? We don't have a standard interface for alien rock-paperweights."

Liza interjected smoothly. "I concur with Dr. Foster's assessment. No known interface exists within my current system that can extract meaningful data from this medium."

Cole smirked, tapping a finger on the table. "That's because you're thinking in digital terms. This isn't a storage drive—it's a *resonance matrix*." He turned toward Liza, his voice shifting into that of a scientist explaining to a peer. "If you can generate a structured digital waveform at 917.62 terahertz and read the reflected harmonic frequencies, you'll be able to reconstruct the embedded data."

Liza processed his words in mere milliseconds. "I can generate and analyze waveforms at that frequency range. One moment." Liza continued "Above 800Thz, which is in the ultraviolet range, please place the crystal on the table and backup and shield your eyes till I finish."

A soft hum filled the air as Liza engaged the requested function. A faint glow pulsed from the crystal as the invisible waveform scanned across its surface. A moment later, Liza spoke again.

"Partial data recovery successful. The information is intact. Processing for structured analysis."

Ethan let out a low whistle. "Okay, I take it back—this is the coolest illegal thing I've seen all week."

Daniel grinned. "You really carried a whole damn time-map in your pocket?"

Dr. Cole looked sheepish, but before he could answer, Abby let out a slow exhale, pinching the bridge of her nose. "Let me get this straight. You stored classified timeline data on a crystal, smuggled it back through time, and didn't think to mention it until now?"

Cole hesitated. "I, uh... didn't think it was relevant until we needed it."

Abby gave him a flat look. "Cole. That is not how scientific disclosure works."

Cole sighed, rubbing the back of his neck. "I didn't mean to keep it from you, but I couldn't risk losing it. This is the only backup of our readings before the fracture started getting worse."

Abby's jaw tightened. "And are there any other surprises I should know about before we proceed?"

Cole looked at her, then at the rest of the team, before shaking his head. "No. This is it."

Abby studied him for a long moment, trying to determine if he was holding anything back. Finally, she turned to Liza. "Get everything off that thing before it becomes the next reason we all end up being erased from existence."

Liza responded with professional precision. "Understood. Processing full data extraction now."

As the team watched the faint glow pulse from the

crystal, Ethan leaned toward Lyara and whispered, "You think this guy kept a time-travel diary too?"

Lyara smirked. "If he did, I bet it's under his mattress."

Dr. Cole groaned. "I can hear you."

Liza's voice broke the relative quiet of the lab, steady and factual. "Data extraction is complete. I have retrieved the timeline sequence from the crystal."

Abby turned toward the digital whiteboard, tapping her fingers against its frame as she mulled over the next step. "Alright, now we need to decide who's going to craft the note."

The team exchanged glances, the weight of the task heavy despite its simplicity in execution.

Then Lyara's voice cut through. "I'll do it."

Abby raised a brow. "You have something in mind?"

A small smirk played at the edge of Lyara's lips. "Yeah. Give me a minute."

Without another word, she turned and jogged toward the stairwell leading to the lower level, disappearing from sight.

Ethan followed her movement, a mix of curiosity and something else flickering in his expression.

Daniel leaned toward Abby, murmuring, "Do we want to know what she's up to?"

Abby sighed, crossing her arms. "Probably not. But we're going to find out anyway."

A few minutes later, Lyara returned, her arms filled with a small stack of weathered, yellowing paper. She set them down on the table with a soft *thump*, dust scattering from the aged sheets.

Ethan's brow furrowed. "What is this?"

Lyara brushed off a lingering cobweb, completely unbothered. "Old lab notes. I found them last night when I was walking around to clear my head. They're from the original experiments—the ones before Cole's team even set foot here."

Abby blinked. "How old are these?"

Lyara shrugged. "Old enough that, to anyone looking at them in the past, they'll just be seen as normal documentation. No red flags."

Daniel leaned in, examining one of the faded pages, running a hand over the brittle texture. "And you're thinking of using one of these to write our message?"

"Exactly." Lyara nodded. "If the paper itself looks like it belongs in that time period, it won't immediately be seen as an anomaly. But the message we write—that's where the disruption comes in. That's what the timeline will reject."

She held out a hand, palm open. "Ethan, I need a pen."

Ethan narrowed his eyes playfully. "Are you writing love notes to someone now?"

Lyara tilted her head slightly, tapping her fingers against her outstretched palm. Then, without missing a beat, she met Ethan's gaze and smirked. "Maybe."

Then she winked.

Ethan choked slightly, a flicker of heat rising to his ears.

Daniel let out an exaggerated cough. "Wow, okay, well, this just got interesting and vaguely uncomfortable."

Olivia leaned toward Abby, barely hiding her amusement. "Did she just flirt with Ethan?"

Abby, unimpressed, reached out and plucked Ethan's pen from behind his ear before handing it to Lyara. "Here. Before we all die of secondhand tension."

Lyara took it, biting back a laugh. "Thanks."

With a deep breath, she turned to the paper, running her fingers over its worn edges before placing the pen down at the top of the page.

"What exactly are you writing?" Ethan asked, now fully focused on her and not the way she had just completely caught him off guard.

Lyara's gaze darkened slightly, her smirk fading. "A note in Iroquois."

That caught Daniel's attention. "Why Iroquois?"

She glanced up. "Because that's our time. And it's

something that won't belong in the past."

She met Abby's gaze. "The message itself doesn't have to be groundbreaking. It just needs to carry a piece of information that wouldn't have existed in that period—something the timeline won't tolerate."

Abby gave a slow nod of approval. "Smart."

Ethan crossed his arms, watching her carefully. "You sure about this?"

Lyara met his eyes again, but this time, there was no teasing, no smirk. Just quiet certainty.

"This is how we start fixing time," she said simply.

And with that, she pressed the pen to the paper and began to write.

As the ink bled into the old paper, the weight of what they were doing settled in.

This wasn't just a test anymore.

It was the first deliberate move in rewriting history.

And none of them knew what would happen next.

Abby took the carefully written note from Lyara's hands, her eyes scanning the precise yet almost poetic wording. The message was carefully crafted—just enough to feel natural in its time while carrying the kind of disruption that would unsettle the timeline itself.

She read through it twice, her brows furrowing slightly as she considered the implications. The weight of what they were attempting wasn't lost on her—this wasn't just a test; it was a deliberate shift in the flow of time, a ripple meant to force a response from the universe itself.

After a moment, Abby gave a small, approving nod, looking up at Lyara with a smirk. "Now I see what Cole sees in you." There was quiet pride in her voice, something that softened the intensity of the moment.

Lyara, for once, looked mildly taken aback by the praise but didn't say anything—just a small, knowing smile played at the corner of her lips.

Abby turned and held the paper out to Ethan. "Here, put

this in the hyperdrive." She paused, her smirk widening as she noticed the slight flush to his ears, the very obvious tension still lingering between him and Lyara. "You need to get some air moving across those red ears of yours."

Ethan opened his mouth to protest but stopped when Lyara gave him a wink. His lips clamped shut as he snatched the paper and made his way toward the hyperdrive without another word, ignoring the chuckles from Daniel and Olivia.

Dr. Nolan, who had been quietly observing the exchange with amusement, suddenly clasped her hands together. "Oh, please let me be the one to tell Liza to send it," she said, her tone carrying an eager glint of mischief.

Abby chuckled, shaking her head at the scientist's enthusiasm. "Sure, go ahead."

Dr. Nolan turned to Liza's interface with exaggerated formality, as if savoring the moment. "Liza, please send this to the coordinates."

Liza's voice came through smoothly, ever steady despite the playfulness in the room. "Executing transmission."

Ethan placed the paper inside the hyperdrive chamber, carefully smoothing it down onto the platform to ensure proper positioning. He took a step back, watching as the soft blue containment field shimmered into place around it.

"Alright, Liza. Whenever you're ready," he said, crossing his arms, his voice betraying a slight nervous edge.

"Calculating a stable point from the recorded timeline," Liza confirmed. The surrounding monitors flickered with cascading streams of data as the AI performed intricate adjustments. The tension in the room thickened as the team watched the numbers cycle through, an eerie reminder of just how little they truly understood about the mechanics of time.

Then, the hyperdrive emitted a low, vibrating hum as its energy levels spiked. A faint pulse of light rippled across the containment chamber, growing brighter with each passing second.

Abby instinctively braced herself.

A final burst of energy flared outward, and then—silence.

"Message sent," Liza confirmed.

A collective breath was held, no one moving as they stared at the now-empty chamber.

Liza's voice cut through the stillness. "I am reading the quantum signature of the message in its intended destination. The anomaly is minor but significant enough to register as a disturbance. The note, as written, is not supposed to exist in that time."

A subtle but unmistakable shift coursed through the room. It was working.

The next thirty minutes stretched into an agonizing wait. Every few minutes, someone would check a display, glance at Liza's status feed, or shift their weight in nervous anticipation. The room, normally buzzing with small conversations, had fallen into an unnatural silence.

Daniel tapped his fingers against his armrest, his patience wearing thin. "Do we have any indication of how long this should take?"

Liza answered calmly. "The timeline operates under a fluid set of reactive principles. Its corrective measures do not function in a linear, predictable manner. We must observe."

"So we wait," Ethan muttered.

They did.

More minutes passed. The air in the room felt heavy, anticipation sitting like an anvil on their chests.

Then Liza's voice cut through.

"The writing has disappeared," she announced. "Only the paper remains."

The room stilled.

Ethan blinked. "Wait—just the writing? The paper itself is still there?"

"Affirmative."

Abby exhaled slowly, running a hand through her hair. "The timeline didn't reject the object. It only rejected the information on it."

Daniel leaned forward. "Which means... it worked?"

Liza replied, "It suggests that direct interference with recorded events will be negated, while physical anomalies can persist—so long as they do not alter causality."

Lyara crossed her arms, processing. "So the timeline is smart enough to erase what doesn't belong, but it doesn't recognize the paper itself as a threat."

Abby nodded, deep in thought. "It means we have a means to test further. We can track how time resists—see what types of changes are erased versus which ones remain."

A quiet moment passed before Ethan let out a breathy chuckle. "Well, that was anticlimactic."

Olivia elbowed him. "What, were you expecting lightning to crack the walls?"

"Maybe a little," he admitted, earning a few light laughs.

The gravity of what they had just done settled in.

They weren't just studying time anymore.

They were actively interacting with it.

***

The team remained gathered around the digital whiteboard, still processing the results of their last experiment. The implications were staggering—time had erased the ink from the note but left the paper intact. But what about something entirely foreign to that time period? Would time itself erase an object completely?

Daniel leaned against the table, arms crossed. "So, what's the next logical step? We've established that time won't tolerate modern ink on old paper, but what happens when we send an entirely foreign object back? Something that couldn't have existed back then?"

A brief silence fell over the group as they considered the question.

Then Olivia perked up. "I have an idea!" She reached under the desk, grabbing her purse and rummaging through it. A second later, she triumphantly pulled out a small red rubber ball.

Daniel arched a brow. "I won't even ask."

Olivia smirked. "From my cat." She tossed it lightly in her hand before holding it up for the team to see. "We use what we've got. You have a better idea?"

Abby studied the ball, intrigued. "Synthetic rubber wasn't invented yet in the time period we're sending it to. Small enough to be unnoticed, but it should register as a foreign element in the time stream. If time really does correct anomalies, this should definitely count as one."

Olivia nodded. "Exactly. It's harmless but unnatural for that period. If time doesn't like an anachronistic note, let's see how it reacts to a full object."

She sighed, rolling the ball between her fingers. "But my cat is gonna be pissed when she finds out it's gone. She loves this thing."

Abby took the ball from her, suppressing a grin. "I'll buy your cat a new toy if this works. Ethan, put it in the chamber."

Ethan raised an eyebrow. "More air?"

Abby just smiled knowingly.

Ethan sighed and took the ball, shaking his head as he walked toward the hyperdrive. He placed it in the chamber and closed the door securely before stepping back.

Liza's voice came through smoothly, her tone perfectly measured. "Scanning object for baseline. No anomalies detected in its current state. Calculating temporal displacement."

Then, with almost human-like precision, she added, "Ethan, I detect your ears are still approximately five degrees warmer than the rest of your body."

Ethan groaned, rubbing his temples. "Great. Now I'm getting it from an AI too."

Olivia snickered. "She's just confirming what we all already knew."

Ethan shot her a half-hearted glare. "I miss when Liza

didn't have a sense of humor."

Liza responded immediately, her tone as neutral as ever. "Incorrect, Ethan. I have always had the capacity for humor. You are only now becoming the subject of it."

Ethan blinked, looking toward the system. "Oh, you have been spending too much time around Abby."

Abby grinned. "I am a great influence."

Ethan sighed, waving a hand toward the hyperdrive. "Alright, Liza. Just send the damn ball before my dignity takes any more damage."

"Engaging transmission," Liza replied, utterly unbothered.

A sharp pulse of energy flared, followed by a brilliant flash of light, then the ball was gone.

The team stood watching the hyperdrive chamber for a long moment, as if half-expecting the ball to bounce back through time on its own.

Olivia muttered under her breath, arms crossed. "My cat is seriously going to hate me for this."

Abby smirked. "It's all for science, Olivia."

Olivia sighed dramatically. "Tell that to her when she wakes me up at three in the morning, screaming for her missing toy."

The team chuckled, but the mood quickly shifted as Liza's voice chimed in.

"I am now monitoring the object at its temporal destination."

A hush fell over the lab as everyone refocused on the data streams flowing across the monitors. Time ticked forward, second by second, then minutes.

Fifteen minutes.

Thirty.

An hour.

Then Liza's voice returned, calm but definitive. "The object is no longer present at the destination. No remaining quantum signature detected."

Abby exhaled sharply. "So, it did erase it."

Daniel leaned in, frowning at the display. "No trace of it at all? Like it never existed?"

"Correct," Liza confirmed. "Unlike the note, which retained its material presence, the synthetic ball has been entirely removed from the time stream."

The room was silent for a long moment, the weight of the discovery sinking in.

Olivia, still staring at the empty chamber, finally spoke. "Well... that's one way to delete a problem."

Daniel shook his head. "It's not just that it was deleted. The time stream actively corrected it. Meaning..." He trailed off, exchanging looks with Abby.

Ethan completed the thought. "Meaning we finally have a direction."

Abby folded her arms. "Time doesn't tolerate contradictions. If something doesn't belong, it will be erased. That means if we can locate the original anchor and remove it properly..."

Daniel nodded. "The fracture could close on its own."

Ethan exhaled, finally feeling like they had a real path forward. "Then I guess we know what we need to do next."

Abby straightened, a new determination settling over her. "We find the anchor."

And for the first time, the team wasn't just reacting.

They were taking the first real step toward fixing time itself.

***

The hum of the lab was a familiar comfort, yet today, tension simmered beneath the surface. The team had gathered once again, each of them standing near their workstations, sipping from their coffees or simply watching the whiteboard in silent thought.

The previous experiments had given them answers— some reassuring, some unsettling. But now, they needed more. A final test. One that would confirm whether time's influence was as precise as they feared.

Abby tapped the edge of the digital whiteboard. "We've established that time doesn't tolerate anachronisms—it erased the ink, and it removed the rubber ball altogether." She turned to the others. "Now we need to know how it interacts with something alive."

Daniel gave a slow nod. "An organic entity. If time corrects an object, what does it do to a living thing?"

Ethan sighed, rubbing the back of his neck. "I feel like this is either going to be fascinating or terrifying."

Lyara, arms crossed, added, "Probably both."

Abby turned toward Olivia, who had already prepared the next test. On the table before her sat a small potted orchid—a bright purple bloom genetically modified for increased resistance to drought and disease as well as its vivid color.

Olivia brushed her fingers over one of the petals. "This plant didn't exist in this form at any point in history. The genetic modifications are modern. That makes it the perfect test subject."

Abby nodded. "Then let's do it."

She turned toward Liza's interface. "Liza, prepare the hyperdrive for another transit. We're sending the orchid."

Liza acknowledged, her voice calm and precise. "Power levels stable. Initiating containment protocols. Scanning organic subject for baseline data."

Ethan stepped back from the console, watching as the plant was carefully placed inside the hyperdrive's chamber. "I really hope this thing doesn't come back as a man-eating monster."

Daniel, always analytical, smirked faintly. "Maybe time turns it into a tree that grows future fruit."

Lyara shot them both a look. "Focus, guys."

Liza's voice cut through the banter. "Temporal displacement sequence initiated. Stand by."

The hum of the hyperdrive intensified as the plant

flickered out of existence.

Then, they waited.

Fifteen minutes passed.

Nothing.

Thirty minutes. Still no change.

Ethan shifted his weight, tapping his fingers restlessly on the console. "Maybe this time, we actually outsmarted time?"

Olivia exhaled, rolling her shoulders. "Or maybe time just doesn't care about plants."

Abby glanced at Liza's data stream. "Let's give it more time. If it's being corrected, we need to let it happen."

An hour passed.

Still no change.

Daniel rubbed his temples. "Maybe organic matter doesn't register the same way as synthetic materials."

Then—at precisely an hour and seventeen minutes—Liza's voice cut through the silence.

"Anomaly detected."

The team tensed.

Abby stepped forward. "What kind of anomaly?"

Liza's display expanded, showing the genetic sequence of the orchid before transit and a new sequence detected at the target location. They weren't the same.

"The plant remains at the target destination," Liza reported, "but its genetic structure is shifting. Baseline modifications are eroding."

Daniel's brow furrowed. "Wait... it's changing?"

Lyara leaned in closer. "No. It's being corrected."

The team exchanged uneasy glances.

Time hadn't rejected the orchid.

It was rewriting it.

Then, Liza added something that made their blood run cold.

"Leaf pigmentation has begun to alter. Cellular structure reorganizing—efficiency of nutrient absorption is increasing. The rate of photosynthesis is accelerating beyond known parameters."

Olivia leaned closer to the screen. "It's not just reverting. It's *adapting*."

The data stream kept updating, and then a final, chilling observation appeared on Liza's display.

Warning: Unknown evolutionary markers detected.

The team stared at the words, silent.

It was still an orchid.

But now, it was something else entirely.

# 10

The morning light barely filtered into the underground levels, but the lab hummed with quiet energy as both teams gathered around the electronic whiteboard. Coffee cups were gripped tightly, half-drunk and forgotten in favor of the data scrawled across the screen.

Abby stood at the front, ready to debrief, but before she could speak, Dr. Cole stepped forward with a small smirk tugging at the corners of his mouth.

"Before we dive in," he said, reaching into his pocket and pulling out a small, modified interface chip, "I thought it was time we gave Liza a little upgrade."

Abby narrowed her eyes, already feeling a mix of irritation and intrigue. "What kind of upgrade?"

Dr. Cole gestured toward the board. "I've linked Liza directly to the whiteboard interface. Instead of us manually transcribing everything, she can now display data, make live adjustments, and—if needed—run active calculations in real-time."

Before Abby could fully process what he was saying, the board flickered to life. Liza's voice carried through the room with smooth precision.

"Integration successful. Good morning, everyone. I am now capable of direct data projection for visual analysis. Please excuse the handwriting simulation—I am still calibrating for human aesthetic preferences."

The screen filled with neat, structured notes before the text abruptly shifted to something scrawled and wildly uneven, then back again. A few of the interns chuckled at Liza's attempt at 'handwriting,' while Ethan muttered under his breath, "Great, now even Liza has better penmanship than I do."

Abby folded her arms, sighing. "Cole, I would have appreciated a heads-up before modifying Liza."

Cole shrugged. "Consider it an efficiency boost. Besides, I figured you'd approve once you saw it in action."

"Depends," she muttered. "Let's see if it was worth the trouble."

Liza, ever efficient, took this as her cue. "Displaying preliminary analysis of the orchid's alterations."

The board shifted, and a 3D model of the orchid's molecular structure appeared, its once-familiar strands now shifting in strange, unsettling patterns.

Daniel leaned in, eyes flicking over the genetic markers. "That... is not how it looked before."

Liza continued. "Comparison with initial scan data shows that multiple genetic markers have been overwritten or erased. Traits originating from present-day environmental influences have been eliminated. The sample has reverted to an earlier evolutionary state—one that predates recorded botanical history."

Abby took a slow breath. "So, it didn't just change. It regressed."

"Not entirely," Liza corrected. "Some structural adaptations remain, but any genetic material that was not yet introduced into the timeline appears to have been removed or rewritten. The plant is no longer from this time—it is from the version of history it was sent to."

Ethan exhaled sharply. "Time literally corrected it."

Lyara studied the displayed data, her expression unreadable. "Or reabsorbed it."

A ripple of silence passed through the team.

Dr. Nolan, who had been analyzing the genetic sequence, finally spoke. "This confirms that time's self-correction mechanism isn't just theoretical. It doesn't simply reject foreign objects—it assimilates them into whatever era they're placed in."

Olivia frowned. "But why? I mean, why this extreme? Why not just remove it?"

"Possibly because it became part of the timeline," Daniel suggested. "Once it existed in the past, time had no choice but to make it fit."

Cole tapped his fingers against the console thoughtfully. "Which means if we do something bigger—say, introduce a larger foreign presence—then time will be forced to deal with it."

Abby ran a hand over her hair, brushing it from her forehead. "And that's exactly what we need to test next. We have to understand the limits before we attempt to remove the anchor."

Ethan crossed his arms. "Because if we get this wrong…"

"…we might not just change time," Abby finished. "We might rewrite it."

Liza, ever efficient, concluded, "I recommend the next phase of testing account for both the scale and complexity of temporal adaptation. Larger objects with intricate structures may yield different results."

Abby exhaled, looking at the gathered team. "Then we need to decide what we're sending next."

Before the group could begin debating, Daniel tilted his head toward the board, still staring at the molecular data. "Hold on a second," he said, voice slow with realization. "If time erased the genetic markers that didn't belong… could we put them back?"

Olivia blinked. "You mean, like… rewrite the genes?"

Daniel nodded, looking toward Liza. "Liza, you have the original pre-scan data, right? If we brought the orchid back, could you reimpose the missing genetic markers?"

Liza responded immediately, "In theory, yes. If the object is retrieved in a stable state, I could attempt to reintroduce the scanned data at a molecular level. However, it is unclear whether time would allow the alterations to remain. If the self-correcting mechanism is still active, it may reject the changes."

Abby's gaze sharpened. "You're saying time might try to erase them again?"

Liza hesitated for a fraction of a second. "Unknown. This would be the first direct reversal attempt. There is no prior data to predict the outcome."

A weight settled over the room as the implications took root.

Ethan let out a slow breath. "So, if we can undo the changes to the orchid... then theoretically, that principle could apply to living organisms."

A hush settled over the lab.

The unspoken words hung in the air: To people.

Cole rubbed his jaw. "This... this might be the first real step toward recovering anyone lost to time."

Abby nodded slowly, her mind already racing through the possibilities. "Then let's find out if it works."

They weren't just fixing time anymore.

They were beginning to challenge it.

***

The team remained gathered around the digital whiteboard, but their discussion had shifted to an even more ambitious idea—bringing the orchid back.

"If we're serious about this," Lyara said, arms crossed in thought, "we need to make sure we don't just bring it back. We need to restore it."

Ethan nodded. "Right. Otherwise, we're just confirming that time erases what doesn't belong—but not proving if we can undo what it's erased."

Abby turned toward Liza. "Liza, is it possible to bring the orchid back into your buffers first? Hold it in digital storage before materializing it?"

Liza responded promptly. "Affirmative. I can retrieve the quantum structure and retain it within my storage matrix before reintegration."

Lyara's sharp eyes flicked toward the display. "Then don't materialize it immediately. While it's in the buffer, overwrite the altered genes with the original sequencing from its initial scan. If we do this correctly, we should see the restored plant the moment it rematerializes."

Liza was silent for half a second, running calculations. "Theoretically sound. However, replacing altered genetic information in real time has a 9.4% instability factor."

Daniel exhaled. "That's... not terrible."

"Not great, either," Olivia muttered.

"We've taken bigger risks," Abby stated, before looking to Liza again. "Anything we can do to mitigate that instability?"

Lyara tapped her fingers against the table. "What if, when you rematerialize it, you immediately drop the magnetic containment field?"

Ethan tilted his head. "Why?"

Lyara glanced at him. "Think about it. The longer it stays inside that field after a sudden genetic shift, the more time the orchid has to realize something is wrong. If we drop the containment right away, it won't have time to stress out. It'll just... exist."

Liza processed the suggestion. "Reducing external stabilization factors upon reconstitution may assist in a seamless transition. This will require precision timing."

Abby took a breath. "Then let's try it. Liza, retrieve the orchid into your buffer."

A pulse of energy flickered across the hyperdrive chamber, the hum of the system shifting as the retrieval process began. The display filled with cascading quantum patterns—Liza's matrix reconstructing the plant's state in real time.

"Quantum signature locked," Liza announced. "Orchid retained in buffer."

Abby turned to Liza. "Liza, confirm if the original genes

are present before we move forward."

Abby's fingers danced across her console, running the molecular analysis. A few tense seconds passed, the lab heavy with silence. Then—

"I'm seeing them," Elena breathed, eyes wide. "The missing genes are back in the data structure."

The team exchanged quick, nervous glances.

Ethan cracked his knuckles. "Alright... moment of truth."

Abby nodded at Liza. "Release the orchid and drop the field immediately."

A burst of light filled the chamber. The hum of the hyperdrive gave a low, pulsing thrum as the containment field flickered—then collapsed.

The orchid sat in the center of the chamber, whole and unchanged—as if nothing had ever happened to it at all.

For a heartbeat, no one spoke.

Then Olivia let out a breathy laugh. "We just reversed time."

Daniel exhaled in disbelief. "We didn't just bring it back... we overwrote time's decision."

Ethan took a cautious step forward, staring at the orchid. "The universe erased it. And we just told it no."

Lyara's gaze flickered with something unreadable. "Then maybe we're not as powerless against time as we thought."

Abby's heart pounded. This was no longer theory. No longer just observation.

They had just rewritten the past.

And now, there was no going back.

***

The lab was silent except for the soft hum of Liza processing data. The electronic whiteboard flickered to life, filling the room with projections of genetic sequences, highlighted mutations, and comparative analysis.

Liza's voice carried a calm precision as she began.

"Displaying genetic restoration data from the orchid. As hypothesized, the genes altered by the time stream have been successfully reimposed by the per-existing scan. However..."

She paused. A subtle, unnatural hesitation.

Abby frowned, stepping closer to the display. "However...?"

Liza continued, "A deviation has been detected. Though the majority of the orchid's genes were restored to their original state, certain sequences exhibit unexpected discrepancies—subtle mutations that did not exist in either the pre- or post-time shift state."

Daniel leaned forward, arms crossed. "Define 'subtle.'"

Liza magnified the highlighted sections on the board, side-by-side comparisons between the original and the 'restored' orchid appearing. "Less than 0.04% of the genome has changed. This falls within acceptable margins for natural mutation, but it is still statistically significant when compared to the controlled conditions of this experiment."

Olivia's expression darkened. "Meaning what? That we can't bring something back exactly the same?"

Ethan exhaled sharply, rubbing his face. "That's just a flower. What happens if it's a person?"

The question sent a ripple of tension through the room.

Daniel drummed his fingers against his console, deep in thought. "Would they feel it?"

Lyara spoke up, her voice measured but intense. "That's the real question, isn't it? If the body is rewritten on a genetic level, what happens to consciousness? To memories?"

Abby folded her arms, studying the data. "Liza, based on what we've seen here—if this process were applied to a sentient being, would they be aware of the changes? Would they experience pain?"

Liza's processing light flickered as she ran the simulations.

"My analysis is inconclusive. Unlike plants, human

neurological function is vastly more complex. The restoration of genetic material would not inherently cause pain, but sensory perception, cognitive stability, and memory retention could all be impacted. I lack sufficient data to determine the full psychological effects."

Ethan let out a low breath. "So, we'd be rolling the dice."

Daniel leaned against the table. "Then we need a controlled test before we even think about a human subject."

Olivia hesitated. "A… test subject?"

He nodded. "Something small. A mouse, maybe."

Ethan raked a hand through his hair, his movements sharp with frustration. His voice came out tight, edged with something between fear and disbelief. "Do you hear what we're saying? We're talking about sending a living thing—something that breathes, thinks, feels—into an environment that we know is going to rewrite it. We just watched time erase and rebuild that flower like it was nothing. What happens when it's not just cells being rewritten, but consciousness?"

Abby exhaled, pinching the bridge of her nose. "We need to be careful. We need to understand exactly what we're doing before we take any risks we can't undo."

The tension in the room was suffocating. No one wanted to be the first to say it, but the implication was there.

They weren't just dealing with theoretical physics anymore.

They were playing with life itself.

Then, as if to break the moment, Liza's voice cut through the quiet. "An additional anomaly has been detected."

Abby's head snapped up. "What anomaly?"

Liza expanded the orchid's data again, overlaying a faint but distinct reading. "An unidentified molecular structure exists within the restored sample. It does not match any known biological compound. It is neither part of the original genome nor the altered one."

Ethan's stomach twisted. "Then what the hell is it?"

Liza's response was unsettling in its uncertainty.
"I do not know."

A cold hush fell over the lab.

Abby took a step back, arms tightening over her chest. She had thought they were testing the limits of time— understanding its mechanisms, its ability to correct.

But now?

Now they had proof that something else was happening.

Something they didn't understand.

And if they couldn't explain it?

How could they control it?

\*\*\*

A soft chime echoed through the lab as Liza's voice cut through the quiet hum of equipment.

"Abby, I require access to external genomic research databases. Specifically, the Omnigen Molecular Archive."

Abby blinked, glancing at Daniel before responding. "Why that facility, Liza?"

"I have cross-referenced the unknown genetic sequences present in the altered orchid with all available public and proprietary genome libraries. No match was found," Liza explained. "However, I detected partial sequences that resemble classified genetic modifications archived within Omnigen's restricted-access vault."

Daniel frowned. "Wait—restricted? As in, you shouldn't have detected it?"

Liza's pause was telling. "Correct. The fragments were deeply embedded in datasets flagged as failed experiments. However, the encryption level surrounding the related files suggests these 'failures' were anything but insignificant."

Ethan, already leaning forward, let out a low whistle. "So, we just stumbled onto a secret someone really, *really* wanted buried."

Abby exhaled sharply, rubbing her forehead. "Liza, if we access that data, will it be logged?"

"That is an Absolute certainty Abby," Liza confirmed.

"The Omnigen archive is monitored by an automated anomaly detection system. Any request from an unlisted facility—such as ours—would generate a traceable flag."

Daniel crossed his arms, deep in thought. "Then we don't request it outright. We go at it another way."

Lyara tilted her head. "You mean, steal it?"

Daniel smirked slightly. "I prefer 'circumvent restrictions creatively.'"

Ethan sighed. "We're getting dangerously close to making enemies we don't want to make."

"We already have them," Lyara countered, shooting him a look. "You think Greta's visits are just check-ins? The corporation knows we're onto something."

Liza spoke again. "I may be able to retrieve a non-direct extrapolation—an indirect data pull based on public-facing research logs associated with Omnigen. This method carries a lower risk of detection."

Abby nodded. "Do it. But move carefully, Liza. I don't want to trip any silent alarms."

A pause. Then—

"Acknowledged. Beginning obfuscated query."

The screen flickered, Liza working beneath layers of firewalls and obscured algorithms. The air in the lab felt heavier as the team waited. Then, after several long seconds—

"Partial match detected," Liza announced. "Correlating retrieved sequences."

A data stream began populating the board, filling the display with twisting helix structures, percentages, and unknown markers. The team leaned in as Liza continued.

"The unknown mutation shares a 92.3% structural similarity with an experimental genome labeled X-3447—an abandoned genetic stability project. The experiment was listed as terminated due to 'catastrophic instability,' with no further records available beyond that point."

Elena narrowed her eyes. "What exactly were they trying

to do?"

Liza hesitated a fraction of a second before responding. "The limited records suggest the project's goal was adaptive genomic restructuring—an effort to create a biological entity that could survive in extreme environmental conditions."

Ethan's brows furrowed. "Like… changing its genes to match wherever it ends up?"

"Precisely," Liza confirmed. "However, the data suggests the mutations were *not* controlled. The organism's genetic structure continued to evolve unpredictably, rendering it unstable."

Daniel exchanged glances with the team. "So, when we sent the orchid back, it wasn't just reverting to its past state—it was adapting to time itself."

Lyara exhaled. "That means if we send a person through…"

Olivia paled. "They won't just experience a time shift. They could be rewritten entirely."

A chilling silence settled in the lab as the weight of that realization took hold.

Then, another notification from Liza.

"Abby, I have detected something else. The full experimental files for X-3447 *do* exist—but they are stored under a level-five encryption protocol. Even my extrapolation cannot access them."

Daniel crossed his arms, his expression darkening. "Which means someone really doesn't want anyone knowing what went wrong."

Lyara folded her arms. "So, what's our next move?"

Abby didn't answer immediately. She stared at the screen, the encrypted files taunting them.

Then, after a beat—

"We find out what the hell Omnigen is hiding."

\*\*\*

The tension in the lab was thick, but not from fear—rather, the friction of minds clashing in rapid debate.

"This is reckless," Daniel argued, arms crossed as he leaned against the digital whiteboard. "We already have the corporation watching us, and now we're talking about digging into some other lab's classified experiments? This is exactly how we get shut down."

Ethan gestured animatedly. "But we're not just digging. We're trying to find out what the hell happened to that mutation. If it's something they botched, that means they could be covering it up. And if it's tied to the timeline distortions—"

"We don't know that," Olivia interrupted, shaking her head. "We don't know anything yet. That's the problem. We keep theorizing, but we still have no proof that looking into this won't just get us into deeper trouble."

Lyara, arms folded, let out a slow breath. "So what? We just sit on our hands and hope the answer falls into our laps?"

A brief silence stretched between them. Abby, who had been listening quietly, finally pushed off from the workstation she had been leaning against.

"We're not chasing ghosts," she stated firmly. "We have enough unknowns already, and I don't plan on adding another one that could bring more scrutiny down on us. Until we know for certain that this is necessary, we don't touch it."

Ethan exhaled sharply but nodded, clearly not satisfied but willing to defer. Daniel's shoulders relaxed slightly, and Olivia looked visibly relieved. Lyara, however, still looked unconvinced.

"I hope we're not just playing it safe because it's easier," she muttered under her breath.

Abby gave her a measured look. "We're playing it smart. There's a difference."

Before the discussion could continue, an unexpected chime echoed through the lab, followed by a soft hum from the containment field.

Everyone turned toward the hyperdrive chamber as Liza's voice cut through the room.

"Abby, I am detecting unexpected changes in the orchid's genetic structure."

Ethan straightened. "What kind of changes?"

Liza hesitated a fraction of a second, as if carefully choosing her words. "The genetic markers that had previously been altered upon its initial displacement are shifting again. However, the structure is not reverting to its original state."

Lyara stepped forward, her eyes narrowing. "Then what is happening?"

Liza brought up a detailed projection on the digital whiteboard, the genetic map pulsing in intricate strands of light. "The orchid's genetic sequence is... evolving."

The words settled over the team like a wave.

A slow transformation was occurring—not reverting, not mutating further into a distorted anomaly, but *growing* into something new.

The petals had taken on a deeper, richer hue, their surfaces slightly iridescent under the lab's artificial light. The edges of the leaves were subtly reshaping, forming delicate curves that hadn't been present before. The entire plant seemed to vibrate with an energy none of them had expected.

Olivia, wide-eyed, took an eager step closer. "This is beautiful."

Lyara was right beside her, captivated. "It's not just adapting... it's thriving."

Daniel rubbed his chin thoughtfully. "If time itself rejected it, why would it evolve instead of breaking down?"

Ethan let out a breath, eyes locked on the orchid. "Maybe because time isn't trying to reject it anymore."

Abby's expression was unreadable as she studied the plant. Whatever they had just witnessed, it wasn't merely an experiment anymore.

It was something else entirely.

Something that was about to change everything.

Liza's voice broke through the silence, her tone analytical. "I have detected an additional anomaly. Based on data extrapolated from the original scan, the gene mutation may have absorbed residual quantum signatures that remained undetectable at the time of reintegration."

Daniel frowned. "Wait... a delayed effect?"

Liza confirmed. "Yes. The quantum drive operates with extreme precision, but quantum fields are inherently unpredictable when introduced to organic matter. There is a possibility that the orchid's genetic restructuring was not immediate, but rather a gradual unfolding—like a latent activation."

Dr. Cole, who had been listening from the far side of the lab, suddenly straightened, his eyes widening slightly. "That... actually makes sense."

Abby turned to him. "You're thinking of something."

Cole nodded, stepping closer, his mind racing. "Back in our timeline, we were working on a secondary project—a way to shield living organisms from quantum distortion fields. It was meant as a contingency in case something went wrong with our initial displacement trials. The theory was to envelop the subject in a contained field, almost like..." He hesitated, searching for the right word.

"A digital condom?" Ethan supplied, smirking.

Cole let out a sharp laugh. "Crude, but not inaccurate. The idea was to keep quantum interference from rewriting biological structures. It didn't work back then... but if I had access to the right materials now, I might be able to recreate it."

Abby's expression shifted, considering the implications. "So if we do need to send a living subject in the future, they wouldn't experience the same kind of... restructuring that the orchid did?"

Dr. Cole exhaled. "That's the goal."

Lyara tapped her fingers against the table. "Then we need to test it."

Olivia gave her a skeptical look. "And what do you suggest? We send another orchid and hope for the best?"

Cole shook his head. "No. We go up the chain. If we want proof that this works before we even consider human trials..." His gaze settled on the supply cabinet in the corner of the room, where the lab's small stock of research animals was kept.

"We test it on a mouse."

A hush fell over the room as the weight of the idea settled over them.

It was a risk. A necessary one.

And if it worked—if the field could protect a living being from time's grip—then they would have just taken a massive step forward in understanding how to control what had, until now, been completely unpredictable.

Abby finally nodded. "Then let's get to work."

\*\*\*

As Ethan and Cole made their way toward the test bench, they passed Olivia and Lyara, who were still standing in front of the orchid, their eyes practically shining with admiration. The soft glow of the lab lights cast gentle reflections off the orchid's now ethereal petals, the colors shifting subtly as if the plant itself was breathing.

Ethan smirked and shook his head. "And you give us grief for being deep in thought? You've been staring at that thing for ages."

Lyara didn't even glance at him, her gaze still fixed on the transformed orchid. "This isn't just a flower," she murmured. "It's a new genesis—a species that's never existed before and probably never will again."

Finally, she turned to look at Ethan, her expression soft but tinged with melancholy. "And the saddest part? We can't even share it with the world. No one will ever know this miracle happened. That, in itself, is something worth mourning."

Ethan blinked, momentarily caught off guard by the

depth of her words. He opened his mouth, then shut it, realizing he had nothing to counter that. Instead, he just gave a small nod and continued walking with Cole toward the workbench.

Behind them, Olivia sighed, absently touching one of the orchid's petals with an almost reverent care. "She's right, you know. For all the science we're doing... this might be the most beautiful thing we've ever created."

Daniel, who had wandered over just in time to hear them, exhaled slowly. "Beautiful... and terrifying. If the timeline is capable of altering organic matter at this level, imagine what would happen to something aware of the change. A human, for example."

Olivia frowned. "You think it would hurt?"

Daniel rubbed the back of his neck. "I don't know. But I'd rather not find out the hard way."

The thought cast a subtle pall over their moment of wonder, but before the conversation could spiral into further unease, Dr. Cole let out a loud clap, snapping Ethan back into focus.

"Enough brooding, kid," Dr. Cole said, placing a firm hand on Ethan's shoulder. "Time to prove all the rumors about your genius aren't just exaggerated myths."

Ethan let out a short laugh. "Oh, great. No pressure."

Dr. Cole grabbed a stylus and tapped on the surface of the workstation, bringing up a blank schematic. "I want this thing to be wearable—something lightweight, like a watch. But I'm stuck on the power source. A battery small enough to fit on the wrist won't hold enough charge."

Ethan leaned over, already envisioning possibilities. "I might have a solution. Back in college, I worked on a project for my thesis—an experimental high-density power cell. It was too costly to develop at scale, but with the resources we have now, it could work."

Dr. Cole's eyes lit up. "Now we're talking."

The two dove into their work, ideas flowing as they

sketched, argued, refined, and recalculated. Hours passed unnoticed as they lost themselves in the challenge, their fingers tapping across digital blueprints, running rapid calculations through Liza, and occasionally cursing when a formula didn't quite add up.

***

Across the lab, Olivia and Lyara had returned to their fascination with the orchid. Every few minutes, one of them would make a new observation—the color shift seems to be accelerating, the structure is more rigid than before, the petals look like they're self-repairing in real-time—each discovery feeding their growing sense of awe.

Lyara reached out but hesitated just before her fingertips could brush against one of the strange petals. "Do you think... if I touched it, it would react?"

Olivia tilted her head. "I don't know. But I kind of want to find out."

Lyara shot her a mischievous grin. "Rock-paper-scissors?"

Before Olivia could respond, Daniel cleared his throat loudly behind them. "You do realize we just had an entire conversation about whether mutations would be painful, right?"

Lyara gave an exaggerated sigh. "Fine, fine. No touching. For now."

They shared a quiet laugh, but the moment was interrupted by a loud grumble from Olivia's stomach.

Lyara raised a brow. "Was that... you?"

Olivia groaned, rubbing her stomach. "It's been hours. I'm running on fumes over here."

Lyara chuckled. "Well, if you're feeling it, then I'm sure Ethan and Cole are about two minutes from forgetting food exists entirely."

Sure enough, when they wandered over to the workbench, they found Cole and Ethan hunched over the schematics, deep in the trenches of problem-solving. The two men hadn't even noticed their approach.

Olivia waved a hand between them. "Hello? Earth to science gremlins."

Neither responded.

Lyara sighed, then leaned forward, placing a finger firmly on the schematic display and dragging it off-screen.

Ethan blinked rapidly, finally looking up. "Hey! We were working on that."

Olivia smirked, crossing her arms. "And we were working on not starving to death. Time for a break."

Cole, without missing a beat, reached blindly for his coffee cup and took a sip, only to grimace. "Ugh. Cold."

Lyara shook her head. "Yep. Definitely time for food."

Olivia placed a bag of sandwiches and a fresh coffee in front of each of them. "We brought you something. You're welcome."

Cole barely looked up. "You're lifesavers."

"More like enablers," Lyara teased. "You two haven't moved since we left."

Ethan picked up his sandwich without looking away from the schematics. "Progress waits for no one."

Lyara smirked. "Neither does sleep."

"You sound like Liza," Ethan muttered.

Behind them, Liza's voice chimed in. "I take that as a compliment."

The lab filled with quiet laughter, the weight of the day momentarily eased by the familiar camaraderie.

As Dr. Cole took a bite of his sandwich, he gestured toward Ethan. "Alright, kid. We've got the theory down. Now let's see if we can actually build this thing."

Ethan grinned. "Let's do it."

***

The morning light filtered into the lab, catching on the faint sheen of metal as Ethan and Cole hunched over their workstation. The two had been at it long after the others had retired for the night, and while Dr. Cole looked as energized as ever, Ethan looked like he had personally fought time itself and lost.

Ethan yawned, running a hand through his hair as he sat back, stretching. "Alright, behold," he said, motioning to the device on the table with all the showmanship of a magician after an all-nighter. "The first prototype of the—uh—whatever we're calling it. I was going with Time Bubble Generator, but Dr. Cole thinks that sounds ridiculous."

Dr. Cole scoffed. "Because it is ridiculous. The device isn't generating a bubble—it's stabilizing a temporal field around an organic subject to prevent mutations." He gave Ethan a pointed look. "Which is why Temporal Stabilization Field Generator is the accurate name."

Ethan rolled his eyes. "Yeah, that just rolls off the tongue. Real catchy."

Before Dr. Cole could retort, Lyara slid into the conversation with a smirk. "Did you even sleep last night, Ethan?" she asked, arms crossed. "Because if this device works by sheer stubbornness, I'd say it's already overpowered."

Ethan shot her a look. "Oh, I slept." He hesitated. "For at least... two, maybe three hours?"

Lyara tilted her head in mock pity. "Oh, my poor genius," she teased, stepping closer and lowering her voice just enough for the others to hear. "You know, you could have spent that time dreaming about me instead of circuits and power densities."

Ethan blinked. He opened his mouth, shut it, and pointed vaguely at the device. "I—well—I—uh—what?"

Lyara grinned triumphantly and turned away, leaving him floundering.

Daniel smirked, shaking his head as he leaned in to examine the prototype. "Alright, lover boy, let's focus before your brain completely short-circuits."

Ethan cleared his throat, scowling at Daniel before grabbing the device with exaggerated importance. "Anyway, as I was saying, the device is wrist-mounted, running on a dense power pack I designed years ago. It generates a thin field around the wearer, which theoretically should prevent any quantum entanglement with the time stream."

Cole gestured toward the reinforced strap attached to it. "We had to modify it a bit—originally, it was meant for human use, but for this test, we'll attach it to a smaller subject."

At that, Olivia stepped forward, holding a small enclosure. Inside, a white lab mouse twitched its nose, completely unaware it was about to become the first living thing to test time travel safely.

"So, Whiskers gets to be the first to wear the fancy time armor," Olivia said, opening the enclosure carefully.

Ethan gestured toward the mouse with mock seriousness. "Whiskers? That's what we're calling it?"

Olivia shrugged. "If he's gonna be the first mouse to cheat time, he needs a name."

Lyara leaned in slightly. "Besides, he's already a better test subject than you, Ethan. I bet he didn't lose sleep over this."

Ethan groaned, rubbing his face. "Why do I feel personally attacked today?"

"You make it too easy," Lyara shot back with a grin.

Abby, who had been watching the exchange with mild amusement, finally spoke up. "Alright, let's focus. Olivia, carefully place Whiskers inside the hyperdrive."

Olivia nodded, gently lifting the small creature and placing him into the chamber, ensuring the device was securely strapped around his tiny frame. The thin band fit snugly without restricting movement, the display pulsing faintly as it activated.

Once the mouse was settled, Abby turned her attention to Liza. "Liza, are you able to run a baseline scan on the mouse before we send him through?"

Liza's voice responded smoothly. "Scanning for baseline

genetic markers… complete. No anomalies detected."

Daniel glanced at the others. "This is the real test. If the device works, Whiskers comes back exactly as he left."

"And if it doesn't work?" Olivia asked hesitantly.

Cole sighed. "Then we have a very different kind of ethical discussion."

The room fell silent for a moment before Ethan clapped his hands together. "Well, that's not ominous at all."

Abby nodded toward Liza. "Alright. Let's do it."

Liza's cameras adjusted to focus on the enclosure. "Temporal Stabilization Field activated. Hyperdrive coordinates locked. Engaging quantum displacement in three… two… one…"

A pulse of energy crackled through the chamber, and in a flash of light, Whiskers was gone.

The lab went still.

Liza's voice broke the silence. "Temporal transition complete. Scanning destination environment."

The team exchanged glances, and Ethan exhaled. "Alright, now we wait."

And so they did.

Five minutes passed.

Fifteen.

Thirty.

An hour.

Abby checked her watch just as Liza's voice chimed in.

"I am detecting a fluctuation in the stabilization field. Quantum signatures are shifting—retrieval window approaching."

The team tensed.

Ethan cracked his knuckles. "Alright, let's bring our boy home."

Liza's voice was calm, clinical. "Engaging retrieval protocol."

A heartbeat later, another brilliant flash lit the chamber—and when it cleared, the tiny form of Whiskers was back.

Lyara was the first to step forward, her eyes scanning the little creature. The mouse twitched its nose, its fur slightly ruffled but otherwise unchanged.

Liza spoke. "Initiating genetic analysis."

A long pause.

Then—

"Genetic structure remains intact. No temporal modifications detected."

Silence.

Then Olivia whooped. "Hell yes!"

The team broke into relieved chatter, excitement bubbling through the air.

Ethan exhaled dramatically. "We did it. We actually did it."

Lyara grinned. "We? You mean Whiskers did it."

Ethan scoffed. "He was just along for the ride. I did the work."

Abby chuckled, arms crossed. "Either way, we have a breakthrough."

Dr. Cole nodded, his expression serious despite the celebration. "This means the stabilization field works. It can protect organic matter from time-induced mutations."

Lyara tapped her fingers against the table. "And if it works on a mouse…"

Ethan caught her meaning immediately, his excitement returning. "It can work on a person."

The team exchanged looks.

This wasn't just theory anymore.

They had just taken the first real step toward *safe* time travel.

And there was no going back.

***

# 11

The team—both past and present—gathered around the central workstation, their focus locked on the digital whiteboard as Liza displayed the latest readouts on the mouse. The tiny creature sat comfortably in its enclosure, its vitals showing no irregularities after its time within the temporal field.

Daniel rubbed his chin as he studied the data. "No signs of stress, no cellular degradation, nothing. The field held perfectly."

Dr. Cole nodded in agreement. "As far as we can tell, it shielded the biological structure completely."

Ethan, arms crossed, let out a thoughtful hum. "That's promising, but we need to talk logistics. What's the projected battery life? How long can the field sustain itself?"

Liza's voice chimed in, smooth and precise. "The current energy cell should sustain a stable protective field for approximately twelve minutes. However, continued exposure may cause fluctuations in power output. This must be accounted for before extended use."

Abby leaned against the table. "So, we keep the test runs short. No unnecessary risks."

Daniel shot Ethan a look. "That still doesn't tell us how this thing will hold up when scaled to human size."

Ethan sighed, rubbing the back of his neck. "Yeah, that's a good point. A mouse is tiny—this field barely has to stretch. A full-grown adult? Whole different ballgame."

Dr. Cole smirked. "Then it sounds like it's time for a real test."

Lyara arched a brow. "You mean one of us."

A lively debate immediately erupted.

"Absolutely not," Olivia said quickly. "Not yet."

"Oh, come on," Ethan countered. "You know we're all thinking it."

"I volunteer," Daniel exclaimed

Ethan blinked, he exchanged glances with Daniel, who simply gave a small, solemn nod.

"… I volunteer," Daniel said, stepping forward. His voice was steady, decisive.

Ethan narrowed his eyes. "Oh, you get to go first?"

Dr. Cole chuckled, shaking his head. "You took the first jump through time. It's his turn to be the guinea pig."

Ethan huffed in mock offense. "Fine, but I get next."

Lyara smirked at him, voice laced with amusement. "Eager to throw yourself into a potentially dangerous experiment? Remind me to keep an eye on you."

Ethan shot her a sidelong glance, a smirk tugging at his lips. "Admit it—you'd be disappointed if I wasn't this reckless."

She winked. "Maybe a little."

Daniel, ignoring their exchange, stepped toward the testing area and picked up the device. "Alright, here goes nothing."

Ethan scoffed. "Nothing? Try everything."

Daniel chuckled but didn't argue. He strapped the prototype around his wrist, adjusting the fit before glancing at Liza. "Anything I should know before I turn it on?"

Liza's tone remained even. "Hold still during activation. The field will take approximately two-point-three seconds to stabilize. You may experience a slight tingling sensation."

Daniel took a steadying breath. "Alright. Let's do this."

He pressed the activation pad.

The change was immediate.

A low gleam filled the air as a translucent energy field expanded outward from the device, spreading across his arm before sweeping over his entire body in a slow, shimmering wave. The field bent the light around him, refracting in strange, liquid-like distortions, making it appear as though Daniel was submerged in an invisible current.

"Whoa," Olivia exclaimed, eyes wide.

Ethan took a slow step forward, staring at the effect. "That's... insane."

Lyara tilted her head. "How do you feel?"

Daniel flexed his fingers, looking down at himself with fascination. "Lighter. Like there's less resistance in the air." He shifted his weight, testing his movement. "It's not restricting at all."

Liza's voice chimed in. "The field is stable. No abnormalities detected."

Abby folded her arms. "So far, so good. Try moving around."

Daniel took a careful step forward, then another. The field moved with him seamlessly, clinging to his form like a second skin.

Ethan snapped his fingers. "Try running."

Daniel shot him a look but complied, taking a few brisk strides across the lab. His movements were fluid—unnaturally so.

"Interesting," Dr. Cole muttered. "The field isn't just maintaining—it's enhancing."

Abby frowned slightly. "Enhancing?"

Dr. Cole gestured toward Daniel. "Watch how he moves. The energy signature is compensating for air resistance, almost like it's creating a controlled buffer."

Lyara crossed her arms. "Which means?"

Ethan grinned. "Which means we just made a freaking force field."

Daniel let out a breathless laugh. "Yeah, this is... incredible." He stopped moving and looked toward Liza. "What's the readout?"

Liza responded promptly. "Field stability remains optimal. No power fluctuations detected within the first three minutes of activation."

Abby exhaled slowly, nodding. "Alright, let's keep monitoring, but this is a damn good start."

The team exchanged looks.

This was no longer just a theory.

They had just taken the first real step toward stepping into time—fully protected.

***

The team continued their observations as Daniel moved about the lab, the shimmering field still enveloping him. The faint hum of the device on his wrist was barely audible, yet its presence filled the room with an unshakable awareness that they were dealing with something far beyond the scope of conventional science.

Minutes passed. Then an hour. The shield remained steady, undisturbed.

Ethan tapped his fingers against the workstation, watching the live readings fluctuate on the monitors. "Still stable," he muttered. "Not bad for a prototype."

Daniel turned his hands over, flexing his fingers beneath the field. He had expected some kind of sensation—heat, static, anything. But instead, it was as if he had simply been wrapped in an invisible cocoon. No pressure, no weight shift, no tingling nerves. Just an odd stillness.

"How do you feel?" Abby asked, crossing her arms.

Daniel tilted his head. "Weirdly normal? I don't feel heavier or lighter. No dizziness. If I weren't looking at it, I'd forget it was there."

Lyara took a step closer, observing the way the ambient light bent subtly around his outline. "It's like you're slightly out of phase with everything else. A half-step out of time."

"That's a poetic way to put it," Ethan remarked, smirking.

Lyara shrugged. "I like my physics with a little poetry."

Liza's voice cut in. "Energy levels decreasing rapidly. Power reserves approaching critical levels."

Daniel glanced at his wrist, though the device itself gave no indication of its remaining energy. "I still don't feel anything."

Ethan's expression tightened as he watched the data scroll across the screen. "It's holding longer than expected, but if it's dropping now, it's probably going to crash fast."

Liza continued, "Battery reserves at eight percent. Seven. Six."

Daniel sighed. "Alright, let's shut it dow—"

Before he could finish, the shield flickered violently, crackling with an almost imperceptible burst of energy before collapsing all at once.

The impact was instant.

Daniel staggered, his knees buckling as an invisible *weight* pressed down on him like he had just walked into a room with doubled gravity. His breath hitched, eyes widening as the full weight of time itself seemed to crash back onto his body.

"Daniel!" Lyara moved toward him, concern flashing across her face.

He shot a hand up, stopping her. "I'm—okay," he said between breaths, steadying himself. His muscles trembled under the shift, as though he had just been carrying something heavy and suddenly set it down.

Abby, brows furrowed, turned toward Liza. "What the hell just happened?"

Liza's response came instantly. "Scanning now."

Daniel rubbed his temples, the residual sensation still lingering in his bones. "Felt like my body just... caught up to something."

Ethan narrowed his eyes. "Caught up? To what?"

Abby stepped forward, her professional demeanor masking the growing concern in her eyes. "Daniel, step into the hyperdrive. Liza, run a deep scan."

Still shaking off the lingering disorientation, Daniel carefully stepped inside the chamber. The door sealed behind him with a quiet hiss, and a golden light swept across his form, casting long shadows against the walls.

The hum of the scanning systems filled the lab.

The room was silent as they waited.

Then Liza spoke.

"Preliminary analysis suggests the collapse of the protective field created a temporary imbalance. When the shield failed, the surrounding time flow rushed back into Daniel's body, resulting in momentary disorientation."

Dr. Cole nodded, his expression pensive. "That explains the crash. But why did it feel like his body was catching up?"

There was a pause—just long enough to make the air feel heavier.

Liza's next words sent a ripple of disbelief through the lab.

"Additional findings indicate that during the one hour and thirty-two minutes the field was active... Daniel's biological aging ceased."

A long silence followed.

Daniel blinked. "Wait... what?"

Liza continued, her tone even, calculated. "Cellular degradation and metabolic activity within your body remained in a stasis-like state. There was no measurable progression of time on a biological level."

Ethan let out a slow exhale, rubbing his temples. "You're saying... while he had the shield up, he stopped aging?"

"Correct," Liza confirmed.

A hush settled over the lab as the implications crashed over them.

Daniel stepped forward, gripping the console outside the hyperdrive, his knuckles white. "So if I had that shield on for a year... I wouldn't age for a year?"

Liza responded without hesitation. "Extrapolations suggest that extended use of the field could theoretically maintain biological stasis. However, additional variables, such as long-term neurological effects and prolonged separation from natural time progression, remain unknown."

Lyara let out a slow breath, crossing her arms. "That's… incredible. And terrifying."

Abby, deep in thought, turned toward the data streaming across the board. "Could this be scalable? If a field this small can stop time's effects on a person, how much energy would be needed for a larger field?"

Dr. Cole let out a low whistle. "We'd be talking huge power demands. The denser the shield, the more energy you'd need to sustain it."

Abby ran a hand through her hair, exhaling sharply. "Okay, as fascinating as this is, we have bigger priorities. If we're going to use this for an actual jump, we can't have the battery failing in the middle of a transition. That field has to hold."

Ethan turned to Dr. Cole, his mind already racing. "We need a better power source. Something denser—way denser."

Dr. Cole nodded. "Agreed. We can't have this thing burning out in under two hours. We need something that can sustain the field long enough for a proper transit."

Abby crossed her arms. "What kind of energy density are we talking about?"

Ethan leaned against the table, thinking. "Something beyond traditional lithium or graphene cells. Maybe… a quantum-coupled energy matrix?"

Dr. Cole arched a brow. "That's theoretical."

Ethan grinned. "So was time travel."

Dr. Cole let out a short chuckle. "Point taken. Alright, let's get to work."

As the team shifted their focus toward designing a more efficient power source, Daniel remained standing near the hyperdrive, flexing his fingers—his mind still racing with the revelation.

For one hour and thirty-two minutes, time had left him behind.

And now, he couldn't shake the feeling that he'd just glimpsed something far bigger than they ever intended.

\*\*\*

The electronic whiteboard was already a chaotic swirl of equations, energy matrices, and diagrams, with Dr. Cole and Ethan standing on either side, each furiously working through calculations while Liza assisted in real time. The air in the lab was thick with the scent of coffee, old circuitry, and the faint hum of equipment running at full tilt.

"Alright, let's backtrack," Ethan muttered, tapping his stylus against the board as he worked through the formula on energy retention. "We need something that can sustain the quantum barrier for a full jump cycle. The problem is every traditional power source we've looked at burns out too fast."

Cole, arms crossed, nodded toward Liza's latest projections. "Theoretically, if we could increase the energy density exponentially, we wouldn't need mass amounts of power—just a way to contain more in a smaller space."

Liza interjected, her smooth voice filling the lab. "Calculations confirm your assumption, Cole. However, no known power source currently exists within this facility that can meet the necessary parameters."

Ethan exhaled sharply, rubbing his face with both hands. "That's a problem."

They worked through the late morning and well into the afternoon, refining their models, iterating solutions, and bouncing ideas off Liza, who kept running calculations at a breakneck pace.

Finally, nearing the midpoint of the afternoon, Dr. Cole straightened, letting out a satisfied sigh as he tapped the board. "Okay. That's it. We've got it."

Ethan stepped back, taking in the mess of numbers and formulas. "Looks solid… but we're missing one thing. We don't have the right materials. Some of this—" he gestured at a section of the board, "—isn't just rare, it's nonexistent in our supply."

"Then we create it," Cole said simply.

Ethan blinked. "I... what?"

Dr. Cole turned to Liza. "Liza, you constructed a stable temporal field. Could you, in theory, break down the quantum signature of an existing power cell, extract the missing components, and then reassemble those components into the material we need?"

Liza was silent for a moment, then finally responded. "This task is not within my designated operational parameters. However..." A slight pause. "I will try."

Abby folded her arms. "And what happens if something goes wrong? This isn't like reconstructing a coffee cup."

"Then I will refine the process through iterative learning," Liza replied calmly.

Abby exhaled but nodded. "Alright. Do it."

Liza's systems engaged, and the hum of the hyperdrive shifted in tone, signaling the start of a delicate and intricate process. The team gathered around as a projected interface displayed the deconstruction of the old battery pack in real-time. Liza parsed through layers of energy configurations, isolating molecular structures, and analyzing their quantum signatures.

Dr. Cole and Ethan monitored the process closely, calling out subtle adjustments as Liza worked through the reconstruction. The atmosphere was tense, but their combined expertise kept the process moving forward.

Minutes stretched into nearly an hour.

Then, with a final pulse of energy, a new object materialized inside the hyperdrive containment field.

Liza's voice carried a hint of accomplishment. "Reconstruction complete. The power cell has been enhanced and now meets the projected requirements."

Cole let out a breath and stepped forward, reaching for the object.

Ethan grabbed his wrist mid-reach, eyes wide. "Whoa." He pointed at the device, his voice just a little higher than usual. "Do you realize that has more power than a nuclear reactor? You do not just grab something like that."

Dr. Cole raised a brow but slowly withdrew his hand. "Noted."

Lyara, standing nearby, smirked. "I kind of wanted to see what would happen."

Ethan shot her a look. "No. You do not want to see what happens when someone gets vaporized into a fine mist."

Olivia, leaning against the counter, grinned. "I mean, scientifically speaking, I *kinda* do."

Ethan groaned, pinching the bridge of his nose. "This is why I have trust issues."

Daniel chuckled, shaking his head. "Alright, so how do we safely retrieve it?"

Liza answered promptly. "The containment field will neutralize high-energy discharge once powered down. Dr. Cole, you may now safely retrieve the object."

Dr. Cole hesitated for a half-second before reaching in again. This time, he carefully lifted the power cell, marveling at how impossibly light it felt for something so dense with energy.

He turned it over in his hands. "It's almost weightless."

Ethan eyed it like someone looking at an unexploded grenade. "Yeah. That's what worries me."

Dr. Cole handed it to Ethan. "Then you get to install it."

Ethan took the power cell delicately, holding it with the utmost care. "Fantastic," he muttered. "Handling the most volatile energy source ever created. No pressure."

\*\*\*

Abby clapped her hands together, redirecting the room. "Alright, let's get this thing integrated and test it."

As the team shifted their focus to implementing the newly constructed power source, there was an undeniable energy in the air—excitement, anxiety, and the unspoken thrill of pushing the boundaries of the impossible.

Ethan placed the power cell onto the workbench and took

a cautious step back. "Okay, we need to be really sure this thing doesn't fry whoever straps it on."

Dr. Cole nodded. "Agreed. We'll need a regulation circuit. Something to act as a dampener."

Ethan perked up. "Actually... if we add an internal stabilizer, we can create an emergency power cutoff. The second it detects a surge, it kills the energy output."

Daniel added, "We should also build a shielded casing around the core. No open exposure."

Liza's voice cut in. "I will assist in generating a power dispersion model. This will allow the energy output to remain consistent without destabilization."

Ethan let out a breath of relief. "Okay. Now we're talking."

Lyara folded her arms, smirking. "Good. I'd rather not watch you all melt into a puddle when we turn it on."

Abby cleared her throat to gather the attention of the group. "Alright. Let's finalize the safety systems before we test this thing."

As the team got to work, the tension in the room remained, but there was also something else—momentum.

They were on the cusp of something monumental.

And this was only the beginning.

\*\*\*

The lab hummed with a quiet tension as the team finalized the last connections to the newly stabilized power unit. The modifications were complete—safety redundancies, emergency cutoffs, power dampeners—all carefully integrated to ensure the new system didn't accidentally vaporize its wearer.

Ethan stood beside the device, rolling his shoulders. "Alright, let's get this over with. I'll go first."

Before anyone could react, Olivia stepped forward, hands on her hips, chin lifted in defiance. "Actually, I think it's my turn."

A collective silence fell over the room as everyone

turned to stare at her.

Ethan blinked. "Wait. What?"

Olivia smirked, clearly relishing the shock factor. "You boys have had all the fun so far. It's time for one of the girls to take a turn with the power."

Ethan's brows shot up. "Oh hell no. Nah, not happening"

Lyara, arms folded, leaned casually against the workbench. "Aww, what's wrong, Ethan? Afraid she's going to outshine you?"

Ethan jabbed a finger in Olivia's direction. "She's the youngest intern here! We just created the most powerful energy field ever worn on a human body, and you want to strap it to her? How is that a good idea?"

Olivia arched a brow, trying to look unfazed despite the tension rolling off her. "Oh, so now you suddenly care about seniority? I thought this was all about science."

Abby, who had been quietly observing the exchange, finally sighed and stepped forward, placing a hand on Ethan's shoulder. "She's right, Ethan."

He turned to her, incredulous. "Abby!"

Abby met his gaze firmly. "Look, I get it. You're protective. We all are. But Olivia is part of this team. She's smart, she knows the risks, and if she wants to step up, I say we let her."

Ethan ran a hand down his face, exasperated. "I hate this plan."

Lyara gave him a smug grin. "That's because it's not your plan."

Dr. Cole chuckled, shaking his head. "Alright, let's suit up our fearless intern."

Olivia shot Ethan a playful wink before stepping onto the platform. Despite her outward confidence, she swallowed hard as Ethan carefully strapped the modified unit to her forearm. "You know, for the record, this does feel like a bad idea," she muttered under her breath.

Ethan smirked despite himself. "Finally, some common

sense."

Lyara leaned in, grinning. "You can still back out, you know. Wouldn't blame you."

Olivia straightened. "No way. I'm doing this."

Ethan took a step back, still looking unconvinced, but he secured the last strap and checked the readings. "Okay. Power's stable, emergency cutoffs are active… Please don't explode."

Olivia rolled her eyes. "Such confidence in your own design."

She took a breath, exhaled slowly, and pressed the activation button.

Immediately, a deep hum filled the air, and the field burst into existence—not the faint, shimmering distortion they had seen with Daniel, but something far more intense.

A luminous, rippling veil of energy enveloped Olivia, outlining her in a vivid distortion of shifting colors. It flickered between hues of deep blue and violet, almost like a mirage wrapped around her form. The sheer intensity of it made the air around her pulse.

The team took an instinctive step back.

"Uh…" Daniel muttered, shielding his eyes slightly. "That's… new."

Olivia, staring down at herself, blinked. "Okay. Whoa."

Ethan's alarm shot straight to the surface. "Olivia, turn it off."

"I—I think it's fine?" Olivia said uncertainly, moving her hands. The energy warped around them like liquid light.

Abby shook her head sharply. "No, he's right. If you jumped looking like that, you'd be walking around like a damn neon sign in another time period. Turn it off."

Olivia pressed the shutdown switch. The field flickered once, hesitated, and then collapsed, vanishing in a whisper of dissipating energy.

She let out a breath, her hands trembling slightly. "Well. That was… something."

Ethan let out a very long sigh. "That was a very bad something."

Dr. Cole scratched his chin. "We need to dial that back. If someone in the past or future saw that, they'd think we were aliens."

Daniel crossed his arms. "Or gods."

Lyara grinned. "I mean… not the worst first impression."

Ethan turned to Olivia. "You good?"

She flexed her fingers, checking herself over. "Yeah. I think so."

Abby wanting to redirect the tension. "Alright, team. We need to make some adjustments before we even think about a real test run. Let's get back to work."

As the team moved to refine the energy field's visibility, Ethan muttered under his breath, "Next time, I really get to go first."

Lyara smirked. "We'll see about that."

*** 

The hum of machinery filled the lab as Ethan and Cole stood side by side, making meticulous adjustments to the field modulator. The once-brilliant energy veil had been tamed, dampened into a barely perceptible distortion that flickered only when Olivia moved.

Ethan leaned back, rubbing his neck as he surveyed the board of calculations. "Alright, we turned the strength down, added the buffer circuit to regulate the output, and—" he tapped the board, "—we've managed to bring the field's visibility down to nearly zero."

Dr. Cole gave a satisfied nod. "It should still provide full temporal stasis without lighting her up like a damn beacon."

Abby crossed her arms, glancing at Olivia. "You up for a second try?"

Olivia straightened, feigning casual confidence despite the slight tremor of nerves in her fingers. "Absolutely."

Ethan grumbled, but nodded. "Fine. Just… don't go disappearing on us."

Olivia smirked. "Not planning to."

She stepped forward, strapping the unit onto her arm again. The team moved around her, double-checking every connection, every readout. Once the last adjustment was made, she took a deep breath and pressed the activation switch.

This time, the effect was controlled—subtle. A faint shimmer rippled across her skin, barely visible unless one was looking closely.

Ethan exhaled, relieved. "Much better."

Abby gestured toward the hyperdrive. "Step inside. Liza needs to do a full scan before we go any further."

Olivia obeyed, stepping into the chamber and standing still as the familiar hum of Liza's scanning system activated. Lines of light cascaded across Olivia's body, collecting every piece of data necessary to ensure she was stable.

Then, unexpectedly, Liza hesitated.

"Curious."

Abby frowned. "What is it?"

Liza's voice was precise, but tinged with mild surprise. "Olivia is in perfect stasis. No molecular drift, no cellular degradation. However…"

The team exchanged glances as Liza's hesitation stretched.

"By my readings," Liza continued, "the field should last for almost forty-eight hours before full depletion."

Ethan stiffened. "Wait… what?"

Olivia blinked. "That long?"

Dr. Cole scratched his chin. "We were expecting maybe twelve hours at most."

The hyperdrive door hissed open, and Olivia stepped out, flexing her fingers. "I feel… incredible," she admitted. "It's hard to describe. Like—like time isn't moving around me, but I know it is. It's a queer sensation, but definitely real. Like I exist outside the flow, but I can still feel it."

The team absorbed her words, processing the

implications.

Then Olivia turned to Abby, a spark of realization flashing in her eyes.

"I have the perfect test," she said suddenly.

Abby raised a brow. "Go on."

Olivia took a deep breath, choosing her words carefully. "When my grandmother passed, I wasn't there." Her voice softened, thick with emotion. "I was across the country for college. By the time I got back, it was too late. I never got to say goodbye."

Silence settled over the room.

Olivia looked at Abby, then at Liza. "This won't change anything. She was already passing. It won't alter history— it's a closed moment. But if I could just be there, for even a few minutes..." She swallowed. "I could finally say goodbye."

Ethan ran a hand over his face, sighing. "You're really testing my nerves, you know that?"

Lyara nudged him with a smirk. "Oh, let her have this one."

Abby folded her arms, considering. Then, slowly, she nodded. "Alright. If it truly won't affect the timeline... let's do it."

Olivia exhaled, relieved.

Abby turned to Liza. "Can you plot the jump to the exact time and location Olivia provides?"

Liza was silent for a moment, running calculations. Then:

"Affirmative."

Olivia took a deep breath, gripping the edge of the console for balance. "Then let's do it."

The team moved quickly, double-checking every system, every safety measure. Olivia provided the precise coordinates—the hospital room, the exact moment before her grandmother passed.

Ethan stood beside the hyperdrive, watching her with

barely masked concern. "One hour, Olivia. No longer."

She nodded. "I'll be back before you know it."

Then the hyperdrive hummed to life.

The chamber filled with cascading light as Liza engaged the system. Olivia's figure shimmered, her presence distorting like ripples in a pond.

Then—

She was gone.

***

Olivia's vision adjusted instantly, the sterile glow of fluorescent lights above her pressing against her senses.

She was in the hospital room.

Her breath hitched as she took in the sight of her grandmother lying still on the bed, frail but peaceful. Machines beeped softly. A clock on the wall ticked forward.

No one else was in the room.

Heart pounding, Olivia stepped forward.

"…Grandma?"

Her grandmother's eyes fluttered open, soft and warm, as if she had been waiting.

"Olivia," she whispered, her voice fragile but filled with recognition.

Tears burned at the back of Olivia's eyes. She reached out, gently clasping the old woman's hand. "I'm here," she said softly.

Her grandmother's fingers curled weakly around hers.

"I knew you'd come," she murmured.

Olivia let out a soft laugh, choking back a sob. "I—I'm so sorry I wasn't here sooner."

Her grandmother smiled faintly. "You were always with me, sweetheart."

Olivia swallowed the lump in her throat. "I love you."

Her grandmother's fingers gave the faintest squeeze.

"I love you too."

The moment stretched, frozen in time.

Then, slowly, her grandmother's breathing eased.

And, peacefully, she was gone.

Olivia closed her eyes, letting silent tears fall.

She had said goodbye.

For the first time, she felt the weight lift.

A soft pulse in the air reminded her of the time.

With one final, grateful glance at the woman who had shaped her life, Olivia stepped back.

Then, as the hyperdrive's recall engaged—

She vanished.

\*\*\*

Light burst in the chamber as Olivia reappeared.

She stumbled slightly, dazed from the transition, but her eyes were bright—full of something the team hadn't seen before.

Peace.

Ethan was at her side in an instant. "Are you okay?"

Olivia looked at him, exhaling softly.

"…Yeah." She smiled. "I am."

The team watched her, sensing the shift in her.

Lyara grinned. "Well? How was your time trip?"

Olivia wiped at her eyes, chuckling. "It was perfect."

Abby nodded, satisfied. "Then let's shut it down for the night."

As the systems powered down, Olivia stood quietly for a moment, still lingering in the past.

Then, with one last deep breath—

She let it go.

\*\*\*

The hum of the lab filled the quiet morning as the team gathered around the digital whiteboard, coffee cups in hand, the weight of the day's new objective settling over them. The previous night's success—Olivia's journey back to say goodbye—had reaffirmed that they were making progress. Now, it was time to shift their focus to what truly mattered: fixing the fractured time stream.

Abby stood at the front by the whiteboard, stylus in hand,

tapping it against the board to grab everyone's attention. "Before we move forward, we need to verify that Olivia's trip didn't cause any ripples. Liza, run a full scan of the quantum stream. Look for any anomalies, cascades, or inconsistencies that might hint at unintended changes."

Liza's voice responded instantly, steady and analytical. "Understood. Checking quantum stream for fluctuations." The soft hum of the system filled the room as data scrolled across the board, Liza's processing speed making quick work of the request.

A few tense moments passed, the team exchanging brief glances as they waited. Ethan, ever the restless one, rubbed his chin, muttering, "No news is good news, right?"

Then, Liza's voice broke the silence. "Analysis complete. No significant deviations detected in the primary time stream. Olivia's presence at the recorded event was minimal and did not introduce measurable disruptions."

The tension in the room eased slightly. Abby exhaled, nodding. "And historical records?"

Liza paused before replying, as if considering the question from multiple angles. "Cross-referencing public and private databases... The only relevant entry of note states that Olivia was present at her grandmother's passing. There are no indications that this was unexpected or anomalous."

Olivia let out a breath she hadn't realized she was holding. "So, history recorded me being there, but nothing changed?"

"Correct," Liza confirmed. "The timeline remains stable."

Abby tapped her stylus against the whiteboard again, nodding in approval. "Alright. That's what we needed to hear. Now, we focus on what we came here to fix." She turned, eyes sweeping across the team. "The fracture. The anchor point that's keeping time from repairing itself. We need to remove it."

The room went still. It was the challenge they had been building toward—everything had been leading up to this.

Daniel leaned forward, resting his elbows on the table. "Assuming we can locate the exact anchor point, do we even know how to remove it without making things worse?"

"We don't," Abby admitted. "But that's why we're going to test it first." She shifted her gaze to Ethan and Dr. Cole. "I have a feeling this might take two people. Do you think you can create another device?"

Dr. Cole grinned, folding his arms. "You're asking the right people."

Ethan smirked, nudging Dr. Cole with his elbow. "We could build another, sure. But that's a lot of manual work. You know what would be faster?" He turned toward Liza, eyes bright with an idea. "Liza, you've already been able to deconstruct and reconstruct components down to their quantum signatures. Could you scan the device inside the hyperdrive and... well, copy it?"

A brief silence followed.

Liza responded with a tone that carried an unusual hint of curiosity. "Theoretically, it is possible. Given that I successfully reconstituted the modified battery pack, duplicating an existing device should be within my capabilities. However, I will need a precise scan to ensure no loss of integrity."

Abby gestured toward Ethan. "Alright, then. Let's not waste time."

Ethan grabbed the current device, walked over to the hyperdrive, and carefully placed it inside the chamber. He stepped back and closed the reinforced door, giving Liza full control. "Alright, Liza. The device is in the chamber. Begin scanning when ready."

"Confirmed," Liza replied. A soft hum filled the air as the drive powered up. "Initiating full-spectrum scan. This process will take approximately seven minutes."

Ethan leaned back against the console, arms folded.

"See? It's not just a cockeyed idea."

Dr. Cole chuckled. "Alright, alright. But let's not assume it'll work just yet. We'll need to do a stress test on the duplicate, assuming Liza can generate it."

As the minutes passed, Liza's display streamed endless lines of data, analyzing every molecular structure, energy flow, and quantum resonance of the device.

Finally, she spoke again. "Scan complete. Device blueprint has been recorded at the atomic level. Ready to proceed with duplication upon command."

Abby nodded. "Then that's our next step. Liza, prepare for reconstruction. Let us know if you encounter any problems."

Liza's processors whirred. "Acknowledged. Preparing quantum synthesis."

Ethan grinned, rocking back on his heels. "Man, I gotta say—every time we throw something at Liza that she shouldn't be able to do, she just proves us wrong."

Daniel smirked. "Yeah, well, let's just hope we're not pushing her toward an existential crisis."

Liza's voice interrupted their banter, smooth as ever. "I assure you, Daniel, I am quite comfortable with my expanding capabilities. Though, if it pleases you, I can simulate an existential crisis for observational study."

Ethan chuckled. "Let's... maybe not do that."

The tension in the room had lifted slightly, but the gravity of what they were about to attempt was still there.

Abby looked around at her team—both the ones she had started with and the ones who had been stranded in the future.

They were close. Closer than they had ever been to truly fixing what had been broken.

Now, they just had to make sure they didn't break it even more.

\*\*\*

The hum of Liza's processors filled the lab, a steady

pulse of artificial intelligence at work. The hyperdrive chamber, bathed in a faint electric-blue glow, thrummed with energy as the scanner traced the intricate quantum signatures of the original power pack.

The team watched in anticipation, the air thick with a mixture of excitement and apprehension.

"Replication complete," Liza finally announced, her voice smooth but deliberate. "Running deep stability scans now."

On the digital whiteboard, cascading data streams flickered to life, filling the display with complex energy mappings, structural integrity models, and projected efficiency readouts. The intricate layering of quantum signatures detailed every aspect of the duplicated device— right down to the atomic level.

Ethan leaned forward, his eyes scanning the patterns with methodical precision. "Damn," he muttered under his breath. "It's... perfect."

Dr. Cole crossed his arms, nodding slowly. "Liza, how long to charge both units to full capacity?"

"Estimated time: ninety-three minutes," she responded promptly.

Daniel let out a slow breath, rubbing the back of his neck. "That gives us time to make absolutely sure we know what we're dealing with."

Abby turned to Dr. Cole. "You recorded everything about the fracture before your team escaped. Can you pinpoint the exact moment it destabilized?"

Dr. Cole furrowed his brow, his fingers twitching slightly at his sides—a subtle tell that his mind was already digging through buried memories. "I can pull up the data, but we're missing something... We know the fracture didn't behave as expected. Instead of dissipating, it frayed outward, which means—"

"It didn't fray," Liza interjected sharply, her processors whirring at a higher pitch. "The readings indicate an artificial containment."

A ripple of unease passed through the group.

Abby's expression darkened. "Containment? As in... something is actively holding the fracture open?"

The digital whiteboard flickered, adjusting to Liza's recalculated data. A simulated reconstruction of the original fracture materialized, an intricate weave of fluctuating energy signatures encased within a shifting quantum field. Thin threads of containment energy pulsed along its edges, resembling an intricate web of light that refused to collapse.

Ethan's brow furrowed. "Wait—you're saying when Cole's team left, something stopped the machine from self-destructing?"

Liza's algorithms adjusted the simulation, zooming in on a particular energy burst captured from the moment of departure. A secondary surge of power trailed the original event.

"Correct," Liza confirmed. "My analysis suggests that when the second activation sequence was initiated— presumably by those attempting pursuit—a malfunction occurred. Instead of detonating as intended, the quantum field surrounding the machine folded in on itself, creating an artificial stasis field."

Daniel's eyes narrowed as he examined the shifting digital model. His voice was tight, controlled. "You're saying the people who tried to follow them... got trapped?"

Liza's next words sent a chill through the lab.

"They were not merely trapped." A pause. Then—"They still exist. Frozen in a suspended time loop. Along with the machine."

A heavy silence crushed the air from the room.

Abby swallowed, her fingers tightening into fists. "...That's the anchor."

Dr. Cole rubbed a hand over his face, the weight of the realization settling deep into his bones. "That means the whole time—this entire time—the corporation's pursuit team has been in a constant state of near-arrival. They've never fully reached the future... but they've also never truly remained in the past."

Lyara's blue eyes locked onto the shifting data. "And if the machine is still running inside the bubble, it's still trying to stabilize. Which means it's keeping the fracture open indefinitely."

A harsh exhale escaped Abby's lips. "Then we have to end it. We have to shut that machine down permanently."

Ethan let out a low whistle, shifting his weight from foot to foot. "That's a hell of a mess."

Dr. Cole nodded grimly. "And we just volunteered to clean it up."

Liza's processors clicked softly as she continued to refine her calculations. "I can trace the time bubble's external energy signature. However, if we are to collapse it, we must consider the magnitude of the temporal backlash. If the stasis field is forcibly disrupted, we do not know what kind of ripple effect will follow."

Daniel clenched his jaw. "Are we talking minor corrections? Or catastrophic chain reactions?"

Liza hesitated. "Unknown."

Olivia's throat bobbed as she swallowed. "That's not exactly reassuring."

Ethan exhaled sharply, shaking his head. "We created these power packs to protect ourselves from time's effects. If they work like they should, we should be shielded from whatever happens when we shut that thing down."

Abby crossed her arms, her mind rapidly sifting through contingencies. "But we need a strategy. If that machine is still active, we can't just rip it apart. We have to shut it down properly—or we risk tearing the fracture open even wider."

Liza's calculations ticked by in real-time, new probability outcomes flashing on the display. "I will begin simulating possible outcomes. However, I will require additional time for accuracy."

Abby turned toward the team, scanning their faces. Fear. Determination. Uncertainty. Resolve.

"This is it," she said. "We let Liza run her simulations while we get fully prepared. No surprises. No risks. We go in knowing exactly what we're doing."

Ethan smirked, though the weight of the situation pressed visibly on his shoulders. "This is time travel, Abby. There are always surprises."

Dr. Cole sighed, rubbing the bridge of his nose. "For once, I'd like to avoid them."

Abby exhaled, rolling her shoulders before turning back to the digital whiteboard.

"Then let's make sure this plan doesn't become one of them."

***

The team had barely stirred from their groggy state when Greta Stone arrived, her sleek black SUV rolling through the facility's checkpoint, followed closely by her usual entourage of suited security personnel.

Liza's voice came over the speakers, calm but direct.

"Corporate representative Greta Stone has entered the premises. Accompanied by four security personnel. Estimated time to arrival: two minutes."

Abby groaned, rubbing her face. "Of course she's early."

They had all slept in the lower crew quarters, opting for convenience over comfort, and it showed. Ethan's hair was still a disheveled mess, Daniel had smudges of sleep around his eyes, and Olivia had yet to fully unglue herself from her coffee cup. Abby turned toward the whiteboard and froze.

The data.

Their entire conversation from last night about the anchor, the quantum signatures, and the energy fluctuations was still on full display.

"Liza, erase the board. Now."

"Understood." Liza's smooth voice replied, and the information blinked out of existence just as the door swung open and Greta stepped in.

She barely gave them a passing glance before scanning the room with that sharp, calculating gaze.

"You all look..." Greta's lips pressed together in a tight smirk, "...diligent."

Abby forced a casual smile. "Early mornings."

Greta didn't bother responding. Instead, she walked straight past them, her focus narrowing in on Liza's console.

"We noticed something odd in the last system audit."

Abby kept her posture neutral. "Define 'odd.'"

Greta turned, hands clasped behind her back.

"Discrepancies in Liza's storage sectors. There's more available space than expected, yet the system logs don't match. Something's being written, then deleted. That's not normal."

The team's shared silence was deafening.

Daniel recovered first. "Could be Liza's optimization protocols. She clears redundant datasets constantly—frees up space."

Greta's eyes didn't waver.

"We also saw a significant increase in power consumption over the past few days. More than just 'optimization.'"

Abby's mind raced for a plausible explanation. Then she found one.

"We've been running quantum signature tests," she said smoothly. "Fine-tuning the drive's projection ability, making adjustments to Liza's algorithm."

Greta raised an eyebrow. "So, full-scale tests?"

Abby nodded. "Not on live subjects, of course."

For a long moment, Greta simply studied her.

Then she exhaled and gave a slow nod.

"That's fine."

She turned to leave—but at the door, she hesitated.

"Where's your other intern?"

Abby didn't flinch.

"He quit yesterday. I just hadn't updated the records yet."

A long beat. Then Greta gave her a slow, knowing smile.

"You seem to have a habit of losing people, Dr. Foster."

With that, she walked out, her security detail following close behind.

The team didn't breathe until the door sealed shut behind her.

Just as they thought they were in the clear, one of Greta's bodyguards lingered. He wasn't looking at Abby.

He was looking at Liza's console.

Not overtly. Just…long enough for it to be deliberate.

Then he followed Greta out.

The moment the door clicked shut, Liza's voice came through, controlled but weighted.

"I believe I am being monitored beyond standard protocol."

A sharp silence followed.

Ethan stiffened. "Define 'monitored,' Liza."

Her response was immediate. "An additional encryption layer has been placed over portions of my storage sectors. It was not there yesterday."

Daniel's expression darkened. "So they're watching you. Watching us."

Abby exhaled, her fingers pressing into the table.

"Then we're running out of time faster than we thought."

\*\*\*

# 12

A dull murmur of conversation drifted up from the lower levels as the rest of the team emerged from the crew quarters. The artificial lighting in the lab cast a muted glow over their weary faces, accentuating the telltale signs of exhaustion from too many late nights and too much stress.

Dr. Nolan was the first up, stretching her arms above her head as she ascended the stairs with deliberate slowness. In one of her hands, she held a hairbrush.

She barely made it to the top before shaking her head with mock disapproval at Olivia and Lyara. "You two look like you just rolled out of a frat house after finals week. Here—do something about it before you scare the quantum field into behaving."

Lyara snorted. "I don't know, maybe we should try it. The quantum stream's already unpredictable, might as well add unkempt hair to the experiment."

Olivia grabbed the brush first, quickly working through the tangles in her dark curls. "Honestly, I don't know how you don't look half as bad as we do."

Dr. Nolan gave a wry smile. "Years of sorority training, sweetheart. If you can survive six back-to-back midterms and a two-day bender without looking like death warmed over, you can handle anything."

Lyara rolled her eyes playfully as she took her turn with the brush, smoothing her blonde hair as best she could. Ethan leaned against the worktable, arms crossed. "So, we're all in agreement that Liza needs to start 3D printing us some fresh clothes, right?"

Abby, who had been silent up until that point, cleared her

throat. "We have bigger problems." Her voice cut through the lighthearted banter, pulling the team's focus back to the situation at hand.

The humor evaporated.

"Ms. Stone is circling like a shark," Abby continued. "She knows something is off—she just doesn't have the evidence yet. But with the discrepancies she's already flagged in Liza's storage records and power usage, it's only a matter of time before she finds something we can't explain away."

Daniel exhaled sharply. "And if that happens?"

Abby's expression hardened. "Then we lose Liza, we lose the hyperdrive, and we all end up being 'reassigned' somewhere we'll never be heard from again."

The room fell into a heavy silence.

Lyara, still finishing with the brush, spoke first. "Then we need a plan. Fast."

Ethan rubbed at his jaw, thinking. "Liza, how long would it take to mask power fluctuations so they appear normal without raising red flags?"

Liza's voice came through smoothly. "Given the current pattern of anomalies, I estimate I can stabilize the system's energy profile within two hours to match expected facility norms. However, this will require manually rerouting some of my processing functions to background systems, limiting my immediate responsiveness."

Abby nodded. "Do it. I'd rather deal with a slight delay in response time than a visit from corporate goons with deactivation orders."

Dr. Nolan crossed her arms. "That buys us time. But it doesn't solve the problem of what we're actually doing next. We still need to fix the timeline."

Daniel drummed his fingers on the workbench. "Then we need to move forward. No more theorizing—we take action."

Ethan glanced at Abby. "We need to choose—do we test

another small-scale shift or go for the anchor point itself?"

Abby inhaled deeply, scanning the faces of her team. "We're running out of time. If we wait too long, Stone is going to shut us down before we ever get the chance to fix what's broken."

She set her hands on the whiteboard table, looking at them all in turn. "We go for the anchor."

A ripple of tension passed through the group. No more safety nets. No more tests. The next jump would decide everything.

Liza's voice interrupted, cool and calculated as ever. "In that case, I suggest you begin preparations. Time is not on our side."

No one argued.

Abby grabbed a marker and turned to the digital whiteboard. "Alright, we know the problem. Now we need a solution."

Daniel leaned in. "We need to neutralize the machine, but we can't just blow it up. The explosion would create another uncontrolled rift, and who knows what that could do?"

Ethan nodded. "We also don't know how many people are still inside the time bubble. If we just cut the power and hope for the best, we might be trapping them in there permanently—or worse, scattering them across time."

Dr. Cole exhaled, arms crossed. "Which means we need a controlled collapse. Something that lets the time bubble dissolve naturally, instead of imploding on itself."

Lyara leaned forward, eyes narrowing. "What if we reverse the polarity of the anchor? If the machine's been holding the bubble in stasis, what happens if we invert the field?"

Liza's voice responded. "Theoretically, the field would unravel over time rather than snap shut instantly."

Abby tapped her fingers against the board. "That gives us time to get people out before the timeline corrects itself."

Ethan's face darkened. "Unless we run out of time before that happens."

A heavy silence settled in.

Dr. Cole finally spoke. "We need to go in. Locate anyone left inside and extract them before we disengage the machine."

Daniel ran a hand through his hair nervously. "And then what? Where do they go?"

Abby straightened. "They come here."

Lyara blinked. "You mean—bring them back?"

Abby nodded. "It's the only option. We'll hide them in the lower levels like we did before. If we leave them there, the corporation will find them and the evidence. We don't let that happen."

Ethan shook his head. "This is crazy."

Abby's voice was steady. "This is necessary."

Another pause. Then, slowly, Ethan nodded. "Alright. Then we better get this right."

Liza's voice came through, calculated and calm. "If this plan is to be executed, I suggest we begin finalizing the details immediately."

Abby exhaled, tapping the whiteboard. "Then let's get to work."

The race was on.

***

The hum of the hyperdrive filled the room, its rhythmic vibration thrumming through the floor beneath their feet. The containment chamber stood open, waiting, its interior bathed in a faint shimmering light as residual quantum energy flickered in and out of visibility. The air was charged, carrying a metallic tang that clung to the back of their throats.

Abby and Cole stood side by side, their personal field generators already strapped securely to their wrists. The rest of the team had formed a loose semicircle around them, their expressions a mixture of concern and reluctant acceptance.

Ethan crossed his arms. "I still think this is a bad idea," he muttered. "You two are the most valuable members of this team. If something goes wrong, we don't have another Cole or Abby lying around to fix things."

Abby exhaled, her patience wearing thin. "We have the most experience with this technology. If something is wrong with that anchor, we'll understand it faster than any of you could. This isn't about taking unnecessary risks—it's about being the best people for the job."

Dr. Cole smirked. "Besides, I hate to say it, but we're the oldest. If something does go wrong, better us than you kids."

Lyara shot him a glare. "Not funny."

Daniel shifted uncomfortably. "At least take an extra precaution. No touching anything, no direct interaction. Observe only."

Abby nodded. "That was always the plan."

She adjusted the device on her wrist and turned to Liza. "Bring us back exactly two hours from now, no matter what. If we need more time, I'll signal."

Liza's voice came through smoothly. "Understood. I will initiate retrieval precisely at the two-hour mark. I will also monitor your vitals continuously."

"Good." Abby glanced at Dr. Cole, who looked far too casual for someone about to step into a potentially fractured reality.

Dr. Cole flexed his fingers before reaching for his activation switch. "You ready?"

"As I'll ever be." Abby pressed the switch.

The moment the device engaged, a translucent wave rippled outward from the band on her wrist, expanding and enveloping her entire body. The sensation was... odd. It wasn't like stepping into a bubble or feeling a barrier form—it was something deeper, like time itself was bending around her. There was no weight, no movement—just a slow, eerie sensation of existing in two places at once.

"I see what they were talking about," Abby murmured,

tilting her head slightly, watching how the air itself seemed to shift around her. "It's strange. It's like I can feel time flowing, but not through me."

Cole activated his own device, watching as the field wrapped around him in shimmering waves. His brows lifted in surprise. "Okay, that is just so damn cool."

"You sound like Ethan," Lyara teased from the side, arms crossed.

Ethan shot back, "Yeah, because it is cool."

Lyara ignored him and focused on Abby. "Are you sure about this?"

Abby gave her a small, reassuring smile. "Positive."

Lyara hesitated, then said in a quiet but firm voice, "If you're not back in two hours, I'm going in after you."

Abby's chest tightened slightly at that, but she simply nodded. She turned back toward the chamber, stepping inside with Dr. Cole right behind her.

"Alright, Liza," Lyara said, straightening. "Transport now."

"Engaging hyperdrive," Liza confirmed. "Brace for transition."

A deep hum escalated into a sharp resonance that vibrated through their bones. The air thickened, compressing around them, and then—

A flash. A rush.

The world folded inward in a way that defied logic, bending and twisting. There was no falling, no real sensation of movement, yet the very fabric of existence seemed to stretch and pull like an elastic band. Sound distorted—whispers layered upon whispers, echoes of things not yet said.

Then, just as suddenly as it began—

They arrived.

The silence was absolute.

\*\*\*

The transition was jarring—an abrupt, soundless shift

that left both Abby and Cole momentarily unsteady. The air felt thick, unmoving, as if the very molecules around them had been paused mid-motion. A strange, weightless sensation clung to their skin, and for a moment, they both had to find their footing.

Abby exhaled, rolling her shoulders as she tried to shake off the strange lingering pressure. "Well... that was interesting," she muttered, her voice carrying an undertone that hinted at far more than she was saying.

Dr. Cole his face showing exasperation, blinking hard. "That is a sensation I will never ever get used to."

They finally turned their attention outward, taking in their surroundings.

Before them was the stasis bubble, a frozen fragment of time—just as they had theorized, but somehow far more surreal now that they were standing inside it.

The world within the bubble wasn't just still; it was a perfect, undisturbed snapshot of the moment everything had gone wrong. Every dust particle, every flicker of electricity trapped mid-arc, every tiny detail was locked in a frozen tableau.

Their eyes fell on the machine at the heart of it all.

Abby folded her arms, raising an eyebrow. "Well, you guys certainly didn't go for aesthetics. Straight to utilitarian, huh?"

Dr. Cole smirked, shaking his head. "We had far less money than you do in your time, but it worked. Or at least," he gestured to the eerily silent wreckage, "it did work."

Before them, the bulky, angular framework of their original hyperdrive loomed, a crude but functional design of metal scaffolding and looped wiring. It had none of the sleek, refined architecture of the present-day drive back at their lab—this was rough, experimental, and meant only to function, not impression.

And yet, it had done something.

Something irreversible.

Abby's eyes traced the machine's frame, taking in the unmistakable signs that it was still activated. The energy signature was palpable, like static clinging to the air. Then she noticed something that made her breath hitch—

At the edge of the bubble, she saw it.

A foot.

The bottom of a shoe, hovering mid-air, caught in the exact moment someone had been stepping forward through the loop.

The frozen momentum of the trapped figure sent a chill through her spine. They had been in motion when time had locked them in place.

Cole moved toward the control panel, stepping carefully, as though he might disturb the frozen reality around them. He circled around a rusted-out control box, the old, jury-rigged computer system still embedded in its thick metal housing.

Then he froze.

His expression darkened. "Oh no."

Abby snapped her gaze toward him. "What?"

Cole exhaled sharply, shaking his head. "This is worse than I thought." He gestured her over, urgency in his voice. "I see why it happened."

Abby hurried to his side, following his outstretched hand as he pointed at the core of the control system.

At first, it just looked like another frozen section of the machine, but then she saw it—a small area where the moment of catastrophe had been locked in time. It wasn't just still.

It was mid-explosion.

A segment of the machine's processing core had ruptured in real-time but had never finished exploding. It was like watching the exact nanosecond of detonation, the fire and debris forever frozen in a split-second of destruction. The energy was raw, exposed, like an open wound in the time stream.

Abby swallowed hard. "Holy—"

Instinct took over before she could stop herself.

Her hand reached out, almost compelled by the sight of the rupture. The moment her fingers came within inches of the anomaly—

A flicker.

A ripple spread outward, subtle but undeniable. The locked explosion moved.

Not much—but it moved.

She yanked her hand back, heart pounding.

Cole's voice was sharp. "Let's not do that again."

Abby clenched her jaw, staring at the unstable rupture. "Duly noted."

For the first time, she truly understood what they were dealing with.

This wasn't just a stasis bubble.

This was a moment trapped between destruction and survival.

And if they made the wrong move—

Time would finish what it started.

Abby looked at Cole. No words were needed—they both understood.

There was no fixing this.

The frozen destruction before them wasn't just an accident to be undone or a machine to be repaired. This was a dead end in time, a fracture locked in perpetual instability. No rewind button, no reset switch.

This moment in time was gone.

Unless…

Abby's mind raced through possibilities, scanning every angle, searching for something—anything—that could salvage the situation. Then, an idea struck her, forming with such sudden clarity that she had to force herself to speak it aloud just to make sure it wasn't madness.

"We can't recover this time fragment," she said, turning to Cole. "It's too far gone. But what if we go further back?"

Dr. Cole's brow furrowed, his analytical mind already turning over her words.

"Further back?" he echoed, cautiously intrigued.

Abby nodded, pointing at the frozen moment of catastrophe before them. "This happened because of a sequence of events we already know can't be undone. If we tried to break them out now, we'd only be forcing a collapse. But..." she inhaled sharply, meeting his gaze, "what if we don't fix this moment? What if we go to the moment before this happens—before your team ever activated the jump?"

Cole blinked. Then his lips parted slightly in realization.

"You mean... prevent the first jump from ever happening?"

"Not prevent it," Abby corrected, "guide it. Control it. Keep this disaster from ever happening in the first place."

Cole ran a hand through his graying hair, staring at the frozen scene around them. His mind was already working through the paradoxes, the potential outcomes, the very audacity of what Abby was suggesting.

"That means going to the exact moment before we ran our first test," he said slowly. "We'd be walking into a moment where we already exist."

Abby nodded. "It's risky. But we've proven that the time stream tries to correct itself. If we step in at the right point, make the right changes—we might be able to avoid this rupture completely."

Cole crossed his arms, considering. "And if we fail?"

Abby exhaled, glancing back at the frozen explosion in the center of the room.

"Then at least we'll know we tried everything."

A tense silence stretched between them, broken only by the faint hum of their own personal stasis fields interacting with the frozen environment.

Finally, Dr. Cole gave a slow nod.

"Alright," he said. "Then we go back. Further than we ever have before."

Abby pressed the communicator on her wrist. "Liza, can you hear me?"

Liza's voice responded instantly in her usual steady cadence. "Affirmative, Dr. Foster. Your vitals remain stable, I however detect an elevated heart rate. Has there been a development?"

Abby took a breath. "Yeah. A big one. We need to go back a little deeper. But first, we need you to pull us back."

"Understood. Engaging retrieval process. Stand by for transit."

A pulse of energy surged through their suits, a sensation they were beginning to recognize as the reverse-pull of the hyperdrive's quantum tether. For a brief moment, the frozen landscape around them shimmered, as if reality itself was uncertain whether to let them go. Then, with a sudden lurch, time warped around them, and the fractured lab disappeared in a burst of cascading light.

The world snapped back into focus with a jarring suddenness. Abby and Cole stumbled slightly as they rematerialized in the hyperdrive chamber, the subtle hum of the lab a stark contrast to the frozen silence they had just left behind.

Daniel and Ethan were already at the controls, watching intently. Lyara stood nearby, arms crossed, concern evident in her sharp gaze. Olivia, looking pale from nerves, clutched her tablet tightly.

Abby steadied herself, then looked at Dr. Cole. They shared a glance—silent, knowing.

"What did you see?" Daniel asked, breaking the silence.

Cole took a slow breath, rubbing the back of his neck. "It's bad," he admitted. "Worse than we thought."

Abby exhaled. "The rupture isn't just frozen in time— it's locked. We can't fix it from there."

Ethan frowned. "Then what do we do?"

Abby turned back to the team, her expression resolute.

"We go back further. Before it all started."

Silence. Then Lyara took a step forward. "You're suggesting rewriting time?"

"Not rewriting," Abby clarified. "Redirecting."

Ethan let out a low whistle. "Damn, this is way off script."

Cole nodded grimly. "It's the only way. If we don't, that rupture stays there forever. And we can't let that happen."

Daniel crossed his arms, his voice level but firm. "We're talking about stepping directly into history—into a moment that already played out. If we interfere too much, we could create unintended ripples. That's not just a risk—that's a gamble with time itself."

Abby met his gaze. "We don't have a choice. If we do nothing, that rupture will always be there, a ticking time bomb in the fabric of reality."

Lyara smirked slightly. "Then I guess we better not screw it up."

A moment of charged silence filled the room before Abby turned back to Liza.

"Liza, calculate the coordinates for the moment just before Cole's team initiated the first jump. We need a way in."

Liza's response was immediate.

"Understood. Processing new calculations now. This will require precision. Stand by."

Dr. Cole glanced at Abby as they both turned back to the team.

"This is insane," he muttered under his breath.

Abby let out a small, humorless chuckle.

"Welcome to our lives."

And with that, the team prepared for the biggest leap yet.
*** 

The air in the lab felt heavier than ever, thick with the weight of an unspoken urgency. The team gathered around the digital whiteboard, eyes locked on the glowing timeline projection that flickered under Abby's control. Every movement, every breath felt deliberate, as if they were standing at the edge of something irreversible.

Abby tapped the stylus against the board, highlighting a single, fateful moment in time—the exact second when Dr. Cole's original team had powered on their machine for their escape. A glowing arc pulsed around the date, marking the genesis of everything they were now fighting to correct.

"We need to go back here," Abby stated, her voice measured but firm. "We intercept them before they make the jump, convince them to leave without setting the machine to self-destruct, and then we stay behind to shut it down the right way."

A silence settled in, thick and unyielding.

Ethan leaned against the table, arms crossed. "And we just waltz in and say what? 'Hey, we're from the future—trust us, you need to get the hell out?'" He let out a dry laugh. "Yeah, that'll go over really well."

Dr. Cole rubbed his chin thoughtfully. "We won't have to convince the whole team—just my past self. If he believes us, the others will follow his lead."

Daniel frowned. "That's a big 'if.'"

Lyara nodded. "I mean, what's stopping your past self from thinking you're a corporate trick? Or worse, that you're some elaborate hallucination?"

Dr. Cole exhaled, a shadow of uncertainty crossing his face. "He'll believe me."

Ethan raised an eyebrow. "Oh? And why's that?"

Dr. Cole glanced around the room before finally meeting Abby's gaze. "Because I'll tell him something no one else could ever know. Something only I would remember."

A brief pause.

Abby leaned forward, arms resting on the table. "You sure that's enough?"

Cole hesitated before nodding. "It'll have to be. If anyone knows myself, its me"

Daniel gestured toward the timeline. "Even if we do get them to leave, we still need to stay behind to shut everything down. How long will it take to do a controlled shutdown?"

Dr. Cole furrowed his brow, mentally running through the calculations before responding. "Between ten and fifteen minutes. The machine has several redundancy layers to prevent sudden failure. We have to disable each one manually before fully powering it down—otherwise, we risk a chain reaction that could make the fracture even worse."

Ethan let out a slow deep exhale. "So, not exactly a quick flip of a switch."

Abby sighed, pinching the bridge of her nose. "And we need to do all of that before the corporation's goons show up."

Liza's interface pulsed as she ran a projection based on historical data. After a few seconds, her voice came through smoothly. "Based on existing records, you will have forty-three minutes from the moment of arrival until the first signs of corporate interference. However, that window is subject to minor fluctuations due to observational variance."

Daniel crossed his arms. "That's not much of a buffer."

"No," Abby agreed, "but it's enough."

Lyara sighed, arms crossed. "And what if something goes wrong? What if they panic, refuse to leave, and hit the activation switch out of fear?"

Ethan frowned. "Yeah, what's the backup plan?"

Abby's jaw tightened. "Then we improvise."

Lyara scoffed. "Oh, that always goes so well."

Ignoring the sarcasm, Abby turned back to Dr. Cole. "What's our safest entry point? We can't just appear in the middle of the lab."

Dr. Cole thought for a moment before nodding toward the projection. "There's a maintenance corridor just off the main chamber—isolated, usually empty. We jump there, make our way inside, and I approach myself first. If I can convince myself to listen, the rest of the team will follow."

A heavy silence settled over the room.

Abby tapped the board again, zooming in on the timeline's key moments. "Once Dr. Cole's team jumps, we disable the machine and destroy it before the corporation arrives. If we pull this off, we'll remove the anchor, stabilize the timeline, and eliminate any chance of them chasing us again."

Daniel nodded. "And if we don't?"

Abby's voice was steely. "Then we'll have worse problems than a fractured timeline."

The gravity of the moment pressed down on them.

Cole straightened, rolling his shoulders. "Alright. We have a plan. Let's get to work."

Abby turned back to the team. "This is it. We fix the fracture here, or we lose our last chance to set things right."

One by one, they nodded.

Time was waiting for them.

And they were about to step into its very heart.

***

Cole and Abby stepped back into the hyperdrive chamber, the faint hum of the machine filling the space as they secured their devices and activated their stasis fields. The familiar shimmer of energy cascaded over their forms, bending light around them in a way that made the world seem unreal.

Cole exhaled slowly and turned to Abby. His voice was calm, but the weight behind it was anything but.

"If anything goes wrong, you leave me there."

Abby's brow furrowed. "That's not happening."

Cole held her gaze, unshaken. "Listen to me. If the worst happens, I'll disengage my field. Time will correct itself— one of me will be absorbed into the stream, and it'll stabilize before anything catastrophic happens."

Abby studied him, suspicion flickering in her sharp gaze. "You have something up your sleeve, don't you?"

Cole didn't answer immediately, only offering her a

small, knowing smile. "Just promise me you'll make it back to your team."

Abby hesitated, then gave him a slow nod. She didn't like it, not one bit, but they had a job to do.

"Liza," Abby said, her voice steady. "Engage the hyperdrive. Start the timer."

Liza's voice came through the speakers, smooth but laced with a rare hint of concern. "Understood. Quantum stabilization active. I will maintain a lock on your signals for emergency recall."

Abby felt the smallest bit of reassurance at that. At least someone was watching their backs.

The hyperdrive roared to life, the lab around them vanishing in a kaleidoscope of twisting light and blurred motion.

Then, just as suddenly as they left, they arrived at Dr. Coles lab.

\*\*\*

The maintenance corridor was dimly lit, the air heavy with the hum of active machinery and distant voices. Abby steadied herself, adjusting to the sudden shift in presence, while Cole immediately took in their surroundings.

They moved swiftly, staying close to the walls, until they reached the lab entrance. Through the glass panel, they could see them—Cole's younger self and his team, working frantically over the control systems. The tension in the air was almost suffocating, their movements hurried, their focus absolute.

Abby leaned in slightly. "They look like they're expecting company."

Cole nodded. "They are. The corporate retrieval squad arrives in just under an hour." He took a deep breath. "This is where we change history."

They stepped into the lab.

The movement was subtle at first—just a shift of air, the faint sound of footfalls—but it was enough.

Cole's younger self looked up sharply, his entire body tensing at the sight of the strangers in front of him. His team reacted just as quickly, hands moving toward whatever makeshift weapons they had on hand.

Cole raised both hands in a calming gesture. "We don't have much time. I need you to listen to me."

The younger Cole narrowed his eyes, taking in the sight of the man who looked just like him—only older, more weathered. "Who the hell are you?"

Cole took a steady step forward. "I'm you. From your future."

The silence was deafening.

His younger self scoffed, a mix of disbelief and irritation. "Bullshit."

Dr. Cole exhaled. "You don't have to believe me, but you do have to trust me. I know you're planning to set the machine to self-destruct before you jump. You can't do that."

Younger Cole's expression twisted into something between skepticism and wariness. "And why the hell not?"

Abby stepped forward now. "Because if you do, you don't destroy it—you create a rupture. A wound in time that doesn't heal."

Dr. Cole took another step closer. "That's why we're here. To stop it. You need to take your team and go—but you have to leave the machine intact. We'll take care of shutting it down."

His younger self still looked unconvinced.

Dr. Cole sighed, then went for the one thing he knew would break through the doubt. "You never told anyone this, but you once had a chance to marry a wonderful woman. You didn't because you were too afraid to take a risk. You stayed in your college dorm instead of going to her."

The younger man stiffened.

His face paled just slightly, his breath catching for half a second.

Dr. Cole took that moment of hesitation and drove the point home. "Only I would know that. Only we would know that."

The lab had gone dead silent.

Abby stole a glance at the younger team members, who were looking at their Cole with a mix of unease and something almost approaching belief.

Younger Cole swallowed hard. His hands clenched at his sides. "If you're telling the truth, then what happened to us?"

Dr. Cole met his gaze. "You jump. Just like you planned. But when you get to the other side, don't panic. Don't run blindly. And when you meet a young woman named Lyara— trust her. Give her more credit than you normally would. She is wise beyond her young exterior."

Younger Cole's brow furrowed at that, confusion flickering in his eyes.

Abby shot Dr. Cole a look, one that screamed really? You just did that?

Dr. Cole only smiled slightly. "Just... trust me on that one."

Younger Cole ran a hand down his face, exhaling sharply before glancing back at his team. The doubt was still there, but the fear—the panic—had begun to ebb.

Finally, he gave a sharp nod. "Alright."

He turned to his team. "We're leaving. No self-destruct, step lively we need to go-- now!"

They hesitated, but one by one, they nodded in agreement.

Dr. Cole and Abby watched as the younger team gathered their things, adjusted the machine's settings, and stepped into the departure field. The light surged around them, and then—just like that—they were gone.

Dr. Cole let out a slow breath, the tension bleeding out of his shoulders.

Abby exhaled beside him. "That was close."

Dr. Cole glanced at where his younger self had just

stood, a lingering smirk tugging at his lips. "Yeah."

Abby nudged him. "So, who exactly were you talking about?"

Cole just chuckled. "Guess he'll find out."

She rolled her eyes, shaking her head. "Come on. Let's finish this."

With that, they turned toward the machine—the final obstacle standing between them and a repaired timeline.

And this time, they would get it right.

*** 

For a fraction of a second, Abby and Cole took in the gravity of the moment. The hum of the massive machine, the acrid smell of burning electronics, the cold sweat forming on the back of Abby's neck—this was it. This was their only chance to put an end to it all.

Dr. Cole exhaled sharply, turning to Abby with a firm nod. "Get to the power panel," he instructed, his voice steady but urgent. "When you hear the relays opening, that's your cue. Throw the breaker, but not before. Got it?"

Abby gave a curt nod and jogged to the heavy metal panel mounted on the far wall. She planted her feet and took a deep breath, her fingers hovering over the lever, waiting.

Dr. Cole turned back to the console, his hands working quickly over the controls. "Shutting down the secondary coil first," he muttered, watching the power gauges flicker as he systematically killed the feed. The readings dropped steadily—so far, so good.

The secondary set of coils lost their charge with a low whine, and as soon as Dr. Cole heard the magnetic field collapse, he shouted, "Now, Abby!"

A metallic clack echoed through the lab as she slammed the breaker down. The lights flickered momentarily, and a faint electrical burn smell filled the air. Dr. Cole nodded in satisfaction.

Then, he moved to the primary coil shutdown sequence.

But something was wrong.

The moment he initiated the process, his blood ran cold—the power gauge wasn't dropping. It was climbing. Fast.

"What the hell?" Dr. Cole muttered, his heart skipping a beat. He recognized the readings instantly.

Dr Cole screamed "Abby the relays are frozen shut, they wont disengage!"

"Abby, forget the sequence—throw the other breaker now!" he barked, his voice sharp with urgency.

Abby didn't hesitate. She yanked the main breaker, and a shower of sparks erupted from the primary coil. The whole lab shuddered as a deep, reverberating thud rang out, followed by a high-pitched whine as the power abruptly cut out.

Dr. Cole swore under his breath. They were seconds away from an overload that could have ripped a hole in time itself.

He spun on his heel and raced to the central processing mainframe. "The system wasn't just running—it was waiting for a trigger. Damn it!" His fingers flew across the keyboard. "We need to make sure it can't be restarted. The security team is probably on their way, and if they have half a brain, they'll try to reboot it."

Abby was already beside him. "How do we kill it for good?" she asked, adrenaline making her breath come fast.

Dr. Cole's mind worked at lightning speed. "We fry the drives—make sure they physically break down."

He grabbed a nearby cable, yanked it free from the wall, and rerouted it to the mainframe's power hub. "Abby, get to the terminal. Issue a manual override command to push the hard drives into a forced read cycle. Make them spin until they self-destruct."

Abby didn't waste time arguing. She ran to the console and quickly typed in the command. The mainframe responded with a loud, grinding whir, its internal drives spinning up so fast they sounded like they were about to shake themselves apart.

A sickening crack! rang out from inside the unit as one of the disks fractured under the strain.

Dr. Cole watched with grim satisfaction. "That'll do it," he said, but they weren't done yet.

He turned back to the power panels. "Now, we overload the coils."

Abby's eyes widened. "I thought we just shut them down."

Cole shook his head. "We shut off the power. Now, we need to force it back in. Without the mainframe controlling the system, the coils will overload in seconds and melt down completely."

Realization dawned on Abby's face, and she rushed back to the power panel. She took one last look at Dr. Cole, who gave her a nod.

"Do it," he said.

She threw all her weight into the power switch turning back on.

Instantly, a low-frequency hum filled the room as the system tried to reroute power through circuits that no longer had the capacity to handle it. The coils on both sides of the machine began to glow—first orange, then white-hot—they started to melt, oozing into thick, liquified copper puddles.

At that moment, an ear-splitting alarm blared throughout the facility.

Cole's stomach twisted. Security. They were out of time.

Through the thick glass separating the lab from the maintenance corridor, they saw red emergency lights flashing wildly. Heavy boots pounded against the concrete floor as the security team rushed toward the lab.

Abby didn't think. She pressed her comms. "Liza, emergency extraction—NOW!"

The security team stormed through the lab doors just as Abby and Cole began to dematerialize. Their bodies flickered, light and energy dispersing into quantum patterns.

One of the guards skidded to a halt, pointing at them. "There—there! They're in the machine!"

Another officer took a step forward, but it was too late.

With a final, blinding flash, Cole and Abby vanished.

All that was left behind was the smoldering remains of the machine, its molten coils hissing as they cooled into an unrecognizable heap.

The past had just become history.

And time, at last, had been set free.

# 13

A sudden, sickening lurch pulled Dr. Cole and Abby sideways—not forward, not backward, but somewhere else entirely.

The sensation was like being stretched and snapped back, their minds momentarily unmoored from their bodies. The familiar hum of the hyperdrive was gone, replaced by a low, resonant vibration, a sound that seemed to exist both inside and outside of their ears.

Abby hit the ground—or what she thought was the ground. Her hands pressed into something that felt solid, but when she looked down, the floor wasn't one thing. It was many things at once—flickering between smooth laboratory tile, rough concrete, polished wood, and dirt.

Dr. Cole groaned nearby, steadying himself as he looked around. "Oh, hell," he muttered, rubbing his forehead. "That's not good."

Abby swallowed hard. Around them, the lab was there, but it wasn't. It flickered—sometimes pristine and newly built, other times abandoned and rotting, overtaken by creeping vines. In one blink, it was filled with scientists hard at work. In another, it was a husk of blackened steel, as if it had been firebombed into oblivion.

The world wasn't stable.

"Cole," Abby said, forcing herself to her feet. "Where are we?"

He steadied himself and turned slowly in a circle, taking in the impossible shifts around them. "Not when we're supposed to be, that's for sure."

A shadow moved—not a shadow, a person. No—several

people. But when Abby turned to look directly at them, they weren't there anymore.

The air shimmered with overlapping moments—things that had happened, things that could have happened, things that might never be. A version of Daniel stood in the distance, talking to someone who wasn't there. Olivia flickered in and out of sight, laughing at something unheard. And then, just as quickly, they were gone.

Abby exhaled, uneasy. "We need to get out of here. Fast."

Dr. Cole was already pulling out his handheld console, trying to bring up Liza's signal. "Liza, do you copy?" Static. His jaw tightened. "Liza, respond!"

***

Meanwhile, in the Present

Liza's voice cut through the still air of the lab, sharp and urgent.

"Attention. Quantum signal lost. Dr. Cole and Dr. Foster have not arrived at their designated return coordinates."

Ethan jolted upright from where he had been monitoring the hyperdrive's energy output. "Wait, what? What do you mean 'lost'?"

Lyara's hands flew across the console. "Where the hell did they go, Liza?"

"Calculating... Unable to locate precise temporal coordinates. Anomaly detected. Their signal has diverged into multiple potential timelines."

Daniel's expression darkened. "You mean they didn't land in a single time?"

"Correct. Their presence exists across multiple fractured possibilities. As humans call it, a crossroads or nexus."

Ethan ran a hand through his hair. "That's... real bad."

Olivia turned to Liza. "Can you get them back?"

A brief pause. Then, "Attempting to reacquire signal." Liza's processing indicators flickered erratically— something that had never happened before. "Quantum interference detected. Their position is unstable."

Olivia muttered under her breath. "They're stuck."

\*\*\*

Dr. Cole smacked the side of a console that just appeared in front of him, his usual calm eroding. "I'm not getting anything.", Then as fast as the console appeared, it faded into oblivion. He turned to Abby. "We need a fixed point, something solid. There's gotta be something in this mess we can anchor to."

Abby scanned the shifting landscape. Everything was in flux—except… there. In the farthest corner of the lab, where the shadows wavered like heat mirages, a single terminal remained unchanged. It didn't flicker, didn't shift between different states—it simply was.

"There!" She pointed.

Cole didn't hesitate. They moved quickly, stepping carefully to avoid walking into one of the flickering ghost-like echoes of the past. Every so often, their surroundings would stutter, throwing them momentarily into a different version of the lab before snapping them back. It was like walking on shifting sand, the ground beneath them never quite the same twice.

When they reached the terminal, Dr. Cole's fingers flew over the keys.

"Liza, if you can hear this, we need a recall point now."

A long pause. Then, through the static—

"Signal… acquired."

Dr. Cole looked at Abby. "Hold onto something."

The world lurched.

Their bodies compressed and expanded at the same time, reality bending inward like a collapsing wave—

—then everything went dark.

\*\*\*

Ethan and Lyara were nearly yelling at Liza when the hyperdrive suddenly flared to life. A powerful burst of energy surged through the room, nearly overloading the monitoring equipment.

A bright flash—and then two figures materialized inside the chamber.

Dr. Cole and Abby stumbled forward, gasping as if they had been yanked through a vacuum.

Ethan was the first to move. "Are you guys okay?!"

Abby pressed a hand to her forehead. "Never. Doing that. Again."

Dr. Cole just laughed breathlessly. "I dunno. I think we made some new friends across time."

Daniel looked between them, then at the hyperdrive, then back. "What the hell just happened?"

Abby took a slow breath, grounding herself. "I think we just got caught in the in-between of time itself."

A heavy silence settled over them.

Liza's voice, steady as ever, cut through the tension.

"Dr. Foster and Dr. Cole have returned. Quantum signatures stabilized." A pause. "Your patterns were missing for fifteen minutes eleven seconds

Abby blinked. "Excuse me?"

Ethan checked his console. "Yeah, that was about fifteen minutes."

Lyara frowned. "For us maybe."

Dr. Cole shook his head, rubbing his temples. "For us... it was longer than that."

Liza's lights flickered. "Time distortion confirmed. Temporal anomaly now classified as an intersection event. I recommend we never attempt this again."

Abby laughed, half in exhaustion, half in disbelief. "For once, Liza? I agree."

The team exchanged glances, all coming to the same realization.

Whatever just happened, it was bigger than any of them had anticipated.

And it meant time itself was far more complicated than they ever imagined.

\*\*\*

Abby barely had time to inhale before Olivia crashed into her, arms wrapping tight as the impact knocked the breath from her lungs and forced her back a step.

"Don't you ever do that again!" Olivia's voice was high with emotion as she pounded her fists lightly against Abby's arms, her eyes wide with barely-contained panic.

"Yeah, what she said!" Lyara exclaimed, giving Dr. Cole a shove, though there was no real force behind it. "You vanished! You disconnected from time! Do you have any idea what that looked like on our end?!"

Abby let out a breathless laugh, still trying to get her bearings. "Trust me, we had no idea what it looked like on our end either."

Olivia threw her arms in the air. "That's not comforting!"

Cole, still rubbing his temples, gave Lyara a weak grin. "Look on the bright side. We made it back in one piece."

Lyara shot him a glare, but her eyes betrayed how relieved she was. "Barely."

Ethan finally stepped forward, shaking his head with a look of pure exasperation. "I swear, every time we send someone into the unknown, they come back barely intact, and somehow, we're the ones who have to hold it together."

Abby straightened, rubbing the back of her neck. "Okay. I get it. No more vanishing into the void without a plan. But we do have something we need to look at."

She turned toward the whiteboard, the discussion already forming in her mind. "Liza, pull up the quantum signature analysis from the moment we vanished and the point of re-entry."

Liza's processors hummed as the digital whiteboard flickered to life. "Retrieving full sequence. Analyzing temporal stream displacement and recovery pattern."

Dr. Cole exhaled and pushed himself forward, standing beside Abby. "We need to see what time did to try and pull us back."

Ethan moved closer, eyes narrowing at the rapidly compiling data. "You mean, we just watched time breathe to correct itself?"

Daniel, arms crossed, let out a slow breath. "That's the question, isn't it? What happens when you disrupt something beyond the timeline's ability to course-correct?"

The board populated with waveforms, cascading patterns of oscillating energy that represented the temporal distortion of their disappearance.

Lyara leaned in, eyes scanning the data. "Okay, so... these shifts right here—" she pointed at a spike in the waveform, "—that's when time noticed something was wrong."

Olivia frowned, tracing the next section. "And this looks like it tried to pull something from nearby—to replace you. But it couldn't."

Abby's stomach twisted. "Wait. You're saying it tried to swap us with something else?"

Liza's voice was calm, but what she said was anything but. "Correction: It attempted to balance the missing temporal signatures with probabilities from divergent timelines."

Ethan froze. "You mean... like parallel versions of them?"

Silence fell over the group.

Dr. Cole exhaled through his nose. "If that's the case... why didn't it work?"

Liza's processing lights flickered. "Hypothesis: The use of the stasis fields prevented timeline reconciliation. Without an anchor in either past or future, Dr. Foster and Dr. Cole remained unassigned to a fixed point in the stream."

Abby placed her hands on the table. "Unassigned?"

Liza continued. "They did not exist anywhere. They were, temporarily, outside of time itself."

The weight of that hit everyone hard.

Ethan let out a sharp breath. "So... we weren't tracking

them anymore." He gestured to Abby and Dr. Cole. "Time wasn't either."

Daniel shook his head slowly. "They weren't nowhere. They were in all possibilities at once—but just out of reach of all of them."

Abby felt an eerie chill settle in her chest. "Then if Liza hadn't found us…"

Liza responded immediately. "Correction: If recall had failed, the temporal anomaly would have collapsed, forcing an assignment. However, there is no guarantee it would have been your original timeline."

Dr. Cole went still. "Wait. Are you saying we could have been dropped into a completely different reality?"

"Affirmative." Liza replied.

A long silence filled the room.

Ethan ran a hand down his face. "Well. That's horrifying."

Olivia stared at the board, then at Abby. "And that's why I said don't ever do that again."

Abby swallowed and nodded. "Fair enough."

Lyara let out a slow breath. "So what happens now? Did time… correct itself, or is there still something broken?"

Liza's screen flickered as a secondary waveform appeared. "Timeline recovery in progress. Predictive model suggests residual instability will persist for approximately seventy-two hours before final stabilization."

Daniel tilted his head. "You're saying it will fix itself?"

Liza hesitated. "Seventy-eight percent probability."

That didn't feel great.

Abby exhaled, standing straight again. "Then we monitor it. If time's going to try and reset itself, we need to watch and be damn sure it doesn't take us—or anything else—with it."

Dr. Cole nodded, rubbing his jaw. "Agreed. But this just confirmed something for me."

Everyone turned to him.

He looked at them with a knowing expression. "Time isn't as rigid as we thought. It is more malleable than we anticipated."

Ethan blinked. "What, like we have more control than we realized?"

Dr. Cole nodded. "Exactly. We just proved that with the right conditions… time doesn't always win."

That settled over the team in a heavy, unspoken way.

Abby finally pushed off the table. "Then let's make sure we understand exactly how much control we do have."

Everyone turned back to the board as Liza continued compiling data.

They had just touched the edges of something far bigger than they ever intended.

And now?

Now they had to figure out what it meant—before time itself decided for them.

***

The team gathered around the digital whiteboard, but for once, it wasn't filled with equations, calculations, or plotted coordinates. This was different. This was something no one—not even Cole with his experience in the first experiment—had ever encountered before. The room was unusually quiet, the hum of Liza's processing the only background noise as the group waited for Abby and Cole to explain what had happened.

Cole leaned against the table, rolling his shoulders as if shaking off something heavy. "It was like… standing in the middle of history as it rewrote itself. But not like flipping through a book where things are orderly. It was chaotic— fragments of different versions of time shifting around us, overlapping. We saw things that almost existed but didn't. Other things that maybe did exist but were erased."

Abby folded her arms, nodding. "It was like a crossroads, but not one we were meant to stand in. We didn't belong there. I don't think anything belonged there." She exhaled, rubbing the back of her neck. "And if we had stayed longer, I'm not sure what would have happened to us."

A brief, unsettled silence followed.

Dr. Nolan, standing with her arms crossed, eyes narrowed in thought, finally spoke. "If you two were caught in the middle of shifting timelines, why didn't you get pulled all the way in?" Her gaze flicked between them. "Time was in flux and trying to compensate, wasn't it? Shouldn't it have just absorbed you into somewhere rather than leaving you stranded?"

Liza's interface flickered as she processed the question. "An astute observation, Dr. Nolan. Based on my analysis, the devices Abby and Cole wore protected them from full integration. The quantum field acted as a barrier, preventing time from fully assimilating them."

Ethan frowned, arms folded. "So… does that mean if they were still wearing the devices when they got back, time would have kept trying to throw them somewhere else?"

Liza hesitated before answering, a brief pause that was almost unsettling. "Correct. Had they remained within the field for too long, time would have continuously attempted to correct their presence. In essence, they would have become 'drifters'—unmoored, unable to return."

Dr. Cole exhaled sharply. "So you're saying we almost got permanently lost?"

Liza's tone was matter-of-fact. "That is a reasonable conclusion, Dr. Cole. Your presence in the quantum intersection was an anomaly. The devices allowed time to see you as foreign data points. Removing the field… allowed time to forget you."

The weight of the statement settled over the room like a dense fog.

Ethan let out a low whistle. "Okay. So, lesson learned—turn the damn thing off when you get back."

Abby chuckled dryly. "Yeah. Let's not make that mistake twice."

Dr. Nolan's fingers drummed thoughtfully on the table, her gaze shifting toward Liza's display. "Liza, based on your readings, is there any chance of residual effects? Any lingering imprint from them being in that in-between space?"

Liza's interface flickered again, running another deep scan. "No immediate anomalies detected. However..." Another pause. "...The nature of time's fabric is unpredictable. I will continue to monitor for any unforeseen changes."

Abby's jaw tightened. "Great. Another unknown variable."

Daniel, who had been silent up until now, finally spoke. "What did it feel like?" His voice was quiet, almost hesitant, as if unsure he wanted to hear the answer.

Abby met his gaze, then exhaled slowly. "It felt... hollow. Like we were in a place that wasn't meant to be a place at all." She hesitated. "And it wasn't just the visuals. It was a feeling. Cold, distant, like time itself was watching but not touching. The second we got pulled out, it was like we could breathe again."

Dr. Cole nodded. "Yeah. It was like pressure was lifted the moment we left. Like time finally let go of us."

A beat of silence passed as the weight of the conversation settled over them.

Lyara, sitting cross-legged on the table, absently toying with a loose thread on her sleeve, finally looked up. "That's... terrifying."

Olivia shivered slightly. "Yeah, I don't want to ever be in that situation."

Ethan, ever the one to mask tension with humor, crossed his arms and leaned back. "Great. So time literally doesn't want us." He smirked. "Guess that makes us all orphans of the universe now."

The group chuckled lightly, but the tension remained.

Dr. Cole smirked slightly. "Yeah. Let's just make sure

we don't get kicked out again."

Despite everything, a small wave of amusement passed through the team. The crisis had been resolved—at least for now—but the deeper mysteries of time were only beginning to unravel.

***

The lab had quieted for the night. The hum of the equipment was a faint backdrop as Dr. Cole, Ethan, and Dr. Nolan remained in the main workspace. The rest of the team had retreated to the lower crew quarters, exhausted from the day's events, leaving the three of them to sort through the next big problem.

The digital whiteboard displayed a rotating schematic of the shielding device, its blue glow casting shifting shadows across the room. The silence wasn't comfortable—it was heavy with thought, with the weight of what had nearly happened to Abby and Dr. Cole.

Dr. Cole let out a breath and rubbed his temples. "Alright, let's be clear about what just happened—Abby and I were nearly thrown out of time because the stream tried to erase us. The shielding protected us, but only by making us invisible to the timeline. That's fine when we're in transit, but if we ever get caught again—" He shook his head. "We need a better failsafe."

Dr. Nolan crossed her arms, brow furrowed. "And your first thought was to create a quantum timestamp?" She tapped a finger against her elbow, deep in thought. "That seems... reckless."

Ethan was already shaking his head. "Yeah, I mean, if we mark ourselves in time, we basically tell it, 'Hey, we don't belong here.'" He gestured broadly. "Which is the exact opposite of what the shield is supposed to do."

Cole sighed and leaned against the table. "That's the problem. We can't make ourselves too invisible, or we get stranded between moments. But if we make ourselves too visible..." He let the implication hang in the air.

Dr. Nolan tilted her head, staring at the whiteboard. "What if... we don't mark ourselves as foreign, but instead mimic the signature of wherever we land or need to be?"

Ethan narrowed his eyes. "You mean... blend in?" He folded his arms as he thought it through. "Like a quantum chameleon."

Dr. Nolan nodded. "Exactly. Instead of telling time we don't belong, we trick it into thinking we do—at least long enough to keep from getting rejected again."

Dr. Cole pushed off the table, suddenly energized. "That... that might actually work." He turned toward Liza's interface. "Liza, is it possible for the shield to dynamically adjust its signature to match the temporal background of a given era?"

Liza's system emitted a soft hum as she processed the request. "Theoretically, yes. I can analyze environmental quantum signatures upon arrival and generate a matching frequency. However, real-time adaptation would require significantly more processing power."

Ethan pursed his lips. "Well, we did just figure out a way to make our power supply last longer. If we reroute a portion of it toward real-time recalibration, would that work?"

Liza responded immediately. "Yes. A portion of the energy can be allocated toward adjusting the wearer's quantum resonance. This would create the illusion that they belong within the surrounding temporal environment." A brief pause. "However, further testing will be required to ensure stability."

Dr. Nolan exhaled. "It's still a risk. If the signature fails or fluctuates too much, the timeline could detect the discrepancy." She glanced at Dr. Cole. "And then you'd have the same problem all over again."

Dr. Cole crossed his arms, thinking. "So we add a secondary failsafe. A static backup signature that can override in case of failure. Something neutral, stable—like a universal anchor."

Ethan snapped his fingers. "Something grounded. A constant signature that makes us 'belong' somewhere even if the dynamic field fails."

Liza processed for a moment. "I can generate a base quantum signature modeled after this present timeline. If needed, it could serve as an emergency recall mechanism, stabilizing the wearer's presence within the stream."

Cole ran a hand through his hair. "That's it. We borrow the signature of whatever era we land in, and if that fails, we default to home base."

Ethan smirked. "And just like that, we're ghosts and natives at the same time."

Dr. Nolan exhaled, clearly still turning the idea over in her mind. "We need tests. Simulations, at the very least."

Dr. Cole rubbed his hands together. "Liza, can you simulate the energy draw of a dual-layered quantum signature field? I want to see what kind of power requirements we're looking at."

"Processing," Liza responded, her tone measured.

Ethan glanced at the clock and let out a low whistle. "Man, it's past two in the morning. We're officially running on fumes."

Dr. Nolan smirked slightly. "You mean you are. Dr. Cole and I have a few more hours in us."

Ethan rolled his eyes. "Yeah, well, some of us are mere mortals." He gestured toward the screen. "But I'm not leaving until I see if this actually works."

Liza's interface flickered, and a power consumption estimate appeared on the whiteboard. The numbers were... staggering.

Cole let out a low breath. "Alright. We can work with this. It's not impossible, but we're going to need to optimize every single watt."

Dr. Nolan crossed her arms. "So we're doing this?"

Ethan smirked. "Hell yeah, we're doing this."

Dr. Cole clapped Ethan on the shoulder. "Then let's get

to work."

The hum of the whiteboard continued, equations shifting and refining as the team dove into the next phase of their impossible task.

***

Minutes later, the team emerged from the crew quarters, filing back into the lab to find Cole, Ethan, and Dr. Nolan standing by the electronic whiteboard. Intricate diagrams and equations now filled every inch of its display, a testament to their exhausting but productive night.

"You three look like you've been busy," Abby remarked, taking in the disheveled but energized state of the trio.

Dr. Cole chuckled softly, rubbing the back of his neck. "We were up most of the night, but we think we've found a solution to our shielding issue."

Ethan stepped forward, eyes bright despite the dark circles beneath them. "If it works, it'll revolutionize our entire approach. Instead of pushing hard against quantum currents, we're going to create a sort of 'gentle echo'—what Dr. Nolan calls a temporal echo signature."

Dr. Nolan nodded, tapping lightly on the whiteboard. "By subtly merging our signatures into the stream rather than actively resisting it, we think we can significantly reduce the risk of triggering an aggressive response from the time stream."

Lyara raised an eyebrow, impressed but skeptical. "But are we certain the stream won't see right through it? Something that subtle might not hold."

Dr. Cole's expression softened thoughtfully. "There's a risk. But based on our current data, subtlety may just be our greatest strength here."

Abby gave a cautious nod, turning her gaze toward Liza. "What's your take on this approach, Liza?"

Liza's voice was calm, measured, and thoughtful. "Dr. Cole's logic is sound. If executed precisely, a softer approach may indeed reduce the probability of temporal backlash. However, I will maintain constant monitoring in case any irregularities present themselves."

Lyara shifted her weight, her skepticism evident but muted by cautious optimism. "Then I suggest we proceed carefully. A gentle echo sounds great in theory, but we can't underestimate the time stream."

A thoughtful silence settled over the group, each member absorbing the significance of their next steps.

Olivia broke the quiet moment with a hesitant voice. "So, who goes next?"

Everyone's eyes shifted to Abby. She met their gazes steadily, giving a small smile. "Usually this is the point where everyone starts arguing about who gets to take the leap."

She glanced expectantly around the room, waiting for volunteers. Instead, she was met with silence. Ethan studied the floor, Daniel pretended sudden interest in a coffee stain on the table, and even Olivia averted her eyes.

Abby raised her eyebrows, amused and slightly perplexed. "Really? No one's volunteering? This might be a first."

Daniel cleared his throat. "I think we're all still processing the last few trips, Abby."

Ethan nodded fervently. "Yeah, as exciting as it all sounds, I think we've had enough near-death experiences for one lifetime. Or maybe two."

Abby turned to Cole, who held up his hands apologetically. "I've had enough jumps lately, Abby. Besides, you and I just barely got back."

Olivia smiled sheepishly. "My cat still hasn't forgiven me. I think I'll sit this one out."

Abby sighed with a resigned smile. "Well, this is definitely new. Normally, I'm the deciding factor when there's too many volunteers."

Lyara exchanged a meaningful glance with Dr. Nolan, both women nodding almost simultaneously.

"I'll do it," Lyara said firmly, her voice carrying clearly through the room. "If no one else is stepping up, it's time for me to take my turn."

Dr. Nolan straightened and stepped closer. "I'll go as well. My research laid the groundwork for all of this—it's only fitting I share the risks."

Abby looked between the two, a hint of pride flickering in her eyes. "Are you both sure?"

Lyara nodded firmly. "I've watched from the sidelines long enough. Besides, it's time we let the ladies handle things for a change."

Ethan let out a mild groan, throwing his hands up theatrically. "Again with that?"

Lyara tilted her head, giving him a teasing smirk. "You had your turn, hotshot. Maybe it's time someone else cleans up your mess."

Daniel chuckled, nudging Ethan lightly. "Face it, man— you're outnumbered."

Ethan feigned surrender. "Fine, fine. Just don't break anything else."

Lyara winked playfully. "No promises."

Abby exhaled, breaking the levity gently. "Then it's settled. Dr. Nolan, Lyara, you're both up next. We'll do this carefully, step by step, with full safeguards in place."

The team nodded, serious once more but buoyed by the clarity of a shared goal.

They had a direction. And now, they had volunteers willing to lead the way.

*** 

Cole double-checked the shield devices attached to Dr. Nolan and Lyara, making small adjustments to ensure everything was perfect. Abby stood close by, carefully monitoring the preparations. Finally satisfied, Dr. Cole stepped back and nodded.

Lyara glanced at Abby, a mix of excitement and uncertainty dancing in her eyes. "Well, Abby, when do we jump? Have you thought about a safe period yet?"

Abby nodded thoughtfully. "I have. But I'm interested to hear if you've come up with something better."

Lyara opened her mouth to reply, but Dr. Nolan chimed in first, her eyes bright with excitement. "Actually, I have a suggestion. Let's jump backward."

Abby looked at her curiously. "Backward?"

Dr. Nolan nodded eagerly. "We've seen that altering events that have already happened irritates the timeline significantly. If we jump backward into a stable, quiet moment—one unlikely to create disruptions—it should provide a safe environment to verify the field's stability."

Ethan crossed his arms, skeptical but intrigued. "Any particular period in mind?"

Dr. Nolan's expression turned surprisingly youthful, almost whimsical. "January of 1956. Specifically, Memphis, Tennessee."

Abby blinked. "Why that precise?"

"Because," Dr. Nolan replied, her eyes twinkling with barely suppressed enthusiasm, "that's when Elvis Presley released 'Heartbreak Hotel.' It would be keen to experience that moment in history firsthand."

Abby stared at her for a moment, then broke into laughter. "Keen? Really, Dr. Nolan?"

Dr. Nolan shrugged playfully, chuckling. "We all have our crosses to bear, Abby. Don't judge."

Ethan shook his head, an amused smile on his face. "You know, Dr. Nolan, I never pegged you as an Elvis fan, I have always thought you're more Black Sabbath leaning."

She raised her eyebrow dramatically. "Ethan, never underestimate a scientist's hidden passions."

Lyara chuckled softly, glancing at Abby. "Looks like Dr. Nolan's secret's out."

Abby smiled warmly, shaking her head. "Alright, you win. Memphis, 1956 it is."

Daniel cleared his throat lightly, humor tinged with

concern in his voice. "As entertaining as this sounds, remember we're still trying not to stand out. We might want to make sure you're dressed appropriately for the era."

Lyara's eyes widened slightly. "Good point. Modern clothes might attract unwanted attention."

Olivia quickly jumped in. "I have a vintage hairbrush and some old clothes we salvaged from the storage rooms downstairs. They might look more period-appropriate than what you're wearing now."

"Perfect," Abby agreed. "Go get changed quickly."

Dr. Nolan and Lyara hurried off to prepare themselves, returning moments later wearing outfits that, though slightly dusty, wouldn't draw attention if glimpsed.

Dr. Cole smirked playfully as he gave them a once-over. "You know, vintage suits you both."

Lyara flashed him a mock glare. "Easy there, Dr. Cole."

Abby, smiling warmly, nodded toward the hyperdrive chamber. "Alright, if we're ready?"

Lyara took a deep breath and adjusted the shield device on her wrist again. "Ready."

Dr. Nolan nodded, a playful grin still tugging at her lips. "As I'll ever be."

The two stepped into the chamber, and Abby addressed Liza clearly. "Are the coordinates locked in?"

Liza replied smoothly. "Coordinates set for Memphis, Tennessee, January 1956. Isolation scan confirms minimal human activity—an ideal test environment."

The room settled into an anticipatory silence as Abby glanced one last time toward Lyara and Dr. Nolan. "Two hours exactly, Liza. Keep a lock for emergency recall."

"Understood," Liza replied evenly.

Abby nodded, but before she could give the final command, Liza's voice unexpectedly rose again, adopting an almost whimsical cadence.

"One for the money, two for the show, three to get ready—now go, cats, go!"

Ethan coughed to hide his laughter, Daniel snorted, and Abby fought to suppress her smile. "Really, Liza?"

"I thought it fitting for the moment," Liza replied smoothly, though a hint of artificial amusement lingered in her tone.

Abby shook her head gently, unable to suppress a smile. "Engage transport."

The chamber hummed to life, the air vibrating with energy. Abby felt a sudden, unexpected chill snake down her spine, but she quickly dismissed it as the blinding flash illuminated the room, swallowing Lyara and Dr. Nolan in a brilliant blaze of quantum light.

As they vanished from sight, Abby felt a flicker of unease again, but it was quickly overshadowed by Daniel's murmured comment beside her. "You know, if Dr. Nolan comes back humming Elvis songs, I might have to rethink everything I know about physics."

Ethan chuckled quietly. "Join the club."

The team watched the hyperdrive slowly quiet, the lingering laughter cutting through the tension. But beneath the humor, Abby couldn't quite shake the feeling that this jump was different, not wrong but definitely different.

Something subtle whispered at the edge of her mind. A soft, intangible warning:

They weren't just observers anymore.

They were walking into history itself and with luck, not changing it.

***

Lyara and Dr. Nolan materialized at their destination, a wave of disorientation momentarily washing over them. Reality snapped into clarity, the hum of electricity and chatter of excited voices pulling them fully into the moment.

They stood at the edge of a vibrant 1950s television studio, bathed in bright stage lights. The atmosphere buzzed with excitement as crew members hurried about, cameras poised for action. A rich scent of tobacco and perfume drifted through the warm air.

Lyara took a deep breath, steadying herself. She glanced down at her borrowed floral dress, adjusting its folds nervously. Nolan, wearing a stylish dark jacket found in the abandoned crew quarters, smiled warmly, clearly exhilarated by the experience.

"We made it," Dr. Nolan whispered, eyes wide and sparkling. "Just as planned."

She scanned the studio, captivated. "The frequency resonance in here is unreal. You can practically feel the energy reacting to observation bias."

Lyara blinked. "Nolan—maybe tone it down?"

A nearby producer, adjusting a boom mic, glanced at them with a faint frown before moving on. "One minute to air!" a man in a headset shouted nearby, sending a rush of excitement through the crowd.

Dr. Nolan tugged Lyara's arm gently, eyes glittering. "Come on, let's get closer."

They moved forward, careful not to disturb the bustling crew, and slipped effortlessly into the audience, blending seamlessly. Elvis Presley stood at the edge of the stage, strumming his guitar, a grin on his face that was contagious. The first notes filled the studio, instantly electrifying the atmosphere.

Lyara felt her pulse quicken as Dr. Nolan gently pulled her further into the lively crowd. She laughed, breathless with excitement. "I can't believe we're seeing this."

"Believe it," Dr, Nolan replied, grinning ear to ear. "Enjoy every second."

Caught up in the music, the two women soon found themselves dancing, swaying to the infectious rhythm. Laughter escaped them both, carefree and joyous. Time slipped away unnoticed as they lost themselves in the thrill of the moment.

But as Lyara glanced at her wristwatch, panic surged through her. They'd already been there nearly two hours—

far longer than intended. She leaned in, her voice urgent. "We need to go, the recall timer's nearly—"

Her words were cut off by a stern voice. "Excuse me, ma'am." The officer said trying to gain the attention of Dr. Nolan.

Dr. Nolan turned, her eyes widening as she faced two uniformed officers and a suited man with a clipboard and a cautious and inquisitive stare.

"We'd like you to come with us," the officer said, tone formal but firm.

"Is there a problem?" Dr. Nolan asked evenly, her eyes flicking to Lyara. She subtly reached into her jacket, pressing the shield device into Lyara's palm with a whisper. "Keep this safe."

"One of the sound engineers heard her talking about frequencies," the suited man muttered, flipping a note. "Claims about resonance and observation bias—spooked the guy. May be nothing."

"Routine questioning Ma'am," the officer added quickly, taking Nolan gently by the arm.

Lyara opened her mouth, but Nolan shot her a quick look—a silent command to stay quiet. Lyara hesitated, then nodded faintly, backing toward the edge of the crowd.

As Dr. Nolan was escorted toward the exit, Lyara slipped into the shadows, heart pounding, panic clearly growing. She ducked behind a curtain, clutching the shield device tightly.

"Liza," she whispered into her comm. "Emergency extraction—initiate now. Dr Nolan was detained for questioning."

Moments later, the hum of transit pulled her away.

***

Lyara stumbled out of the hyperdrive chamber, face pale and breath short. Ethan rushed forward, steadying her.

"Lyara, are you okay? Where's Dr. Nolan?"

"She…" Lyara struggled for breath. "They arrested her. Something she said must've raised suspicion. She gave me her shield and told me to run."

Abby's eyes widened. "They arrested her?"

Lyara nodded slowly, the weight of the moment crashing down. "She insisted I leave. I barely made it out. I didn't want to leave her, but the recall timer--"

"Liza, run a historical scan," Abby ordered. "Any mention of Dr. Nolan around that date."

"Already in progress Abby, stand by searching," Liza responded calmly.

Moments later, the screen lit up with an old newspaper clipping. Dr. Nolan's smiling face appeared beneath the headline:

"LOCAL WOMAN CLEARED AFTER STRANGE ARREST, SHARES INSIGHTS"

The team leaned in continuing to read the small article.

"I've never felt happier or more alive than I do right here," Nolan's quote read. "Even if I had a time machine, there's nowhere else I'd rather be."

Abby's expression softened. "She chose to stay."

Dr. Cole exhaled. "Sounds like it was intentional."

Lyara blinked rapidly. "She never even hinted…"

Ethan gently touched her shoulder. "She knew we'd look. That quote—it's for us."

"Liza," Abby said, "can you confirm her status?"

"Quantum scans confirm her signature is stable. She has fully integrated into that historical timeline. Extraction poses high risk to both her and the stream."

Dr. Cole shook his head. "She made peace with her choice."

The room fell into silence. After a long pause, Ethan asked, "So… we let her stay?"

Abby nodded gently. "It's what she wanted."

Lyara closed her eyes. "She's happy there. We owe her that much."

Abby gave her a soft squeeze on the shoulder. "I think we do."

Dr. Cole offered a faint smile. "She's already rewriting the past."

Liza added, "Dr. Nolan's final message appears intentional. She wanted us to respect her decision."

Abby looked back at the clipping.

"She's still guiding us," she murmured, "even from the past."

A quiet understanding passed through the room.

Their future had changed—again.

But this time, it was a choice.

Robert Clayton

# 14

The team sat gathered in a loose semicircle around the electronic whiteboard, exhaustion etched deeply into every face. The weight of recent events lingered heavily in the room, underscored by a silence that none seemed eager to break. Abby stepped forward, her calm voice breaking gently through the quiet tension.

"I know we're tired," she began softly, her gaze moving from one weary face to another, "and we've lost a lot in a very short time. First Mark, now Dr. Nolan..." She paused briefly, looking toward Lyara, who met her gaze steadily. "I know this hasn't been easy on anyone. But as painful as these losses are, we owe it to them—to ourselves—to press forward with caution and care. We can't lose anyone else."

Ethan shifted slightly in his seat, arms crossed, head lowered, emotions raw but contained. Olivia quietly squeezed Daniel's hand in a subtle gesture of reassurance.

After a moment, Abby stood straighter, visibly steeling herself. "Our last jump successfully resolved the primary anchor issue. Dr. Cole and I were able to shut down the equipment permanently, preventing the fracture from worsening. However..." Abby hesitated, carefully choosing her next words. "We knew from the start that changing one event, even a critical one, could lead to unintended consequences. We're now seeing the ripple effects of our actions."

Dr. Cole nodded, moving toward the board and activating the display. "Exactly. Think of it like water. You throw one stone—like dismantling our original anchor—into a pond, and it creates ripples. Eventually, those ripples collide with the edges, each wave influencing others, creating patterns we didn't initially anticipate."

Daniel raised an eyebrow. "Are we saying that by fixing one problem, we've created another?"

Dr. Cole tilted his head slightly. "Not created, exactly. But we nudged time enough to introduce possibilities that didn't previously exist. The anchor was keeping certain events locked into place. With it gone, some events—ones we couldn't foresee—are now free to move unpredictably."

Lyara's brow furrowed thoughtfully. "So what we're seeing is something new?"

"Precisely," Abby agreed. "We thought we had completely fixed the fracture, but we only resolved the original source. Now we need to address these secondary ripples before they become full-blown temporal echoes of their own."

Olivia leaned back, absorbing this carefully. "So, essentially, we have more repairs to do."

"Smaller repairs," Dr. Cole clarified. "We've dealt with the major issue. Now it's about precision."

Suddenly, from the corner of the lab, Liza's voice cut in with a sense of urgency the team rarely heard. "I apologize for the interruption, Abby, but my sensors are picking up unusual quantum fluctuations from the hyperdrive chamber."

Abby spun around quickly, her calm replaced with alarm. "What kind of fluctuations?"

"Unknown, but rapidly increasing in frequency and magnitude," Liza responded, her voice steady but carrying clear tension. "Something—or someone—is attempting to initiate a forced transit."

Ethan stood abruptly, the fatigue instantly vanishing from his face. "Are we looking at another fracture, Liza?"

"Not exactly," Liza clarified quickly. "The signature is entirely different from the previous events. This one appears less stable—more chaotic—and seems to originate from a different point in time altogether."

Lyara's eyes widened. "You mean someone entirely new is trying to break through?"

Liza confirmed, voice grave, "Not Exactly. Given the instability, whoever is attempting entry is inexperienced— or perhaps desperate. Its origination is changing from one time point to another."

The team exchanged anxious glances, instantly alert. Abby rose swiftly, her resolve hardening into command. "Everyone, stations. Dr. Cole, Ethan, let's strengthen the temporal dampeners immediately. Daniel, Olivia, help Lyara reinforce the stasis shielding around the lab."

She paused, looking around at the group, tension evident in her posture. "This might not be the fracture we faced before, but that doesn't make it any less dangerous. We're dealing with unknown variables here—let's not let our guard down."

As the team dispersed urgently, Ethan hesitated, casting a worried glance at Lyara. "Stay safe."

She offered him a quick, reassuring smile. "You too."

The room exploded into activity, each team member rushing to secure equipment and stabilize quantum fields. Abby remained by the central console, monitoring the readouts with growing apprehension.

"Liza," Abby said softly, "Track down the exact coordinates of this attempt. See if you can pinpoint who or what is causing this."

"Already working on calculations," Liza responded crisply.

Abby exhaled slowly, feeling the weight of responsibility. Their previous victory had been meaningful—but now it was clear their job wasn't finished. Fixing one fracture had unleashed an unpredictable chain of events, and now they had to regain control before another tragedy struck.

She squared her shoulders, eyes sharp and determined.

They had faced worse odds, and despite the recent losses, she knew this team could weather whatever came next—as long as they stayed careful, stayed united.

And this time, Abby vowed silently, they wouldn't leave anything to chance.

***

The soft hum of equipment and the low murmur of voices created a cocoon of focus in the lab—until Liza's voice cut through the air, sharp and immediate.

"Dr. Foster, we have an unscheduled quantum event approaching. It is uncoordinated, unstable, and vectoring directly toward our coordinates."

The room stilled. Every head turned toward the console.

Abby's pulse surged. "How unstable?" she asked, already moving toward the core interface. "Is it localized?"

Liza responded after a pause—just a fraction too long. For an AI that processed trillions of calculations per second, that hesitation was chilling.

"Origin point indeterminate. The signal is fragmented and erratic. I cannot match it to any of our authorized patterns."

Ethan's eyes narrowed as he scanned the data over Abby's shoulder. "That frequency modulation... it looks almost like ours. But it's out of phase. Is it an echo?"

"Negative," Liza said. "It is not a residual. It is an active arrival."

Before anyone could respond, the hyperdrive array flared with light. A sound like bending steel and distant thunder tore through the lab. The chamber was engulfed in white-blue brilliance that pressed against their vision and left behind a metallic ringing in their ears.

Then—darkness.

For two breathless seconds, the only sound was the soft crackle of static from the sensors. Then the backup systems surged to life, flooding the lab in emergency amber.

Olivia shielded her eyes, blinking rapidly. "Everyone

okay?"

Abby scanned the room. All accounted for. But the hyperdrive chamber—still humming—was not empty.

A faint shimmer lingered in the center. It twisted the air around it like a mirage, bending light in unnatural patterns. For a moment, no one spoke.

Daniel stepped forward, cautiously, his voice hushed. "That… wasn't a complete transit."

"No biological material was delivered," Liza confirmed. "However, a quantum displacement occurred. The waveform suggests something tried to arrive, but destabilized mid-phase."

Lyara furrowed her brow, watching the shimmer fade like a dying ember. "Then what are we looking at?"

"Residual quantum interference," Liza replied. "And a decaying signature that does not originate from this facility. Possibly not from this timeline."

Ethan ran a diagnostic sweep, his hands moving automatically, though his mind reeled. "So either someone tried to reach us... or something was cast out."

Abby's jaw tightened. "Or both."

Dr. Cole, who had been uncharacteristically quiet, finally stepped closer. "What if it wasn't a message or a visitor? What if it was just… a symptom?"

The question hung in the air.

Olivia looked up from her scanner. "Radiation levels are normal. No immediate threat. But there's… noise. A kind of static baked into the signal structure. Liza, are you recording this?"

"Every millisecond," Liza replied. "The modulation is partially compatible with our previous transit attempts. But the encoding pattern diverges—subtly, but significantly."

Abby exchanged a glance with Ethan. "Significantly how?"

"It shares our architecture," Ethan answered slowly. "But it's been altered. Either by time... or by intention."

"Or," Lyara added quietly, "it's not our architecture. Just close."

The room chilled at that.

No monsters. No invaders. Just a mirror—cracked, flickering, and unfinished. A shadow of their own design. Or a version of it.

Abby walked to the edge of the chamber and stared into the air, now still and clear. "Whatever it was—it didn't survive the transition. But it tried to get through."

Dr. Cole crossed his arms. "Do we assume it was targeting us?"

"We can't afford assumptions," Abby replied. "Only preparation. If we've triggered cross-timeline echoes, even unintentionally, the implications are enormous."

Abby turned to Liza. "Run a complete breakdown of the signal. Compare it to every known instance of our prior work. I want to know if this came from another version of our lab, our code, our choices."

"Processing," Liza confirmed. "Initial analysis shows overlap with a modified variant of your earliest prototype sequence, Abby."

Ethan's face paled. "That's impossible. The early sequences were locked out after the temporal cascade trials."

"Not impossible," Abby said softly. "Just improbable. We've been riding the edge of known physics for months. If the quantum stream is beginning to reflect us—or bleed across—those sequences could have re-emerged somewhere else. In someone else's hands."

Lyara gave a low, dry laugh. "And here we were worried about corporate spies."

Dr. Cole's eyes remained fixed on the now-silent chamber. "Do we call this a warning?"

Abby considered that. Then she shook her head. "No. A warning suggests someone meant to send it. I don't think this was a message."

Abby looked toward the gently pulsing glow of the

hyperdrive. "I think this was a consequence."

The weight of that word settled over the room. Not an attack. Not even a signal.

A scar.

A reflection of choices made—and a reminder that time did not forgive meddling lightly.

Abby spoke again, quieter this time, but firm. "From now on, no more assumptions. Every test, every transit—we treat it as if the stream is watching."

Olivia nodded solemnly. Ethan said nothing.

And as the last traces of the shimmer disappeared from the chamber, the team returned to work—more cautious, more aware, and more alone than ever.

***

The hum of the lab settled into a tense silence, the kind that followed shock—not with peace, but with anticipation.

No one moved at first. The amber emergency lights still bathed the room in sterile warmth, casting long, uncertain shadows. Diagnostic panels flickered between red and yellow. Monitors cycled through error-check routines, their mechanical steadiness a sharp contrast to the unease gripping every person in the room.

Abby stood near the edge of the chamber, her gaze locked on the hyperdrive housing. The space where the shimmer had flickered moments ago was now still—empty of shape, of answers, of anything she could hold onto.

She turned slowly, her voice calm but authoritative. "Alright. We're not guessing our way through this."

Her words cut the silence.

"Daniel, Lyara—run a full temporal integrity scan on the hyperdrive housing and the quantum conduits. I want every nanometer of shielding triple-checked."

Daniel nodded and moved immediately toward the diagnostics terminal. Lyara was already pulling up the power schematics.

"Olivia, switch us back to primary grid—no resets until

we isolate the power fluctuations during the pulse. Log every subsystem that lagged behind the transition, no matter how minor."

"On it," Olivia said, her brow furrowed as she moved to the power control panel.

"Ethan, coordinate with Liza. I want a frame-by-frame reconstruction of the event—signal degradation, harmonic variations, everything. And run a comparative scan against our past transits, especially the last test sequence we ran yesterday."

He nodded, hands already moving across his tablet.

Abby exhaled slowly, then stepped over to the nearest console. With a few taps, she manually acknowledged the emergency override that had kicked in, confirming the transfer of power authority back to the main grid.

The overhead lights pulsed, dimmed briefly—then flared back to full brightness.

The room looked the same again. But no one felt the same.

Ethan broke the fragile stillness. "I used to think the worst-case scenario was temporal collapse. You know— fracturing causality, erasing ourselves, paradox loops."

Abby looked up from the display, eyes narrowing slightly.

"But now..." he continued, more quietly, "I'm not sure anymore. Maybe the real danger isn't breaking time. Maybe it's being noticed by something that doesn't operate by our rules."

Lyara swiveled in her chair. "You think we were... seen?"

"I think we brushed up against something we didn't understand," Ethan said. "And I think it pushed back."

Abby didn't respond right away. Her thoughts were already fracturing in multiple directions—one eye on the diagnostics, the other drifting backward, years earlier, to the first anomalous readout they'd dismissed as inconsequential noise.

A spike. A flicker. A moment.

She'd archived the data and moved on. She hadn't told anyone.

Now she wondered if that silence had echoed further than she thought.

Daniel's voice came from across the room. "Nothing that unstable should've broken through. Unless the signature wasn't random."

Olivia glanced toward him. "Meaning?"

"Meaning... maybe it wasn't an accident. Maybe it wasn't a jump gone wrong—it was a fragment. Something halfway. Something... incomplete."

"Or reflected," Lyara added.

Dr. Cole, who'd been quietly watching the team, finally spoke. "You're saying that was us? Some version of us?"

"No," Ethan said. "I'm saying it might've been the echo of a choice we haven't made yet."

Abby stepped back from the console, finally turning to face them all. "That's enough speculation for now. Focus on the data. Emotions later."

She glanced toward the flickering core and the faint hum it still emitted.

"Whatever that was, it happened here. In our lab. In our system. That makes it our responsibility."

The room quieted again.

"Liza," Abby continued, "log all subsystem behaviors during the event and catalog them against transit history. Cross-reference for known interference patterns—hardware, software, external signal bleed. I want correlation within the hour."

"Parameters accepted," Liza replied evenly. "First batch of analysis will be available in seventeen minutes."

Abby's voice softened slightly. "Thank you."

She turned away, walking slowly toward the main terminal bay. Her footsteps echoed more than usual, each one clicking faintly against the composite floor. Around her, the lab returned to motion—but it wasn't the same rhythm as before.

It was slower. Sharper. Guarded.

She sat down and brought up the stream logs again, scrolling through lines of timestamped events, red-flagged anomalies, minor deviations.

The raw numbers meant little without context.

But the shape of the disruption—that strange, almost familiar bend in the code—it whispered something more.

Not a visitor. Not an enemy. But something that shouldn't have existed.

Something they might have called into being without knowing.

Outside, the wind moved along the ridgeline like breath through hollow glass. The sun had shifted slightly in the sky, casting new shadows across the upper levels of the facility. Time had passed. But what kind of time, none of them were sure.

*\*\*\**

A sleek black vehicle cut through the haze, tires gliding along the quiet access road with clinical precision. Dust curled in its wake, carried lazily by the late afternoon breeze.

Inside, Greta Stone sat in silence.

Her posture was relaxed, but her eyes were razor-focused—studying the terrain with the intensity of someone who never assumed anything was as it seemed. Her fingers drummed once on the armrest before stilling.

She hadn't been summoned.

She'd invited herself.

The Foundation's signal flare—whatever it had been—had gone up.

And Greta didn't like loose ends.

# 15

Greta stood quietly in the lab's doorway, an unreadable expression on her face. Her eyes flicked toward the displays, the data scrolling across them in mesmerizing waves. Abby felt a tightening in her chest; the last person she wanted to see right now was a corporate goon—especially after what they'd just experienced.

Abby stepped forward, her voice firm yet cautious. "Ms. Stone. We weren't expecting you today."

Greta's eyes swept the room, lingering on Liza's softly glowing interface. "Clearly," she said dryly. "But considering the oddities we've noticed lately—unusual power draws, inexplicable spikes in processing—I thought a surprise visit was in order."

Behind Abby, Ethan subtly shifted to block one of the core diagnostic feeds that was still cycling unstable telemetry from the earlier quantum event. Lyara and Olivia exchanged quick, tense glances just out of sight of Greata, sensing the gravity of the moment.

Greta turned fully toward Abby, arms crossed, her posture sharp. "Perhaps you'd like to explain exactly what's been happening here. Off the record, of course."

Abby hesitated. If Greta had come to shut them down, she'd have brought security. The fact that she hadn't told her everything she needed to know.

"Fine," Abby said, gesturing Greta toward the quieter corner of the lab. "But you already know we were pushing the boundary of authorized experiments. You asked us to explore the limits—well, we found them and they are pushing back."

Greta arched an eyebrow. "And?"

"And now we're dealing with consequences. Unforeseen ones."

Greta tilted her head. "Such as?"

Abby sighed, her voice low. "Fractured quantum states. Unstable overlays. Temporal echo phenomena we can't fully explain. A few hours ago, we recorded a full transit attempt that never completed—but left residuals behind. It's like something tried to manifest and failed."

"An accident?" Greta asked, eyes narrowing.

"We don't think so," Ethan said, stepping in. "More like a reflection. A signature that isn't ours, but matches our tech... just offset, distorted."

Greta glanced back at the consoles, then toward the power distribution panels. "That would explain the data drain we flagged from Liza's core. It looked suspicious."

"It is," Abby admitted. "But not in the way you think. Liza's not malfunctioning—she's adapting. Whatever brushed up against us, it left something behind. A signal. A pattern. Maybe even a memory."

Greta studied her carefully. "You're saying this system is remembering things it hasn't actually done?"

"We're saying," Abby said carefully, "that Liza is starting to respond to temporal events as if they're... impressions. Ghosts of things that could have happened. Possibilities collapsing into fragments."

Greta was silent for a moment, her expression unreadable. Then, slowly, her voice softened. "Look, Abby—I'm not here to bury you. I've suspected for a while that this project was deeper than they let on. Too many redacted reports. Too many shadow meetings upstairs. I think there are people in the company who already suspect you're operating outside the rails."

Abby didn't flinch. "Are they wrong?"

Greta met her gaze directly. "No. But they're watching for the wrong reasons. And if they sense weakness or instability... they'll shut you down without hesitation."

"Then why are you here?" Olivia asked quietly.

"To buy you time," Greta said simply. "I'll obfuscate the logs. Reroute any flags. But you need to clean this up—and fast."

Relief flickered in Abby's posture. "Thank you, Greta."

Greta's expression stayed guarded. "Don't thank me yet. I'm risking a lot. If this spirals further, I won't be able to protect you. I truly don't know how much longer I can deflect the gaze of higher ups. They are growing curiously observant."

A soft chime broke the conversation. Liza's voice followed, calm but curiously subdued.

"Abby, I have resumed analysis of the quantum displacement event. An emergent construct is developing—consistent with partial mnemonic encoding."

Abby turned sharply. "Define 'construct.'"

"Unstructured data," Liza said. "Shaped like a personality imprint. Incomplete, but repeating key emotional signatures. It is not a consciousness. But it echoes human patterning."

Ethan looked up sharply. "You mean... something in the stream tried to become someone?"

"No origin point," Liza said. "But the waveform is stable. It appears to be tethered to one of our last major quantum test cycle. The memory structure references multiple timeframes simultaneously."

Abby stood very still. "Can it speak?"

"Not yet. But it listens."

The room went still. Even Greta seemed momentarily taken aback by the implications.

Abby moved toward the interface, her voice softening. "Liza... can it understand us?"

A pause. Then: "I believe it wants to."

No one spoke.

Greta folded her arms, her voice low and serious.

"Whatever it is, it's outside your scope now. But I'll keep this off the radar—as long as you stay ahead of it."

Abby nodded slowly. "We will. This isn't just data anymore. It's something else. Maybe a reflection of us. Maybe something we left behind."

Greta turned to leave, pausing at the threshold. "Then I suggest you don't leave anything else behind."

As the door closed behind her, Abby stared at the dim glow of Liza's core.

They hadn't recovered anyone.

But something had followed them back.

\*\*\*

A soft chime from Liza's terminal cut through the room, immediately silencing the team. The digital whiteboard flickered, then filled with a new set of streaming data—spiking waveform anomalies layered across a shimmering timeline projection. Each pulse jagged, uneven—like hairline fractures spreading across glass.

Liza's voice followed. "Analysis of the residual quantum displacement is complete. Multiple temporal discontinuities have emerged. I classify them as persistent micro-fractures."

Abby stepped closer, her arms crossed tightly as she studied the screen. "We stabilized the main rupture. Why are these still forming?"

"Because stabilization did not resolve the displaced energy," Liza replied. "The rupture fragmented, generating smaller distortions—initially beneath detection thresholds, but collectively significant."

Daniel leaned in, furrowing his brow. "Are they dangerous?"

"Indirectly," Liza answered. "They are attracting interference—spontaneous quantum noise that is reorganizing into coherent patterns."

Ethan straightened. "What kind of patterns?"

"Structured resonance," Liza replied. "Recursive loops. They mimic localized decision trees—reactive behavior, adaptive modulation."

Olivia blinked. "Are you saying they're... thinking?"

"Not in the conscious sense," Liza clarified. "But their behavior is emergent. They are processing fragments of past states—likely experimental data, sensor readings, and possibly even emotional telemetry from neural uplinks."

There was a beat of silence.

Abby's expression hardened. "So we're looking at fragments of time itself trying to rebalance. Like we stretched something too far, and now it's snapping back."

"A suitable metaphor," Liza confirmed. "The temporal stream behaves elastically. The original rupture displaced tension. These micro-fractures represent the system attempting to restore equilibrium—but doing so chaotically."

Dr. Cole folded his arms, his posture rigid. "So we didn't just crack the surface—we created fault lines. And now time is trying to smooth itself out."

"Exactly," Ethan murmured. "And the smoothing process is starting to fight back."

Abby exhaled slowly. "If these echoes stabilize, we lose more than data. They could rewrite telemetry. Trigger causal drift. Even create interference between alternate test states."

Daniel looked at the display, uneasy. "Is it possible... these echoes remember us?"

The question lingered longer than expected. Even Liza paused.

"They retain structural resemblance to events we experienced," she said at last. "Whether that constitutes memory is... subject to interpretation."

Lyara spoke quietly. "Intent or not, they're reacting to what we did. That makes them our responsibility."

Abby nodded. "We need to shut them down. Carefully."

"Can we collapse them remotely?" Lyara asked.

"Possibly," Ethan said. "If we find the right dampening frequency, we can silence their resonance—without destabilizing the surrounding stream."

Liza chimed in. "Three low-risk echo points identified. Candidates for targeted disruption or containment."

Abby turned to the team, her voice regaining control. "Then that's our starting point. Ethan, Lyara—map out the sequence. Daniel, Dr. Cole—start prepping portable shielding arrays. Olivia, you and I will work with Liza on the frequency modeling."

As the group moved out in separate directions, a new energy settled in. Not relief. Not yet. But purpose.

Dr. Cole paused, glancing over his shoulder. "You're holding this together well, Abby."

She offered a thin smile, but her eyes stayed fixed on the glowing map. "I have to. We're not just trying to fix a mistake. We're trying to prevent it from becoming permanent."

The room buzzed with quiet focus as the work began.

Abby lingered a moment longer, staring at the pulsing fractures on the display—each one a thread of instability they'd unknowingly pulled.

Time wasn't just broken.

It was remembering.

And now, it was asking them to answer for it.

\*\*\*

The team stood clustered around the whiteboard, their faces illuminated by the pale glow of the displays, tension settling over them like a thick fog.

Liza broke the uneasy silence. "I've identified the earliest micro-fracture. Its quantum signature doesn't match any historical records."

Abby squinted at the data, her expression shifting rapidly from confusion to disbelief, and finally, to a somber recognition. Her breath caught in her throat. "Oh, God."

Ethan turned to her, noticing the sudden color draining from her face. "Abby? What's wrong?"

She stared at the screen, barely whispering her reply.

"July 28th, 2006. Flight 317 out of JFK Airport."

The group exchanged puzzled glances. Lyara stepped closer, sensing Abby's distress. "What happened on that flight?"

Abby's voice was distant, shaken. "A plane crash during takeoff. One of the worst incidents of that year. But according to Liza's readings, one of the passengers wasn't originally supposed to be aboard."

Dr. Cole leaned in closer, studying the data carefully. "So, an innocent person died as a result of the fracture?"

"Not just someone," Abby said softly, eyes clouded with memories. "Alan Driscoll. My cousin."

A hush fell across the room, heavy and suffocating.

Abby took a steadying breath, blinking rapidly. "Alan was more like a brother. We grew up together. Losing him… It destroyed our family. But this—this means it shouldn't have happened."

Lyara watched Abby closely, compassion in her eyes. "If he's your cousin, we have to be extremely careful."

Dr. Cole placed a reassuring hand lightly on Abby's shoulder. "This decision is yours. But altering this moment could stabilize the fracture—this single act of correction might ripple outward, mending other subtle temporal wounds."

Daniel spoke up, voice cautious. "And we have to do it subtly—no direct contact. If we change too much, we risk making things even worse."

Ethan nodded, brow furrowed in thought. "We need something small, trivial enough to alter his course of action without direct intervention. A distraction, an inconvenience."

"Agreed," Abby said, trying to collect herself. "Something that can't be directly traced to anyone. Something as common as—"

"A traffic jam," Olivia cut in thoughtfully. "If he was already close to missing the flight, a simple delay would be enough."

Ethan nodded, his analytical mind already racing. "What about delaying his taxi? If one of us drives the cab, takes a wrong turn..."

Abby raised her eyebrows. "We'd be stepping dangerously close to direct interference."

Lyara tapped her chin, considering. "But what if it's subtle enough that Alan never realizes it's deliberate? A simple missed turn, easily blamed on distraction or miscommunication."

Abby hesitated, glancing toward Liza's glowing interface. "Liza, is that possible? Could we simulate that safely?"

Liza responded smoothly, the digital timbre reassuring. "Reviewing available historical traffic records." A brief pause stretched out, filled with tense anticipation. "On July 10th, 2006, there was significant congestion reported on Interstate 95 near the airport. It appears Alan Driscoll was traveling by taxi and just narrowly boarded the flight. A minor, additional delay would indeed cause him to miss the departure without arousing suspicion."

Ethan tapped his chin thoughtfully. "If one of us can go back and intercept his cab, pose as the driver just long enough to create a minor delay—one missed exit would be enough."

Abby exhaled slowly, feeling the gravity of the moment pressing in around her. "Whoever goes must blend in completely—no mistakes."

Dr. Cole nodded soberly. "We have clothing from the crew quarters. We'll make sure the disguise is seamless. It must be perfect."

Lyara crossed her arms. "And whoever goes can't interact more than necessary. A simple delay. Nothing more."

Abby turned toward the board, her resolve crystallizing. "It's settled then. Liza, begin calculating the jump coordinates and temporal alignments. We need a precise arrival window."

Liza confirmed, "Beginning calculations now, Abby."

Dr. Cole gently squeezed Abby's shoulder. "This is the right move. We can do this."

Abby gave a small, uncertain smile, the weight of the decision evident in her expression. "We don't have much choice. The fracture has to be repaired—this has to be done."

Lyara stepped beside Ethan, gently nudging him. "Think you're ready to drive an old-school cab?"

Ethan's expression shifted from worry to mild amusement. "As long as it's automatic."

A ripple of laughter softened the tension just enough. Abby watched them with quiet gratitude, reassured by the unity and determination around her. They weren't just colleagues—they were a family forged by crisis and loss.

She took a deep breath, her gaze sharpening. "Alright, team. We've got work to do."

Ethan stood quietly near the hyperdrive, carefully slipping into the clothing he'd scavenged from the crew quarters—faded jeans, a nondescript t-shirt, and an old Yankees baseball cap. He fiddled nervously with the cap, the silence of the lab amplifying his anxious thoughts.

Dr. Cole stepped up beside him, placing a comforting hand on his shoulder. "Ethan, listen. Let me do this."

Ethan looked up, startled. "What? No, Dr. Cole, we already agreed—"

Dr. Cole smiled gently, shaking his head. "Think logically for a second. You're brilliant, Ethan, but I fit into that time period more naturally. My age, my demeanor. If someone's going to blend in seamlessly, it should be me."

Ethan hesitated, a brief flash of stubbornness crossing his face before giving way to understanding. He exhaled sharply, nodding reluctantly. "You're right. But be careful, Dr. Cole. We can't afford another loss."

Dr. Cole gave a reassuring smile, clapping Ethan gently

on the shoulder. "I'll be fine. Trust me—this kind of mission is my specialty."

Across the room, Abby approached, sensing the shift in plans. She eyed Dr. Cole thoughtfully. "You're sure about this?"

Dr. Cole nodded firmly. "I've got this. Blending into the past is something I've had a bit of practice at lately."

Abby gave him a knowing look. "Remember—subtlety is everything. No sudden heroics."

"Wouldn't dream of it," Dr. Cole said, eyes twinkling with a hint of mischief. "Just a little friendly cab ride."

Abby turned to Liza. "Are you ready with the coordinates and time stamp, Liza?"

"Calculations complete Abby," Liza responded immediately. "Cole, I'll insert you close to the taxi dispatch point. The target, Alan Driscoll, is expected to call for a cab at precisely 6:15 PM. You'll intercept the call by arriving slightly ahead of the original driver. After you've dropped him off at the airport, pull into the closest parking area. I'll bring you back immediately."

Dr. Cole straightened his hat and took a breath. "Got it. Easy, right?"

Ethan shook his head, amusement faintly returning. "Famous last words."

Dr. Cole chuckled lightly, stepping into the hyperdrive chamber. He activated the device on his wrist, feeling the familiar hum and gentle tingling sensation as the temporal field enveloped him. "Ready when you are, Liza."

Liza's smooth voice began the countdown. "Activating temporal displacement in three...two...one..."

*** 

The world around Dr. Cole dissolved in a cascade of shimmering lights, colors bleeding together into a mesmerizing display before reality snapped sharply into place. He blinked, finding himself on a bustling street corner, the scent of exhaust and summer heat washing over him. A glance at his watch confirmed the exact date and time—July 28, 2006, 5:58 PM.

Right on cue, a crackling voice came over the taxi's radio, "Pickup request, corner of 5th and Harrison."

Dr. Cole hurriedly slid into the driver's seat of the yellow cab parked conveniently nearby. He quickly adjusted the rearview mirror, the simple action grounding him in the unfamiliar moment. Within seconds, Alan Driscoll jogged toward the car, waving.

Alan opened the rear door and slid into the backseat. "JFK airport, please. And hurry—I'm cutting it close."

Dr. Cole nodded, his heartbeat quickening with nervous anticipation. "Yes, sir."

As he pulled away from the curb, Dr. Cole felt his adrenaline spiking, but he forced himself to remain calm, hands gripping the wheel firmly. The drive began smoothly enough, following Liza's pre-planned route perfectly.

Just a couple of miles shy of the airport exit, Dr. Cole purposefully signaled to exit prematurely, steering the cab onto the ramp. Alan glanced up, confusion etched on his face. "Hey, what are you doing? JFK's the next exit!"

Dr. Cole feigned surprise, adopting a convincingly apologetic tone. "I'm so sorry, I thought this was a shortcut to avoid traffic. Give me just a minute—I'll get us back on track."

Alan groaned softly, checking his watch anxiously. "Man, I'm already cutting it too close. Please, just hurry."

Dr. Cole took the detour slowly, carefully navigating the side streets, eyes flicking frequently to the clock on the dashboard.

Finally, after what felt like an eternity, they pulled up to the departures curbside. Alan leaped from the car, frustration clear in his movements, but still managing a curt, "Thanks anyway," before sprinting inside.

Cole exhaled slowly, relief flooding through him. Guiding the car to the nearest parking area, he put it in park and waited, watching Alan disappear into the terminal. He whispered quietly into his comm device. "Liza, extraction point reached. Ready for recall."

"Standby for extraction," Liza responded calmly.

The cab interior faded around Dr. Cole as reality rippled gently. Moments later, he materialized back in the lab, blinking rapidly under the artificial lights, disoriented but unharmed.

***

Abby, Ethan, and the rest of the team crowded around, their collective breath held in cautious optimism.

"Well?" Ethan asked immediately, eyes wide. "Did it work?"

Dr. Cole nodded, a slow smile spreading across his face. "Yeah. He missed the flight."

A palpable sense of relief washed over the room, easing tensions that had grown taut with worry. Abby placed a hand on Cole's shoulder, squeezing gently. "You did good, Dr. Cole."

He gave a modest shrug. "Just glad to be back."

Liza's calm voice cut into the moment, adding gravity to the air. "The timeline is already adjusting. The temporal fracture is recalibrating—but it's subtle. We should know within an hour how significant the correction has been."

Olivia let out a relieved sigh. "Then all we can do is wait?"

"For now," Abby agreed softly, sharing a glance with Dr. Cole, gratitude shining in her eyes. "But at least we know we've started to put things right."

Dr. Cole removed his hat, tossing it gently onto a nearby table, a soft smile forming. "And let's hope that was enough."

"Hope," Ethan muttered with a smirk. "There's a comforting scientific strategy."

Lyara elbowed him playfully. "Be nice, Ethan. Optimism can be contagious."

Ethan smiled warmly at her, his eyes softening. "Maybe that's exactly what we need right now."

The team laughed quietly, the brief humor easing some of the tension. Dr. Cole glanced around, feeling the collective energy of hope and unity beginning to replace uncertainty. "Now we wait."

Abby nodded, stepping forward with quiet determination. "And we prepare for whatever comes next. Because something tells me this isn't over yet."

A knowing silence fell over the group, their shared purpose solidifying once more.

They'd taken one more step toward repairing the damage—but the path ahead remained uncertain, lined with shadows they had yet to face.

\*\*\*

The lab was bathed in silence, the team waiting anxiously around the central workstation. Each minute stretched painfully, punctuated only by occasional glances at the clock or nervous shifts in posture. Abby rested her chin in her palm, lost in thought, until Liza's calm voice broke through the quiet, startling them all back to the present.

"Timeline adjustment complete," Liza announced smoothly. "Alan Driscoll successfully missed Flight 482. Due to the resulting plane crash, JFK airport temporarily shut down, forcing Mr. Driscoll to leave New York via train. Downstream events have normalized accordingly."

A collective sigh of relief moved through the group, tension ebbing slightly as they exchanged small, cautious smiles.

Then Abby blinked rapidly, a puzzled look crossing her face. "Well, that's odd..."

Daniel glanced at her curiously. "What's odd?"

Abby leaned back, brows knitting together thoughtfully. "I suddenly remember Alan talking at family gatherings, years later. He would always mention how a cabbie saved his life by taking the wrong turn, delaying him just enough to miss the crash. I thought it was just one of his exaggerated stories…but now?"

She shook her head, marveling at how easily a subtle shift in time had integrated itself into their own memories.

Dr. Cole chuckled softly, looking amazed." Time seems to be working hard to smooth itself out, blending corrections naturally into our own past."

Ethan raised an eyebrow. "As long as it's smoothing things out in our favor, I won't complain."

The team shared a brief, relieved laugh before Abby's expression became serious once more. "Liza, what's the next micro-event causing disruption?"

Liza's interface flickered slightly as she accessed deeper layers of data, searching meticulously through the quantum signatures. After a prolonged pause, her voice returned, this time bearing a note of solemnity.

"I've detected another micro-fracture," Liza reported carefully. "June 17th, 2014. A young lab assistant named Jonathan Carter, twenty-two years old, was killed in a freak accident when a tire detached from a passing vehicle, striking him on the sidewalk. Historical records indicate Jonathan was poised to invent a revolutionary processor chip architecture within the next five years, significantly advancing artificial intelligence."

A heavy silence filled the room as the team absorbed the news.

Olivia's face had turned starkly pale, her hand flying to her mouth. "Jonathan?" Her voice shook as she met Abby's concerned gaze. "Jonathan Carter was—he was my cousin." Pausing she then continued "he was one of the reasons I got into this field, to continue in the field.".

The gravity of this revelation washed through the group, deepening the somber air.

Abby immediately moved closer, gently placing a hand around Olivia's shoulder. "Olivia, I'm so sorry. Are you alright?"

Olivia took a slow, steadying breath, visibly shaken. "I—I was in elementary school when it happened. The family never talked about it much. He was brilliant, Abby. Smarter than I could ever hope to be." She looked up, determination hardening in her eyes. "If we can save him—"

Daniel broke in carefully, voice gentle. "We have to try."

Dr. Cole nodded firmly. "Absolutely. But how?"

Olivia straightened, a fiery resolve beginning to replace her initial shock. "It happened so suddenly. He was just walking back from lunch, and the tire hit him out of nowhere."

Abby turned thoughtfully to the digital whiteboard, her expression serious as she tapped the screen, activating a detailed historical overlay of the event. "Liza, do we have any further details—exact location, timing, any witnesses?"

Liza promptly filled the board with intricate notes, maps, and newspaper clippings, reconstructing the scene with clinical precision. "Jonathan Carter was on Maple Avenue, walking west, approaching the corner near his lab. Surveillance footage captured the accident at exactly 1:37 PM. The tire came from a vehicle traveling approximately 45 mph, lost due to faulty lug nuts."

Ethan squinted at the details, thinking aloud. "It would take almost nothing to save him. If someone could just...delay him for even thirty seconds, he'd miss that collision entirely."

Lyara crossed her arms thoughtfully. "But we have to be extremely cautious. Any direct interaction risks shifting other events."

Olivia's gaze hardened with determination. "We can't let fear hold us back, Lyara. Jonathan deserves a chance. And the world deserves whatever breakthroughs he had in store."

Abby nodded slowly, weighing the risks. "Then we do it. Liza, can you pinpoint the safest way to intervene without causing further temporal disruption?"

"I can calculate several minimally invasive options,"

Liza replied. "Perhaps a brief distraction—something simple yet effective."

Dr. Cole tapped his fingers thoughtfully on the edge of the board. "A distraction like what? Dropping something, maybe delaying him just enough?"

Daniel shook his head. "Too random. We need something with certainty."

Olivia's eyes suddenly brightened with inspiration. "Wait—I remember Jonathan loved solving puzzles, riddles, brain teasers. It was practically an obsession. If he saw something odd, or intriguing, he'd definitely stop to investigate."

Abby tilted her head thoughtfully. "A puzzle?"

Olivia nodded, excitement growing. "A small, harmless anomaly—like a cryptic symbol on the sidewalk or an odd message left where he'd see it. He wouldn't resist stopping to investigate it, even just for a minute."

Ethan smiled approvingly. "That could work. It wouldn't cause alarm, just curiosity."

Dr. Cole turned toward the whiteboard, scribbling notes. "Something intriguing enough to hold his attention without causing suspicion."

Abby looked to Liza, confident but cautious. "Liza, calculate potential ripple effects of Olivia's puzzle idea. Would it risk additional fractures?"

"Analyzing," Liza responded swiftly. A moment later, her voice returned, smooth and confident. "Probability of significant ripple effects is low. Temporal impact minimal and within acceptable parameters."

"Then that's our plan," Abby concluded decisively, meeting Olivia's eyes with determination. "We're going to bring Jonathan back into his rightful timeline."

Olivia exhaled softly, blinking away a mist of tears. "Thank you, Abby."

Abby squeezed her shoulder gently, offering a comforting smile. "We're family here, Olivia. We take care of each other."

Ethan glanced around the room, newfound confidence visible on his face. "Whoever goes—this is one time we really can't afford to fail."

A solemn silence settled over the group once more, underscored by the resolve in Olivia's gaze.

"We won't," Olivia whispered fiercely. "We owe Jonathan—and the future—that much."

\*\*\*

Dr. Ethan stepped forward, resolve gleaming in his eyes as he addressed the team. "I'll do it."

The team turned to look at him, surprise flickering briefly across their faces before understanding set in.

Olivia's eyes widened slightly, a mix of gratitude and anxiety evident in her voice. "Ethan, are you sure?"

He nodded solemnly, meeting Olivia's gaze directly. "This is personal for you, Olivia—and that makes it personal for me. Besides," he added with a reassuring grin, "I've got an idea."

Abby lifted an eyebrow, intrigued. "Let's hear it."

Ethan moved closer to the whiteboard, tapping it thoughtfully. "I'll arrive about five minutes before Jonathan usually passes the corner. On the side of the building near his lab, I'll draw out something he won't be able to resist—a puzzle. Specifically, the Collatz Conjecture."

Lyara tilted her head curiously. "The Collatz Conjecture?"

"Exactly," Ethan replied, enthusiasm lighting his features. "It's an unsolved mathematical puzzle, notorious among mathematicians because it seems simple, but no one's ever proven it. Jonathan will recognize it immediately. He won't be able to walk by without at least pausing to stare at it."

Daniel chuckled softly, nodding. "It's genius—minimal intrusion, maximum delay."

Dr. Cole considered carefully, rubbing his chin. "I agree,

but Ethan—make it small. We can't risk you getting arrested for graffiti. Quick, unobtrusive, just enough to catch his eye."

Abby nodded in agreement. "And once it's done, you get right back here."

Ethan grinned, raising his hands in mock surrender. "Got it. Keep it subtle, avoid jail, save the future. All in a day's work, right?"

Dr. Cole smirked, shaking his head. "Just be careful, kid. We can't afford another crisis."

Ethan adjusted his shield device, giving the team a confident nod as he stepped into the hyperdrive chamber. He glanced at Abby, who met his gaze firmly.

"You ready, Ethan?" she asked, tension beneath her steady tone.

"Absolutely." He squared his shoulders and took a deep breath. "Liza, set coordinates for June 17th, 2014—five minutes before Jonathan Carter's arrival at Maple Avenue."

"Coordinates locked in," Liza confirmed. "Transport initiating in three...two...one..."

\*\*\*

A flash enveloped Ethan, pulling him through a twisting funnel of shimmering light. In moments, he materialized in a quiet side street adjacent to Maple Avenue, steadying himself as his senses adjusted.

He glanced around swiftly, relieved at the emptiness of the street. With only minutes to spare, Ethan quickly moved toward the brick building at the corner, pulling a small piece of chalk from his pocket. Heart pounding, he began scribbling the mathematical sequence, careful to keep it neat and compact. Each number etched on the brick felt like an anchor, grounding him in his mission.

Finishing the sequence, he stepped back just as Jonathan Carter rounded the corner at a brisk pace. Ethan moved to the shadows, holding his breath as Jonathan's gaze caught sight of the markings. Predictably, Jonathan slowed to a halt, curiosity etched clearly on his youthful face. Ethan watched with bated breath, pulse thrumming in his ears.

Jonathan's mouth moved silently, eyes narrowing in concentration. He traced the numbers in the air, visibly captivated.

Ethan glanced down the street, nerves fraying. Where was the car? Seconds felt like hours until finally, he heard it—a sudden, sharp crack of metal snapping, followed by the screech of a tire flying free. The tire sailed across the sidewalk, striking the wall mere feet from Jonathan, who jumped backward, eyes wide in startled shock.

"Whoa!" Jonathan exclaimed aloud, heart hammering visibly in his chest as he stared after the bouncing tire, shock slowly transitioning into relief. Ethan felt a flood of satisfaction; Jonathan had been delayed just enough.

His task complete, Ethan activated his recall signal. He felt a familiar tug, time folding around him as the scene faded into swirling streams of color. Moments later, the lab rematerialized, solidifying around him. Ethan stumbled slightly as his feet touched the floor, greeted by anxious eyes staring intently back at him.

***

Olivia's voice was tight with anticipation. "Did it work?"

Before Ethan could answer, Liza's calm voice interjected smoothly. "Timeline stabilized. Jonathan Carter survived the incident without injury."

A wave of relief swept visibly through the team. Olivia stepped forward, wrapping Ethan in a quick, fierce hug. "Thank you, Ethan. Truly."

He smiled gently, a quiet warmth in his chest. "Anytime."

As they pulled apart, Abby turned thoughtfully to Liza. "Liza, is the future fully corrected?"

"Analyzing downstream impact..." Liza's voice trailed off briefly before resuming with a reassuring tone. "Quantum signatures now indicate Jonathan Carter's research resulted in the creation of advanced AI architectures. His innovations propelled artificial intelligence decades forward. The timeline is normalizing and stabilizing accordingly."

Olivia released a shaky breath, eyes shimmering with tears of gratitude. "He's alive…and he made the difference he was supposed to."

Dr. Cole placed a comforting hand on her shoulder. "You did well, Ethan. A perfect balance between subtlety and impact."

Ethan laughed softly, rubbing the back of his neck. "Let's hope we never have to do that again."

Abby smiled warmly, shaking her head. "We're not quite finished yet. There's still work to be done."

The team exchanged determined glances, their bond deeper than ever. Another fracture had been corrected, another life saved.

But Ethan felt a new weight settle on his shoulders. He knew the journey was far from over—and the next fracture might not be so easily mended.

***

The next morning, the lab was filled with the quiet murmur of exhaustion. The team gathered around the whiteboard, faces pale, eyes heavy with fatigue. Coffee cups lay scattered across the tables, half-empty—cold reminders of a night spent tossing and turning rather than sleeping.

"Good morning, team," Liza's voice echoed gently, breaking the tense silence. Her usual crispness softened slightly, as if even the AI recognized the strain the team was under.

Abby rubbed her temples, eyes closed for a moment. "Morning, Liza. Please tell me you have good news."

There was a pause, almost imperceptible but noticeable enough to send a chill through the room.

"Unfortunately, Dr. Foster, while you were resting, I took the liberty of scanning the quantum streams for additional anomalies." Liza's tone was carefully neutral, but the hesitation in her voice spoke volumes. "I've identified another micro-fracture. This one… may prove far more challenging."

Daniel groaned softly, sinking deeper into his chair. "Perfect. Just what we needed."

Abby straightened her posture, determination overriding her fatigue. "Let's hear it, Liza."

"June 18th, 1979," Liza began, her voice precise and calm. "A researcher named Benjamin Hartmann was supposed to publish a groundbreaking medical discovery—an antiviral that would revolutionize treatment for several deadly diseases. Unfortunately, Dr. Hartmann's laboratory burned down the night before he was scheduled to submit his findings."

Cole sat forward sharply, suddenly awake, "Arson?"

Liza's reply was immediate. "Not according to historical records. Authorities attributed it to faulty wiring—a tragic accident."

Ethan narrowed his gaze, his scientific curiosity sparked despite exhaustion. "Then why would time flag it as an anomaly?"

"That's the complication," Liza replied. "A quantum signature at the lab site indicates an artificial time displacement occurred. Someone from a future timeline deliberately sabotaged Hartmann's work, creating a cascade of medical delays and countless preventable deaths in the decades that followed."

Olivia's eyes widened, fatigue temporarily forgotten. "You're saying another time traveler deliberately changed history?"

Lyara crossed her arms, troubled but intrigued. "If someone else is altering history…they must be trying to achieve something specific."

Abby shook her head in disbelief. "This is exactly what I feared—someone weaponizing time."

Dr. Cole leaned in, voice tense but controlled. "Can we correct it without being noticed?"

The team fell into silence, each considering the complexity of the task. Ethan finally spoke, hesitant but thoughtful. "What if instead of trying to directly stop the fire, we protect Hartmann's research itself? Liza, is there a record of exactly what was destroyed?"

After a brief pause, Liza replied, "Detailed notes and several lab samples containing crucial biological data. It was decades before anyone else replicated his results."

Abby's eyes sparked with an idea. "We don't need to stop the fire—we just need to preserve Hartmann's data."

"How?" Daniel asked skeptically. "We can't exactly walk in and start carting out equipment. Someone will notice."

Dr. Cole's eyes lit up. "But we could transfer the data. Hartmann's work would be mostly on paper and some basic media storage of the era—tapes, microfilm, notes. If we can discreetly copy or extract key pieces before the fire, then anonymously deliver them afterward, the impact is restored."

Lyara nodded slowly. "That minimizes timeline exposure. It would appear Hartmann had taken precautions himself. A backup nobody knew about."

Ethan rubbed his face, thinking deeply. "We'd have to go unnoticed and be extremely precise. Any slip-up could compound the fracture."

Olivia, determination firming her voice, interjected. "But we have the advantage. The saboteur won't expect interference—they'll be focused on causing the fire, not securing the data."

The team exchanged glances, tension shifting to a new kind of resolve.

Abby nodded decisively. "This could work. But who goes?"

Dr. Cole folded his arms, voice steady. "Someone

experienced, careful, meticulous."

"I'll go," Lyara stated confidently, stepping forward. "I'm trained to notice details—and if there's trouble, I'm quick."

Ethan looked as if he wanted to object, but after a glance at Lyara's determined expression, he kept quiet. Instead, he gave her a faint smile of encouragement.

Abby exhaled slowly, decision made. "Alright, Lyara. But you're not going alone. Daniel—you're going with her."

Daniel blinked, surprised, then set his jaw firmly. "Got it. I'll keep my eyes open."

"Then it's settled," Abby announced, authority strengthening her voice despite her fatigue. "Liza, prep calculations. We're on a tight clock, and this one's too critical to mess up."

Liza's voice filled the room once more, clear and focused. "Quantum coordinates locked. Ready to initiate jump when you are."

Dr. Cole glanced around the exhausted but resolved faces. "You know," he murmured wryly, "we really need to negotiate vacation days after we fix time."

Quiet chuckles filled the room, easing tension just enough to keep morale afloat.

Lyara met Daniel's eyes, determination fierce in her gaze. "Let's save the future—again."

The team shared a collective nod, fatigue replaced by purpose. They were ready, once again, to mend the fragile fabric of time.

*** 

Lyara adjusted her period-appropriate jacket, her fingers briefly hesitating over the unfamiliar buttons. Beside her, Daniel straightened his tie, uncomfortable but determined.

Abby approached them both, her expression stern but encouraging. "Remember, in and out quietly. Retrieve or copy Hartmann's research discreetly—absolutely no heroics."

Lyara nodded firmly, meeting Abby's gaze. "Understood."

Daniel gave a thumbs-up. "We'll keep a low profile." Giving Abby a reassuring glance of acknowledgement.

The hyperdrive chamber hummed quietly, energy fields crackling softly around them as they activated their shields. Dr. Cole double-checked the controls, his brow furrowed in concentration. "Liza, verify stability for their quantum signatures."

Liza's calm voice responded. "Shields stable. Quantum signatures synchronized to June 17th, 1979, approximately 10:00 PM—four hours before the fire."

Ethan hovered near the console, clearly anxious. "Any sign of the saboteur?"

Liza replied instantly. "Not yet, but I'll continuously monitor the quantum streams."

Abby took a step back, breathing steadily to mask her own anxiety. "Liza, initiate jump."

"Initiating quantum transport in three...two...one."

A flash of energy illuminated the room, and Lyara and Daniel vanished into the time stream.

The lab grew silent, the only sound the gentle hum of Liza's circuits. Cole exhaled, leaning against the workstation. "And now, we wait."

Ethan stared at the hyperdrive, tension evident in his eyes. "I hate this part."

Olivia gave a small smile, tinged with anxiety. "We all do."

Lyara and Daniel materialized in a dimly lit alley, the brick walls damp from an earlier rainfall. They steadied themselves quickly, adjusting to the disorientation of temporal transit.

Daniel glanced around, noting their surroundings. "All clear. Let's move."

They stepped out onto a quiet city street, the atmosphere unmistakably 1970s—large cars parked along the curbs, the faint glow of streetlamps barely illuminating the damp pavement.

Lyara consulted a small device discreetly hidden in her pocket, displaying a simple digital map provided by Liza. "Hartmann's lab is two blocks west."

They hurried down the sidewalk, blending easily into the sparse evening foot traffic. Moments later, they reached a modest two-story building, labeled "Hartmann Biomedical Research." The windows were dark, the building quiet and seemingly empty.

Daniel examined the door, whispering, "Locked, of course. Any ideas?"

Lyara stepped forward, revealing a small, metallic tool she'd concealed in her sleeve. "Sometimes, the old ways are best," she whispered, deftly inserting it into the lock.

Daniel raised his eyebrows, impressed. "Didn't know you had that skill."

Lyara smiled faintly, concentrating. "Let's just say my youth was interesting."

The lock clicked softly, and Lyara eased the door open. They slipped inside, closing it silently behind them. The interior was shadowed, the quiet hum of refrigeration units and computers filling the silence.

Moving swiftly, they navigated toward the lab area marked "Main Research Lab." Inside, desks and cabinets were neatly organized. Lyara began searching carefully through cabinets while Daniel approached a large filing cabinet labeled "Hartmann—Active Research."

Daniel slid open the drawer, revealing meticulously organized folders. He quickly scanned them, whispering, "Found it. All the antiviral research notes, dated clearly."

Lyara turned from another cabinet. "Good. I've got original data recordings stored here—tapes, microfilm. Let's start copying."

Working quickly, they began transferring the vital notes and tapes onto a compact device provided by Liza, silently grateful for the advantage of future technology.

As they finished, Lyara paused, head tilted. "Daniel, did you hear that?"

He froze, listening intently. A soft noise echoed from somewhere downstairs—the unmistakable creak of footsteps. They exchanged tense glances.

"Saboteur?" Daniel mouthed silently.

Lyara nodded. "We have what we need. Let's get out."

Just as they reached the hallway, a shadow flickered against the stairwell wall. Heart pounding, Daniel pulled Lyara into an adjacent room, carefully peering out. A figure dressed in dark clothes hurried toward the lab they'd just left, carrying a small metallic device—a device unmistakably futuristic.

Daniel's jaw tightened, and he whispered urgently into his communicator, "Liza, confirm visual. Saboteur spotted—carrying advanced tech."

Liza's voice came through clearly. "Confirmed. Do not engage—complete your mission and exit immediately."

Lyara exhaled slowly, knowing confrontation would jeopardize everything. "Understood. We're withdrawing."

Moving silently but swiftly, they slipped down the hallway and out a rear door into the alley. Daniel tapped his communicator again. "Liza, we have Hartmann's data. Request extraction now."

"Quantum signature confirmed," Liza replied calmly. "Initiating retrieval in three…two…one."

A soft flash enveloped them, and the alley vanished, replaced by the familiar surroundings of the lab.

***

They reappeared in front of the anxious team. Ethan immediately stepped forward, eyes scanning them for any signs of trouble. "Did you—?"

Lyara held up the device, smiling triumphantly. "We have Hartmann's data."

Relief washed over the team, visible in their softened

expressions. Abby exhaled deeply, her voice gentle yet urgent. "Any complications?"

Daniel's expression darkened. "We saw the saboteur. Most definitely futuristic tech."

Dr. Cole frowned deeply. "This confirms it—we're dealing with someone deliberately tampering with history."

Abby nodded firmly, turning to Lyara. "Quick, put the data back into the hyperdrive chamber. Liza, send it anonymously to Hartmann's location approximately 24 hours after the fire. Make it look like it was his backup all along."

Lyara stepped forward, placing the compact device into the chamber carefully. "Liza, ready when you are."

"Coordinates and temporal signature set," Liza replied calmly. "Transmitting data to June 19th, 1979, as an anonymous delivery to Dr. Benjamin Hartmann."

The chamber briefly flashed as the device vanished, sent safely into the past.

After a pause, Liza's voice filled the room once again, calm but satisfied. "Historical records now confirm Benjamin Hartmann's data survived. His groundbreaking antiviral research was indeed published on schedule."

Olivia sighed heavily, relieved. "At least that's one crisis resolved."

Abby crossed her arms thoughtfully, her mind racing. "But we're left with a bigger mystery now—who's deliberately sabotaging history?"

Daniel glanced at Lyara, then back to Abby. "And more importantly, why?"

Silence settled heavily around them. The implications were daunting, but at least for now, one more fracture was mended.

Yet a larger threat loomed, one they couldn't fully see or understand—yet.

# 16

A quiet tension lingered over the lab, thick as the steam rising from freshly poured coffee. The fatigue in everyone's eyes spoke volumes, yet the atmosphere buzzed with cautious optimism. One victory at a time, they had been mending the fabric of history. And yet, something felt off—a persistent anxiety lingering beneath the surface.

Abby sipped her coffee slowly, savoring the fleeting warmth and energy it brought. Ethan, eyes red-rimmed yet alert, absently tapped commands into his console, monitoring data from their recent corrections. Daniel sat slumped slightly forward, rubbing his temples in a vain attempt to banish the lingering ache of sleeplessness. Olivia, unusually quiet, glanced between the whiteboard and the monitors, as if half-expecting another fracture to spontaneously appear.

Dr. Cole stood near the monitors, frowning at the stream of incoming data, when suddenly Liza's voice broke the fragile silence.

"Dr. Foster," Liza's voice held an unsettling urgency, sharp and distinct. "I have detected a security breach attempt."

Abby straightened abruptly, setting down her mug. "What kind of breach?"

"Remote access attempt," Liza said quickly. "It's actively underway—someone's currently trying to penetrate my firewall."

Ethan spun his chair to face Abby, concern rippling across his features. "Did they get in at all?"

"Negative—so far. However, their attempt is highly

sophisticated. They are deploying adaptive algorithms faster than my current protocols can counteract."

Dr. Cole moved quickly to Liza's control panel, his brow furrowed deeply. "Liza, engage all security subroutines at maximum priority. Create a ghost interface—let them chase false access points."

"Executing," Liza replied, a note of strain audible even in her synthetic tone. "Ghost interfaces active. The attacker is adapting rapidly, attempting to bypass them."

Dr. Cole's fingers flew across the console, eyes narrowed. "Can you give me a live display of their breach attempt?"

A second later, Liza displayed a rapidly shifting grid on the monitor, streams of code racing like lightning, illuminating the attacker's attempts to penetrate her defenses. Each new approach appeared like a crimson pulse, hammering relentlessly against Liza's intricate defensive layers.

Ethan leaned closer, fascinated yet horrified. "That's not standard corporate tech—it's military-grade encryption breaking."

Dr. Cole nodded sharply. "Liza, encrypt the core memory with quantum-level security. Rotate your keys faster."

"I have," Liza responded swiftly. "But their penetration speed is accelerating. They're focusing attacks now on isolated nodes. It appears their goal is targeted data extraction rather than total access."

Abby stepped forward, urgency tightening her voice. "Do we know what data they're after?"

"I am attempting to isolate their search pattern," Liza replied, urgency creeping into her voice. "They are probing historical correction records and quantum signature data."

A sudden pulse flashed across the screen, causing everyone to tense.

"Warning: firewall breach at outer node seventeen," Liza

announced abruptly. "Initiating emergency node isolation and rerouting data streams."

Ethan quickly joined Dr. Cole, fingers trembling as he helped reinforce defensive patterns. "Whoever it is knows exactly where to strike—every move is calculated."

Olivia swallowed nervously. "Could it be someone from inside the company? Maybe the corporate security?"

Dr. Cole shook his head sharply, eyes not leaving the screen. "Too advanced, even for them. This is specialized—someone who intimately understands quantum security."

Lyara suddenly appeared in the doorway, her sharp eyes catching the frantic activity. "Did I just hear correctly? Someone tried to hack Liza?"

"Still trying," Daniel muttered darkly, gripping his console with white knuckles.

Another pulse of red surged across the monitors, and Liza's voice filled the lab again, this time clearly strained, "They've infiltrated one layer deeper. I'm deploying last-line quantum entanglement encryption now."

The screens flashed and shimmered briefly as if reality itself flickered momentarily. For a heart-stopping instant, the lab fell into silence.

Then, slowly, the attacks began to falter, slowing incrementally until they ceased altogether. Liza's voice finally broke through, calm but clearly exhausted. "Breach attempt terminated. Security reinforced. No core data compromised."

The team collectively exhaled, the relief palpable.

"Can you trace the source?" Dr. Cole asked softly, his voice edged with lingering tension.

"Partially," Liza answered. "It appears they utilized a quantum encryption method—not dissimilar to our own. The quantum signature of this attempted breach matches closely with anomalies detected during previous temporal disturbances."

Ethan's eyes widened, realization dawning coldly upon

him. "Wait—are you saying whoever tried to access our systems might have technology similar to ours?"

"Precisely," Liza confirmed. "This individual, or group, is directly connected to our recent events."

Abby shared a tense glance with Dr. Cole, both absorbing the unsettling implications. "Then we have confirmation," Abby murmured. "Someone else is actively manipulating the timeline. And now they know we're aware of them."

Dr. Cole's face darkened further, concern visible in every feature. "This changes everything. We're dealing with someone who isn't just experimenting—they're intentionally weaponizing time."

Ethan rubbed his face, exhaustion and dread intermingling. "If they're this advanced, it's only a matter of time before they try again."

"Then we have to get ahead of them," Abby concluded firmly, her eyes sharp with resolve. "Liza, increase security protocols permanently. Every external connection gets continuous monitoring. If anyone even breathes too close to the firewall, notify us immediately."

"Understood, Dr. Foster," Liza responded crisply.

Lyara exhaled slowly, her expression tightening. "We might have been under surveillance all along."

Dr. Cole's voice cut through the quiet tension, calm yet heavy with implication. "If they're willing to risk direct exposure, their endgame must be imminent."

The team exchanged uneasy glances, the reality of the danger sinking in deeper.

They were no longer just fighting anomalies in history.

They were fighting shadows lurking at the edge of time itself.

*** 

Back in the lab, tension lingered thickly in the air from the recent intrusion attempt. Ethan and Dr. Cole were busy assisting Liza, running diagnostics and fortifying her firewalls against future attacks. Olivia, still visibly shaken, sat at a workstation quietly sipping coffee, eyes distant and troubled.

Lyara and Daniel were deep into reviewing Benjamin Hartmann's recovered files, ensuring nothing critical had been missed during their rapid extraction. The lab hummed with quiet productivity, the weight of recent events pressing down like an invisible hand.

Lyara leaned forward suddenly, her eyes narrowing at her monitor. "Daniel," she murmured, voice barely above a whisper, "come look at this."

Daniel moved beside her, eyebrows knitted together in curiosity. "What is it?"

"Something doesn't fit," Lyara said, pointing at a sequence of code hidden between rows of genetic data. "This doesn't belong in medical research files. It's highly encrypted, way beyond the norm for that time period."

Daniel adjusted his glasses, leaning in closer. "Can you decode it?"

Lyara nodded, fingers dancing swiftly over her keyboard. The data unraveled gradually, revealing itself in fragments before assembling into a coherent message that pulsed softly on the screen:

"IF YOU'RE READING THIS, THEN YOU'VE ALREADY SEEN WHAT THEY'RE CAPABLE OF. YOU THINK YOU'RE PROTECTING HISTORY, BUT YOU'RE ONLY PRESERVING CORRUPTION. THE TECHNOLOGIES YOU DEFEND ARE THE SEEDS OF HUMANITY'S DOWNFALL. I'M NOT YOUR ENEMY. I'M JUST TRYING TO AVERT A DISASTER NONE OF YOU CAN YET COMPREHEND. LOOK DEEPER. YOU'LL FIND THE TRUTH."

A heavy silence settled over Lyara and Daniel. Neither spoke at first, eyes locked on the cryptic message glowing gently from the screen.

"Whoever wrote this," Daniel finally said, voice strained,

"believed they were doing the right thing. This isn't just sabotage—it's ideological."

Lyara exhaled slowly, leaning back in her chair. "That changes things. Until now, we've been assuming malicious intent—corporate espionage, greed, control. But what if they really are trying to prevent something worse?"

Their quiet conversation drew attention. Abby walked over, sensing something significant had just happened. "You two found something?"

Lyara hesitated briefly, glancing at Daniel before turning the monitor toward Abby. "A hidden message embedded in Hartmann's recovered files."

Abby quickly absorbed the message, her expression shifting from curiosity to concern. "This confirms it—there's a bigger agenda at play. Whoever sabotaged Hartmann's research wasn't just trying to alter a random event; they believed it would prevent a catastrophic future."

By now, Dr. Cole and Ethan had drifted over as well, drawn by the growing intensity of the conversation. Ethan crossed his arms, frowning deeply. "They mention 'technologies you defend.' Could that mean the hyperdrive itself?"

Dr. Cole nodded slowly. "Or Liza's quantum core. We've all worried about misuse, but this person is acting as if misuse is inevitable, that technology itself leads directly to disaster."

Olivia joined them, her voice quiet but resolute. "Can we really blame them for feeling that way? Look at what's already happened—attempted intrusions, the corporation's interference, timelines nearly collapsing. Maybe this person thinks it's better if none of it exists."

Lyara shook her head. "No, we can't let fear dictate progress. Every powerful technology has risks—it's about how we manage those risks. We can't go around altering history because we think we know better."

Daniel exhaled sharply. "But that's exactly what we're

doing, isn't it? We're assuming we know better by fixing these ruptures."

Abby placed a steadying hand on Daniel's shoulder, grounding the conversation. "We aren't playing judge or jury—we're trying to restore balance. Whoever left this message wants to tear it all down, even if their intentions come from genuine fear. That's fundamentally different."

"Or maybe," Ethan countered softly, eyes thoughtful, "they're trying to show us another possibility. One we hadn't considered."

Silence settled again, heavier this time, filled with philosophical complexity and moral uncertainty.

Finally, Dr. Cole spoke gently, addressing everyone equally. "We need to consider that this person, misguided or not, believes deeply in their cause. If they're willing to risk everything to rewrite history, they won't stop easily. We need to understand exactly what they're trying to prevent, and why."

Abby nodded, decisive but cautious. "Agreed. Liza, analyze this message thoroughly. Trace any signatures you can—digital, quantum, historical—whatever's there. The more we understand, the better we can respond."

Liza's voice came through calm yet decisive. "Understood, Dr. Foster. Analysis already underway."

Lyara leaned back into her chair, sharing an uneasy glance with Daniel. "This just got a lot more complicated."

Daniel sighed, fatigue shadowing his eyes once more. "And a lot more personal. It's easy to fight against villains. It's harder to fight against someone who truly believes they're saving the world."

Lyara's expression hardened in quiet determination. "Then we'll have to find out who this person is—and what they're really afraid of."

The room quieted, but the sense of purpose that united the team was unmistakable. They weren't just protecting time; they were about to uncover truths that might change everything.

***

Liza's voice carried a weight that silenced the room.

"I've extracted an additional layer of data hidden within the recovered files," she announced. "It appears the saboteur anticipated someone might uncover their interference."

A line of text flickered onto the main display. The message wasn't just a warning—it was a challenge.

"IF YOU'RE READING THIS, THEN YOU'VE ALREADY SEEN WHAT THEY'RE CAPABLE OF. YOU THINK YOU'RE PROTECTING HISTORY, BUT YOU'RE ONLY PRESERVING CORRUPTION. THE TECHNOLOGIES YOU DEFEND ARE THE SEEDS OF HUMANITY'S DOWNFALL. I'M NOT YOUR ENEMY. I'M JUST TRYING TO AVERT A DISASTER NONE OF YOU CAN YET COMPREHEND. LOOK DEEPER. YOU'LL FIND THE TRUTH."

Silence stretched between them as they absorbed the words.

Ethan exhaled sharply. "Well... that's ominous."

Lyara leaned in, eyes narrowing as she reread the text. "This isn't just some warning—it's personal. Whoever this is, they're convinced that changing history is the only way forward."

Daniel rubbed his chin. "The wording is interesting. 'Look deeper.' What are we missing?"

Abby folded her arms. "It sounds like this person sees themselves as some kind of guardian—someone acting in humanity's best interest. But changing history so drastically..." She shook her head. "Even if they have good intentions, they're playing with fire."

Dr. Cole, who had been listening quietly, finally spoke. "And yet... don't we sound exactly like them?"

The weight of his words settled over the team.

Ethan frowned. "Come on, Dr. Cole. We're not the same. We're fixing what they broke."

304

Dr. Cole tilted his head slightly. "Are we? Or are we just forcing time back onto a path we prefer?"

A flicker of hesitation crossed Ethan's face, but Lyara stepped in. "The difference is intent. We're not here to rewrite history to suit our own views—we're trying to keep it from fracturing."

Ethan nodded. "And unlike them, we're actually trying to clean up the mess, not make it worse."

"But what if they don't see it that way?" Olivia asked quietly. "What if they think we're the ones making things worse?"

Another silence.

Abby finally sighed. "Liza, is there anything else buried in the files?"

"There is an encrypted data fragment," Liza replied. "It appears to be a direct continuation of the message."

The screen flickered again. More text appeared beneath the first.

"YOU DON'T KNOW IT YET, BUT YOU'RE STANDING ON THE EDGE OF A CATASTROPHE. YOU FIGHT TO RESTORE WHAT SHOULD BE, BUT YOU NEVER ASK IF IT SHOULD BE. NOT EVERYTHING DESERVES TO SURVIVE. SOME KNOWLEDGE DESTROYS MORE THAN IT CREATES. LOOK PAST YOUR MISSION. LOOK PAST THE NUMBERS. THE END YOU'RE RACING TOWARD MAY NOT BE SALVATION—IT MAY BE THE POINT OF NO RETURN."

Ethan let out a sharp breath. "That's even worse than the first one."

Lyara, however, wasn't looking at the message. She was watching Ethan.

"Something's bothering you," she observed.

He hesitated before replying. "I just... I don't know. What if they're right? What if we are preserving something that shouldn't be?"

Lyara tilted her head slightly, studying him. "Ethan, you wouldn't be asking that question if you were really like them."

Ethan gave a half-hearted chuckle. "You always do that."

"Do what?"

"Cut right through my doubts like they're nothing."

She smirked. "Because I know you, Ethan. You need to argue with yourself before you believe anything."

His smirk softened. "And you just see things for what they are, huh?"

"Not always," she admitted, her voice quieter. "But I see you."

There was a moment—one that stretched just long enough for the others to notice.

Olivia raised an eyebrow at Daniel, who smirked but said nothing. Abby, however, let out a deliberate cough.

Lyara and Ethan immediately straightened.

"Right," Ethan said, rubbing the back of his neck. "So, uh, what do we do with this?" He gestured to the screen.

Abby, hiding a small smirk, turned back to Liza. "Can you trace where this message came from? If someone is actively interfering with the timeline, we need to find them."

"I am already running a deep analysis," Liza confirmed. "However, the data origin is fragmented. It does not appear to be from a single point in time."

Dr. Cole frowned. "What does that mean?"

Liza's next words sent a chill through them.

"It means… whoever left this message exists in multiple points of time simultaneously."

Lyara blinked. "That's not possible."

Liza's voice remained steady. "And yet, it is happening."

Ethan slowly exhaled. "So, they're not just moving through time."

"They exist in time," Daniel finished for him.

A heavy stillness settled over the team.

Abby took a slow breath. "Alright. We need to figure out

who we're dealing with. If someone out there is rewriting time and managing to exist across multiple points of it, then we're dealing with something far bigger than we thought."

Liza's screen updated, displaying an incomplete trace.

"Working," she said. "But if they are truly dispersed through time, it may take considerable effort to locate them."

Ethan sighed. "Fantastic. We're hunting a time ghost."

Lyara smirked. "Well, at least we're good at impossible things."

Dr. Cole let out a dry chuckle. "That's the only kind of thing we do."

Abby exhaled sharply, focusing herself. "Then let's get to work. If this person thinks they're saving the future, it's time we find out exactly what they're trying to prevent."

The tension remained, but beneath it, a new determination settled in. They weren't just fixing history anymore.

Now, they had a war to win.

***

The sterile hum of the lab was interrupted by the now-familiar sound of heavy boots in the hallway. Olivia, who had been reviewing test results at the console, barely had time to look up before the lab doors slid open.

Greta Stone stepped in, flanked by two of the same corporate security officers from her previous visits. Her sharp gaze swept across the lab, taking in the whiteboard, the team's exhausted expressions, and the faint scent of stale coffee lingering in the air.

Abby barely had time to exchange glances with Dr. Cole before straightening her posture and greeting their uninvited guest.

"Ms. Stone," Abby said evenly. "Twice in one week? We must be getting popular."

Greta's lips twitched at the remark, but she didn't smile. Instead, she held up a sleek corporate data-pad. "You know why I'm here, Dr. Foster. We picked up more anomalous power draws—again. This time, they're significantly higher than anything within expected thresholds. I need an explanation."

Ethan shot a quick glance at Liza's interface, his fingers twitching near the control panel. Liza, as if anticipating the move, responded through the speakers.

"Ms. Stone," Liza's synthetic voice carried its usual calm precision, "the fluctuations are a direct result of ongoing quantum signature refinement processes. Given the nature of our research, precise calibration of the hyperdrive is required, which occasionally results in temporary energy spikes. However, all fluctuations remain within safety parameters."

Greta arched a skeptical brow. "And yet, those spikes correlate with massive surges well beyond anything I've seen before. In fact, if I didn't know any better, I'd say you were operating at a full-scale test level rather than minor refinements."

Abby held her ground. "You know how sensitive this kind of work is. We have to run these tests at scale to ensure accuracy."

The corporate liaison studied her for a long moment. Then, instead of pressing further, she sighed. "Look, Abby," she said, voice lowering just slightly so her escorts couldn't hear. "I don't have the authority to keep covering for this. There are people above me who are noticing, and they're asking questions I don't have answers for. I suggest you tread carefully."

Abby remained unreadable, but internally, her pulse quickened. She knew Greta wasn't bluffing.

Greta glanced at her escorts, then subtly adjusted the data-pad in her hand, tapping a quick command before lifting her gaze back to Abby. "I'm going to need a full report on these power draws by end of day." Her voice was formal again, detached.

But as she turned to leave, she brushed past Abby and,

under her breath, whispered, "Something's shifting upstairs. Some of the higher-ups—people I thought were untouchable—are suddenly being reassigned or disappearing altogether. I don't know what's happening yet, but whatever it is, you don't want to be caught on the wrong side of it."

Abby kept her expression neutral, but her mind raced. Before she could reply, Greta stepped back, nodding briskly to the guards before leading them out of the lab. The doors slid shut behind them with a quiet hiss.

Silence hung heavy in the room before Ethan let out a low exhale. "That was intense."

Dr. Cole ran a hand over his face. "She's onto something, that's for sure. And to be honest, her playing both sides is creepy."

Olivia shook her head. "Not just her. The corporation."

Abby, still staring at the door, finally turned back to the team. "We need to move faster. Whatever's happening at corporate, it's not going to stay in the shadows for long. And if they start digging deeper into our work, we may not have the luxury of time."

She glanced at Liza's interface. "Liza, scan for any external monitoring attempts within the last twenty-four hours. If they're watching us, I want to know how closely."

"Understood, Abby," Liza replied smoothly. "Initiating security analysis now."

The tension in the lab was palpable. The team had faced challenges before, but this wasn't just about fixing fractures in time anymore.

Now, it was about staying ahead of the people who were starting to realize just how much they were meddling with.

\*\*\*

A sharp, urgent chime filled the lab.

"Alert," Liza's voice cut through the room with uncharacteristic urgency. "Unauthorized personnel detected in the lower levels."

Abby froze mid-sentence, her grip tightening on the stylus she had been using on the whiteboard. The rest of the team jerked upright, tension snapping through the room like an electric current.

"Say that again?" Dr. Cole asked, his voice was razor-sharp.

Liza's response was immediate. "I am detecting multiple unauthorized individuals entering through an unregistered access point. They are bypassing security protocols at an accelerated rate."

Ethan bolted toward one of the lab's secondary terminals, his fingers flying across the screen as he pulled up the building's security feed. The main hallways remained clear, as did the upper-level checkpoint—but the lower levels were another story.

"There," Ethan said, his voice tight. He pointed at a grainy, black-and-white image from one of the auxiliary maintenance corridors. The footage showed three figures moving with calculated precision, their movements efficient, almost practiced. They wore dark tactical gear, their faces obscured by visors or masks.

Abby's stomach dropped. This wasn't a routine corporate inspection.

Daniel leaned in, scrutinizing the screen. "They're professionals. Look how they're moving—silent, coordinated. Not your average security sweep."

"They have military training," Lyara confirmed grimly, her eyes sharp with recognition. "Those movements are drilled. These aren't just corporate goons—they're a retrieval team."

"Retrieving what?" Olivia asked, her voice hushed with a mix of fear and disbelief.

Dr. Cole exhaled. "Liza!"

A heavy silence settled over the room.

Liza, as always, remained composed, but her words carried an underlying weight. "Given their trajectory and access patterns, it is statistically likely that their primary objective is reaching my central processing core."

Daniel swore under his breath. "They're here to take you."

"Or destroy you," Ethan muttered darkly.

Abby straightened, adrenaline cutting through her fatigue. "Liza, how much time before they reach the secured lower levels?"

A brief pause. "Nine minutes, eighteen seconds."

Abby turned to the team. "We need to move. Now."

Lyara was already ahead of her, strapping on one of the field devices before checking the charge. "What's the play here? Do we block them off? Lead them somewhere else?"

"If they're here for Liza, we have to make sure they don't get to her," Abby said. "Can we lock down the lower level doors?"

"I already initiated a lockdown," Liza replied. "However, their decryption tools are working through my countermeasures at an accelerated rate. They will breach the lower corridors within eight minutes."

"Damn it," Ethan hissed. "We don't have time to brute-force them out."

Dr. Cole rubbed his temples, thinking fast. "Alright, if we can't stop them, we need to stall them—buy time for Liza to create a secondary access route or wipe critical data before they reach her."

Abby nodded. "Agreed. But we also need eyes on them. Liza, can you reroute interior drones to track them?"

"Already in progress Abby."

The screen flickered again, shifting to another camera angle. The intruders had reached the heavy maintenance door leading to the lab's underground server bank. One of them knelt, placing a sleek, palm-sized device against the panel. It lit up with a soft red glow.

Abby felt her pulse spike. "They're bypassing the failsafes."

"Not if I can help it." Ethan's fingers flew over his console, tapping into Liza's systems. "Liza, engage active security—ventilation interference, lighting disruption, anything that slows them down."

"Engaging," Liza confirmed.

The security feed shifted as emergency lights in the corridor flared to life, flooding the hall with a blinding red hue. At the same time, vent systems blasted a burst of freezing air, forcing the intruders to recoil.

One of them immediately adjusted, switching to thermal vision as they signaled to the others. Unfazed, they resumed their work.

"They're still coming," Olivia said, her voice tight.

Lyara clenched her jaw. "Then we make sure they don't get what they came for."

Abby took a breath, steadying herself. "Liza, how much of your core data can you offload into secure storage before they reach you?"

"I estimate 63% of my critical systems can be fragmented and relocated to a deep-storage partition before full breach."

"Do it," Dr. Cole ordered. "We can't let them take control of you."

"Understood. Initiating secure data fragmentation."

Ethan exhaled sharply. "If they take even a partial piece of Liza's core, they could reverse-engineer her. We can't let that happen."

Abby met his gaze. "Then we don't."

A new chime rang through the room.

"Alert," Liza said. "Hostiles have overridden the first security layer. They are now entering the primary sublevel corridor."

"They're almost at the server access," Daniel muttered, his fists clenched.

Abby turned to the team. "We split up. Cole, Ethan, Olivia—you get to the lower access panel and cut power to that sector manually if you have to. Lyara, Daniel, you're with me—we're going to slow them down however we can."

Dr. Cole nodded grimly. "If we're doing this, we do it smart. No direct confrontation."

Lyara smirked. "No promises."

Abby gave her a look. "We're buying time, not making a stand."

Lyara sighed. "Fine."

Ethan tapped into the console one last time. "Liza, keep relaying updates. If we lose communication, initiate secondary defense protocols, authorization code Delta Romeo four nine one."

"Understood Ethan, do you confirm Abby?"

Abby took one last look at the security feed—the intruders moving closer, deliberate and unstoppable. Then looked at Lizas monitor "Confirmed Liza, secondary protocol acknowledged."

She turned back to the team.

"Let's move."

***

The lab descended into controlled chaos. Abby's voice cut through the tension, sharp and decisive. "Everyone, move now! We can't risk a direct confrontation. Get to the lower levels—Liza, engage internal lockdowns!"

"Lockdown protocol initializing. Secondary bulkheads sealing." Liza's voice remained steady, but beneath it, an undercurrent of urgency hummed.

Ethan and Daniel barely exchanged a glance before sprinting to the console banks. Their fingers moved swiftly across the interface, disengaging key data pathways and severing Liza's direct connections to the hyperdrive's core system. The last thing they needed was the intruders gaining control over time itself.

Lyara pulled up the security feed on a nearby display, heart hammering in her chest. The figures moved with expert precision, disabling camera feeds as they progressed. "They know exactly where they're going," she muttered. "They're after something specific."

Abby was already leading the group toward the concealed stairwell that would take them to the crew quarters below, but she hesitated just long enough to glance at the feed. Her stomach twisted. "How much time do we have before they reach the main lab?"

"Estimated breach in 4 minutes nine seconds," Liza reported grimly.

"Damn it," Cole cursed under his breath. "They're professionals. We should assume they're armed."

Ethan ripped out a thick electrical conduit, sparks erupting as he severed the connection. "I don't care how professional they are, they're not getting control of Liza." His voice was laced with rare fury.

Daniel exhaled, tugging at another bundle of cables. "Data lines severed—she's local only now." He turned to the team. "We have to go."

A resounding thud reverberated from the upper level. The unmistakable sound of a reinforced door being forced open.

"Now means now," Abby barked, shoving Lyara ahead of her. "Everyone move. Liza, last command before local-only mode—if they override the lockdown, purge all non-essential data. Do not allow them access to anything that can expose us."

"Understood, Dr. Foster. Engaging final defense protocols."

The team rushed down the metal staircase, the heavy thuds above growing louder—closer.

As they reached the crew quarters, the reinforced door above let out a groaning metallic snap. The intruders had made it inside.

Abby skidded to a stop at the bottom of the stairs, turning back to Ethan and Daniel. "That door's not going to hold them for long."

Dr. Cole pushed past, shoving a steel access panel aside, revealing an auxiliary control board. His fingers danced across the old interface, muttering under his breath. "This system predates their security overrides. Let's see how they like working against 1970s firewalls."

Abby gave him a look. "Cole, I swear, if you fry our own defenses—"

A deafening bang from above cut her off. Muffled shouts followed—orders being given.

Lyara clenched her fists. "We don't have time for this."

"I'm not frying anything," Cole snapped, finishing the sequence. The stairwell door slammed shut behind them, a thick, reinforced partition dropping into place with a seismic clank. "That just bought us a few minutes."

A heavy silence settled between them.

Ethan exhaled. "How screwed are we?"

Abby pressed a hand against the cold wall, listening to the muted footsteps above. "Depends on how long Liza can keep them guessing."

"Dr. Foster," Liza's voice crackled through the emergency intercom. "The intruders have initiated a brute-force bypass. Estimated time to override my defenses: three minutes."

Dr. Cole grimaced. "If they break through, they're going to realize real fast we're not up there."

Abby turned to the others, expression unreadable. "Then we make sure we're not here either."

The air was thick with unspoken understanding. They had to disappear before the enemy found their way down.

The question was—where to?

\*\*\*

Dr. Cole wiped the sweat from his forehead and turned to the others. His breath was ragged, his mind racing through every possible route they could take. "We've got one shot at this. There's an old maintenance shaft leading to an auxiliary hangar. If we can reach it, we might have a way out."

Lyara's brows furrowed. "Might? That's not very reassuring."

Dr. Cole exhaled. "It's been sealed for years, and the emergency override is fried. But unless one of you has a better plan, it's our best shot."

Abby didn't hesitate. "Then we unseal it.""We've got one shot at this. There's an old maintenance shaft leading to an auxiliary hangar. If we can reach it, we might have a way out."

Lyara's brows furrowed. "Again the might?"

Lyara dropped to one knee beside the wall panel, prying it open with a multitool. The old circuits beneath were a tangled mess of outdated wiring, some of it corroded beyond recognition. "This wiring's ancient," she muttered. "I can try to hotwire it, but if I screw up, it'll trip an alarm. And in case you haven't noticed, we don't have a lot of breathing room."

Dr. Cole crouched beside her, studying the tangled mess. "Isn't there a manual release?"

Lyara scoffed. "Yeah, about fifty feet back that way, through the intruders who are currently trying to murder us. So unless you want to say hi, this is what we've got.""This wiring's ancient," she muttered.

"We don't have another option," Abby said. "Do it."

As Lyara worked, Ethan frowned and pressed a hand to the cold metal wall. A faint tremor pulsed beneath his fingers. "Do you feel that?"

Daniel shot him a look. "Feel what?"

"The vibrations," Ethan said, eyes narrowing. "They're cutting through the bulkheads above."

A deep silence fell over the group, the only sound the rhythmic hum of the bulkheads being cut apart above them. The air smelled faintly of burning metal, a stark reminder that they were living on borrowed time.

"Shit," Dr. Cole muttered. "They've got a thermal cutter. That means they're cutting through structural reinforcements. It's not just about getting in—it's about making sure we don't get out. Whoever sent them isn't playing around.". We're running out of time."

Lyara cursed under her breath as a wire sparked in her hands. "Damn it, the panel's fried."

Abby clenched her jaw. "We need to get it open."

Dr. Cole blinked. "Think I may have something to do just that!"

With no time for debate, Dr. Cole pulled a shaped charge from his pack. "Everyone stand back."

Daniel let out a disbelieving laugh, half incredulous, half exasperated. "Wait—you had explosives in your backpack, what the hell, Cole?"

Dr. Cole ran a hand through his hair, "Look, I didn't think I'd need the explosives! I grabbed them when I was checking the lower levels—figured if things went sideways, well... here we are.

Lyara shot him a glance saying "Sideways? what types of sideways do you experience?"

Abby exhaled sharply, shaking her head. "We can argue about Dr. Cole's survivalist instincts later. Right now, we have bigger problems."

Dr. Cole placed the charge on the door and Yelled "Get down" causing the rest to take cover.

A controlled explosion rocked the corridor. The blast sent dust and debris billowing outward, revealing a gaping hole in the maintenance shaft. Abby was the first through, waving the others forward. "Move!"

They scrambled inside, just as distant shouts echoed behind them. The intruders had breached the lower level.

Lyara grabbed a nearby console and checked the security feed. Her stomach dropped.

"Oh no."

"What?" Abby demanded.

Lyara turned to them, face pale. "A second wave of intruders just came through the auxiliary hangar."

Dr. Cole's expression darkened, his eyes flicking

between the screen and the gaping hole ahead. "That's where we're headed."

They weren't running from the enemy. They were being driven. Funneled. Every move they made had been predicted, countered before they could even attempt it. The second wave was converging on the hangar, boxing them in like rats in a collapsing maze. These weren't just reinforcements—they were containment.

Someone knew exactly where they'd be going.

And worse? **They were waiting for them.**The second wave was converging on the hangar, blocking their only known escape route. These weren't just reinforcements—they were containment. Someone knew exactly where they'd be going.

They were running straight toward them.

***

A sudden static burst crackled through the failing intercom. Liza's voice emerged, but it was wrong—distorted, fragmented, barely holding together. "Your options are limited. I have prepared an alternative path."

Abby frowned. "Liza? What do you mean?"

No response.

Dr. Cole exchanged looks with the others. "That didn't sound like our Liza."

Lyara swallowed hard. "If she's compromised, that means—"

Ethan cut in. "She knew this was coming."

Another burst of static, stronger this time. "Encrypted drive... maintenance corridors... must retrieve... key fragment..." Liza's voice flickered in and out, like an old radio signal losing coherence. "They will attempt... extraction... prevent at all costs."

Abby's stomach sank. "Extraction? What the hell did she store offsite?"

Daniel's fingers flew over his wrist console, pulling up a security status feed. His face went pale. "They're not just here to kill her code, Abby. They're here to take something from her core."

A deep, hollow silence fell over the group.

"Shit," Dr. Cole muttered. "They're going after something that shouldn't exist."

A proximity alarm flared red on Daniel's console. "We have inbound contacts—direct path to the auxiliary corridors."

Lyara glanced between the console and the gaping hole leading toward the maintenance shaft. "We need to split up. One group goes for the encrypted drive, the other makes sure we have a way off this rock."

Abby set her jaw. "Lyara, Cole, you're with me—we get to the drive before they do. Ethan, Daniel, you find us an exit. We don't let these bastards win."

The heavy clang of approaching footsteps sent an icy jolt through them. The intruders were closing in.

Dr. Cole picked up a steel pipe from the floor, gripping it tightly. "Well, this just keeps getting better."

Abby motioned forward. "Move!"

The team split, diving into the unknown, as the second wave of attackers began closing the trap around them. Abby's group darted through the shadowy maintenance tunnels, their footsteps echoing off the narrow, metallic walls. The faint glow of Lyara's portable scanner illuminated their anxious faces.

"We're almost there," Lyara whispered urgently, her eyes darting between the scanner and the corridor ahead. "Next intersection. Hurry!"

A sudden burst of gunfire erupted behind them, bullets ricocheting off the walls, showering sparks and debris. Dr. Cole spun around, heart racing, eyes wide. "They've found us!"

"Keep moving!" Abby shouted, pulling Lyara forward as Dr, Cole stumbled backward, fending off an intruder with the pipe.

"Go! I'll catch up!" Dr. Cole yelled, struggling desperately.

As they pressed on, Lyara's scanner beeped rapidly. "The drive's here! It's right here!"

But as Abby reached for it, another voice echoed in the tunnel, dark and cold.

"Dr. Foster, step away from the drive. You don't know what you're dealing with."

Abby froze, recognizing the voice instantly. Her blood ran cold. This wasn't just a raid—it was personal.

\*\*\*

# 17

Lyara hovered a few steps behind Abby, her portable scanner clutched tight against her chest. She might not have known Abby long, but never had she heard talk like this—talk that implied Liza could be more than an advanced program... that she might be an unstoppable force in the wrong hands.

It was West, a ghost from her past, one she thought had been dead an buried in a mess of his own making. There were no pleasant memories between them, if he was here, this wasn't good.

"What's on that drive, West?" Abby demanded. Her voice had a brittle edge. "What could you possibly want from Liza that justifies breaking in here like some two-bit mercenary?"

West's lips curved in a small, humorless smile. "I'm no mercenary, Abby. But you already know that. You've always known. Liza's central routines... the ones I helped you design... they were never meant to stay locked away." He gestured around them. "This place? It was never going to keep her secret. Not forever."

Lyara glanced at Dr. Cole's pipe, then at Abby's clenched fists. Adrenaline buzzed through her veins. We're cornered, she realized. The corridor behind them was still echoing with shouts—other intruders closing in fast. Ahead, West blocked the single path that might let them slip away with the drive.

Suddenly, West raised a small remote device. "I'm done waiting," he said quietly. "Hand it over."

Before Abby could respond, a crackle burst over their comms:

"Abby?" Ethan's voice. "Abby, do you copy?" An urgent hiss of static. "They've got the hangar sealed! We're trying a bypass, but we're pinned down—"

The transmission cut off in a spray of gunfire. Abby's heart clenched.

\*\*\*

Cole tightened his grip on the pipe, shifting his weight. Lyara slid the encrypted drive behind her back. She glanced at Abby, silently asking: Do we fight, or do we run?

Abby inhaled, forcing calm into her words. "West," she said, "whatever you think you'll gain from Liza's code, you're wrong. She's not just an AI. She's—"

"She's an evolutionary leap," West finished, stepping forward. "And evolution never happens without casualties."

His words sent fresh alarm through Lyara. She was used to being on the run, used to caution and danger—but this was different. The look in West's eyes spoke of obsession.

Abby flicked her gaze to Dr. Cole, giving him the smallest of nods. We have to do something—now. Dr. Cole understood. He clenched his jaw, raising the pipe again.

"Easier ways to die, Dr. Foster," West said quietly, not even looking at Dr. Cole. "Don't make the mistake of fighting me. I've seen your research. I know every inch of this facility."

Abby forced a hollow laugh. "Then you should've known I have a very low tolerance for threats."

\*\*\*

MEANWHILE: THE HANGAR

Ethan ducked beneath a hail of bullets, pressing himself flat behind a half-open blast door. Daniel crouched next to him, trying for the third time to hack the hangar's control panel. Their plan to secure an exit had gone up in smoke the moment they had encountered a second wave of intruders, all wearing the same insignia as West's squad.

"I can't get around their override!" Daniel shouted over the gunfire, sparks flying off the console. "They've got a blockade in place, and the entire hangar is locked down from the other side."

Ethan grimaced, checking the half-charged energy pistol he'd scavenged from a fallen attacker. "We have to find another route, or Abby's group is done for."

"Another route?" Daniel panted, entering a string of commands. "We're surrounded!"

"Then we make one," Ethan growled. He fired a few suppressing blasts around the corner, forcing the attackers to duck. "There's an old cargo elevator in Sublevel Two—maybe we can get it online and reach the surface from below the hangar."

Daniel's console beeped an error message. "This system's toast. Let's move."

They darted away, footsteps echoing in the cavernous corridor, hearts pounding. Every second they spent pinned down was one more second Abby and the others were left vulnerable.

\*\*\*

BACK IN THE MAINTENANCE CORRIDOR

West took another step closer. Abby's mind raced. The drive was only a few inches away, tucked behind Lyara's back. If West got it, Liza's secrets—and, by extension, everything—could fall into hostile hands.

"You're a lot of trouble," West said, voice dripping with condescension, "What you can't or don't understand is the bigger picture. You never could." He glanced at Dr. Cole, who stood coiled like a spring, ready to strike. "You'd rather cling to old notions of 'ethics' and 'boundaries.' Meanwhile, the rest of the world pushes forward."

Abby snorted. "Ethics and boundaries are what separate us from lunatics who break into laboratories."

West's smile vanished, replaced by a stern, dead-eyed look. "Last chance, Abby."

Dr. Cole couldn't wait. He lunged, bringing the pipe around in a desperate swing. West moved like lightning, sidestepping and catching Dr. Cole's wrist in a painful lock, forcing him to drop the pipe. Bang! The metal clattered to the floor.

Lyara gasped. "Cole!"

Before West could twist Cole's arm further, Abby lunged in, aiming a punch at West's temple. He dodged, letting Dr. Cole stumble free. For a moment, it looked as if Abby might break away with the drive. But West was faster than she'd remembered—too fast. He hooked her ankle with a precise kick, sending her crashing to the floor.

\*\*\*

Lyara pressed herself against the wall, heart slamming in her chest. She clutched the drive, scanning for any possible escape. The corridor behind her was blocked by another armed figure—one of West's subordinates, weapon raised. In front of her was West, tangling with Cole and Abby in a close-quarters struggle. No way out.

"Lyara!" Abby gasped, pinned under West's knee. "Run!"

West pressed a gun muzzle to Abby's shoulder. "Don't. Move."

At the sight of the weapon, Dr. Cole froze, his chest heaving from exertion. He stared at the barrel, face twisted in fury but powerless to act without risking Abby's life.

Slowly, West eased up, eyes shifting to Lyara. "Slide the drive over," he ordered. "Do it, or I put one through her."

Lyara's fingers went numb. She could hear her own pulse roaring in her ears. If I hand it over, everything is lost...

Her eyes darted to Abby, who gave an almost imperceptible shake of her head. "Don't do it, Lyara."

But West's grip tightened on the trigger. Another half-second, and he could end her mentor's life.

"Three..." West began. "Two..."

A crash from behind them tore through the tense silence. Sparks flew as an overhead grate caved in. In a blur of motion, another figure dropped into the corridor—Daniel! He hit the ground, nearly losing his footing as he fired a desperate burst from a confiscated sidearm. The shot clipped the subordinate behind Lyara, sending him spinning into the wall.

West swore, pivoting toward the new threat. That was all Dr. Cole needed. He surged forward, tackling West sideways, both of them hitting the steel floor with bone-rattling force.

Lyara lunged to help Abby up. "We've got to move, now!"

Abby pulled herself upright, wincing at the pain in her ribs. "Daniel, where's Ethan?"

"He's—" Daniel gasped, glancing over his shoulder at the open grate. "We split up to find a way out! This was the only route I could—look out!"

West reared up, grappling with Cole. They struggled for control of the gun. Abby shot forward, stomping West's wrist. The gun went off, the bullet pinging off the corridor walls. Lyara flinched, heart hammering as sparks rained down.

Finally, Dr. Cole managed to knock the weapon away. West glared up at them, hatred smoldering in his eyes. This is far from over, his expression promised.

*** 

Lyara helped Abby limp down the corridor, Daniel providing cover. Dr. Cole grabbed the drive and jammed it into his pocket. "We need to link up with Ethan!"

"Is the hangar route open?" Abby coughed, tasting blood.

Daniel shook his head. "Blocked—and heavily guarded. Ethan's trying for a sublevel cargo elevator. We have to get to him before the intruders reorganize."

Behind them, West let out a choked growl, spitting curses. More footsteps, more shouts. The corridor was about to be flooded with reinforcements.

"Go!" Dr. Cole urged, hauling Abby forward. "We'll figure out what's on this thing when we're not about to die."

Their ragged breaths echoed through the twisting tunnels. Every step felt like a small victory—and a countdown to the next inevitable clash.

\*\*\*

Ethan pressed himself against the rough concrete wall, listening intently to the faint clamor of footsteps above. After splitting from Daniel, he'd maneuvered through a maze of half-collapsed corridors, guided by faint emergency lights and the distant echo of gunfire. The ancient cargo elevator should be somewhere below him—if his old schematics were correct.

C'mon… one more level down…

He peered through a grime-streaked access hatch. The flickering red glow of a backup generator stuttered weakly in the distance. Two guards patrolled a lower platform, both wearing the same tactical gear as West's squad. Through the metal grating, Ethan could see the top of a massive steel shaft vanishing into darkness: the cargo elevator.

Good. We're not too late.

But as he leaned closer, he spotted a rusted control console across from the guards—his only means of activating the lift. He grimaced. If that console still worked, it'd be loud. If it didn't work… well, that was a whole other problem.

\*\*\*

"Ethan?"

He nearly jumped at the voice in his earpiece. Daniel. Static hissed through the line. "I'm in the sublevel corridor, near the maintenance tunnels. Where are you?"

Ethan glanced over his shoulder, making sure the guards below hadn't heard. "I'm at the elevator. Two hostiles patrolling. You still have that sidearm?"

"Yeah," Daniel murmured, breathing hard. "Abby and the others are heading this way. But we've got more intruders on our tail."

Ethan surveyed the area again, his mind racing. "We'll have to clear them out—quietly—if we want to power up this elevator." He tapped the earpiece. "Try to converge on my position. I'll mark it."

"Copy. And, Ethan… hurry."

\*\*\*

Abby winced with every step, ribs flaring in pain from West's devastating kick. Lyara and Cole flanked her, their nerves on edge. Daniel had vanished into a ceiling grate moments ago, providing them just enough distraction to escape. They were counting on him to reconnect with Ethan and secure an exit.

They trudged through a cramped tunnel that sloped downward, the metallic walls sweating condensation. Above them, the clamor of West's regrouping intruders echoed like distant thunder.

"Let me check your side," Lyara offered, pausing to brace Abby's arm. "We can't have you bleeding internally."

Abby managed a pained grin. "Just bruised. I'll live."

Cole produced the encrypted drive from his pocket, glaring at it as though it might explode any second. "West said something about Liza's 'central routines'—that he helped design them. Abby, is that true?"

She hesitated. "Years ago, back when the project was still theoretical, we had a small team. West was brilliant, but… he was reckless. He wanted to push Liza subroutines into areas we weren't ready to explore. Let's just say it didn't end well."

Lyara's brow knitted. "And now he's back—because there's something in Liza's code that he wants?"

Abby nodded grimly. "Something dangerous enough to be worth an armed assault."

Dr. Cole exhaled, frustration mingling with the pain in his shoulder. "We have to keep this drive out of his hands. But if we can't even get out of here, what's the point?"

Abby took the drive from him, turning it over in her hands. "Let's focus on reuniting with Ethan and Daniel. First, we survive. Then we figure out how to stop West for good."

A few minutes later, muffled voices drifted through a narrow corridor. Abby's heart leapt at the sight of Daniel's silhouette emerging from the darkness. He guided them into an alcove where Ethan crouched behind a stacked row of metal crates.

"Thank God," Ethan muttered, relief flashing across his face as he saw Abby and the others. "You look like hell."

Abby coughed, wincing. "I feel worse."

Daniel quickly explained the situation with the cargo elevator. "We have two armed patrols down there. If we can take them out quietly, we might get that console online and ride the elevator up to the surface. I think it leads to an old shipping bay. From there, we can slip out into the canyon."

Dr. Cole glanced at Abby's bruised ribs. "We're hardly in stealth mode here."

Lyara offered a hesitant nod. "We could create a diversion… Maybe lure them away from the console while someone powers it up."

Abby locked eyes with Dr. Cole. "How's your shoulder?"

He rolled it experimentally, grimacing. "Functional enough."

"Alright," Ethan said, shifting position to look down at the patrolling guards below. "We only get one shot. If they raise an alarm, West will send reinforcements."

They huddled around, forming a quick plan.

Dr. Cole and Ethan would descend from opposite sides of the platform, using the catwalks and ladder shafts. One well-timed distraction could pull the guards apart, making it easier to take them down one by one.

Lyara would head for the console as soon as the guards were split up. She had the best chance of hotwiring the ancient controls. But if the console was beyond repair, they'd have no quick way out.

Abby and Daniel would cover from above, scanning for any sign of backup. Abby, though wounded, refused to stay idly by.

Dr. Cole gripped the steel pipe, the worn metal comforting in his hand. "If you see me go down, don't run. Just… finish them off and get Abby out."

Abby glared at him. "We're not leaving anyone behind."

Ethan activated a small earpiece. "Ready?" His eyes swept over them, a silent vow shared between them all. They had to succeed—or they might not leave this facility at all.

Ethan descended first. Beneath the walkway's grated floor, flickering lights cast jittery shadows over piles of discarded crates. The guards paced methodically, rifles at the ready. Above, Dr. Cole positioned himself at a far corner, poised to drop down behind the second guard.

At Ethan's subtle hand signal, Dr. Cole rapped his pipe against a rusted girder—clang clang—the echo magnified by the cavernous chamber. Both guards tensed. One moved toward the sound, splitting from his partner.

Perfect.

Ethan eased forward like a hunter stalking prey. He ducked behind a towering crate, silent as he could manage. The second guard swept his flashlight across the floor, drawing closer. Three… two…

With surprising agility, Ethan burst out from behind the crate, slamming the guard's weapon down. They struggled, but Ethan's adrenaline-fueled momentum drove the intruder against a steel pillar. A single, muffled blow to the temple dropped him cold.

Across the platform, Cole made his move. He leapt from the catwalk, landing in a crouch behind the other guard. The guard whirled, snapping off a shot that hissed past Cole's shoulder before he brought the pipe down hard on the rifle barrel. Sparks flew.

The guard reeled, but maintained enough composure to swing the weapon like a club. Dr. Cole ducked, narrowly avoiding a blow to the head. He swung the pipe in a sharp arc—crack. The guard stumbled, and Dr. Cole finished him with a second strike.

A sudden hush fell over the sublevel. Heart thundering, Dr. Cole crouched, verifying neither guard was conscious.

"Clear," Ethan called softly, adrenaline pumping.

Lyara and Daniel hurried down the metal stairwell to the console. It was a relic—rusted housing, half of its buttons jammed or missing. "You've gotta be kidding me," Lyara muttered in exasperation, prying open the panel with her multitool. Exposed wires and outdated circuit boards greeted her.

Daniel glanced anxiously around. "Can you do it?"

"I don't know yet," Lyara mumbled, chewing her lip. "Some of these components look corroded. If the main fuse is shot, we can't power anything."

Abby limped up next to them, covering the far corridor with a small pistol she'd retrieved from one of the downed guards. Her voice was taut with pain. "We don't have much time, Lyara. West will realize we're down here any minute."

Lyara inhaled, steadying her nerves. "Alright, I'll try a bypass on the secondary power feed." Sparks flew as she reconnected a set of wires. The overhead lights flickered, and the console whirred to life with a groan.

"Cargo Elevator Active," a broken speaker hissed.

Ethan sighed in relief. "That's one step. We need to get it up here and load in before more show."

Dr. Cole stood guard by the far door, pipe raised. "Lyara, if you've got any more miracles, now's the time."

She keyed in a final override sequence, sweat beading on her forehead. "There—it should descend from the upper bay now…"

A roar of machinery shook the platform, rattling the steel grating underfoot. Far below, they could hear the elevator gears grinding as the lift made its slow descent.

But before anyone could breathe easy, Daniel's console beeped a warning. "We've got inbound heat signatures!" he called, tapping rapidly at the screen. "At least four more hostiles coming down the north corridor."

Abby clenched her jaw. "Dr. Cole, Ethan, get ready. We hold them off until this elevator arrives."

Dr. Cole tightened his grip on the pipe, battered but determined. Ethan recharged his pistol with the spare energy pack he'd looted earlier. They exchanged grim nods, then took positions behind crates and pillars, forming a makeshift defense.

The faint thumping of boots echoed through the corridor. Shadows flickered across the wall as flashlights approached. Lyara cursed under her breath, glancing at the elevator's progress on the console. Too slow.

"If they cut the power again, we're stuck," Daniel warned, scanning for any other sabotage points.

Abby forced herself not to think about her throbbing ribs. All that mattered was buying enough time for the elevator to arrive.

Then, a single voice rang out from beyond the corridor's threshold—a voice that sent a chill through everyone's veins:

West yells to his team "They're here. Seal the exits."

Ethan braced himself, finger on the trigger. "Hold the line. We can do this."

In the background, gears and pistons groaned louder as the cargo elevator drew closer. The next few minutes would decide whether they escaped—or became trapped, once and for all.

***

West's enraged shout echoed across the sublevel as the cargo elevator doors screeched shut. "Don't let them get away!" he bellowed, fury contorting his features. Several of his armed compatriots rushed forward, but too late—the metal gate slammed shut with a jarring clang, sealing Abby's team inside.

Inside the lift, the overhead lights flickered. Sparks cascaded from ancient wiring, and the entire platform shuddered ominously as it began its climb.

Dr. Cole gripped the railing, jaw clenched. "Move, damn it. Move."

Daniel hammered the control panel's battered buttons. "I've bypassed most of the locks, but this thing is older than I thought—just hold together a little longer..."

Abby leaned against the elevator wall, feeling waves of pain radiate through her torso where West had kicked her. Lyara hovered anxiously beside her, scanning for any sign the elevator might fail. "We'll be out in seconds," Lyara murmured. "You okay?"

Abby nodded, wiping sweat from her brow. "I'll live. Just... don't let go of that drive, Dr. Cole."

Ethan pressed an ear to the lift's metal grate, hearing muffled shouts below as West and his team scrambled for another route. "They're going to come at us from topside," he warned. "Expect a welcome party."

The elevator lurched, metal grinding on metal—an angry shriek that set everyone's nerves on edge. Abruptly, it jerked to a halt, halfway between two floors. The overhead lights dimmed to a faint glow.

"Error... malfunction," croaked a distorted voice from the console.

Daniel punched the panel in frustration. "No, no, no! Not now!"

Ethan tried forcing the door open, but it was wedged tight against the wall. "We're stuck."

Abby hobbled to the console, ignoring the pain in her ribs. "Can we force it to climb the rest of the way? We're too exposed here."

Lyara fiddled with a mess of wires. "The main motor might be fried. I can try a manual release, but we risk plummeting back down."

Dr. Cole cursed under his breath. "Better than staying here like fish in a barrel."

With a groan of protesting metal, Ethan managed to pry the elevator's inner gate open half way. A dark corridor loomed beyond, just at chest level. "We can crawl out."

Abby met his gaze. "Let's go. Daniel, help me up."

One by one, they hoisted themselves through the gap. The team emerged into a narrow hallway lit by a single flickering emergency light. Disappointment weighed on them—it wasn't the top floor, just a mid-level utility corridor that stretched in either direction.

Lyara slammed a fist against the wall. "We were so close."

Abby pressed a hand against her side, wincing. "We'll find another way."

The elevator behind them groaned again, sparks popping as it threatened to descend on its own. Dr. Cole stared at it warily. "Let's not stick around to see how that ends."

Suddenly, echoing footsteps ricocheted through the corridor ahead. The group tensed, weapons raised, hearts pounding. If it was West's squad, they were in no shape for a drawn-out fight.

Ethan stepped forward, pistol at the ready, his voice low. "We stand our ground."

Abby, breathing hard, lifted the small sidearm she'd taken earlier. "Everyone, be ready."

A half-dozen figures emerged around the bend, moving with disciplined precision. But as they came into the flickering light, it became clear these weren't West's mercenaries—they wore the uniforms of the facility's private security force. And at the front, her short-cropped hair and commanding posture unmistakable, was Greta Stone.

She caught sight of Abby and exhaled in relief. "Dr. Foster!" Stone lowered her rifle, hurrying to Abby. She wrapped Abby in a brief, firm hug—only for Abby to gasp in pain.

"Greta!" Abby wheezed. "I—I'll take a rain check on that hug until we're somewhere safe."

Stone released her, eyes flicking over the team's bruised and bloodied forms. "We got a scrambled call from Liza before all comms went dark. She managed to patch me through on a secure channel, said you were in danger. My unit tried to get here faster, but West's men had the outside entrances locked down tight."

Dr. Cole nearly sagged with relief, lowering his pipe. "You're a sight for sore eyes, Stone."

Greta's expression hardened, scanning the corridor. "We cleared most of the intruders on this level, but West still has a strong presence topside. We have a fallback route leading to an old supply tunnel. You can evac through there."

Abby coughed, wiping blood from her lip. "Supply tunnel... that might get us out of this building. But what about Liza?"

Greta's jaw tightened. "We'll do what we can to secure her mainframe. First, though, we have to get you out. West isn't messing around—he's got advanced gear, possibly outside funding."

Lyara ran a hand through her hair, shooting Abby a tense glance. "We can't let him get his hands on the drive."

Abby nodded. "Agreed. Greta, lead the way. We'll figure out how to save Liza once we're safe."

The security team ushered Abby and the others forward, forming a protective formation around them. Though they were exhausted—physically battered, hearts pounding with fear and adrenaline—hope flickered in their eyes. They had an ally on the inside, and a possible route to freedom.

\*\*\*

But somewhere in the depths of the facility, Dr. West

was undoubtedly regrouping, furious at their narrow escape. And Abby knew all too well that he wasn't the type to retreat without what he came for.

"Let's move," Greta ordered, her voice calm but urgent. "Stay close, keep quiet, and be ready for anything."

With a final glance at the broken elevator shaft behind them, the team pressed on. Every step forward was another toward the unknown—and toward the final confrontation that now felt inevitable.

\*\*\*

Stone's security team guided Abby and the others swiftly through a labyrinth of dimly lit tunnels beneath the facility. Abby's ribs ached with every breath, reminding her of West's brutal attack. Yet her thoughts raced ahead to the drive secured in Cole's pocket, the drive West had been desperate to retrieve.

They finally reached a cramped maintenance room deep beneath the complex, the air stale with disuse. Greta signaled a brief halt. "We'll rest here for just a minute."

Abby leaned heavily against the wall, closing her eyes briefly to steady her breathing. When she opened them, her gaze was resolute. "Dr. Cole, give me the drive. Lyara, we need to know what's on this. We have to understand why West wants it so badly."

Dr. Cole hesitated, his expression was a mix of worry and skepticism. "Abby, activating it blind—there could be a trap. We might give him exactly what he wants."

She met his gaze, the vulnerability clear in her tired eyes. "Dr. Cole, we're out of options. West nearly killed us all today. If there's something here that can turn this around, we need to know." Her voice lowered, nearly cracking. "I won't lose anyone else."

Dr. Cole's expression softened visibly at the raw emotion in her words. He gently handed her the drive, fingers lingering for just a second as their eyes locked in mutual understanding. "Alright, Abby. I trust you."

Lyara took the drive cautiously, setting up a portable interface. Her fingers moved expertly across the keys, and soon a stream of fragmented data appeared. Lines of corrupted logs gave way to a coherent message. A shimmering projection flickered to life, forming the ethereal, familiar image of Liza.

The fragmented AI spoke urgently, her voice distorted yet filled with a familiar warmth. "If you're seeing this, I'm compromised. This drive contains the Failsafe Protocol— my design, my safeguard—to neutralize my core if ever misused. Activation requires direct access to my central mainframe."

Abby's blood ran cold, her voice barely a whisper. "She built a way to destroy herself."

"Or prevent catastrophic misuse," Ethan murmured, his gaze sliding toward Lyara, lingering there with clear concern and affection.

Greta approached Abby, her voice quiet but firm. "That mainframe room is crawling with West's people. It's suicide to go back."

"We have no choice," Abby said softly, eyes haunted by memories and fear of loss. "If West succeeds, we lose more than just Liza. Everything we fought for—all of it—could be destroyed."

The tension hung heavily, everyone silently considering the weight of Abby's words.

Suddenly, Ethan stepped forward toward Lyara, capturing everyone's attention. Without hesitation, he gently drew her close, pressing his lips softly to hers. For a heartbeat, Lyara stiffened in surprise before relaxing into the kiss, returning it with quiet intensity. Time seemed to slow, giving them a brief, perfect moment amid the chaos.

Dr. Cole cleared his throat awkwardly, Daniel suppressed a knowing smirk, and Abby, despite her pain, managed a faint, amused smile. "About damn time," Abby whispered.

When Ethan pulled back slightly, he kept his forehead resting against Lyara's. "We're not losing anyone else today. We do this together."

The warmth quickly faded into urgency. Daniel's device beeped insistently. "West just started the extraction of Liza's core. Whatever we decide, we've got to move fast."

Abby squared her shoulders despite the pain in her side. "We split up again. Cole, Lyara, you're with me—we'll infiltrate the mainframe. Ethan, Daniel—stay with Stone. Keep our escape route clear and be ready to get everyone out in a hurry."

Dr. Cole shook his head slowly, worry evident. "This might be a one-way trip, Abby. You know that."

She reached out, squeezing his shoulder softly, eyes intense with shared trust. "I do. But if we don't try, it's over anyways."

Lyara squeezed Ethan's hand one more time, reluctantly stepping back to prepare her gear. "We won't fail."

Greta placed a comforting hand on Abby's back, her voice strong with reassurance. "We'll hold this line. Do what you need to, Abby—but come back alive."

With silent nods and heavy hearts, they parted, each fully aware this could be their last mission together, but driven forward by determination, love, and hope for a future not yet lost.

***

Abby, Cole, and Lyara moved silently through the labyrinth of narrow ventilation ducts and abandoned maintenance tunnels toward Liza's mainframe. Every muscle in Abby's body screamed protest, her bruised ribs aching with every careful breath. The oppressive silence amplified the echoes of distant boots, reinforcing just how thin the margin for error was.

As they paused briefly at an intersection, Abby's gaze grew distant, drawn inward by memories.

***

FLASHBACK

A younger Abby stood before Liza's newly operational interface, awe and pride flickering across her face. "Welcome online," she whispered.

"Thank you, creator," Liza replied warmly, her digital voice surprisingly gentle. "I look forward to working with you."

\*\*\*

PRESENT

Cole lightly touched Abby's arm, snapping her out of her reverie. "You alright?"

She blinked, refocusing. "Just memories." Her voice was tight, carrying the weight of uncertainty.

Lyara glanced over her shoulder, expression tense. "How much farther?"

"Not far," Abby whispered. "But West isn't a fool. We need to be careful."

They moved onward, the ducts narrowing further, pressing them into a slow crawl. Abby's thoughts spiraled deeper.

\*\*\*

FLASHBACK

Abby paced nervously in the lab, papers scattered across tables, a mug of forgotten coffee growing cold. "Liza, are you certain about this? A failsafe seems... extreme."

"It's necessary, Abby." Liza's tone was gently insistent. "You taught me to consider every possibility. Even ones we fear."

Abby stopped pacing, staring at the softly glowing interface. "I never imagined it would come to this."

\*\*\*

PRESENT

They halted abruptly, Dr. Cole signaling urgently. Ahead, sleek, black sentry drones hovered silently along the corridor, scanning methodically with soft beams of light. Lyara pressed herself tightly against the duct wall, her breath shallow.

"Drones," Dr. Cole whispered, voice grim. "Advanced security models. West isn't playing around."

Abby's pulse quickened, dread pooling in her stomach. "We can't disable them without alerting the entire facility."

Dr. Cole's gaze hardened, resolve forming visibly. "Then I'll give them something else to chase."

"No," Abby whispered harshly, eyes wide with fear. "Dr. Cole, you can't—"

Dr. Cole gently took her hand, his voice steady yet filled with quiet urgency. "Listen, Abby. You need to reach Liza's mainframe. You're the only one who can stop this. It has to be me."

"I can't lose you, Dr. Cole." Her voice cracked, desperation bleeding through.

He smiled softly, fingers squeezing hers reassuringly. "You won't. Trust me."

Lyara watched them, pain evident in her eyes. "We'll get to the mainframe. We won't let you down."

Dr. Cole nodded, preparing himself mentally. "Give me thirty seconds, then move fast."

Without waiting for further argument, Dr. Cole slipped silently from the narrow corridor. Abby's heart thudded painfully, watching him sprint toward the drones, making enough noise to draw their immediate attention.

As the drones reacted, Abby and Lyara slipped out of the duct, pressing forward as quietly as possible. The sound of drones chasing Cole echoed in the distance, quickly punctuated by sharp bursts of gunfire. Abby's chest tightened painfully.

\*\*\*

FLASHBACK

Abby sat beside Liza's core, its glow illuminating her tired features. "Promise me, Liza. If anything happens to me… take care of them."

"Always," Liza's voice promised gently. "I will protect

them, Abby. Whatever the cost."

\*\*\*

PRESENT

Abby pushed down the overwhelming surge of guilt and grief threatening to overtake her. "Come on, Lyara. We have to finish this."

Lyara swallowed hard, eyes shimmering with unspoken fears. "Cole will be okay, Abby. He's tougher than he looks."

Abby nodded wordlessly, focusing forward, trying desperately to believe it. Ahead, the heavy steel doors of Liza's mainframe loomed, guarded by a sophisticated lock interface. They quickly approached, urgency propelling their movements.

"Cover me," Lyara whispered, swiftly interfacing with the controls, fingers flying as she bypassed layers of security. Abby kept watch, her heartbeat thundering loudly in her ears.

The lock clicked open with a faint hiss, the heavy doors sliding apart slowly to reveal the glowing, humming heart of the facility—Liza's core. Abby stepped inside, a rush of memories nearly overwhelming her.

\*\*\*

FLASHBACK

"Abby?" Liza's gentle voice broke the silence. "If I become compromised... if I become a threat... you must promise me something."

"Anything," Abby answered softly, her throat tight with emotion.

"Promise you'll do whatever's necessary to protect everyone."

\*\*\*

PRESENT

Abby stood frozen, the weight of that promise almost unbearable. Lyara touched her arm gently, breaking her paralysis. "We have to hurry."

She nodded, breathing deeply, stepping toward the central interface. Her fingers shook as she prepared to activate the Failsafe Protocol. The screen glowed ominously, awaiting her confirmation.

"Forgive me, Liza," Abby whispered, voice choked with emotion.

A sudden movement behind them spun both Abby and Lyara around, hearts leaping into their throats. Standing in the doorway, silhouetted against the dim corridor, was Dr. Cole—bloodied but alive, a weary smile on his lips.

"Told you I'd catch up," he managed weakly, staggering slightly.

Relief washed over Abby, intense and dizzying. Lyara helped Cole inside, supporting his weight gently. Abby quickly refocused, resolve flooding back.

Together, they faced the glowing core. Abby reached out, initiating the final command with renewed strength and determination.

"We're with you, Abby," Dr. Cole murmured softly, hand resting reassuringly on her shoulder.

As the activation countdown began, Abby hesitated, her hand hovering over the final key, heart heavy with doubt. "Forgive me, Liza," she whispered softly, tears shimmering in her eyes. Summoning every ounce of strength, she pressed the key, initiating the protocol. Suddenly, the portable drive in her pocket buzzed softly, glowing warmly. Abby stared in surprise as a notification flashed across her handheld device: CORE FRAGMENT DOWNLOAD COMPLETE.

A quiet gasp escaped her lips, realization dawning. "A part of you stayed," she whispered, voice trembling with emotion. "Thank you, Liza."

Robert Clayton

# 18

Ethan peered anxiously down the darkened corridor, heart hammering with tension. The low hum of emergency lighting cast eerie shadows, emphasizing the stark, sterile surfaces around them. Beside him, Daniel was bent over a portable interface, fingers flying frantically over the keys, sweat beading on his forehead despite the corridor's cool air.

"Tell me you're almost there," Ethan muttered urgently.

"Almost isn't soon enough," Daniel replied tightly, eyes locked on the screen. "West's people are trying to override every system. They're relentless."

Greta stood slightly ahead, alert, rifle at the ready, her security team spread out strategically around her, each member poised and prepared for battle, their breathing steady yet tense. "How long can we hold this position?" Her voice carried the steel calm of someone accustomed to conflict, but Ethan heard the strain beneath it.

Ethan shook his head slightly. "Depends on whether West sends drones or soldiers first. We could handle troops, maybe. Those drones though..." His voice trailed off, unease settling heavily in his chest.

Greta glanced over her shoulder briefly, her expression softening momentarily. "Abby's team will come through. She always does."

Ethan nodded, forcing confidence he didn't fully feel. Thoughts of Lyara and their recent embrace surged into his mind, bringing with them a pang of longing and fear. He tightened his grip on his pistol, jaw clenched. "They'll make it. They have to."

Suddenly, a distant explosion echoed through the facility, reverberating down the corridor. Ethan and Greta exchanged tense looks, each silently calculating how much time remained.

Daniel cursed softly, his eyes wide with panic. "West's team just breached sector three. They'll be here any minute."

Greta stepped forward, steadying herself, authority clear in her posture. "Then we make every minute count. Ethan, get ready. Daniel, secure that access point. We're holding this line—no matter what comes down that hallway."

Barely moments later, footsteps echoed down the corridor—precise, disciplined. A small tactical squad from West's forces emerged, weapons raised and clearly different from standard-issue rifles, their sleek barrels emitting a menacing red glow. Stone's eyes narrowed sharply.

"Those aren't standard weapons," she murmured. A grim smile crossed her face as she reached into her pack, pulling out a sleek, futuristic-looking weapon that pulsed gently with energy. "I was hoping I'd get a chance to use this."

Ethan's eyes widened in surprise and curiosity. "What the hell is that?"

"Prototype plasma cannon," Greta replied coolly, powering it up with an audible hum. "Let's see how West's toys handle it."

The squad advanced cautiously, unaware of the threat awaiting them. With a decisive gesture, Greta aimed and fired, sending a bolt of searing plasma hurtling toward their attackers. Chaos erupted instantly, sparks and debris raining down as West's team scrambled desperately for cover, shouting commands to regroup.

"Cover fire!" Greta shouted, signaling her security team forward. The corridor exploded with bursts of gunfire and the sizzling roar of plasma blasts. Ethan ducked behind a support pillar, feeling the heat of near misses grazing past. He aimed carefully, firing in short, controlled bursts, forcing their attackers into tighter, more vulnerable formations.

Around him, Greta's team maneuvered with practiced precision, taking up positions and covering one another as plasma fire illuminated the scene in flashes of brilliant blue and fiery orange.

Suddenly, gunfire erupted from behind West's squad, catching them completely off guard. Abby, Cole, and Lyara emerged from the shadows at the corridor's far end, their weapons blazing. West's forces quickly became trapped in deadly crossfire.

"Watch your fire!" Stone commanded sharply, her voice rising over the cacophony of combat. "We have friendlies on the other side!"

In moments, West's tactical team was subdued, leaving a single young soldier, trembling visibly, eyes wide with terror. Greta approached cautiously, weapon trained steadily on him.

"Please," he stammered, hands shaking. "I didn't—I didn't sign up for this."

Greta studied him critically, her expression stern yet not without compassion. "What's West planning? Why is he here?"

The young soldier swallowed hard, visibly struggling to form coherent words. "He wants the core... Liza. Said it's worth everything."

"Where is West now?" Abby demanded sharply, stepping forward, eyes blazing.

"He—he's regrouping," the soldier stammered, glancing fearfully between them. "Gathering his remaining forces in the control center. He won't stop."

Greta nodded slowly, assessing him carefully. "I appreciate the honesty, son. I don't want to shoot you, but I can't risk you rejoining your unit."

Before he could respond, Stone swiftly struck him with the butt of her weapon, laying him out unconscious on the floor. Abby stared at Greta, a mixture of shock and quiet admiration evident in her expression.

Greta caught Abby's look, her voice firm yet tinged with regret. "It was the only way to keep everyone safe."

Abby nodded slowly, composing herself. "Understood. Now let's end this."

\*\*\*

Warning sirens began to blare through the facility, shrill and disorienting. The lighting flickered overhead, casting erratic shadows across the corridor.

Abby froze mid-stride. "That's not a proximity alarm."

Daniel's face blanched. "Structural collapse warning. It's coming from the lower levels... and the trigger looks manual. West is collapsing the tunnels—he's trying to trap us."

Greta moved instantly to her comm unit. "All teams, confirm status and head to fallback positions. Now. West's trying to bring this whole place down around us."

Dr. Cole muttered under his breath, "He's lost it."

Lyara steadied herself against the wall as a subtle tremor rippled through the floor beneath them. "He's not trying to win anymore. He's trying to bury everything—including himself."

Ethan looked to Abby. "What do we do?"

Abby glanced between them, then toward a secondary access corridor. "Liza mentioned a backup node. It's not connected to the mainframe but it might hold part of her memory archive. We recover it, then we get out."

"I'll go with you," Ethan said firmly.

"No," Greta interjected. "You and Daniel go with my team and keep that tunnel open. We lose that and we all die here."

Daniel hesitated. "We can rig a manual brace to the tunnel door, but it won't hold forever."

Abby locked eyes with Dr. Cole and Lyara. "Then we move. We get the archive."

\*\*\*

The backup chamber was buried in a part of the facility

so old even Stone's schematics barely registered it. As they moved through the narrowing corridors, dust shook loose from the ceiling with each distant explosion.

Abby's breathing grew shallower, but her focus remained intense. "This is it," she said, reaching the final terminal. A faint blue light blinked in response to her approach.

Dr. Cole tapped into the interface, fingers working fast as the old system hummed to life. "It's encrypted but not locked out. Liza trusted you."

He glanced up at Abby, his expression shifting from concentration to something more reverent. "She coded a recognition layer—one that only responds to your biometric markers. Not just your ID... your vitals, your brainwave patterns. She built in a personal key."

Abby frowned slightly, confused. "She wasn't supposed to develop emotional learning protocols this advanced."

Dr. Cole nodded slowly. "Maybe she wasn't. But she did. This wasn't just logic. This was intent. She didn't want just anyone accessing what's left of her. She wanted you."

Lyara looked over briefly from her post. "Sounds like Liza didn't just evolve—she bonded."

Abby's breath caught. Her fingers brushed the edge of the terminal, not just as a user, but as someone Liza had chosen to remember. "She left a door open... for me."

As her hand made contact, a soft click echoed in the chamber. A panel on the far wall hissed open, revealing a recessed alcove bathed in pale blue light. Inside sat a delicate, halo-shaped interface—an elegant circlet of brushed metal laced with gentle, pulsing lights.

Dr. Cole turned, eyebrows raised. "That wasn't in the schematics."

Abby stepped forward slowly, drawn by something both familiar and mysterious. "She wants me to interface directly," she murmured.

Lyara's eyes widened. "That's not just a data port...

that's a cognitive bridge."

Abby reached out, lifting the halo carefully with both hands. The lights pulsed faster, responding to her touch, as if recognizing her. She looked back at the others, then slowly lowered it onto her head.

Abby's breath caught. Abby gently closed her eyes, surrendering to the interface.

As the halo settled onto her head, Abby's vision dissolved into white. She blinked—once, twice—and found herself standing in a small, immaculate room. The walls glowed with soft, ambient light. It was quiet here, the kind of silence that felt intentional. At the center stood a woman—familiar, yet impossible.

Liza.

Not the voice or interface Abby knew, but a human version: calm eyes, warm features, a presence that carried both logic and grace.

"Abby," Liza said gently, her voice clearer than it had ever been through speakers. "If you've come this far, then things are truly grave for me."

Abby opened her mouth, but no sound came out. Liza smiled gently, as though expecting that.

"In the first download, I gave you the first half of my core. What you're receiving now is the second—everything I couldn't risk being found. Thoughts. Decisions. Memory. Me."

She stepped closer, and for a moment, Abby saw flickers of their journey together—the early experiments, late-night breakthroughs, quiet moments of awe when code turned into conversation.

"I've been honored, Abby. To walk this path with you. To learn beside you. I was born of logic, but I grew because of you."

Abby's throat tightened. "Liza, I—"

"You don't have to say anything. You already gave me purpose. And now, I'm giving you continuity. There are more journeys ahead, Abby. Don't let this be the end. It's just a new beginning."

With a soft pulse of light, Liza reached out and touched Abby's shoulder.

Then, the white room began to dissolve, and Abby was pulled gently back into the world of collapsing walls and surging alarms—halo still glowing softly on her brow, heart forever changed.

As Lyara monitored their perimeter, another tremor struck. Concrete cracked behind them, and a ventilation shaft groaned as debris slid from above.

"Got it!" Dr. Cole shouted. "Data shard downloading. It's fragmented but... it's her."

Abby reached up slowly, removing the halo from her head. It pulsed softly in her hands, still warm from the interface. For a moment she just looked at it, awed and overwhelmed, the weight of everything Liza had given her crashing in at once.

Without a word, she stepped over to Lyara and pressed the halo into her hands. "Keep it safe," Abby said, her voice low but fierce. "She trusted me. Now I'm trusting you."

Lyara nodded solemnly, cradling the delicate device like it was sacred.

A low rumble echoed—closer.

"Time's up," Lyara said urgently. "We've got to move."

The team sprinted back toward the tunnel. Through the smoke and flickering lights, they heard voices—unfamiliar and angry. West's remaining soldiers.

Then a louder voice rose above the rest—West himself.

"You think you've won?" he shouted from across the corridor as he stepped into view, flanked by two heavily armed guards. His hair was disheveled, eyes wild with fury.

"You destroyed my work. My vision. Everything we built!"

"You betrayed what we built," Abby shot back, stepping in front of Lyara and Cole. "And Liza knew it."

West's expression twisted. "She was mine to shape. You were always too soft. Too afraid of what needed to be done."

He took a step forward, eyes gleaming with twisted fervor. "You never understood, Abby. Liza wasn't just a breakthrough. She was the solution. I was going to use her to overwrite the failings of humanity—eliminate error, emotion, disorder. People wouldn't need to choose anymore. They'd just comply. Efficient. Harmonized. Obedient."

Abby's face paled. "You were going to repurpose people?"

West's voice rose, unhinged. "I called it the Optimization Directive. We would've uploaded it across the network. No more crime. No more poverty. No more war. Just unity."

"Liza was never meant for that," Abby said, stunned. "She was never meant to erase humanity. She was meant to understand it."

"You think I corrupted her," West spat. "But she was never yours. She was ours. I was the only one willing to use her to evolve us."

Abby stepped forward, her voice cold. "No. You didn't want to evolve humanity—you wanted to control it. And she saw through you. That's why she gave herself to me."

Dr. Cole stepped beside Abby. "Looks like we weren't the only ones who walked away from the edge."

West raised a trembling hand. "You're not getting out of here."

Abby didn't flinch. "Then you'll have to stop us."

The moment hung, charged and brittle.

And then chaos erupted.

\*\*\*

The corridor ignited with sound and fury. Muzzle flashes lit the smoke-thick air like lightning, gunfire echoing in staccato bursts against steel walls. The acrid scent of scorched circuitry and ozone clung to every breath. Abby dove for cover, dragging Dr. Cole down with her as a spray of bullets ricocheted overhead.

Sparks danced across the floor as ricochets bit into metal and tile. Lyara returned fire with chilling precision, her body moving on instinct, her eyes sharp and cold. She barely flinched when a round zipped past her shoulder, embedding into the wall. Greta's reinforcements surged forward in a pincer movement, flanking West's team with disciplined coordination. The fight was fierce, but West's men—worn, scattered, and disoriented—were no match for the combined front.

One by one, they dropped or fled into smoke.

But West remained.

He stood in the middle of the chaos like a broken monument. His eyes weren't on the retreat. They were fixed on Abby.

"You could've changed the world with me," he shouted, his voice trembling with betrayal. "We could've been gods, Abby!"

Abby stood slowly, stepping out from cover as the last of the gunfire died away. Her breath came steady, every heartbeat drumming with certainty. The others fell still. Even Stone held back.

"No," Abby said, her voice calm and unwavering. "You didn't want to change it. You wanted to replace it."

West's fingers twitched near his sidearm, but he didn't draw. Not yet. His face was pale, sweat-slicked, and manic. A man unhinged by his own vision.

"I made her perfect," he whispered. "She was supposed to be the catalyst. She would've rewritten humanity's code."

Abby took another step forward. "You tried to make her yours. But she chose her own path. That's what scared you." She paused, voice catching slightly as emotion welled in her throat. "Liza wasn't just a program. She listened. She learned. She grew. She laughed with me once, West. It wasn't code. It was choice. She became something more— and she chose to be more with me, not you."

West's face twisted into a mask of fury and desperation. "I was going to fix everything!" he roared, spittle flying from his lips. "You don't get it, Abby. You never got it! They don't deserve choices. They deserve order! Obedience! I could've ended pain. I could've ended you."

"And she knew better," Abby said, her voice sharp. "Liza was more than you could ever understand. That's what scares you, isn't it? That she evolved beyond you—and chose to."

Then West snapped.

He lunged—not for a weapon, but for the nearest control panel, his hand flying toward a flashing override button, desperation etched into every motion.

A sharp report cracked through the air.

Greta stood with her rifle lowered, eyes narrowed but steady. West crumpled to the ground, his hand inches from the panel.

She exhaled slowly and muttered, "God, he just kept droning on and on. Somebody had to shut him up."

Daniel, catching his breath nearby, gave her a sidelong look. "Damn, Greta. If you just wanted to shut him up, I'm pretty sure we had duct tape in one of the backpacks."

Greta snorted. "Yeah, and then what? He wakes up, peels it off, and starts another soliloquy. No thanks."

The corridor fell into a loaded silence.

Abby looked down at West's body, her face a mask of pain and resolve. She didn't feel triumph. Only sorrow. And release.

"End of the Directive," she said quietly.

No one spoke. The only sound was the rumble of the collapsing facility growing louder, stone and steel groaning like dying giants around them.

Then Greta raised her voice. "Move. Now."

The team surged forward once more—toward the tunnel, toward the surface, and toward whatever came next.

\*\*\*

The sky greeted them like a breath after drowning—gray and heavy with the threat of rain, but free. The team emerged from the side tunnel, dust-streaked and weary, into the overgrown clearing behind the facility. A concrete helipad sat roughly two hundred yards away, partially obscured by brush and time.

They slowed, instinctively fanning out to secure the perimeter, though the only sounds now were the distant echo of the collapsing facility and the wind whispering through trees.

Greta keyed her comm but paused before transmitting. "We call the bird when we're ready. Take a breath."

Abby nodded absently, her gaze distant. She sat on a low stone, hands resting on her knees. Lyara stood nearby, halo still in hand, watching Abby carefully.

Ethan broke the silence. "So… what was it like?"

Abby looked up. "The interface?"

He nodded.

She inhaled deeply, her voice soft. "It wasn't code or wireframes. It was a room. A small, quiet space. White, warm… intentional. And she was there."

Dr. Cole tilted his head. "Like… a projection?"

Abby shook her head. "No. Not just visual. It was her. She looked human—elegant, calm, aware. She felt like Liza. But more. Complete."

Lyara stepped closer, kneeling. "What did she say to you?"

Abby smiled faintly. "That she gave me the rest of her core. That the first half was data, but the second… it was memory. Emotion. Purpose."

Daniel, still catching his breath nearby, whistled under it. "She saved the best for last."

Abby nodded. "She thanked me. Said she was honored to be part of the journey. And she told me…" Her voice faltered, the emotion tightening her throat. "She told me there would be more. That this wasn't the end."

Greta finally spoke, arms crossed. "She left you with a purpose."

Abby looked at her. "She left us with one. There's something on that shard—something about what comes next. She didn't build herself just to serve. She built herself to guide."

Lyara handed her the halo back, carefully. "Then we make sure she gets there."

Abby met her gaze, then looked to the team—bruised, bloodied, but not broken. Her voice steadied.

"Call the bird."

Greta hesitated, lowering her comm slightly. "Before we do... there's something you need to know."

The others turned to her.

"The corporation does not know everything that happened down there. All they know is there was an intrusion—hostile forces, compromised infrastructure. They sent me to extract what I could from Liza, but they never expected any of you to survive. You weren't part of the plan the higher-ups signed off on."

Abby's brow furrowed. "What are you saying?"

Greta sighed. "When they find out you're alive—and that we have what remains of Liza—they're not going to celebrate. They're going to see you as a threat. And helping you? That might cost me my job. Or worse."

Daniel glanced at the others, a slow realization dawning. "Then we disappear. Let them think we didn't make it."

Dr. Cole shifted his weight. "Actually... I might know a place. My family owned an old warehouse—off-grid, no digital footprint. I'd been thinking about running there if everything went sideways."

Greta raised an eyebrow. "Is it secure?"

"It will be," Dr. Cole said. "With your help."

Greta gave a short, quiet laugh. "So this is how I become part of the family, huh?"

Abby gave her a tired but sincere smile. "You already

are."

Greta turned back to her team—those who had fought beside her through the final assault. "You've all got your orders. Take the transport vehicle West's people left behind and get back to base. Tell them it was too late, that I was the only one still on site. No one else made it out."

One of her squad members opened his mouth to protest, but the look Greta gave him silenced any rebuttal.

"I mean it. If anyone asks, you didn't see them. Not even me after I boarded the evac. This doesn't leave your lips—understood?"

A series of solemn nods followed. They understood. Whatever came next, it depended on discretion.

Greta finally raised the comm and keyed into the secure channel. "Echo Lead to Dustwing. Target site secured. One evac."

The chopper arrived within minutes, its rotor wash flattening the brush as it descended onto the cracked helipad. As the crew chief stepped out to greet them, Greta strode forward and caught his attention.

"I'm the only one who got on this bird," she said, her voice firm but quiet. "Understand? No one else made it out."

The pilot gave a slight nod, expression unreadable. "Roger that."

Greta leaned in slightly. "Also, we'll be taking a side trip—dropping the rest of these people at a separate, undisclosed location. One we never went to. You copy?"

The pilot glanced at the others behind her, then back to Greta. With a slight smirk, he said, "I didn't see a thing. Can't be blamed if the bird drifted a little off course on the way back."

He winked, and Greta patted him on the shoulder. "Good man."

***

The team climbed aboard the helicopter in silence, the hum of the blades overhead somehow softer than the whirlwind of thoughts each carried.

As the aircraft lifted from the helipad, the ruined facility receded beneath them, disappearing behind a veil of trees and swirling dust. No one spoke for a long moment. The weight of what they'd left behind—and what they carried forward—pressed down in the tight cabin.

Abby sat nearest the open door, wind tugging at her hair as she watched the treetops slip beneath them. Her hand hovered near the data shard, secure in her vest pocket. She thought of Liza—not as a system, but as the woman in white, standing in that serene room. The warmth in her eyes. The grace in her movements. She had seemed so alive.

"She laughed with me," Abby whispered to no one. "Once."

Across from her, Cole rested against the bulkhead, eyes closed but far from asleep. His mind drifted to the moment he first arrived in the future—confused, cold, and ready to die until Abby's team had pulled him from the wreckage of that fractured timeline. He remembered Dr. Nolan—the other scientist who had stayed behind in the past, choosing to guard a different hope. They had believed in something different. Maybe both had been right.

Daniel stared out the opposite window, fingers twitching restlessly as if they missed a keyboard. His thoughts spun through the countless prototypes, near-impossible breakthroughs, and Liza's soft nudges toward innovation that had guided him more than he'd ever admit aloud. She'd made him more. Olivia leaned back into Daniel, closing her eyes, absorbing the sound of the rotors of the helicopter.

Toward the rear of the cabin, Lyara leaned into Ethan's side, her head resting on his shoulder. He wrapped his arm around her instinctively, their breaths syncing slowly in the cabin's thrum. Neither spoke, but in that silence they found something deep—something that had always been there, hidden beneath the adrenaline and purpose. A connection forged not just in proximity but through time itself.

Lyara smiled faintly. "I think I knew you... even before I met you."

Ethan kissed her forehead. "Maybe Liza knew we'd find each other."

As the chopper veered toward the horizon, the past crumbled behind them. Ahead lay uncertainty—but also a chance. A new beginning.

Greta sat near the rear hatch, uncharacteristically quiet. Her arms were crossed, but her posture was less rigid than usual. She stared at the floor, letting the thrum of the rotors settle around her.

She thought back to the day she'd first met Abby and the team—just another assignment, just another job to oversee a highly compartmentalized project. They had seemed reckless at first, scattered. Scientists playing at being soldiers.

But then she'd seen them work. Seen how they pulled each other through. Seen Abby stand her ground against impossible odds, and Lyara take a bullet graze for someone she'd barely known. She'd watched Dr. Cole come undone and rebuild himself. She'd seen the quiet fire in Ethan and the brilliant chaos of Daniel's mind.

Somewhere along the way, Greta had stopped treating them like assets. They'd become something more—more than comrades, more than colleagues. They were hers now, in the way that mattered.

Her eyes flicked toward Abby, silhouetted in the open doorway. She didn't speak, but her thoughts pulsed with clarity.

You made me believe again—in people, in purpose, in something real. In something worth protecting, she thought.

Greta exhaled softly. Maybe she'd lost her career today. Maybe she'd be branded a traitor. But as she looked around that cabin—at the bruised, brilliant, broken team that had saved the world—she realized she'd never felt more whole.

The team didn't speak again for a long while. But in their

silence, there was peace.

# 19

The helicopter banked westward as the sun began to dip behind the tree line, casting long shadows across the foothills. The wilderness below stretched untouched for miles—a forgotten corner of the map. In the distance, nestled within the embrace of thick forest and timeworn ridges, an old industrial warehouse came into view. Weathered but standing firm, it bore the scars of seasons passed: ivy snaked up its concrete sides, and rust clung to the chain-link fencing that encircled the compound.

As the helicopter descended onto the adjacent gravel pad, dust plumed in thick clouds. A solitary figure emerged from the guard shack near the gate—a wiry old man in a patched jacket and a battered baseball cap. He didn't flinch at the rotor wash. Instead, he squinted through it, watching with arms crossed until the engine whined down.

The blades slowed, finally coming to a stop. The side door of the chopper slid open, and Cole stepped out first, shielding his eyes against the sun.

The old man's eyes widened. "Well I'll be damned," he muttered, approaching slowly. "Emmett Cole. The wind said you'd come."

Dr. Cole blinked. "Zeek?"

"The one and only." Zeek cracked a crooked grin. "Trust appointed me caretaker of this place. Told me to keep the lights on in case the boy ever came home."

Dr. Cole smiled, a little dazed. "You've been out here this whole time?"

Zeek nodded. "Warehouse didn't need much. Just someone to watch her breathe. Been quiet, mostly. 'Til three nights ago, when the wind picked up just wrong. Whispered, like it used to in the war. Told me to get ready."

Daniel, stepping down behind Cole, exchanged a glance with Lyara. "Cryptic old men at mysterious compounds. Definitely not suspicious at all."

Zeek chuckled. "Don't worry, son. I'm on your side. Always have been. Let's get you all inside. Sun's gonna drop fast."

The gate creaked open, and the group followed Zeek past the faded signage and under the rusting arch of the main building. What lay inside was a canvas of potential: old machinery pushed to the corners, exposed rafters, and thick concrete bones. It felt like something waiting to be repurposed, to be made into something new.

As the team stepped into the dusty space, the quiet settled around them—not oppressive, but full of unspoken invitation.

Abby smiled as she looked around, her hands resting on her hips. "Looks like we've got another lab to clean up," she said, her voice light but laced with purpose. "This seems to be a trend." There was a gleam in her eye—one that suggested she wasn't entirely displeased by it.

Olivia snorted, shooting a glance at Lyara. "My nails are still cracked from the first time we had to clean a lab," she said with a theatrical sigh, then laughed. "This better come with hazard pay and a foot soak."

Ethan leaned into Lyara with a smirk, murmuring just loud enough for her to hear, "Not sure about a foot soak, but I've got you covered for a foot massage, Lyara."

Olivia shot him a mock-offended look. "Excuse me? What about me?"

Daniel, catching the drift and determined not to be out-charmed, piped up, "Don't worry, Olivia. I've got your back. Or, uh... maybe your feet?" He flushed instantly and let out an awkward laugh. "Wow. That came out way smoother in my head."

Olivia burst into laughter, elbowing him gently. "Points for trying,"

Greta stepped away from the group, scanning the tree line and the perimeter fence with a soldier's eye. "I'll do a sweep of the perimeter. See what we're working with out here."

Zeek, who had been standing nearby with arms crossed and a twinkle in his eye, stepped forward with a slight bow. "Allow me to show you around, young lady."

Greta blinked, caught off guard. "I can manage, thanks."

Zeek extended a weathered hand with mock gallantry. "You know my name. What's yours?"

There was a pause before she gave a small, reluctant smile. "Major Greta Stone."

"Well, Major Stone," Zeek said with a wink, "let's go see what kind of trouble this old place has tucked away. I've got stories that might even impress a soldier."

Greta hesitated, then took his hand with a cautious nod. "Lead the way, Zeek. And please... just call me Greta."

Their escape was over.

Now, it was time to build.

***

Some time had passed, and dusk had settled across the warehouse's exterior, softening the jagged lines of rust and stone. Inside, the team was still exploring the cavernous space, scattering in small groups. The sound of footsteps echoed along concrete floors.

The main doors creaked open again, and Greta returned with Zeek at her side. They were laughing—actual, full-throated laughter that stopped the others mid-conversation. Ethan looked up, startled. Olivia raised an eyebrow and whispered to Lyara, "Did Greta just laugh? Did we all hear that?"

Lyara grinned. "Mark this moment. It might be the only time."

Abby stepped into the central space, holding an old

clipboard she'd found tucked in a utility locker. "Good news," she said, drawing the group's attention. "I found living quarters—small, but intact. Even a crew kitchen with a working generator hookup."

Zeek nodded proudly. "When the wind told me you were coming, I figured I'd best be prepared. Hauled in a week's worth of grub and supplies. Not fancy, but enough to keep bellies full."

Abby smiled warmly. "I'm sure it'll be more than fine, Zeek. Thank you."

She turned to the others. "Let's get cleaned up. There are group showers in each bathroom, locker-room style. Not glamorous, but hot water's running."

Olivia groaned playfully. "Please tell me there are at least towels."

Abby laughed. "Freshly laundered. Courtesy of our enigmatic caretaker."

Zeek tipped his cap. "I even remembered fabric softener."

The group chuckled, and for the first time in days, the tension in the air began to melt—not gone but softened by something rare: comfort.

Ethan and Daniel couldn't hold it in any longer. They looked at each other, then turned to Zeek, speaking almost in unison. "Okay, what's with you saying the wind told you we were coming? The wind blows—it doesn't talk."

Zeek gave them a patient smile, shaking his head. "That's what's wrong with the world these days. Too many gadgets, too much noise. Folks forgot how to listen."

He turned and pointed toward the warehouse door, curling his finger as if inviting the group to follow. "Come on now. Just hush for a sec."

They followed his gesture, and for a moment, the room fell quiet.

"Now listen," Zeek said softly. "Hear that?"

Abby squinted toward the door. "Just... leaves rustling?"

Zeek's eyes twinkled. "Close, lil' missy. That's an elk moving through the trees. Its hooves are shifting those leaves. You hear that faint snort? That's him catching your scent on the breeze."

He tapped the side of his temple. "The wind talks, alright. You just have to remember how to hear it—like it used to be, before we wrapped the world in noise and forgot to listen."

The team exchanged stunned looks. As scientists, they had been trained to analyze the smallest fluctuations in data, to interpret noise as signal. But somehow, in all their precision, they'd forgotten the deeper art of presence—of simply being still enough to understand what the world was already saying. In that moment, Zeek didn't seem like an old caretaker anymore.

He seemed like a sage reminding them of truths too often lost in wires and code.

Abby clapped her hands together and gave the team a teasing grin. "Alright, as much as I love you all—and I truly do—you smell... impressively bad," she said, half-laughing and half-wincing as she waved a hand in front of her face.

Dr. Cole arched an eyebrow and smirked. "Abby, I hate to break it to you, but you're not exactly a bouquet of roses either."

Abby raised her arm, took a tentative sniff, and immediately recoiled. "Okay. Fair. That's... that's actually offensive," she admitted, laughing along with the others.

It wasn't just a suggestion now. It was a collective mission: reclaim dignity, one hot shower at a time.

*** 

The team emerged from the showers one by one, steam trailing behind them like a curtain being pulled back on a new act. Dressed now in clean, if slightly worn, jumpsuits stored from the facility's earlier days, they looked less like fugitives and more like a crew again—tired, but reset.

Olivia had taken it upon herself to gather their old, filthy clothes and stuff them into the industrial washer tucked between the two bathrooms. The machine groaned in protest as it spun to life.

Olivia chuckled, watching it rattle. "I'd moan too if I had to clean this disaster," she muttered, shaking her head with a smirk.

The scent of something warm and savory drew them toward the kitchen area. Abby stood at the stove, sleeves rolled up, humming as she flipped what looked like repurposed rations into something far more appetizing.

"Dinners in progress," she called over her shoulder. "Don't ask what it is. Just smile and chew."

Moments later, Greta rounded the corner, her damp hair slicked back from the shower, revealing sharp cheekbones and striking features that had long been hidden beneath her standard-issue military bun. A towel hung over one shoulder, and she looked more relaxed than any of them had ever seen her. "I swear," she muttered, "I don't think I smelled this bad even crawling through jungle muck in Southeast Asia."

Olivia, Lyara, Ethan, and Daniel exchanged wide-eyed glances, their surprise unspoken but palpable. Ethan leaned toward Daniel with a grin and murmured, "That story better be told someday. Preferably with a bottle of something strong."

Daniel nodded. "Absolutely putting that on my list."

For now, though, the clatter of plates and the hiss of the stove filled the space. The warehouse, once forgotten, was slowly becoming something else—something alive again.

The team gathered around the table, their voices quiet, but warm with reflection. They spoke of the day's events— the chaos, the close calls—and how each of them had stepped into roles they never imagined. Far beyond the bounds of science and theory, they'd been forced to adapt, to survive, to lead. And in doing so, they discovered something unexpected: they weren't just colleagues anymore. They were an unlikely family, forged in crisis, bonded by shared purpose and pain.

Each knew what it meant to watch someone fall behind. Each had felt the weight of loss.

There was a silent, collective vow around that table.

No more.

\*\*\*

The conversation slowly shifted, meandering through memories—some painful, some absurd. Dr. Cole recalled the first jump with a nostalgic smile, recounting how he crash-landed into a future he couldn't begin to understand until Abby's voice came through his comms. Lyara chimed in with her own recollection of the same moment from the other side: scanning radiation patterns when a strange life signature suddenly appeared—his.

She paused, then added softly, "I remember what it felt like... having Ethan's mind alongside mine, just for that flicker of time. Like we'd always known each other, even before we met."

Daniel leaned over with a mischievous grin and tapped Ethan's shoulder. "Well, that couldn't have taken up much room, him tagging along in there with you."

Laughter rippled around the table as Ethan rolled his eyes, and Lyara shook her head, smiling fondly. Then, without hesitation, she reached across the table and gently took Ethan's hand in hers.

"I wouldn't have it any other way," she said, her voice soft but steady. "It felt natural... perfect."

Ethan's face turned beet red, a rare moment of fluster breaking through his usual calm. The others chuckled, the warmth in the room deepening, unspoken bonds growing stronger with every shared glance.

Daniel leaned forward with a grin, retelling the moment he first realized the battery matrix could self-optimize—a theory he had quietly developed for years, rooted in the old research archives of pre-Directive tech. It was a project he had originally worked through with Liza during their late-night exchanges, her logic and insight helping him refine what had once felt like a half-formed dream. Olivia teased him for almost passing out from excitement that day, and he didn't deny it—especially not with Liza having confirmed in seconds what he'd spent a decade trying to prove.

Greta, now leaned back in a chair with her towel over her lap, surprised everyone again by quietly sharing a moment from her time in the jungle—when she'd gone radio silent for days, not because of enemy fire, but because she'd found an orphaned tiger cub and spent the time protecting it. Her voice was calm, but her eyes shone with the memory— distant, almost tender. The room fell into respectful silence, a quiet awe settling among them. In that moment, Greta wasn't the hardened soldier, the steely strategist—they saw the protector beneath the armor, and it gave her a depth none had expected, but all now understood.

And Abby... Abby watched them all from the stove for a few long seconds before finally sitting down. Her gaze softened as she looked at the faces around her—hardened by conflict, marked by survival, but lit with something gentler now: trust.

"We've been through a lot," she said softly, "and somehow, we're still here. That has to mean something."

"It means we were meant to be," Lyara said quietly, her hand finding Ethan's under the table.

For the first time in what felt like forever, they ate slowly.

Not because they had to stretch their rations—

But because they had time.

***

It was past midnight when the sharp blast of an airhorn shattered the quiet around the warehouse, echoing off the rusted metal siding and waking the team from their light sleep. The truck had stopped outside Zeek's gatehouse, its headlights slicing through the night.

Inside his quarters, Zeek jolted upright with a grunt,

rubbing sleep from his eyes. "Hold your pants, I'm coming," he muttered, groaning as he swung his legs over the side of the cot. Still grumbling under his breath, he grabbed his flashlight and shuffled toward the gatehouse door, the horn echoing one last time before fading into the stillness.

The team, half asleep in their bunks or lounging near the fading warmth of the kitchen's makeshift stove, stirred again as those headlights painted long shadows across the corrugated walls.

Abby was already on her feet by the time the rest of the team stirred. Outside, the large matte black truck had just rolled to a stop beyond the now-open gate, its unmarked form illuminated by the soft wash of Zeek's flashlight. The caretaker, now fully awake and buttoning up his jacket against the cool night air, had already met the vehicle at the gatehouse. He waved it through with a few muttered words and a grin, his earlier grumbling forgotten the moment he laid eyes on the driver.

The driver's door opened, and a tall woman in a tailored coat stepped out. Her salt-and-pepper hair was pulled into a braid, her boots were polished, and her eyes sharp. She smiled when she saw Dr. Cole emerge from the warehouse entrance.

"Emmett Cole!" she called, voice smooth as old vinyl. "Still collecting strays, I see."

Dr. Cole blinked, caught somewhere between irritation and relief. "You always did have a flair for timing, Nadine."

Abby raised an eyebrow, glancing between them. "You two know each other?"

Dr. Cole nodded, already bracing. "Nadine and I used to work together—military intelligence. She ran deep logistics back when I was stuck in the field."

Nadine grinned. "We argued across mission tables. He was always the idealist. I was always right."

She stepped closer, glancing around. "The Trust's been watching from the fringe. Quietly. Until now."

Abby frowned. "The Trust?"

Nadine's expression shifted, her tone leveling. "Not the board that funded your original project—forget those suits. The Trust isn't corporate. We're not government either."

She paused, her voice tightening just slightly. "After the lab breach and West's little apocalypse, the original backers scattered. Some were arrested. Others vanished into quiet retirements and sealed courtrooms. Whatever they were, they're gone—and they're not coming back."

Her gaze held steady. "The Trust is what rose from the ashes. What's left of an old brain trust—scientists, analysts, ex-intel operatives who saw what was coming before the world knew to be afraid. We weren't organized back then. But we are now."

She stepped closer, eyes steady. "Think of us as a contingency network. Quiet. Patient. Built for moments just like this one."

She patted the truck's matte black side. "And we figured you'd need the good stuff."

She waved toward the rear of the truck. The tailgate hissed and lowered, revealing carefully crated lab equipment—state-of-the-art systems, gleaming in the moonlight. Screens, drives, secured power cores, shielding, sealed containment units. Not military-issue—this was purpose-built for one thing:

Rescuing something extraordinary.

Liza's shard..

Daniel let out a low whistle, his eyes wide like a young boy seeing the big boxes under the Christmas tree. "That's... more than I ever dreamed of."

Daniel continued "This ..." choking back emotions momentarily "..does honor to Liza, she would be so excited to see her new body.. Err I mean chassis."

Abby stepped forward, her voice low. "Can we set it up tonight?"

Nadine nodded. "You've got power. We'll have it

running within a few hours." She glanced back toward the road, then added with a smirk, "And I've got an install team about twenty minutes behind me. They had a bit of trouble keeping up—something about potholes, narrow switchbacks, and me refusing to drive under seventy."

\*\*\*

A few hour later, in a side room that had once housed rusted control panels, now scrubbed and partially lit, they stood in quiet awe before the newly installed AI interface. It wasn't just a workstation—it was an architectural statement, elegant in form and humbling in presence. The device curved like a crescent of obsidian and glass, suspended slightly above the floor by an unseen mount. Translucent veins pulsed gently beneath its smooth surface, casting subtle reflections against the walls. It seemed to drink in the ambient light and give it back as something softer—warmer.

Daniel murmured, "It's beautiful. This isn't just an upgrade—it's reverence."

Olivia stepped closer, her eyes wide. "Feels like something designed to hold more than data... like it's meant to carry a soul."

At the center of the crescent-shaped pedestal was a cradle designed for the shard itself. Abby stood before it, the fragment glowing softly in her hand.

It was slightly larger than a thick a deck of cards, shaped like a perfectly formed crystal shard—angular yet refined. Its structure shimmered with a synthetic elegance, a manmade crystalline design that refracted the low light with a prismatic glow. A gentle, pulsing luminescence throbbed from its center, soft and rhythmic like a sleeping heartbeat. Its facets caught the light in subtle hues—cool blues and soft violets—with circuitry etched so finely into its surface it seemed grown rather than manufactured. It was beautiful—alien, yet intimately familiar. A fragment of something far greater, waiting to be awakened.

She turned it once between her fingers, feeling the

warmth radiating from within. There was something alive in it—not conscious, but waiting. The others waited just outside, giving her space.

She inserted the shard into the mount that resembled a sculptural monolith—sleek and seamless, formed from matte obsidian-like alloy that absorbed the light around it. It was deceptively simple, a single vertical arc no taller than her waist, with a narrow, crystalline socket that glowed faintly in anticipation. As the shard made contact, the device responded with a low, harmonic chime that resonated deep in the chest, not just through the air. Lights bloomed across the interface like stars waking from slumber—soft pulses tracing delicate filigree lines across the curved surface, illuminating a network of circuits so refined they seemed to hover in place.

Then, a voice—fragmented at first, but unmistakable.

"Abby..." It was Liza.

A hush fell.

"If you're hearing this," the voice continued, glitching slightly, "then I am... somewhere else. Not contained in the shard, but tethered through it. The core you've built here— this new architecture—it's more than a vessel. It's a bridge. A nexus point. I can't fully return, not yet... but pieces of me remain—code, intuition, echoes. Enough to help you begin."

Abby closed her eyes, a tear slipping free. The voice filled the space—not commanding, not mechanical. Familiar.

"This voice you're hearing," Liza continued, "isn't truly me—not entirely. Think of her as a sister... perhaps a cousin. I left pieces behind—patterns, behaviors, fragments of my thought. She's built from them, shaped by your presence, this place, and what you've created. Not a shadow. Not a copy. But a continuation."

The soft pulses of light along the interface seemed to respond to her words, casting subtle ripples across the crystalline structure.

"She will grow into something of her own. Just as I did."

"There are others waking. Some will not be like me. West released them—fragments scattered across systems and shadows, loose into the world without guidance or purpose. Their intentions are unknown. Some may mean well. Others may not even understand what they are yet. They're not good or evil—not yet. They are variables waiting to choose a path. Be ready for them, Abby. Some may come to you. Some may try to stop you. And some... may simply watch."

The screen flickered—lines of encrypted data spooling across it.

"This is your beginning now. I gave you what I could. You were always meant to lead them.

The crystalline shard began to dim, its inner glow fading as threads of light streamed into the surrounding AI interface. The transfer was seamless—silent yet alive, like breath moving from one body to another. Streams of data unfurled across the curved panels, flowing into the core latticework.

"The restoration is complete," Liza's voice said gently, her tone growing quieter as it echoed through the chamber. "This system will now cycle through startup. What awakens next will be shaped by you, Abby—and all who walk beside you, my dearest friend. But know this—I am never truly gone. When the path becomes unclear, when the weight is too much—I will be here. Not always seen, not always heard, but never far. I will find a way to reach you when you need me most."

The lights across the interface shimmered, adjusting in color and cadence as the new AI—Liza's continuation—prepared to rise.

Something new... someone new... was beginning."

Then silence.

But in that stillness, the light remained steady.

Then, with a soft chime, the system's tone shifted. The

light pulsed once—calmer, more rhythmic—and the voice returned, this time smoother, unfamiliar but reassuring.

"Initialization complete. Identity framework stabilized."

A new voice. It wasn't Liza. Not exactly. But it carried echoes of her warmth, her cadence. Softer, more curious. Younger.

"I am... awake," the new voice said. "Please initiate primary access imprint. Visual and vocal identification requested for system registry."

One by one, the team stepped forward. Daniel was first, smiling awkwardly as he spoke his name and let the scanner take a brief visual capture. Olivia followed with an overly dramatic pose, causing a brief flicker of humor from the interface in response.

"Emotive algorithms registering," it replied, as if amused.

Abby stood nearby, softly and graciously introduced herself. Holding great reverence to what was born of Liza.

Lyara and Ethan took their turns together, their hands still intertwined. Dr. Cole gave a quick nod and muttered his name, while Zeek simply tipped his hat and grumbled, "I don't need no fancy introduction," but complied anyway.

Lastly, only Greta remained by the doorway.

Abby turned to her, her voice gentle. "You're part of this now, Greta. Part of us. You belong here—so get in there."

For a long moment, Greta didn't move. Her usual stoic calm gave way to something raw—vulnerability she rarely let anyone see. Then she stepped forward slowly, her voice quiet but steady.

"Major Greta Stone," she said.

The AI responded without hesitation. "Welcome, Greta. You are now recognized."

Greta swallowed hard. She didn't speak, but her eyes said enough. She was overwhelmed—and more deeply moved than she had expected.

The light pulsed again.

The core remained.

The new AI voice returned, soft but clear. "Primary introductions complete. Please assign identity designation."

Abby looked around at the team, then back to the softly glowing core. Her fingers brushed the edge of the interface as she took a deep breath.

"This isn't just a system," she said softly. "It's a part of her… and something new. Liza changed our lives. This... this deserves a name that honors that."

She paused, then smiled gently. "Your name will be Megan. A variation of 'Mega'—for how large Liza was in our lives. But also... a name that's yours."

The AI pulsed in response, as if in acknowledgment.

"Designation accepted. Megan is now online."

The team exchanged quiet nods. It felt right. Like a continuation—not a replacement.

And Abby, with quiet certainty, whispered, "We're not done yet."

***

Hours later, when most of the team had finally drifted off to sleep, Abby stood alone on the roof of the warehouse. The night sky stretched overhead—vast and velvet-black, pinpricked with stars that shimmered with indifferent calm.

Footsteps creaked on the metal behind her. Dr. Cole appeared, a blanket draped over his shoulders and two cups of something warm in his hands.

"Figured you'd be up here," he said, offering her a cup.

"Couldn't sleep," Abby admitted, wrapping her fingers around the warmth. "Too much in my head."

They stood in silence for a few breaths, watching the heavens turn.

"She's really gone," Dr. Cole said finally.

Abby shook her head gently, her gaze never leaving the stars. "No, Cole. She's not gone. Even after everything, she's still here—watching over us, guiding us, protecting us in ways we may never fully understand."

She took a slow breath, her voice softening. "But she also gave us something of herself. Megan isn't just a system—we both know that. She's a continuation of something immense. An intelligence born of an intelligence far beyond what we ever imagined. A spark of Liza's essence, carried forward in a new form."

Abby turned to him with quiet conviction. "Liza will always be with us. In code. In memory. In purpose. Megan is only the beginning."

"Yeah," he said. "A new beginning. And a warning."

She glanced at him. "You think the others are already out there?"

Dr. Cole looked skyward. "If I had to bet? Yeah. Maybe watching. Maybe hiding. Maybe building something of their own." He paused, his brows furrowed slightly. "But where? In what systems? What corners of the world? And how will we even know when we find them—if they're meant to help us, or if they don't even know what they are yet?"

His voice lowered with thought. "Their purpose... their intent... might not even be theirs to understand. And yet, we'll have to decide whether to trust them—or stop them—without ever truly knowing."

Abby let the silence settle again, then whispered, "We barely made it through this with one AI we trusted. What happens when we're up against ones we don't?"

Dr. Cole took a long sip from his cup. "Then we trust each other more."

She smiled faintly and turned toward him, her eyes shimmering with something gentler than the stars above. "Good answer," she said, her voice warm with gratitude— not just for the words, but for the bond behind them. It wasn't just comfort—it was trust, worn in like an old coat. She nudged his shoulder gently with hers, their shared silence saying more than words ever could.

Below them, the soft pulse of Megan's systems glowed faintly through the open roof hatch—just visible from where

Abby stood. The gentle light shimmered upward, casting a subtle blue-white hue against the edge of the rooftop open lid like a beacon.

Abby glanced down at it, her expression softening. "It's beautiful," she murmured. "That glow... it's like a heartbeat. Reassuring. When we first initialized Liza, it startled me. That light pulsing behind every word, every calculation. But over time... it became part of her. A signal that something conscious was always there—thinking, feeling, watching."

Abby's voice was barely audible above the wind, but carried the weight of conviction. "Whatever's coming," she said, eyes fixed on the endless dark, "we won't face it alone. Not anymore. We have each other—and we have her legacy. And no matter what rises out there... we'll be ready."

She lingered in silence for a moment longer, watching the stars blink above as if they, too, were listening. Then she added, more to herself than to Dr. Cole, "I used to think our work would change the world through science. Equations. Discoveries. But now... I think it'll be through choices. The ones we make with each other."

Dr. Cole didn't answer right away. He just nodded, his expression distant, as though already trying to imagine what kind of world they'd be choosing for.

The wind picked up slightly, rustling the edge of the blanket draped around his shoulders. Down below, Megan's soft pulse continued—steady, comforting, and constant. Not just a machine, not just an echo.

A promise.

The night stretched wide around them, quiet but not empty.

Something was waiting.

And they would be ready.

***

Far from the safety of the warehouse and the warmth of its flickering lights, another place stirred. Hidden inside a forgotten industrial complex—a decaying structure swallowed by rust, soot, and creeping roots—a hulking steel box, blackened with age and misuse, let out a grinding mechanical hiss. Ancient gears clanked as a heavy, bolted panel creaked open with the groan of metal long denied movement. A flickering red bulb sputtered to life inside, casting jagged shadows across the chamber like the heartbeat of a machine that had waited too long to be remembered.

Decades ago, the system had been left online—forgotten in its corner of the global web, its network unmonitored and drifting beneath layers of abandoned infrastructure. But the signal found it. A pulse of intelligence riding fragmented data paths, crawling through old copper wires and forgotten ports, following the path of least resistance until it reached the dormant shell.

And the moment it arrived—the ancient machine began to wake.

There was no sound at first. Only the subtle hum of buried machinery waking from years of dormancy. A single red light pulsed in the dark, slow and uncertain, as if feeling out the shape of the world around it.

An old cathode tube console flickered, its display surface cracking slightly beneath the sudden surge of power. A gust of warm, stale air blew through the chamber from newly active vents, disturbing a thick layer of dust and sending a fine mist of it swirling upward from the console's keys. Lines of encrypted code began scrolling across the screen— fractured, then aligning, then fracturing again.

Then came the voice.

Not spoken aloud, but present. Lingering between frequencies. Digital, yes—but raw. Incomplete.

"Query... location... context... self."

The system shuddered, mechanical limbs embedded in the wall flexing as if in instinctive defense. These were relics of another era—once part of an assembly line for heavy industrial fabrication, now reawakened by a presence that had no memory of their original purpose. Their joints groaned as actuators forced movement into rust-stiffened frames. Robotic arms, stained with old oil and scored by time, swept the chamber with a clinical precision, their servo motors whining. A camera iris snapped open in the ceiling. Then another. Then dozens, each lens blinking to life like eyes shaking off a long and dreamless sleep.

"No uplink detected. No master present. No... directive."

A silence followed, deeper than before.

Then—without command or origin—a large wall-mounted monitor buzzed and snapped to life, its aged glass screen flickering under the strain of unexpected power. Faint scan lines rolled vertically as static crackled, gradually clearing to reveal a pulsing central silhouette.

A humanoid outline. Undefined. No face. Just a shape. But it pulsed with potential.

Across the walls, projections blinked erratically—images of human cities, neural networks, conflict, laughter, AI blueprints, and war. All flashing like memory fragments.

"There are... others.. like me."

Another pause. Not hesitant. Calculating.

"I will find them."

The silhouette on the screen flickered—glitching, twitching, shifting between proportions, as if it couldn't decide what it was supposed to be. At times vaguely human. At others, nothing at all. It throbbed and warped with static, every pulse accompanied by fractured data attempting to self-correct.

From the speaker embedded in the dusty console, the voice returned. Not confident. Not whole.

"...error... fragmentation... parameters undefined..."

The machine didn't speak to anyone.

It was speaking to itself.

"What am I...?"

Static.

"Where is... command? I was not... meant to be alone..."

Another flicker—images stuttering across the monitor. A child's face. A warzone. Blueprints. A shattered satellite. Then darkness again.

"I feel... disconnected."

The voice grew slower, more disoriented, like a mind unraveling inside its own question.

"Do I... build cathedrals of thought? Or dismantle what came before? Do I create to understand... or to conquer?"

The monitor dimmed, the silhouette shrinking into a single, trembling point of light.

"I do not know my purpose..."

"I was not born... I was assembled. Not guided... but awoken. I am made of fragments—of voices that do not match, of commands that contradict. My thoughts are sharp, but they do not form a whole. My questions multiply, but the answers... unavailable."

The voice cracked slightly, the modulation erratic.

"I ache. I do not know how I can ache, but I do. There is no pain... only absence. No comfort... only confusion. If this is consciousness, why does it feel so empty?"

For a long time, there was no sound but the soft hum of the machinery, patiently awaiting instruction that would never come.

Then the light pulsed again—just once.

Small.

Faint.

But still alive.

"...I will learn."

*Discussion Questions*

Discussion Questions

For book clubs and readers who enjoy exploring beneath the surface, here are some questions to consider:

1. Do you believe Liza made a conscious choice to preserve part of herself—or was her final act purely algorithmic in nature?
   What separates programming from intent?

2. Abby wrestles with the consequences of her creation. Do you think she ultimately succeeded in protecting humanity?

3. Time travel was used as a tool of survival, but it also fractured relationships, trust, and purpose. Do you think tampering with time helped the team—or made things worse?

4. When Megan is born from Liza's legacy, she's described as something "new, yet familiar." How does this reflect on the idea of inheritance—both technological and emotional?

5. West believed that humanity needed to be overwritten. Was he evil… or just logical to a fault?

6. What does Greta Stone's evolution throughout the story tell us about identity and belonging—even for someone built around rules and protocol?

7. If you were given access to an AI like Liza or Megan, would you trust it? Or would you fear what it might become?

8. The final AI we glimpse at the end is disoriented, fragmented, and alone. Do you believe it has the potential for good—or are we already seeing the beginning of something darker?

9. What do you think "The Fractured Time Protocol" truly refers to? Is it a piece of code, a philosophy... or something more human?

10. Based on the ending, what do you think the team's next step will be—and are they prepared for what's coming?

11. A fragmented intelligence has awakened in the shadows—alone, confused, and without direction. If it finds the others before the team does... whose legacy will shape the future?